The Mine Safety Trilogy
Part II

The Mine Safety Trilogy
Part II

The Case of the Abnormal White Center

William B. Moran

PALMETTO
PUBLISHING
Charleston, SC
www.PalmettoPublishing.com

Copyright © 2025 by William B. Moran

All rights reserved.

No portion of this book may be reproduced, stored in a retrieval system, or transmitted in any form by any means—electronic, mechanical, photocopy, recording, or other—except for brief quotations in printed reviews, without prior permission of the author.

Paperback ISBN: 9798822985995
eBook ISBN: 9798822986008

This is a work of fiction. As such, the characters in this novel are completely fictional. No real persons or events are portrayed. References to places and to organizations, while they may exist, are similarly fictional.

CHAPTER 1

Mount Hope, West Virginia

It had slipped out of her hands. She tried to catch it, but it escaped her grasp and immediately began rolling across the lab floor, almost scurrying away as if it had a mind of its own. She chased after it but the round disc, which was about the size of a fifty-cent piece, was too quick, as it found refuge under a nearby cabinet. Naturally, it went far enough under the cabinet so that it was out of the reach of her hand. Donna Nelson, only three weeks at her new job as an MSHA technician, was embarrassed over her clumsiness. And, of course, the whole event was watched by her supervisor, Greg Balkum, the director of MSHA's Health Technology Center in Mount Hope, West Virginia.

Wouldn't you know it, she thought, awkwardly conscious of his obvious disapproving evaluation of her klutzy side. She noticed the look on his face, more irritated over the small mishap, than taking it in stride. Couldn't he see it as humorous? Like he would never drop something. Right!

Now on her knees, her hands adding support and balance as she tilted her head sideways, while peering under the cabinet where the disc had fled, she couldn't see it.

Balkum continued to watch the event. He was not above noticing what a fine, well-rounded, ass she had. Her form-fitting tights displaying its shape, no different really than if she had been naked from the waist down.

Realizing that her approach would not succeed, she arose and grabbed a wooden yardstick from a nearby table. Returning to the disc's hiding place,

THE CASE OF THE ABNORMAL WHITE CENTER

she swept the yardstick under the cabinet and, after one pass, the little bastard came out, this time on its side, the harder to be retrieved she thought.

Balkum, unable to resist a second viewing of her derriere, again appreciated the beautiful presentation. Luckily, he had both sufficient time and the good sense to avert his gaze before she arose.

Righting herself, blushed over her mistake, she returned to the work cabinet where she had first grabbed the disc, this time being ultracareful so that there would be no encore performance. She took a clean cloth to wipe off the dirt particles and fuzz that the disc had collected in its escape attempt. Though a cleaning crew appeared nightly, they did not routinely sweep under the recesses of the cabinets, a fact attested to by the dust bunnies and other small particles which had clung to the sleeves of her top, making a fine mess on her cotton shirt.

Nearby, Balkum continued to watch the event. Conscious of his continued presence, she thought, couldn't he just get back to his own tasks? Hey, show's over!

Had she known Balkum was leering at her posterior, she would have been seriously irritated. She entertained no such suspicions but, at only 34 years, and attentive to her health and fitness, she was not oblivious to stares. A petite brunette, divorced with one pre-teen boy, she remained fit, determined to avoid the middle-age weight gain which so many in her age group succumbed. Naively, she believed that the workplace environment had changed in the last decade, transformed into a place where it was to be about – work. Despite that view, she did allow her own inconsistency in applying her standard for the separation that was to be observed between work and sexual attraction between employees, as there was a young man in the Center that she had grown to favor.

Having returned to her work station, poised on her stool, her facial redness now ebbing, she resumed her task – evaluating the dust sample in the cassette. These samples were important and she undertook her task with the seriousness it called for. As if underground coal mining were not hazardous enough for those miners who spent years in that darkness and managed to escape serious injury or death, that inhaled coal dust could still kill them after prolonged exposure, the particles blocking the exchange of air in their lungs. They would literally suffocate from it.

Making matters worse, her drop had cracked the case and now it was partially open, the two normally sealed halves split. She knew the mishap would need to be reported to Balkum.

The task before her was not complex; she was to weigh the cassette and then compare it with its original weight. If over a certain amount, the cassette would reveal excessive exposure to the deadly dust.

It was then that she noticed something unusual. Though she had been examining the cassettes for only a few weeks, this one stood out from all the others. Right there, in the center of the filter, was a donut shaped white hole, with almost no dust on it. That was clearly abnormal; every other cassette, regardless of the weighing task, had the dust evenly spread over the filter. Not this one. Not at all.

Green, but intuitive, she spoke up, asking Balkum, who was then on the far side of the lab, to come over, advising, "Sir, I need you to take a look at this cassette."

Balkum, mildly annoyed that his own task was being interrupted, walked over to her work table.

"What's up, Miss Nelson?" he asked, displaying a reverence for her that he had ignored, twice, only moments before.

"Sir, I dropped this cassette a moment ago," unaware that he had watched the whole event, though his focus was entirely upon her physique. "When I returned to my lab table, I found something odd. Please take a look at this," she requested, showing him the open cassette, the filter in full display.

She added no commentary, deciding it was best not to express her concern. *Let him tell me if it matters, or not,* she thought, not wanting to influence his take.

Balkum looked at the cassette and, in all his years of doing this, he had never seen a cassette with such an appearance. *Very peculiar white center in the filter,* he immediately observed. *Outside the circle, the filter had the expected coal dust particles.*

He paused, silently considering what was before him, then he spoke.

THE CASE OF THE ABNORMAL WHITE CENTER

"I see the cassette is cracked," pretending that he had not witnessed her earlier slip and drop of it. "I saw that you dropped something earlier," he disclosed. "If that was a cassette you dropped, perhaps when it fell to the floor the accident created that abnormal center," he speculated.

She picked up on his word choice – he did say "abnormal center," she thought, exactly her reaction.

Balkum continued to peer at the cassette. His sense was that something was amiss. Privately he contemplated that a dropped cassette could impact the filter's appearance, but not in this way, not with a white center like that.

"Let's see," he continued, "where did this dust sample come from?"

Donna did not hesitate. "It's from the Eagle Coal and Coke mine," she informed. "We have eleven other samples from them to review, all taken during the same sampling period there," pointing to the labeled container holding the other samples.

Balkum, a serious look on his face, spoke without hesitation. "Let's take a look at them." Then, he added for emphasis, "Right now," to be sure she understood it was important.

They began reviewing the cassettes together and, to their growing dismay, each of them had abnormal centers. That was definitely not normal. Further, Donna had only dropped that one; all the others were in their intact state. None of them were cracked, nor were there any other signs of damage to them.

When they were done, Balkum and Nelson looked at each other; their faces displaying mutual concern. Though the abnormal center was new to her and though her experience in her new job was limited, the same could not be said for Balkum. No, he had been examining these cassettes for years and, in all that time, he had never seen a filter, and now 12 of them, with that appearance.

"Donna," he said, "I need to think about this for a while. I don't want you to say anything about this to any of the other techs. In fact, I don't want you to speak of this to anyone in the office."

Sensitive to the potential gravity involved, Nelson responded simply, "Understood, sir."

"In the meantime," he continued, "I want you to turn your attention to the other Pennsylvania coal mine dust samples. We need to see if this was an aberration or something else," his voice trailing off at the end. "Of course, I need not tell you to be alert to any abnormal centers, should they arise." He then added, "I hope there will not be more. This has never happened before. See me periodically as you review the samples from those other mine operators."

"Yes, sir," she responded obediently. "I will notify you periodically," she continued, employing the word he used. She smiled, "I don't want to pester you, so I'll use my judgment for updating you."

He was satisfied with her response. The unexpected development and their exchanges helped him get to know his new employee better and he was impressed with her.

Balkum then returned to his office to contemplate the development. He didn't want to think the worst. It was only one batch. But the odds that all of the 12 cassettes would look that way did not add up. At a minimum it called for a closer look at the previous submissions from the Eagle Coal and Coke Mine. That involved more than simply weighing them, which was the customary practice.

The key for now was to keep this quiet until more information could be gathered. That also meant it was important to sternly reemphasize to Nelson that she was not to mention this to anyone. No exceptions.

Life's experiences had taught him that, in an office of this small size, just telling one other person would quickly spread to others, the information uncapped. Nor would the information stay within the office. Before long, some well-intentioned soul would mention this to people outside the Technology Center and from there, like a wildfire, the mining operators would learn of it. That needed to be prevented.

Filled with nervous energy over the discovery, Nelson immediately set to work examining the numerous other coal dust cassette samples from various Pennsylvania mines. She began with the Gurling Mine.

As customary, she did weigh them. It was part of the routine practice, but with her first look at the cassettes from this entirely different mine she was wide-eyed – each of the 12 cassettes from that mine also had those abnormal white centers. Balkum had already confirmed that they shouldn't look like that. But, apart from his concerns, on its face, it obviously made no sense for such an appearance – a filter inside a case, designed to catch dust particles and the center, the *very* center, of that filter remaining white? Nothing would rationally account for such an uneven distribution of the dust particles, especially with the center, of all places, remaining white. Couldn't happen.

Her suspicions grew with each atypical cassette and, along with that, purely from a weight standpoint, all of the cassettes passed – none had excessive weight. Therefore, presumptively, there was no overexposure to coal dust from the miners who wore them on their shift.

She had an urge to march right down to Balkum's office to let him know of the latest news, but she resisted the temptation because he had asked that her reports be made periodically, not breathlessly with each few examined cassettes. Suppressing that urge, there was also a pull for her to examine the next batch pronto.

The next one was from the Meadow Crossing Mine. Better to have at least one more mine's samples reviewed, she thought, before seeing him. Though not all of that mine's twelve had the abnormal white centers, eleven did. And the appearance of those was nearly identical to the first two batches. Visually, they all could have come from the same mine, all having the distinctive white centers, though she was sure, upon double-checking, that they were indeed all from different mines. Aware of the importance of segregating the cassettes, she was ultra-careful to keep each mine's cassette samples in their own container.

That made two more in a row following the samples she and Balkum had just reviewed. That could not be happenstance, she thought. Though there were many dozens of other dust sample cassettes yet to examine from various mines, she did not feel that visiting Balkum at this point would be unwelcome. She was perceptive enough to realize that he was not dismissive of that first batch. Plainly, he displayed a look of concern with the appearance of the first group alone.

She walked down to his office, finding the door was shut, as usual. Being closed, it sent a message to the staff, quite intended by Balkum. He was friendly enough to the office employees, perhaps courteous was the more apt description, but he still wanted to maintain some distance with those under him. He was the head of the office and having the door closed reinforced that there was a hierarchy, with him at the apex. Knocking, he answered simply, "Come in."

"Mr. Balkum," she began without any greeting, "I thought you would want to know that the next two batches I examined were from the Meadow Crossing and Gurling mines, and both of them had the same white centers. It was 12 for 12 with Gurling and 11 out of 12 for Meadow."

He looked at her. It was at once alarming news, but yet not surprising. Instinctively, as he walked back to his office that morning, his gut told him that something serious was up. Over his long experience in mining, which included working in mines for nearly two decades, as well as eleven years with MSHA, he knew full well that mine operators were not angels. Sure, some tried to run safe mines but, to survive, production had to be king. Because of that, corners would need to be cut at times. Repairs, other than those that hurt production, would have to take a back seat.

As for this respirable dust requirement, about which none of the operators were pleased, real compliance with it would obviously impact production negatively.

"More government interference," he had heard more than a few mine operators grouse. Their reasoning was without apology. Okay, a few conceded, miners might inhale some dust. Well, it wasn't supposed to be an office! It was dirty work but that was part of the package. These people, by and large, had minimal formal education, and taking that into consideration, they were paid handsomely. Just try and find a job with equivalent pay for these workers, they would inform the purists. It wouldn't happen. Risks and all, those employees should be grateful. Period.

This was not a fluke, not three out of three, he realized. Arising from his chair, he told her, "I need to see these first-hand. Let's go down to your work station."

It did not take long for him to assess the two new sample batches. They obviously presented the same condition; their uniformity so stark, it almost made one think that they came from the same mine.

Balkum knew something was up and that there could be no innocent explanation. Those samples Donna had examined came from different mines and different ownership. Further, they arrived on different days, eliminating the remote possibility of mailing mishandling. Last, this was new, no previous samples, none, had these white centers.

Did it seem far-fetched to think that mine owners could collaborate in presenting such a fraud? Not at all.

Years ago, when Congress decided the fines for safety and health violations needed to be increased, virtually all mines decided to challenge *every* citation. It was a coordinated effort, all to impede the government from pursuing civil penalties. And it was not speculation, as a few mine operators were foolish enough to admit the scheme to MSHA.

"Well, Donna, I want you to continue to examine as many batches as you can today. Take meticulous notes and be sure that you keep each mine's samples segregated from any others. You can be sure they will claim chain of custody issues. Do you know about that?"

"Only vaguely," she admitted, "but I understand the gist of it what it means."

"Good, because they will claim that you mixed up samples from different mines."

As this was basic procedure, he realized that it might come across as a lack of confidence that she would perform those tasks carefully, so he added, "I'm sure you would perform these reviews that way. I only add the reminder because you can see how important this is, given what you've discovered. If these troublesome centers continue to appear, and many mines are involved, you can imagine how the knives will come out, questioning your diligence."

She nodded. "I get it Mr. Balkum. I will be extra careful, not rushing the review, nor commingling samples from different mines," she added.

He smiled benevolently, appreciating her reassurance. Continuing to worry that the discovery could be leaked, he added, "One more thing. It's also very important. I know I've said this before but you must be careful not to breath a word of this to anyone else in the building. No one," he added for emphasis.

Again, she nodded. "I won't. Promise. I appreciate the potential significance of this."

THE MINE SAFETY TRILOGY PART II

Satisfied, Balkum again expressed his thanks for her reassurance to keep this quiet. "Good. I'm confident you will. So, during the last hour of the day, drop by and give me an update on your subsequent reviews of these cassettes."

"Yes, sir," she answered. "I'm going to get right on it."

As he walked back to his office, he felt no joy in this discovery. Part of him hoped the three results so far would simply be anomalies, statistical oddities, random clusters, which can happen, but nothing more than that.

If that were the case, the problem could be easily solved. The office would merely casually contact those few mines and indicate the samples had been 'lost' in the mail. It would be a lie, of course, but he didn't want to alert them that there were any questions about their samples.

But what if that were not the case? What if there were dozens of mines involved, or more?

It was worrisome, but he resolved not to jump the gun. He would simply have to wait and see what Nelson came up with at day's end. It would not end there, he knew. He would direct that she continue her particularized review all week. By then, the picture would be clearer, one way or the other. Still, he could not help but begin to contemplate the appropriate next steps, if the grim picture were to continue.

Though there were many other tasks for him at hand, this development continued to occupy his attention. He closed his office door, and sat back in his chair, propping his feet up on an opened desk drawer, a footrest, though uncomfortable. Rubbing his temples, he tried to think through the best way to proceed. At 53 years, and therefore not near retirement, if this grew into a coordinated, massive, effort by underground coal mines, this would be the biggest event in his many years of running the center.

He did not relish the idea. The mining companies, he knew, would fight back forcefully. They had the wherewithal to secure the top legal firms and spare no expense in retaining their services. It would be an exhausting experience. Graying and losing a lot of that hair, he also had not paid attention to his overall health. And while he had no major maladies, he did carry around an extra thirty or so pounds, over his five-foot ten-inch height, all of it collected around his middle, as it had with his father before him. When he was young, he swore not to let that happen. But, beginning in his mid-forties, each year he would gain a few pounds. A quick diet would shed a few of them, but they would reappear once he was off it.

A reminder of the progression, each year at his annual physical, his doctor would admonish him for his incremental, but consistent, weight gain, which was about three to four pounds per year. Over time the pounds added up and now displayed themselves prominently, a fact he would be reminded of each time he bought a new pair of trousers at the store. Just like his dad after all.

At week's end, Nelson came to Balkum's office, as instructed. She had visited with him every day during the week, a custom they had informally adopted, for a brief update. The news continued to be worrisome. While there were a few exceptions, cassettes with no abnormal centers, they were so few that they constituted the anomalies, not the other way around.

She had been diligent in her assigned task. With each additional sample displaying the abnormal white centers, her energy to turn to the next batch grew. She was also conscious to follow Balkum's admonition that she was not to tell a soul about the nature of her work or her findings. At each day's end she would lock up her tabulations for the mine samples reviewed.

When Friday arrived, she had completed review of 64 sample submissions. Of those, 58 had the "AWC's," the shorthand expression she had created to describe the concerning displays. It made no sense, she knew instinctively, for the filters to have such an appearance. If anything, she thought, the centers should be darker from the collected dust, not lighter. And, even if one could, for the sake of argument, assert that some of the white centers in the filters just developed that way, the sheer number of them and the uniformity of their displays, pointed to anything but a chance occurrence.

When she presented the information to him, he was not surprised, especially since her visits during the week were consistent. Clearly, something was going on. His concern now more heightened that none of this leak out, he reminded her yet again that this information was to be closely held. She didn't need the reminder, but it underscored the seriousness of the discoveries. Privately, she knew that she would not even disclose the news to any family or friends; Balkum would expect no less.

Mindful that there were a large number of samples yet to be reviewed, and that this required that the reviews would need to be distributed to at least some of the other technicians in the office, Balkum spoke to the new week ahead. "Next week," he advised, "I will have no choice but to add some of the other techs to begin reviewing the sample submissions. You can't do this alone, there are too many. I will have to alert them to pay attention to any abnormalities in the filters. I won't be too specific, because I don't want to be accused of steering anyone to conclusions. I'm not sure whom I will add for these reviews but my concern is that those selected will also not disclose the information to anyone, not even to others in the lab. Trust is important."

Nelson nodded, glad that his remark affirmed his trust in her.

"On Monday, I'll go over with you those I am considering to add to our review team."

That was a first, calling those involved part of the "review team." She was pleased to be a part of it. While, before this discovery, much of her lab work could be described as routine, and, to be frank, dull, this matter certainly was not.

"You're new, but I need your sense of the trustworthiness for the techs we add to the review team. It's imperative that they will also keep this absolutely quiet," Balkum continued.

Another compliment, she thought, elevating her to evaluating those who could be added to the team as trustworthy.

When Monday arrived, Balkum called Donna and two other technicians, Daniel Tucker and Tom Grasser to his office. Only Nelson knew the purpose. Before they had arrived, Balkum disclosed to Nelson the names of the techs he planned to add to the review team. She informed that she didn't know either one very well, but had no reason to oppose their inclusion.

While Balkum could not be sure of it, he considered Tucker and Grasser as good candidates to trust. They had both been employed at the Center for several years. During that time, they had performed their jobs satisfactorily and there had been no problems with either one; they showed up on time, worked a full day, and left the office as soon as the day ended.

Dispensing with the usual chatter before meetings, he told them there was a need to closely examine the dust samples. He then displayed two examples of the cassettes that had caught his attention, so that they could see firsthand what they could look like. He reminded them that these were examples; they were not to lock in to these as the only type of odd samples.

Acting as if all three of them had been doing this work for a long period, though only Tucker and Grasser had, not Nelson, he reminded them to rely on their experience in viewing the dust filters.

Nelson quietly listened, having the good sense to act as if she was hearing about this for the first time, saying nothing unless and until Balkum disclosed her prior involvement.

Balkum emphasized two things. First, no one was assuming that a white center meant there had been any tampering, though privately he knew it to be highly likely that was exactly what was going on. Still, it was important to present himself before this group as one who was merely gathering information. Conclusions would be down the road.

"You may not find any cassettes with a white or whitish center," he added, his remark intended to convey that he had no predetermined outcome. He just wanted them to pay attention to the possibility. "And if you do find some, that doesn't necessarily mean anything either. Could be a bunch of reasons for that."

His second point, the one he particularly wanted them to follow, was that no one was to disclose to anyone, in or out of the office, about this issue. "And so, we have to be true professionals. For now, we're just seeing if any of these white center filters show up."

All three nodded their understanding of their assignment and the rules they were to follow. Balkum then designated Nelson as the lead. He believed it was the appropriate decision, given that she made the first discovery of this.

Neither Tucker nor Grasser liked hearing that news. Silently, privately, unaware of each other's reaction, they resented her elevation above them. Between the two of them they had been employed at the lab for several years, with her experience made up of only weeks. And so now, this woman, still wet behind the ears at this office, would be overseeing them? As they saw it, it was another sign of the ugly times they were experiencing – white guys taking a back seat to every other group. Their view ignored that Balkum, the head of the office, was both male and white.

The meeting did not take long and, at its end, Nelson was asked to stay, as the other two were dismissed, a fact they both sourly noted. Balkum took only a few minutes to outline the procedure she was to employ in assigning samples for review by the two other technicians. He emphasized that she was to scrupulously keep records of the samples she assigned to them, as well as to continue with the same detail for her own reviews

Though he kept his feelings to himself, as he walked back to his cubicle, Tucker continued to brood over the matter. He didn't like it one bit. It was just not fair. Some sort of payback for the slight would be justified, he thought. Before he came to work with MSHA he had been employed by coal mines. Friendships from those days continued, and should there be something amiss with this cassette business, he would discretely alert those pals about it. He had no qualms about such disclosures. Balkum's warning be damned. Besides Balkum would never learn that he was the source. His friends could be trusted.

Following the new assignment for review of the dust sample cassettes, as the end of the next two weeks approached, Balkum directed that the trio of technicians convene for a review. Donna had been receiving updates each day from Tucker and Grasser, though that rigorous daily review only served to highlight that, at least for this task, she was their supervisor, irritating both of them. Though unhappy about her superior status, having no choice, they kept quiet about it. Didn't mean they had to be cheery towards her though, which they were not. Though elevated above them for this task, the fact was she wasn't their boss. A business-like demeanor was the watchword for them.

She picked up on it of course; the coldness in their interactions – it wasn't hard to detect it. Knowing the friction was insoluble – they couldn't accept the new hierarchy – she decided to ignore it as best she could, keeping her focus on the results as they came in.

THE CASE OF THE ABNORMAL WHITE CENTER

Depending on one's perspective, the results, after two weeks, were not good. They were exciting, if one sensed that they were uncovering massive, coordinated corruption, but depressing at the same time, if it revealed how low people could go – unscrupulous behavior by so many underground coal mines, not to mention the life-shortening damage to miners' lungs resulting from it.

With each of the three technicians averaging samples from some 20 mines per week, they had more than 120 mines for which they had scrutinized the cassette samples. The task was easier in one respect, as they were looking for a specific trait, what they all now routinely called the AWCs. Still, it was tedious, reviewing, what seemed endlessly, one cassette after another. And it wasn't as if each cassette presented a clear call. Some seemed to have an abnormal white center, but they were difficult to assess. They didn't seem normal, but their centers were not as unquestionably white as most. All three of them had been experiencing the same phenomenon. Some of the cassettes were too close to make a call as being suspect.

After Nelson realized that some of the questionable determinations persisted, though not large percentage-wise, and that each of the techs had encountered these, she alerted Balkum to the development during the first week of their cassette reviews.

He took it in stride. The numbers of those that were clear-cut, AWCs for which there was no doubt, were north of 80%. Though she had already made note of those that were disputable, Balkum instructed her to segregate, within each mine's samples, those for which no clear call could be made and to tell Tucker and Grasser to do the same.

Donna informed that she had already been doing that, realizing that the obvious AWCs had to be separated from the rest. For the others, the few that were not so obviously having white centers, she had been informally putting them aside, wrapping a rubber band around those that were unclear. But now, with his express direction, she responded that she would create separate containers for each mine, three to be precise; those that appeared normal, the majority with the AWCs, and those for which a solid assessment could not be made. It made sense to have something more formal than her rubber band arrangement. She would have the others do the same.

Balkum liked her approach. It was the same he would use if he were a reviewer. His admiration was growing; she was fitting in well for someone so new to the lab. And it was fortuitous that her momentary clumsiness led to the astounding discovery. He affirmed that she was to advise Tucker and Grasser to start the same approach immediately. Not clueless, that they would likely resent receiving instructions from her, he added that when she gave them those instructions to tell them that she was conveying this from him, which was true. In that way, she would be viewed as a messenger, not as the one giving the orders. They still wouldn't like it, with all their seniority over her, but it would go down a bit easier if presented that way.

Following the meeting, she did not delay in conveying the new procedure Balkum had just put in place. She was careful to be diplomatic, describing it as news she had just received from their boss. He asked, she told them, that she was to convey the procedure and that it was for each of them to follow. She described that, for each mine's samples, they were to create three containers; those unequivocally identified as AWCs in one and a separate container for those showing no abnormality and last, the third container for those where it was unclear if an AWC was present. She tried to present a friendly mien, her attempt to display that they were equals, all part of the team, working under Greg's supervision.

Tucker and Grasser received the instructions impassively, displaying neither warmth nor irritation. They nodded, adding words sparingly.

"Will do," Grasser responded.

"Understood," said Tucker.

As they returned to their work stations, and seeing that Donna was not nearby, Tucker whispered to Grasser, "Mind the orders from our f'ing new boss, Tom," he said contemptuously.

"Got it, Dan," he answered. "It's just the way things are," he added, more accepting of the arrangement than his fellow worker.

In the following week, and then in the week after that, the information conveyed by all three technicians was consistent with the previous findings. It was obvious that something was foul. Now the number of mines that had been reviewed had doubled, at nearly 250, and what they were staring at was undeniable – something was afoot, something not explainable as an accident or attributable to a claim that there could be so many defects with the cassettes. The same manufacturer had been making them all along and when Balkum examined older samples from those mines and from others, there were no such abnormalities. He knew that tampering was the only rational explanation, but he was not about to say that out loud.

Upon digesting the updated cassette samples' review, Balkum instructed the three technicians to continue their efforts as before. He took the time to remind them again, in what was conveyed this time as a warning, that they were not under any circumstances to disclose the information to anyone. "Not to anyone, not a soul," he repeated to them so that there could be no doubt, no claimed misunderstanding, about the secrecy that was to be maintained. Emphasizing the directive, he then added, "Understood?"

Underscoring the importance of his command, he required an affirmative response that they got his message. All confirmed that the instructions were received, but Tucker squirmed inside, while keeping an expressionless visage.

At odds with his stern instruction, Balkum then tried to dispel the natural conclusion that something corrupt was at work. "And none of this is to suggest that anything nefarious is going on. We make no presumptions. Just trying to see how often these things are occurring, then see if we can figure out why. Could be a host of innocent explanations."

As the meeting ended, none of the technicians were buying Balkum's attempt to downplay the events.

When, two weeks later and again two weeks after that, with the review now approaching 500 mines, Balkum knew that the next step was then required, the results so overwhelming that procrastination could not be an option. He called Doug Green, with the Mine Safety and Health Division of the Office of the Solicitor. They were not strangers, having met on several occasions over the years at both agency and industry health conferences. It did not take long to describe the results that had been uncovered, and it took no lobbying to persuade Green that there was a problem demanding further inquiry.

As Balkum had leaped over a few rungs in the MSHA hierarchy by calling Green directly, he raised that concern to him as well.

Green assured him he would take care of that. No worries in that department, he told him.

Three weeks later, with the number of mines having AWCs in their dust cassettes then approaching 800, Green and two other attorneys from the Solicitor's Office arrived at Balkum's Health Technology Center. Green, brought along attorneys Jake Sanford, and Karl Czarnecki. From the MSHA health division they also brought along two specialists with experience in the dust cassettes. None had been to the little town within Wild and Wonderful West Virginia with a population less than 1500. Little more than a five-hour drive from the Mine Safety headquarters in Arlington, Virginia, the quintet was anxious to see the samples that had caused such consternation in Balkum's office.

Balkum greeted them in the parking lot and from there they proceeded to the modest one floor building which housed the Technology Center. It made little sense to have the facility located in such an obscure town, but that was the practice for politicians of all stripes – do what you can for your constituents, especially in shrinking, economically starving, little towns like Mount Hope. The citizens appreciated it. Small as it was, it still offered some relief for the economic decline the state had been facing over decades.

They assembled in Balkum's office. An acknowledgement of appreciation for Donna Nelson's role in first spotting the issue, he had invited her to join the group. As his office was cramped, some had to stand, while Balkum made his succinct presentation, showing them, without delay, representative samples. He began by displaying normal cassette samples, a baseline, so that they could appreciate the abnormal results with them.

Once that was established, he displayed the white center dust cassettes, a stark contrast from the non-suspect samples. He made a point of noting that the AWCs before them came from different mine operations. This was by design, to show them results from unrelated mine operators. In that way, they could not question whether they just happened to be quirks from a single mine's operations. No, these samples all came from entirely different ownerships.

THE CASE OF THE ABNORMAL WHITE CENTER

Besides, as Balkum would later emphasize in summing up the results, they now had a number approaching 800 mines displaying these AWCs, making it impossible to conjure up some innocent explanation for this phenomenon.

All agreed, including the health specialists from headquarters, that what was before them involved tampering. Results of that order – they don't just come out of the blue. Given those huge numbers, Balkum had persuasively ruled out guiltless explanations. The sheer number of mines involved solidly confirmed that conclusion.

When the presentation was completed, Green asked to speak with Balkum privately. The others were ushered out, with Balkum instructing Donna to use the time for introducing the group to the other technicians involved in the review. Given the modest size of the facility, all staff had been aware of the presence of the visitors, a rare occurrence at this remote location and it had created a small buzz, especially because the word got out that they came from D.C. Apart from the two other techs within the office, who surmised the reason for the visit, the other employees were in the dark, though the group's presence sparked much gossip over it. People don't come from Washington without a reason, they realized.

Nelson brought the guests to Tucker and Grasser's work stations but, as she was again in charge for the moment, asked that they all go to the lunchroom. Though the two fellow techs were peeved that they were once more taking orders from someone so junior to them, they had no choice but to obediently follow Nelson. Once there, she closed the door and introduced the group to her fellow technicians.

Another insult, the two thought, upon only now being informed of the reason for the headquarters' visitors. Donna reviewed what had occurred moments earlier in the chief's office and that he had directed her to introduce the others on the team to the visitors while he conferred with Attorney Green.

Before long, Balkum appeared with Green in the lunchroom, introducing him as the lead of the visitors from Washington.

Green said only a few words, expressing appreciation for the efforts of the technicians, but he consciously avoided any grand statement about what these AWCs meant. Describing the results as 'interesting,' he was studiously noncommittal, expressing vaguely that they would need further study and examination. However, it was obvious that he viewed the matter seriously, as he spotlighted Balkum's earlier multiple admonitions that this was not to be discussed with anyone, as any leaks could undermine a fair and impartial review of the results.

Balkum then spoke up about the mandatory secrecy, noting, "As I have instructed before, when I told you not to discuss this with anyone, that includes any other employees in our office." Underscoring the confidentiality, he again required an affirmative response. "We all understand this, right?' Dutifully, all acknowledged the requirement, with Tucker only nodding, while Grasser and Nelson voiced their commitment to the order.

It was just after the noon hour when the visitors were ready for their return trip to their D.C. headquarters. With the roundtrip distance alone making for a very long day, Green politely declined the invitation to join Balkum and Nelson for lunch at one of the two local cafés. As they were assembling around their car, bringing along some representative samples of the suspect cassettes, all properly labeled to ensure there would be no chain of custody issues raised down the road, Green informed that he would be in touch before long, but Balkum, seasoned as he was, understood that meant at least a few weeks would pass.

Later that afternoon, Balkum reconvened his group of technicians. The meeting was brief. Though he began by praising their work, a diplomatic move on his part, his purpose was twofold; to instruct them to continue their diligent efforts, but more importantly to reinforce yet again that none of this was to be discussed out of the office, nor even outside of their group.

All again acknowledged his renewed admonition, which had now been repeated several times. But with his resentment running high, despite his promise, it made Tucker more resolved to alert a former mining buddy.

At the end of the day, only Tucker remained at the office. Normally, he was out the door without delay. Just to be certain that his fellow workers had all left, he took a tour around the small facility, to make sure that he was the lone employee. Thus assured, he noted that only the nightly cleaning crew was then arriving.

They were not an issue. Tucker was dismissive of them. 'Dumb-asses' he called them when talking with Grasser. "Learn to speak fucking English, for Christ's sake!" he would complain to his friend, ironically revealing his own low level of vocabulary. "Stealing our jobs is what they're fucking doing!" he would gripe. The F word made frequent appearances when he spoke about issues that animated him.

Confident of his privacy, upon returning to his work station, he dialed out to his long-time friend, Ricky Slone, Bobcat Creek Colliery's director of safety.

"Hey there, Ricky, my bud, how'r they hangin," he began.

Not immediately recognizing the caller's voice, Slone responded cautiously, "Hello?"

"It's me, Danny Tucker, you ol' dog," he replied, realizing that Slone was uncertain who was on the line.

As he spoke, Martina Reyes, the lead for the cleaner crew, was emptying the trash cans next to Tucker and Grasser's work stations. Tucker stopped to look at her. She looked clueless. Dumb fuck, he thought, probably the only two words she would comprehend.

Slone then picked up who was on the phone. "Oh, sorry Danny, didn't know for sure who it was. I'm good, my friend. I'm really good. And you?" he asked realizing that the time of the call was odd.

"Same here, just fine," he reassured. "I called for a reason," he continued, realizing that Ricky was curious about the nature of the call.

"Not surprised, my friend, not surprised. So what's up, I'm all ears."

Cautious, Tucker looked around, eyeing the nearby cleaning woman again, concluding that her vacuous appearance meant she posed no threat, assuming she could even comprehend more than limited English.

"Well, I'm the only one in the office now," he advised, as if Reyes was no more than a robot. "But, I got to be cautious, so I can't say much. I just want to alert you to be careful with your dust samples, okay? Be careful with them," he repeated for emphasis.

Martina, seriously underestimated by Tucker, had been in the states for eight years. She had picked up a lot of English in that time. Though she had never communicated with him beyond a nod or a smile, she read his name, right there, on the nameplate for his cubicle. She had also learned, too frequently, of those Americans who had contempt for newcomers of her background. And she was legal, proud to be a citizen too and, most recently, had voted in her first state-wide election. Though she didn't know why dust samples were important, ironically now dusting the work spaces herself, she was keen enough to realize by the tone of his voice that something secretive was involved. To lull Tucker, she was able to adopt the vacant, clueless look, on her face that gringos like him expected them to have. It wasn't so hard to mislead this Mr. Tucker.

The disclosure was enough for Slone. He didn't need a sledgehammer to understand the message. It was a heads-up, a warning to be sure. Slone was very much aware of his mine's dust sampling practices. Thinking ahead and now instantly worried, in case the call was being recorded, he kept his response vague, as unrevealing as he could manage. "Got it. Got it. Thank you."

Though he had known Tucker for years, he had to be cautious. Maybe Tucker had been co-opted. Trust no one when it came to his mine's operations was his rule.

Protectively, he added, "We're always very careful with our samples as you know," imparting a tone of innocence. "We're just as concerned as anyone 'bout protecting our miners' health. We give it a high priority, but it's always good to get a friendly reminder, my friend."

Tucker was not dense either. It was obvious that, despite Ricky's innocuous response, his friend got the message, loud and clear. Mission accomplished. And screw you too, Balkum! he thought, while oblivious that even his old buddy was wary about the friendly warning he delivered.

His task completed, he still eyed that nearby nameless cleaning woman, while concluding again that she was a virtual deaf mute, unable to grasp his words, much less to express them. He felt quite safe. He was, effectively, alone in the office. Besides, if anyone else were to overhear that conversation, Tucker continued, he could maintain that it was completely innocent, with no intent to provide any advance warning.

Yet, that his mind would call up that foreboding thought made him squirm. Advance warnings could get a mine into big trouble. The twist here was that advance warnings referred to miners or their supervisors warning that

THE CASE OF THE ABNORMAL WHITE CENTER

an MSHA inspector was on site. Do that and a criminal proceeding could be the result. But an MSHA employee giving the advance warning? Though it only applied to warnings regarding an inspection that was about to start, he was now nervous that his words to Slone would be labeled as the same thing. And that would be quite a case. The newspapers would shout about such a thing. A government employee violating the safety act he was to protect! Whether labeled as an advance warning or not, if anyone found out about the call he would be in a heap of trouble.

"Okay," Tucker wrapped up the call, attempting to reinforce the idea that it was just a call between friends and some general safety advice, like he would offer to anyone. "Take care, my friend. We'll keep in touch as usual."

"You bet, Danny. Have a good night."

Almost immediately after he hung up Tucker's worry persisted. Misgivings over his act started in. Should he have made the call? Had he acted rashly? Was it stupid to have done so? If ever discovered, his job would be over. True, he considered Slone to be a friend, but still what if ol' Ricky were to blab, to god knows who, that the call came from him? It was possible. Slone, he knew from their years together, could be crafty and he knew how to protect himself for sure. A knot formed in his gut, an unanticipated reaction of dread, the opposite of the feeling he expected to have, given his good Samaritan deed. Too late now, he thought, regretting his call.

CHAPTER 2

Balkum had been patient, waiting for a response from the Mine Safety and Health Headquarters' Office of the Solicitor in D.C. His long government experience had taught him that the administrative wheels turn slowly, methodically. He did not expect a rapid reply. Besides, he knew this was no ordinary matter. Properly, it would require a lot of close scrutiny at many levels within the Solicitor's Office and the Mine Safety and Health Administration.

Another factor, learned from his years of experience in government, had educated him that, because the Republicans presently held sway in Washington and especially as that party was in the White House too, there would be a pushback. Charging a business, any business, with wrongdoing, met with reluctance from the Grand Old Party. That was not surprising, as they were the party of business, so if there was a way to sink this investigation, or at least sugar-coat it, that would be the route taken. So, he waited, while instructing his tech trio to continue their review of the dust sample cassettes.

One problem had appeared of late. Rather abruptly, some of the mines which had regularly displayed the AWCs now started delivering cassettes without that issue.

From Donna's regular report updates, she informed her boss of this development and that Tucker and Grasser's review of the samples had found the same thing; the AWCs were dropping dramatically – the number of mines without AWCs was now growing substantially.

Something, Balkum knew, was up. It was plain that somehow the information had been leaked. He recognized that now, with Washington involved, it could have come out of there, but there was also a possibility that someone in his own office was behind it. Though he expected that there would be denials from all three when asked if any of them had broken their promise of silence, he still decided to call them to his office. Perhaps, like a good poker player, he could detect a tell from one of them when speaking face to face. Even if he could not sense anything, as was likely, he still had to make the inquiry. If he had an inkling that one of them had crossed the line, he could follow-up by checking their office phone call logs.

As expected, when they convened, and he raised the issue of disclosing the AWCs to anyone in or out of the office, all three declared their fealty, asserting that they had kept their promise to Balkum. Scrutinizing their faces as they made the denials, he was unable to ferret out whether any of them had transgressed. While the problem remained, he decided to reinforce that the whole matter was to be kept private. All nodded their understanding of the standing order.

Upon leaving the office, Tucker was relieved that no accusation had been leveled at him. It was hard enough to remain expressionless when Balkum hit them with the news. He had broken into a sweat, but it was not obvious until after he left the boss' office. Too late, he now viewed his call to Slone as a serious mistake, but at least he had the good sense not to compound that error by confiding with Grasser about what he had done. Still, it left him edgy. What might follow if this whole AWC thing became a big deal? Might he get caught up in it? To save their own hides, he knew that people will often give up others and his old buddy Ricky would not be above that, though he would express feeling "real bad" that he had to inform on Tucker.

Donna, though without sin herself, was upset at the apparent betrayal. She considered that it was at least possible that either Tucker or Grasser could have been behind it. She was relieved when Balkum, trusting her in a conversation later that same day about the issue, pointed out that the leak could well have come from those in DC who now knew of the investigation. It was clear that, wherever the source of the leak, he knew it was not from her.

It was a month to the day of the Solicitor's visit to the Mount Hope Technology Center that Balkum received the call from Doug Green.

"We're going ahead with it, Greg," he announced. "Off the record, we had some resistance from the Assistant Secretary, as you might have expected given his political affiliation, but given the numbers of AWCs, he didn't have much choice."

"Good to hear, Doug," Balkum replied. "I thought with so many of them, they would have to bring civil penalties. And, of course, as you probably anticipated, we had a large number of AWCs continue after your visit."`

"No surprise about that," he confirmed. "More instances only serve to strengthen our case."

"However, there is one issue that's come up," Balkum advised. "In fact, I was planning on calling you about it this week."

"You have my attention. What's going on?"

"Just last week there was a dramatic change. The number of AWC's started to drop significantly. And, this week they have almost entirely dried up. So, the cassettes that are coming in now, those with the abnormal center, they're down to a trickle. Now, without the AWCs, the majority are showing excessive dust exposure, which as you know, was the norm until the AWCs started appearing. But the abnormal centers, they're virtually gone."

Green was taken aback by the news but he did not feel it would hurt the cases about to be filed. "Somebody leaked this Greg, obviously," he said tersely. "Trust, it's a hard thing to come by. I'm disappointed naturally, but it's not a blow to our litigating position."

"Just so you know," Balkum informed, "I called in my three techs, who have been examining the dust cassettes. From their review of recent samples, each of them was fully aware of the development. You may recall that I was alerted to the whole AWC thing by my tech Donna Nelson, whom you met. I trust her. The other two, I can't be sure, but they all denied any breach of their promise to keep this matter secret. If they were lying, they did a good job. I just couldn't tell."

"That's all you could do, Greg," Green comforted him. "There are few confessions in real life. Mostly they're in TV crime dramas. If it's any consolation, remember that the leaked information could've come out of headquarters too. They're not above doing that out here, you know."

"Hadn't thought much about that," Balkum acknowledged, "My inclination was to think the source was from my office."

"Well, we're unlikely to find out where it came from," Green continued. "But if you stop to think about it, it seems to help our case more than hurt it."

Balkum, unsure how that could be, replied, "I'm not sure I understand."

"Think about it. We have a ton of these AWC cases. Then, almost on signal, which I literally mean there must have been a signal from someone, they stop. The AWC's disappear. How would that look to whichever administrative law judge is assigned to these? Shows consciousness of guilt to me. The attorneys I assign to bring these cases will make that point forcefully. I'll make sure of it."

"You're right," he replied, "the way the spigot was flowing and then suddenly it stops. The logic you noted seems inescapable."

"You can expect the official announcement in a few days. I'd prefer if you'd keep this between us until then, even from the techs in your office."

"I won't mention this to a soul, but I sure appreciate the heads-up."

"Thanks, I knew you would. We have a lot of work ahead of us once this gets launched. With so many large coal companies involved, you can expect a tidal wave of a defense. So much money will be involved with the civil penalties we'll be seeking, they won't care about the legal fees."

He continued, "Watch your back, too. Defending cases like these are not limited to the facts and evidence. Expect it to get personal, Greg. After the announcement, you should convey a similar message to your techs. If any of them are caught using drugs, busted in a massage parlor, or any other kind of trouble, the defense will use that to its fullest extent. If they can smear you or your office, they will."

Balkum, lacking background in such matters, hadn't considered that a defense would resort to such low tactics. He took the warning seriously.

Ending the call, Green expressed, "So, we'll be in touch, to say the least. If we don't screw up the case in some major way, I think we'll prevail. Take care, Greg."

The call over, Balkum leaned back in his chair, pleased that charges would be made. With such a solid case, he was confident that the mines would be held to account.

The following week, the big brass of the Department of Labor assembled within its Hall of Honor to announce the action against a slew of coal mine operators. The press had been summoned. Remarkably, only a few hints had been disclosed about the nature of the upcoming news and even those were limited to the select group of reporters who had developed connections with the Department. They were advised only that it would be a significant announcement, that it involved underground coal mines, and that it was a major enforcement action. But that was all; the details were not disclosed, heightening the anticipation. Frantic efforts were made to learn more from DOL sources, but to no effect.

The soon to be identified coal mine operators knew full well what was coming. They had assumed that their corrupt practices would never be noticed by the employees who received the dust samples. Those government automatons would simply weigh the cassettes, find that the dust levels had not been exceeded, and move on to the next batch of samples. That the origin of all this would come from the discovery by a nondescript tech lab out of the hinterlands of West Virginia was not on anyone's list.

That it was to be a substantial news event was confirmed just by the high level of the officials who were present. The Secretary of Labor, Roberto Costa, led the group. His remarks were brief; he was there primarily to introduce those who would be giving the details. True to his party, and the Republican occupant in the White House, he began by stating that there appeared to have been tampering with some coal dust sampling in some underground coal mines, but he immediately noted that these were charges only and that, consistent with due process, no one should presume that any of the mines actually engaged in any wrongdoing. Upon identifying those within the Mine Safety and Health Administration who would speak after him and provide details of the charges, Costa skedaddled from the Hall.

The Assistant Secretary of Labor for Mine Safety, Forest B. Ford II, then followed. He too took a non-committal tact, the same approach presented by his boss, Costa. Though occupying the top position within Mine Safety, Ford had already established himself on the mining industry side of the equation by instituting the "single penalty" assessment. The term, intentionally non-descriptive, was a boon to mine operators, as it brought about $25.00 penalties for violations which were deemed not reasonably likely to result in a reasonably serious injury or illness. Less than a parking ticket, it meant that if an injury or illness was not deemed to be reasonably serious, the operator would walk away with a penalty that would not encourage compliance, not when the penalty was cheaper to pay than the cost of following the safety or health requirements.

It was not until Delbert Findlay, the Deputy Assistant Secretary, took the podium that the enormity of the charges was finally revealed. On their face, the numbers were staggering: some 1,500 underground coal mines had been charged, involving 800 mine operators. The press was introduced to a new term, "AWCs", and that it stood for "abnormal white centers" in the cassettes that contained the filters. Those filters, Findlay informed, were designed to capture the amount of dust a miner was inhaling during the course of a shift.

For some of these AWCs, it was explained, the amount of the dust collected was less than the typical dust exposure on a city street corner, making underground coal mines a cleaner environment to work in than outdoors. Quiet guffaws could be heard among the press upon hearing that revelation. Forest Ford looked sternly at Findlay, his comment about the mine air purity being a departure from the script to be followed.

With the news conference presenting only the bare bones of the charges, the news media was left with waiting until the civil penalty petitions were filed. They were anxious to see the names of the mine operations but that anticipation was offset by the large number of mines already announced to be involved. With all those mine operators soon to be named and with the huge number of underground mines involved, only a relative few would not have to face litigation. As the media began to disperse, the conversations among the reporters reached the obvious conclusion – with that many mine operators cited, there had to be a choreographed effort to falsify the dust measurements.

That same day, far away from the hubbub at the Labor Department headquarters, fourteen attorneys had gathered at the law offices of Watkins, Lewis, Porter, Cooley and Young. That firm, headed by two seasoned litigators, Winston Malthan and Milo Krakovich, under an agreement reached with the other law firms engaged by the wealth of the mine operators, had been designated to lead the defense of the AWC cases. All of the assembled attorneys had known of the impending charges for two weeks and there had been no delay in preparing the defense. The two addressed the gathering of their fellow barristers. Designed to impress visitors, they had gathered in the firm's large conference room, a rich wood-paneled place for which no expense had been spared.

Malthan began, "I welcome all of you and I appreciate that we have reached a consensus that Milo and I will be the lead attorneys." Stroking the group's considerable self-regard, he was quick to add, "That's a formality however. We know this is a team effort and the two of us, and the many associates in our firm who will be working around the clock, will draw upon your considerable expertise and strategies for defeating these unwarranted and unfounded actions."

It was pure fluff, as all knew, but still welcomed by them, feeding the overflow of immense egos in the room. They acknowledged the accolades, nodding to Malthan and Krakovich and to each other, a mutual admiration fest. However, the venerable group had a secondary motive in acceding to the Watkins Firm leading the defense – if it failed and the mines had to eat the enormous fines being sought by the Labor Department, they could easily blame that firm for the adverse outcome. Sharks will be sharks, collectively they silently thought, without shame.

Malthan continued, "We've already secured the services of several experts. They know the ins and outs of all the issues surrounding particles, filters and dust collection. Several samples from the dust collection devices have already been demanded by us. We received them and they've been sent to the experts for their analysis."

'Analysis,' all knew, was a code word, meaning starting the process of casting doubts on the samples. "In addition," he continued, "we have already filed our initial discovery request, demanding representative samples from each mine charged with these violations. Those cassettes, alleged to have been tampered, will be delivered to our experts within the next ten days."

Getting ahead of himself, because the 'experts' had not begun their work yet, Malthan, feeling the moment of authority, added, "Those experts will make mincemeat out of the unfounded complaints."

Contradicting his pronounced confidence that there was no substance to the government's claims, he then added, "Furthermore, the science, I have been told by two of the experts, is so complex, that any judges assigned to these cases will have their heads spinning with the highly technical testimony they will be presenting. They won't know up from down, they tell me. And if there is utter confusion, no judge will be able to conclude that the cassettes were tampered."

A few of the group glanced briefly at one another, conveying their recognition that Malthan's confidence that there was no solid case was immediately undercut by the firm's other strategy of overwhelming any judge who would hear the case.

Milo also recognized that his colleague had gone too far, as he noted the poor reaction of a few to the last remark. To avoid displaying his reaction, he took to looking down at his notepad. He would have stayed with the weak case argument, avoiding the fallback strategy that they could win by creating such confusion for the judge that it would become incomprehensible.

One of the attorneys, representing a large coal mine, then spoke up, "So, Winston, we don't know which judges have been assigned these cases?"

"That's true," Krakovich interjected, not wanting Malthan to hog up the entire speaking time before the group. The two were equals and he wanted to be sure that the assembled group knew that. "And we have thought about that as well. If there are several judges assigned, we will move to consolidate the cases so that they will be heard by one judge. As we will point out to the Chief Judge, the logic supports the move. If there were to be more than one judge assigned, there could be conflicting and completely inconsistent results. As the government is claiming tampering, there must be a somewhat unified theory how that occurred."

"Isn't that a bit risky?" as an attorney representing a different coal mine, then spoke up, the first one having broken the ice, wresting the domination of their meeting that Malthan and Krakovich had tried to accomplish. "Putting our eggs in one basket and all?"

Smoothly, Krakovich tried to assuage the valid concern, while trying to regain control of the group. The last thing he and Malthan wanted was to have too much questioning about their approach. Yes, on paper, they were a team with no captains, but in reality, the Watkins firm was in charge.

Putting forth a personal touch, addressing the questioner by his first name, Milo responded, "Jim, your point is well taken, but here are two things to consider. First, we may not have a choice – the Chief Judge may assign all these to one judge anyway. And we are confident that, if that occurs, we will prevail. Second, if more than one judge assigned, we will work that to our advantage as well. In that scenario we will look to sweep the table so to speak, victories with both judges. But if that doesn't happen, as long as we win one, we still have a strong case that the inconsistent results mean that there are deep flaws if one is not a win," avoiding using the word 'loss.'

Then, contradicting his silent misgivings over his partner having gone too far, Milo then double downed on the claim. "And, again, we believe we will win if it's one judge or two hearing these. As Winston mentioned, the experts we have lined up, well, I'll put it less delicately than he did, those experts will flood the record with so much sh …,", he stopped before uttering the word, an expletive being unfitting in the stately conference room they occupied, "with so much *science*," he continued, a broad smile coming across his face as he completed the sentence, "that any judge or judges will throw up their hands, unable to make heads or tails of the whole thing. And so, faced with the burden of the preponderance of the evidence, the Secretary will lose."

Collectively, the group smiled, a look of self-satisfaction then spread through the room. Nice to have tigers like these two coming to the fight, several thought.

More importantly, for the purposes of Malthan and Krakovich, they had quelled the brief challenge to their leadership role.

Shifting gears, the two knew there was an uncomfortable matter that they had to address. Ignoring it would only make matters worse, as the subject was on the minds of all the attorneys in the room – the absent, but very present, elephant in the room. One large operator, Eagle Coal and Coke, with fifteen mines, sprinkled through West Virginia and Pennsylvania, had not joined the others in the litigation defense.

Krakovich could not be sure what, if anything, was up, but it did not fit that the Eagle Coal operation was conspicuously without a representative at their gathering. Always guarded in his behavior, he had the cautious good sense not to inquire of the firm that typically handled Eagle Coal and Coke mine safety and health cases about their absence. He would soon find out.

Though communications between all the cited mines had been extremely circumspect, and at a time well before the Solicitor had filed the civil penalty actions, and therefore before the Watkins firm had been formally engaged, all the mines knew the identities of their compatriots. Eagle Coal and Coke had been with them from the start, as they collaborated about the techniques to assure that the dust samples passed. But now, with their noticeable absence, it made the whole lot of them uncomfortable when they met in the Watkins firm's prestigious conference room but with no counsel from Eagle Coal and Coke in attendance.

"There's one more subject we need to address," Milo began. "I imagine it's been on your minds. I'm referring to Eagle Coal and Coke. And rest assured, we've reached out to them. Now, as you've no doubt noted, we don't have a representative for them with us to date, but that doesn't mean that our brother mine won't be joining our group, as I expect they will," he declared, though his instincts told him otherwise.

"But let's consider if, for whatever reason, they go it alone," he then paused for effect. "I'm here to tell you that it won't harm our case one bit. Not one bit," he added for emphasis. "Heck, wouldn't matter even if a few mines did get jittery."

He continued, "The success in our trial does not depend on decisions that Eagle Coal, or anyone else, makes. It would be insulting to all of you to suggest that you never considered whether the decision by some other mine in this dust matter could impact the merits of our case. While we may momentarily think about such a development, we would promptly dismiss it because we all know that things don't work that way. Each case has to stand on its own. That's basic law."

For emphasis, he repeated, "Each case must stand on its own. And, who knows, maybe Eagle did tamper, God forbid," he said with the innocence of a saint. "So, we take care of our own yard. Winston and I are confident we will prevail against these unwarranted charges, whatever ill-advised decision Eagle might take."

The members of the group then looked at one another, reassured by Krakovich's peptalk. Collectively, they nodded, pacified by Milo's reassurance.

Having ended on that high note, the two recognized that it was the appropriate time to call the meeting to a close. Following Krakovich's words, Malthan then picked up, "So, that's about it for now. We will be in close touch, perhaps more often than you might wish," he added with his practiced broad smile. "We will need your consultation and input each step of the way," he claimed, again stroking the crowded egos in the room, while not meaning those words at all. "For now, there will be an unavoidable lull as we wait to receive the representative dust cassette samples and the equipment used to capture those faulty samples. And then, it will be several months before we start to receive the experts' evaluations of the claimed AWCs. I want you to know that if anything of importance comes along, you will be informed about such matters without delay."

Again, the group seemed content with the presentation and the direction the defense would take.

Krakovich had the last word. Ever gracious, he had perfected a polished, gentle demeanor, completely at odds with his ruthless underbelly. "And now, if you will, please let's all proceed directly to our dining room where we have a delicious catered lunch waiting for us. Bon appétit," he intoned, with his gentle smile, while stretching the limits of his sincerity and French.

CHAPTER 3

The team from the Solicitor's Office, having observed the parade of notables at the Labor Department's Great Hall, had now all returned to their separate quarters in Arlington, Virginia. Though the leaders had made their largely uninformative pronouncements, the real work, enormous as it was, had yet to be done. They had the raw numbers, now nearly 5,000 incidents of AWCs, encompassing involvement of slightly more than 800 mines. That amounted to about half of the underground coal mines in Kentucky, West Virginia and Pennsylvania. The Solicitor's Office had served nearly all of those mines having those suspicious dust cassettes and each of them had forcefully denied the charges. Of course, the team led by the Watkins firm were well aware of the claims, having issued the denials.

Three weeks after the Department of Labor's announcement, the Solicitor made a news splash, announcing that Eagle Coal and Coke had admitted to tampering with the dust cassettes, a huge victory for MSHA. Not only that, Eagle agreed to pay a half a million dollars civil penalty for the hundreds of tampered cassettes involved. "All of the cassettes," the Solicitor somberly noted, carefully not displaying his glee when before the press, "all of them," he soberly repeated for emphasis, "had the AWCs."

Upon learning of the news, Milo and Winston arranged a conference call that same day with all the attorneys in their group. Milo took the lead when the call began, immediately acting as if the news was not a surprise and, in the same breath, that it was of no consequence. "As I mentioned when we were all together in Washington just a few weeks ago, it was always a possibility that Eagle Coal might get weak-kneed and settle. But recall that I said at the time

THE CASE OF THE ABNORMAL WHITE CENTER

it doesn't matter for us what others may do, however misguided such decisions come about. So, as they say, no worries. We will prevail, full stop," he asserted imperiously. He then continued, "I'm pleased to take questions any of you may have about this."

Several members from the group had spoken with one another before the call from Milo and Winston. Though some of the attorneys were now re-evaluating whether a settlement would be the wiser course, their respective mine operator employers had all advised them to continue with the Watkins leadership. They had their orders, the operators unwavering. Besides, when they returned to brief their mine owners following their recent group meeting, they told them of the possibility that Eagle Coal might fold and settle with the Secretary, but that it would not threaten their cases. So, the development was not a surprise to the operators.

This was no time to switch horses, several mine operators advised. Memorably, one operator remarked, "in for a penny, in for a pound." Though less confident than their mine employers, the lawyers took their orders. Some, nervous whether Eagle Creek portended their mines' fate, thought of their own expression, the one about having made their own bed. Now, more than an expression, they had to lie in it.

Only a few had questions, but as they had the marching orders from their mine operator employers, even those were not really questions as much as seeking reassurance from Milo and Winston, that all would still end well. The two, knowing that some hand-holding would be needed given the development, obliged fully. It amounted to repeating what had already been said, but they realized that was the nature of reassurance, saying yet again that it would end well.

Once the call had ended, Milo and Winston met to share their assessment of it. Both were satisfied, but to avoid any renegades among the group, they agreed it was best to convene a new in-person meeting in D.C., to forestall any risk that a mutiny could develop. They waited a few days and then called for a second meeting, using the ruse that it was to update 'the team,' as they liked to refer to them, on some new developments. There was some news, but before the Eagle Mine settlement, it would have been relayed by telephone.

A week later, they all gathered once more in the Watkins firm's conference room. This time the effect of the grand surroundings had a diminished impact. The mission was to restore backbone among the newly timid. The two masters of ceremony knew they had to reestablish the correctness of their position – stay the course, and all the mines would prevail. If several started to peel off, the defense and the wherewithal to pay for the costly retained experts would be cramped.

A few spoke up without hesitation after Winston and Milo made their opening remarks. The questions, expressing their considerable worry, confirmed to the two that the decision for this second in-person meeting was prudent.

"Eagle Coal and Coke is a large operation," one of the attorneys noted. She continued, "They will be disclosing how the samples were altered. That won't be news to us," she noted, with all secure in the knowledge that their undisguised discussion could be unhindered, as they were protected by the attorney-client privilege. "It will be of immense use to the government as they proceed against the rest of us. They will seek to enter all of it in the record and I don't see how any judge presiding in our cases can put that kind of information aside."

The group seemed to concur with the grim new assessment. Making matters worse, fearful that the Eagle Coal and Coke news was a harbinger of their own fate, the group's assessment of the two chieftains before them was now more critical. That Krakovich smile, so genteel, so smooth, had lost some of its charm. Now it felt more like a salesman's grin, the type that made buyers wary, not reassured. And, he had that small religious cross thing on his tie. What was that all about?

As for Malthan, his smile was not heartening at all. Instead, his attempt to project confidence looked frozen, as if the expression had been painted on his face.

Krakovich, seeing the worry on their faces, took on the persuasion effort with vigor. Just as much was at stake here as when before a jury. It required a masterful, smooth presentation, but he felt completely up to it.

"Now, now," he began with a soft, comforting tone, "I get it. Winston gets it. You're concerned about Eagle Coal and Coke. Some lingering worries. We're aware of your questions, but we don't share your concerns. I don't know why they folded, but I can tell you this, it was a foolish and needlessly expensive decision. They were too fainthearted. Had they been with us, it wouldn't have happened."

The group listened; they would at least hear out the rebuttal to their collective concerns.

"Remember," Milo continued, "we all know," presenting himself as an educator to the irresolute, "that no judge can simply look to one party's settlement and use that against us. It could never be expressly acknowledged that such a settlement had any effect on that judge's evaluation of the evidence. Doing that would constitute plainly reversible error and the government would be back to square one. Plus, the matter would then be assigned to a new judge. Painfully aware of what happened, any new judge would be duly chastened by the previous judge's reversal."

Intentionally pausing, he let that thought sink in for a moment. "So, our cases will come down to the evidence at *our* hearings. And we can all agree that's how it should be. As we told you when we last met, that evidence will be formidable. Hate to repeat myself, but with the experts we have retained, all with credentials that would impress any judge, the defenses will make that judge or judges' heads swim. Remember, the burden is on the government. They have to prevail by the preponderance, *by the preponderance*," he repeated for emphasis, "of the evidence. We are confident that burden won't be met."

"And, yes," he then added, "the government will have their own experts, but our team, the best in all of the United States, will be able to help us refute their claims. Remember too, the experts the government will present will be second tier. For a case like this, they will have to rely substantially on their own people, out of that lab in Mount Hope. We have already looked into the educational and career background of the head of that office. Let me be blunt; it is not impressive. Not saying he's a nobody, but our experts will have the upper hand by far. He will not fare well on cross-examination; I can tell you that."

Listening to Milo's presentation, the group seemed to relax, their initial, upright and stiff postures, now easing back in the rich leather chairs. A few then poured more coffee in their cups and the Danish started to be consumed, though initially it had been untouched.

"So, I am telling you all," Milo continued, now sensing the tide turning in his favor, "this is not the time to fret." Careful not to go too far, he considered for a moment whether to include his next point. With little time to contemplate the decision, he then added, "And while we're focusing for a moment on the concerns y'all have, let's not ignore the other side of the coin. If there were to be a settlement, it would require an admission that every one of the mines we represent knew damn well what they were doing. Talk about sending a message that those operations were callous, not caring a whit about what all that coal dust was doing to the lungs of their miners. That would forever taint the public's view of the industry in a way it has never experienced before."

He paused, letting the message sink in, then added, "Mine disasters, they cause horror with the public for sure, but it's never bled over to an indictment of all mines. No, through no small efforts, those events have been tagged on the individual mine where a disaster occurred.

And then, time, our good friend, time, has the effect of causing the public to move on, the memory of a disaster, outside of the particular small community affected, fades. But this, this one, especially if it's the essentially the entire coal mine industry that's been involved in a coordinated scheme, I can tell you that the public will not forget that, not at all. And Congress will step in too, you can be sure of that. Think of the expenses you will all bear if that happens. So, you can all see, far too much is at stake here."

He had brought them around. Scattered involuntary nods began around the room. Though some still worried, it did seem that, on balance, it was wiser to go ahead.

Milo sensed it, proud of his persuasive skills. Though he admired Winston, he knew that he was the better one to make the pitch. He could not resist one last word on the subject, his boastful ego at work. "And don't tell me that there are moral issues involved here, because there simply are not. These miners, they're making more money than any of the other people in their communities.

THE CASE OF THE ABNORMAL WHITE CENTER

Among the best paid. Why, comparatively, they're rich in those places. Living the good life is what they're doin'.

"Beyond that, sure, I'll allow that coal dust isn't a good thing, but it comes with the work. Now doesn't it! Dust and coal mining, they're inseparable. To meet the government's coal dust exposure levels, it's fantasy, pure and simple. You can't mine and be productive if those unrealistic dust level standards were to be met. And when those miners get home, what do they do? Why the vast majority, they smoke cigarettes that's what they do. So, it's hypocritical to whine about some dust exposure while inhaling those cancer sticks, I tell you."

Taking in that last remark, though not a one in the room was a smoker, the group felt uncomfortable with Krakovich's last observation. Though he was correct, at least as to the inconsistency of worrying about coal dust exposure while smoking cigarettes, admittedly endemic in poorer towns, it did not escape many of them that one problem did not excuse the other. Smoking was a choice, a poor one, but sucking in that dust, often laden with silica quartz, that was no choice on their part. They either accepted it or they found another job paying far less for those with minimal education.

Krakovich sensed that his last observation had landed with a thud and needing a recovery, so he decided to use the time-honored practice of litigators – end on a high note. "So, my friends, *we will win* this litigation I assure you. Winston and I will keep you up to date and answer any questions you may have as this proceeds." He ended with an insincere remark. "We will continue to need your input and advice as we proceed," his wide grin, a rehearsed look, developed over years of practice, accompanying his close.

Then, he continued seamlessly, "With those concerns now laid to rest, I want to speak to you about the real reason we called you back." It was a complete lie, of course, but as Milo assessed the group's collective reaction, they seemed attentive, not dismissive of him. "We have some great initial news from our top-notch scientists studying this bogus white center business. Two of them, completely unrelated to one another, operating out of different scientific labs, have concluded that there are many, I repeat, many, harmless reasons that can cause these things to occur. There will be more, but just this news itself means we already have a strong hand in our defense."

The group listened respectfully and, as it was good news, it was well-received. But these litigators were experienced and they knew full well that cross-examination can have a withering effect on direct testimony. Beyond that, they also knew that the Secretary would have his own expert witnesses.

Milo continued, "And there is more good news. Early results from our statistical expert demonstrate that these white centers appear with the same frequency at all mines. It just happens is what, no doubt due to manufacturing quirks. We'll be updating you regularly on these positive developments."

Though he couldn't be sure, it seemed that the group had been pacified. "Now, having put your concerns to rest and relayed the great scientific news, let's all partake in our five-star lunch spread.

The luncheon went well, the food having sated their worries about losing the litigation.

Having put out that fire, once the group had departed, the two resumed their strategy for the litigation. This was a two-pronged offensive – hyper-vigilance over the experts they had retained and a coming blitzkrieg mounted against the experts the Secretary would provide.

At this point, they knew of only one, that Balkum fellow out of Mount Hope. He would qualify as an expert, as the standard for meeting that label was low – one only need to know more than the average person to be deemed an expert. But cross-examination, done right, could demolish anyone qualified as an expert.

The preliminary information on Balkum was that he had the background to meet the threshold, but his education and career were not very impressive. Though the head of that small tech center office, in truth, he was only a mid-level bureaucrat. As such, his testimony would pale by comparison to the resumes and experience brought by the experts the Watkins firm had retained.

CHAPTER 4

When the issuance of the civil penalty petitions began, the numbers so large, the Solicitor's docket office was temporarily overwhelmed. It required some reorganization within that office to manage the onslaught of paper. Two clerks were assigned to deal solely with the task. To avoid cases being misdirected, no one else was to attend to the AWC cases. The Chief Judge for the office of administrative law judges, Edward Blandford II, had directed the arrangement. Having confidence with the chief clerk in the docket office, Jean-Ellen Phelps, he was satisfied with it. Beyond that order, he took a hands-off approach. If there were problems with the case, he could direct any criticisms to the presiding judge.

His focus was upon which judge, or perhaps which judges, should be assigned to the tidal wave of cases for these matters. Seasoned as he was, Blandford quickly discarded the idea of multiple judges handling the matters. True, it would be an enormous lift for any single judge to be assigned so many dockets, but the risk of different judges reaching conflicting conclusions would create insoluble havoc. No, it would have to be one judge, together with the reassurance to the unlucky person so designated that it would be the only matter on his plate and that there would be no pressure as to scheduling them for hearing.

He chose the most senior judge in the office, Charles Gray.

The Honorable Charles Gray, having a life-long outsized view of himself, never lacked for confidence. His physical appearance added to that self-image. With a height of six feet four inches, he had not spoiled that imposing look by being overweight. Though not obese, he was not in any sense fit. Exercise was not part of his routine, nor had it been for decades. His face was, some might say, distinguished for his sixty-four years. Though his hair had thinned significantly everywhere across his head, at least he did not have that typical bare spot on the back, the frequent starting point for baldness, nor did he need to employ a comb-over.

A federal administrative law judge for twenty-three years, his entire judicial career had been presiding in mine safety cases. Now, he was nearing retirement, though he had not decided on a firm date for it.

Yet, he felt cheated in his career. A judge all those years and not much to show for it financially.

His home was a modest three-bedroom ranch, which he frankly regarded as being on the low end of that description. Calling it modest was too generous. It was one of those split foyer arrangements. From the start, he had always hated that house. But his wife, Millie, wanted it and she prevailed on the decision, now more than 30 years ago. It had such a poorly designed floor plan; upon entering the front door, only a miniscule foyer presented itself, an area of some five by six feet. And at that point, one was only technically in the house. To access any practical use within it, one had to choose to either go up a flight, a climb of some eight stairs to the living quarters, or go down the same number of steps to the basement. Awful. Who thought of such arrangements?

That dwelling, such as it was, represented his largest asset, apart from whatever his federal retirement would bring. Though the mortgage had been paid off, the value of the house remained low. The neighborhood he lived in was safe, but it was packed with homes of similar modest value, and given the nature of the house itself, that meant he could never realize much from any sale, even though its location, in Alexandria, Virginia, was near to D.C. And by no means was it in a toney part of that city. It was all part of his feeling cheated, the damn thing had never appreciated significantly. Never mind that, while not rich in any sense, he was better off than most Americans. He still viewed his glass as half-empty.

Those drawbacks with his home were compounded by the unending maintenance costs. There was that inescapable need for painting the exterior every five or so years. It was a big expense and that process always involved some areas of rotten wood which had to be torn out and replaced. The roof had already been replaced once and it was clear that, not too many years ahead, that would be needed once again. With a house like that, even upgrading the windows, which had also been done, did not change the essential character of the place. Lipstick on a pig, he often thought, when thinking about the place.

Married almost 38 years, they were unable to have children. Though he presumed the problem was hers, testing revealed that it was his low sperm count that was the obstacle. The technology for in vitro fertilization was new during her child-bearing years and the cost was prohibitive. Artificial insemination was an alternative, but for them it meant someone else's sperm would have to be used, an entirely unacceptable method to him. As he saw it, that was only a step away from endorsing her having an affair. It wouldn't be his child, he told her. So, both unhappy with the news and a solution unacceptable to Charles, the outcome was no children.

Yet, the marriage did not dissolve. For him, as he well knew, a new wife would not overcome the problem, as he was the issue.

As if that weren't enough, his wife, Millie, had contracted multiple sclerosis, now a decade ago. It took a long time before the diagnosis was made, as her early symptoms did not reveal the condition. Vision issues were the start of it, some blurring and then some generalized chronic pain too. Later she developed some memory problems. The doctors made guesses, which is all they were, during the early years. Then, slowly, inexorably, other symptoms appeared. Millie kept telling people that her energy levels were low, but none of her varied symptoms produced a solid diagnosis. It was not until several years later, when new problems surfaced, bladder and balance issues, that they were given the news that she had MS. It was, the medical authorities explained, a diagnosis of exclusion. There was no "test" for the illness. It was particularly cruel in a way because it wouldn't kill her in the short term. Instead, it would take her apart, function by function, on a schedule that no one could predict.

Of course, he felt terrible about it. He was not cold-hearted. He loved his wife and had been true to her. But her condition impacted him, too, being the sole caregiver. All those meds, expensive as all get out, helped keep them from growing a retirement nest egg. As the condition progressed, her care needs grew with that. This meant that his work day's end only signaled the start of what was effectively his second job – the unrelenting care she required, with those duties increasing year by year.

He accepted all of that, but the intimate side of their marriage had also withered away. Mostly, she was just too tired for that, and the interest for it wasn't there anymore either. He was informed that this was a common symptom of the illness too, as if he needed to be told that. He still wanted sex, needed it, but when she did consent it was without any enthusiasm, a marital concession by her to have it from time to time, while her minimal participation made her disinterest plain.

Part of him, his illogical side, was angered by it, but he had remorse over those feelings too; his wife had a serious illness, how could he be angry at her?

That left little for him to be cheery about at the close of each night. Sitting there, in their too small living room, watching TV, while careful to keep the volume low so as not to disturb her sleep, his only solace was alcohol, usually a glass of wine. To be more precise, his nightly dose was a hearty glass of the red grape variety. Half-watching what was on the set, he would brood over his situation, an unhappy state to end his evening. He would have had more, but on work nights, he managed to exercise sufficient self-control to limit his intake. The weekends, Friday and Saturday nights, did not impose that restriction, though he still tried to limit himself, fearful that he might succumb to the grip of the grape, as his uncle, now deceased, had.

It was early on a Wednesday, when the Chief Judge of the Office of Administrative Law Judges summoned Gray to his office. That was an unusual event in itself. Most communication between the "Chief," as he liked to be called, was impromptu, brought about upon passing one another in the office hallways. As if destined to be a chief of something, the dignified name his parents selected, Edward, the second yet, seemed to herald that one day he would be important. Few viewed his position as fulfilling that prediction, but Blandford had a high regard for himself. Privately, however, that self-regard was not unbounded. He retained enough sense to know that, ability-wise, he was already over his head and this was as far as he would climb. So be it, he would think to himself, the title of "Chief," was enough reassurance to his ego.

"Come in, come in, Charles," Blandford greeted him warmly, presenting an atypical level of friendliness, an approach that set Gray's antennae on alert.

"How are things going?" a smile accompanying his ostensible interest. He did not wait for a reply, nor want one. "Reasonably well, I hope," he continued, not caring a whit about Gray's circumstances. He knew there was some sort of health issue with his wife, but his only true focus was that the office was running smoothly so that there would be no flak coming from his superiors, the Mine Safety and Health Review Commissioners.

Gray responded in kind, fully aware that Blandford's announced interest was empty. "Fine, just fine, thank you," he answered politely.

That formality out of the way, Blandford wasted no time getting to business. "Tell you why I called you in," he continued. "We just received a big case. I'm sure you've read about it in the papers and the local news stations."

Gray acknowledged that he was aware of the stories. There was no confusion, he knew it was the dust tampering case.

Blandford continued, "In terms of the number of coal mines charged and the enormous number of citations involved, it's the single biggest case we've ever had," he informed. Blandford had no idea whether that claim was true. Nearly everything the Chief spouted was based on something someone else had told him. He merely echoed information.

"The Solicitor has filed a civil penalty against some 800 mine operators, big and small. Thousands of citations are involved. As you know, the Secretary is claiming that the mines manipulated their coal dust sampling. The cases, they've all been consolidated by my order."

Gray knew what was coming. This was not simply a meeting to dispense information.

Blandford moved right to it. "So, I'm assigning these matters to you, Charles. Given your long experience in the office, I decided you're the best person to preside in this."

By using the description, "decided," he was making it clear that this was not something he was considering, the decision had been made.

"Course, this means that it will be your only case until it's completed. I will have all the other cases in your docket reassigned. The majority of them will be going to our newest judge, Richard Larkin."

Gray was not happy about the assignment. Rather than welcoming the complexity of such a case, his predominant thought was the enormous amount of work that it would entail. He much preferred the busy, but not overwhelming, amount of work that his docket had reliably involved. Now this had been thrust upon him.

Blandford saw that Gray showed no enthusiasm. Didn't matter. There was no bargaining. He was issuing an order, not starting a negotiation.

Still, he tried to put a gloss on it. "Gonna be a real feather in your cap, Charles, a case of such prominence and publicity."

Gray's attitude was unchanged. He just listened, aware that Blandford was not about to reconsider the assignment.

The Chief continued, "Your law clerk will assist you full-time during this. He won't be sharing his time with any other judge while this matter is before you," he added, hoping that Gray would be pleased by the full-time clerk assistance.

Gray welcomed that news. It would help, but it wouldn't alter the grind he would be facing.

Not wanting to prolong the meeting, Blandford brought it to a close. "Well, that's about it, Charles," he continued, signaling that it was over. As he arose from his chair, emphasizing that the matter had been concluded, he made another compliment, "You're the best for this one," he stroked.

Gray dispensed with any acknowledgement to the empty praise. Still, as he then arose from his chair, he knew that, having said little, some words were required. "The docket office will be delivering the cases today?" he inquired.

"Yes, absolutely," Blandford reassured. "They're already loading the files in carts. You can expect them by early this afternoon."

Resigned to the unwelcome assignment, as he departed Gray offered the required respectful response. "Okay, I'll begin examining them today then."

"Good, good, Charles," he responded. "Let me know of anything you need."

The files were delivered, as promised, not long after lunch. Five carts, each full of case files and more on the way, Jean Ellen announced. The sight of so many files only served to make Gray gloomier about the task ahead. Too bad, he thought, that it was not quite yet the time for retirement.

Looking out his office window, contemplating the first steps for the enormous assignment, he heard a voice. "Knock, knock," came the verbal announcement. "Mind if I visit, Charles?"

Recognizing the caller's voice, Gray swiveled around in his chair to welcome the visitor, Richard Larkin, the newest judge in the office. "Sure, please come in, Richard," he responded cordially.

Larkin took a seat on Gray's office couch, respectfully avoiding using the coffee table in front of it as a footrest, though he employed it that way in his own office. The judges all had offices that spoke of their relative importance; spacious with an impressive desk of good size, several wood cabinets along two walls for books and papers, and a modest, round, business table with four chairs, suitable for small meetings. There was nothing chintzy about the furnishings.

"I just got a bunch of your cases, Charles, reassigned to me from Blandford," he informed.

Larkin knew something was up. Thirty of Gray's cases had just been delivered to his office. That was an unusual development. Occasionally a case or two would be reassigned from one judge to another, but that was prompted by the need to consolidate dockets arising out of the same inspection or for some other practical reason. This was quite different; with the delivery of so many cases all at once, there had to be a reason for it. Aware that Gray was near retirement age, he hoped that the case reassignments did not signal some health issue for his colleague.

"What gives?" he asked simply.

Gray was forthcoming. After all, there was nothing secret about his new assignment.

"I knew you would be receiving a number of my cases," he informed. "It's not just you, other judges in the office will be reassigned my cases too. As of now I have but one case, or to be more accurate, hundreds of cases, but all with the same issue. The Secretary is claiming that coal mine operators, not all of them of course, but more than 800 of them, tampered with the coal dust collection samplings."

Larkin then recalled the announcement. Somehow, he did not pay close attention to it, and in the weeks since then, it had dropped from his radar. He was embarrassed by his lapse. Trying to recover from his forgetfulness, he responded, "That is big news."

He was surprised, both by the large number of mines involved, and more fundamentally that anyone would monkey around with the dust sampling. He didn't think that way and, though he was not a rookie, it was still difficult to imagine that, if this actually happened, mine operators, and so many of them, would do such a thing.

But he then privately chastised himself for being taken aback. One would have thought that after all that happened to him at the Freedom Mine in Idaho, nearly losing his life, he would have routinely presumed the worst about mine operators' behavior.

Gray ignored that his colleague had forgotten about the charges. His focus was on the burden that he had just be given.

"Have to think this through," Gray continued. "I've never had a case of this order. And you just know that it will receive a lot of press. I'll need to consult some sources on complex litigation, and how to deal with multiple respondents and all that. And then there's the inevitable technical aspects that will come with it. A lot of scientific information, I'm sure. I'll have to become reasonably knowledgeable about all of that too, at least enough that I can pass as being able to grasp it. I have no scientific background, so that will be a challenge in itself."

Larkin listened, silently agreeing that this would be a daunting matter, while relieved that it had not been assigned to him. He was new at this administrative law judge role. Sure, he could do it, if it fell in his lap. He would have to become competent in all its aspects, just as Gray had remarked, but as he was still green, he was completely content with the garden variety mine safety and health civil penalties which were the staple of the office's workload.

"Charles," he then spoke up, "I don't pretend to have the experience you have, but I'm offering to help. Someone you can bounce ideas off, for instance. Quandaries you may encounter. Really anything, I'm available. Can't say I'll have some brilliant thoughts, but I'll try to be useful."

Gray appreciated the suggestion. "Thanks, Richard. Always good to hear what others have to say."

Now apprised about what was going on and relieved that there was no health issue for his fellow judge, it seemed to be an appropriate time to end the conversation, so Larkin then bid his colleague a good afternoon.

Though Larkin was a new judge, Gray was very much aware of his prior experience, as was everyone in the office and, for that matter, all who worked for MSHA and in the mining industry too. They all knew of Larkin's fame from that deadly event in Idaho. Gray had sized him up early on when he joined the office, and was glad that Larkin didn't consider himself to be a celebrity. If anything, he observed that new judge downplayed it, wanting to move on and avoid having it define his career.

Larkin had settled down in the months after that memorable Christmas week in the Gem State. He had kept his promise too, visiting the site where Nancy had been cremated, but with nothing to show for the trip. He was left to gaze out in the field where the coroner's administrative officer told him that her ashes had been spread. Moved to tears, he knelt at the site, offering a prayer for her. He could only hope that, somehow, she knew of his presence and that his feelings for her were genuine.

On a later visit, in the spring of the following year, he returned to the area again, this time to see Coralee and her children. She and her brood were thrilled that he came back. He stayed four days on that trip, seeing them each day, and one evening Coralee and he had dinner, just the two of them, in downtown Wallace.

Returning to Wallace was difficult with all the memories there. The brothels, he had read, had since been shut down, an FBI raid closing them. Wisely, he knew that mentioning his experience at one of those establishments would not be well-received by Coralee, his secret remaining intact. In fact, he had never divulged those experiences to a soul.

With the local police aware of his contact with a brothel, and considering him a troublemaker, they had no use for him, and so he was worried that he might be spotted by someone while they dined. To his relief, no one did. The dinner was pleasant but the strong chemistry they initially felt, when the circumstances of her husband's death were first learned, had waned during his absence. When he dropped her off following their dinner, both knew that that things had changed and, aware of that, he made no attempt to bed her that evening.

He was a different man ever since Nancy. The idea that a woman from a brothel would fundamentally change him, no longer viewing women as conquests, was ironic to say the least.

The next day, when the visit was at its end, both realized that, at least for now, a deeper relationship did not seem to be in their immediate future. Added to the lessened chemistry, being on opposite coasts and with such different backgrounds, the chances to rekindle those earlier feelings seemed remote. Though bound by the tragic and ugly death of her husband, Orlin, that was not enough to carry it forward. At least not now, not so soon. They agreed the time and circumstances were not right, though neither wanted the door to be shut for a possible future connection.

As the months passed and the calls between them grew less frequent, by the summer of that year, Larkin had started dating Sandy Catton, at first sporadically, and then, without forethought, by fall, it had transitioned into exclusively seeing each other.

By autumn, he had mentioned to Coralee that he had been dating someone in D.C. and she informed that, just recently, she too had started dating again, a natural occurrence for both. It provided them with mutual relief, in a sense, freeing them from any implication that there was something brewing for a relationship to develop. That had been put on hold, both excused from any guilt as they were free to see others, yet without closing any doors for what the future might hold.

Acting on that mutual absolution, Larkin had recently moved to Sandy's apartment. That arrangement brought with it Sandy's adopted young daughter, a three year old. Unable to have children, Sandy and her then husband had decided to adopt. Though it seemed like a joyous development, it was not long after the arrival of the tot, given the name Sophia, that her husband decided fatherhood was not for him, an inopportune time to reach that late conclusion. A year later, the divorce was finalized and it was then just the two of them in her apartment. She had become accustomed to the change, realizing that the adoption was an effort to disguise their own unhappiness as a couple. As the months went by, she actually welcomed his departure and took to her newcomer without any regrets. Her little one was bouncy and bright, and Sandy looked forward to each day with her new daughter.

Now, with the addition of Richard, it felt like a more complete family. Yes, it was a stereotyped idea, but whether ingrained in her culturally or just the way it progressed, she was happy with it. It was so much better now than it had been with spouse number one, as she privately referred to him, dropping his name from her thoughts. For her, the homelife was satisfying, now including in the bedroom. Better yet, Richard had no hesitancy over the 'bonus' to the relationship – young Sophia. For a man who not so long ago was a vacuous prowler, always seeking his next conquest, it was a monumental change.

Other developments in his career followed Larkin's Idaho experience. He had enough trial experience to qualify for a position as a federal administrative law judge. Openings to be added to the roster of qualified people for such positions were rare and it was unpredictable when they would occur. Applications for positions to become judges were conducted by the Office of Personnel Management. One had to act fast when such matters developed and he did not delay. His reputation, fame really, though never mentioned in the process of his application, propelled him to a high ranking on the list of candidates. It was not long after qualifying that the Mine Review Commission offered him a judicial appointment.

With Larkin having departed, Gray stared at the carts. All those cases, it was daunting just looking at them. At this time of day, he could have deferred any work until the next day. While tempted, admonishing himself for that attitude, he muttered, "have to start at some point."

He picked up the first case file. The Majestic Mine, in Eastern Kentucky was charged with tampering with twenty dust sample cassettes. The civil penalty petition sought $2,000 per violation, an amount that caught the mine's attention, especially because there was a citation for each. Penalties of a few hundred dollars, those never really bothered mining operations. Of course, from his many years of experience, he knew they would try and whittle down the amount, even for those low dollar penalty assessments. It was just the way the game was played. But when penalties entered the realm of a thousand dollars or more per citation, and if there were several of them in a given docket, then the mine attorneys would be called in. It was worth it, dollar-wise, as there would usually be some give from MSHA. For the mine operator attorneys, it was a matter of finding that line between going to trial, and the costs that option would bring, compared with how much they could reduce the original assessment.

Flipping through the pages of the file, the essence of the case was plain – the petition alleged that the mine had finagled with the samples in some manner, with the result of dust levels which not only met the federal standard but were amazingly below the maximum exposure.

A shorthand expression was also used in the penalty petitions to describe the cassettes' condition; they all had "abnormal white centers" in the filters, "AWCs," as they were now routinely described by the Secretary.

While the core of the charge was easy to understand, Gray knew that would be the only aspect that would be simple. There would be an elaborate defense, with a mountain of scientific evidence presented by both sides. He dreaded that, both from the daunting task of comprehending it and being able to separate the rubbish science from the genuine.

He reached for the next file. Forest Creek, also out of Eastern Kentucky. It did not take long to realize that it was fundamentally the same – intentionally monkeying with the dust cassette apparatus. In a sense it made the cases more manageable, meddling with the sampling being the common theme. Of course, he realized that the manner in which an abnormal white center could be created might vary from case to case, but their overarching similarity – tampering of one sort or another, caused him to begin considering how best to proceed. He would give that some thought, together with reading up on complex litigation manuals.

After two weeks of reviewing files, though more kept arriving by the day, Gray had arrived at a preliminary plan on the best way to proceed. During that time he had consulted some articles on handling complex cases, as this matter was plainly that, both in terms of the number of mines involved and the scientific issues.

Upon learning of Gray's assignment and that it encompassed all the AWC cases, the Watkins firm had already notified Gray that it would be acting on behalf of all the named respondents, a development the judge welcomed, as it would avoid the unwieldy spectacle of too many counsels at the hearings.

It always rankled Gray that these proceedings were called "hearings." Bullshit, he thought, they were trials. Yes, they were judge-only proceedings, as there was no jury, but plain and simple, they were still trials, virtually indistinguishable from any state or federal trials. But, because they arose in an administrative law forum, they'd always be named 'hearings.'

At least his title was 'judge.' It used to be that they were called "presiding officers," a far less impressive designation than "judge."

Nomenclature aside, it was undeniable that they were essentially indistinguishable from civil trials. Attorneys were representing the parties in the vast majority of the cases. There were rules of evidence applied and they were nearly the same as those in federal district trials. A transcript was created and post-hearing briefs were submitted. At the hearing, meaning at the *trial*, the judge behaved in the same manner as in any civil litigation, making rulings on objections of all manner, determining the admissibility of documents, and otherwise controlling the proceedings.

Moving with deliberate speed, Gray set the first preliminary conference a mere four weeks after his assignment to the cases. The purpose would be to outline the rules that would be employed, along with a rough outline of the anticipated timeline.

Larkin, who had developed the habit of dropping by Gray's office at least once each week, learned of the upcoming preliminary meeting and again offered whatever help he could provide.

That first session, held in the Mine Commission's own hearing room, was uneventful, as it was largely procedural, but it gave everyone the chance to size up their respective opponents, and for Milo and Winston, their first in-person view of Gray pertaining to this case.

CHAPTER 5

It was early November when the first day of the hearing began. Though Washington weather in November could still be moderate, frequently reaching the upper 50s, the mornings were a reminder that winter was soon approaching with temperatures often in the mid-30s.

As Gray walked to the courthouse that day, it was one of those crisp mornings. He enjoyed it, invigorating him in a way that the commute and morning coffee had failed to achieve and giving him enough time to collect his thoughts for the day ahead.

This matter was unlike anything he had experienced in his many years of administrative trials. Befitting the seriousness and the scale of this litigation, impacting so many of the eastern coal mines, the Commission had been able to secure use of the E. Barrett Prettyman Federal Courthouse, which was less than ten blocks from the White House, with Gray's own office not much further away. That was a feat because it was expected that the hearing would last at least a month.

Though he had walked by that courthouse often, when the weather cooperated, on his route for a lunchtime walk, down to the Washington Monument and then around the National Mall, he had never entered this federal courthouse.

Once past the guards and directed to his loaned chambers, he took a moment to acquaint himself with the new setting. As it was nearly nine, he wanted to make an on-time appearance, especially on the first day. Checking his watch, he made his entry precisely on schedule, sending a signal both of his importance, as well as the significance of the matter that was about to get underway. The grandeur of the courtroom immediately impressed him, though he presented a demeanor that the setting was customary to him.

Upon taking the bench, he first stood as he laid down his papers along with a large accordion file, acting as if he did not notice the large number of people before him. Then, assuming his chair, and the lofty position he then held above everyone, he looked at the counsel tables, nodding acknowledgement of the lawyers' presence. Everyone had respectfully stood upon his entry, even those who were simply observers. He counted the number of attorneys before him. Eleven. Six were at the Respondent's table, five on the government's side. He never had so many attorneys in a case, not by a long shot. In all his years of presiding in Mine Act cases, four attorneys, in total, was the previous high. It was, he thought, quite a spectacle, with so many lawyers squeezed in at their respective counsel tables.

With practiced gravitas, he then spoke his first words. "Good morning," he said, expressed without cheer or somberness, only a matter of fact greeting. "I am Charles Gray, the presiding judge in this matter." He then added, "Please be seated."

As he looked out beyond the counsel tables, he also saw that some number of unidentified persons, a dozen or so, he estimated, were also present, apparently just curious members of the public, presumably aware of the issue because of the press coverage it had already received.

Nearly all his previous hearings had no spectators, another indication of the significance of this case. Gray couldn't help but notice that among those, a handful of people in the public seating area appeared, from their informal attire, to be working folks. Perhaps, he considered, they might be miners.

Then one of those from the spectator seating area raised his hand and spoke up. "Good morning, your honor," he began, "I'm Joshua Robinson, business reporter with the Washington Sentinel." Having identified himself, he asked for permission to approach the bench. Gray nodded in response, beckoning him to come forward. Handing his card to the judge, he spoke. "Your honor, we realize this is an important case. For that reason, our paper will be here each day to cover the proceedings."

THE CASE OF THE ABNORMAL WHITE CENTER

Already a heady experience, reinforcing the importance of the case, the reporter's announcement felt at once both exhilarating and daunting to Gray. Exhilarating, because he realized that the daily presence of the Capitol's major newspaper underscored its importance and, by extension, his importance, as he was the center of it all. But those facts were intimidating too. Relying upon his long tenure of hearing administrative cases bolstered his confidence, helping him overcome his private jitters.

Gray then asked the court reporter if she was ready, receiving word that she was. He then announced that they were on the record, whereupon he stated the names of the parties to the litigation and the docket number.

Calling upon that extensive experience, he knew it was important to quickly establish that he was running the show, so to speak, and he did that without hesitation. Immediately upon beginning the proceeding, he invoked his authority in an unassailable manner, instructing that there could only be three attorneys per side at their respective counsel tables.

He then waited patiently, while there were hurried discussions at each table, as the sides determined who would remain. In a short time, the musical chairs were established and the unwieldly initial arrangement was corrected. Gray had established from the start that he was in charge of this proceeding.

The lead team for the Secretary consisted of Jake Sanford, Doug Green, and Carl Czarnecki, the same team that visited the Mount Hope Technology Center at the start.

For the Respondents, Winston Malthan and Milo Krakovich remained at their counsel table, a para-legal, rounding out the allowed number of three. Winston and Milo, having no shortage of self-confidence, didn't want another lawyer with them at the table. As they saw it, any lawyer from the group that was theoretically part of the defense team would only invite an opportunity to muck things up, raising the risk of dissension within the team. They had all the wisdom needed to handle the case, thank you very much; the other lawyers, ostensibly part of their 'team,' were, truth be told, figureheads.

Gray then turned to the trimmed counsel tables, inquiring, "Are the parties set to proceed?"

Both sides affirmed they were ready and with that Gray made his opening remarks. He was careful to describe the charges neutrally, that it was *alleged* the Respondents had intentionally altered the dust collecting discs so as to misrepresent the level of dust actually inhaled during the miners' shifts for which collections were made. He emphasized that the burden of proof was on the Secretary of Labor, and that the burden applied is the preponderance of the evidence. Though understood only vaguely by most of the public, all the lawyers knew well its meaning and Gray was not about to insult them by stating aloud that it meant the Secretary had to establish that it was more likely than not that tampering occurred.

Though there were preliminary discussions about the mine to be chosen for the first trial, Gray in effect issued an edict, announcing that the significance of the mine selected would be more than just being the first in the long line of cases charging hundreds of mines with tampering. Further, he reminded the parties that he had informed that the choice of the first mine case to be tried would be made by him, not the parties. This was not news – in an order issued earlier, he had advised the parties that the Bobcat Creek Colliery would be that first one. The outcome of that case would also determine the issues common to all the rest. That meant that a failure to prove tampering in that case would also likely defeat tampering charges for the others.

On two counts, the Secretary didn't like it. Afterall, he was the prosecutor and for that reason, asserted that he, not the judge, should choose the first mine to go to trial. As for the outcome controlling the common issues for every case, he objected to that as too broad. The cases, they argued, weren't fungible, there were many ways to commit fraudulent dust samples.

The judge, after hearing the Secretary's objections, stood by his ruling. Defending his decision, he noted that, as the judge, he was the impartial neutral in the case. In that role, his choice would be immune from challenges that the selection was unfair. In contrast, he observed that choices for the first mine trial from either side would be subject to such claims. He then added the undeniable; the Secretary had to be prepared to prove their claim against any of the more than 800 mines they had charged. To assert otherwise would be tantamount to admitting that some of their cases were questionable.

THE CASE OF THE ABNORMAL WHITE CENTER

Upon hearing that comment, Sanford, recognizing that he could hardly dispute it, relented, responding with "Thank you, your honor," conceding the point.

Gray then announced that his selection for the first hearing would be as he had directed – the Bobcat Creek Colliery Mine out of Mingo County, West Virginia. Both sides recognized that it was a logical choice. According to the Secretary, the Bobcat Mine had 78 cassettes with those abnormal white centers; those AWC's. At $1,700 assessed for each citation, if the Secretary prevailed, the mine would face a fine exceeding $132,600. And that was just one mine among the hundreds of cases he had brought.

Though the Secretary had no choice but to agree to what was in effect a test case, the judge correctly observed that, with a such a large number of AWC's, it seemed fair to consider this first case as representative of the issues that would be present in each of the cases. As the Court's determinations in this case would necessarily have an impact on the others, it was no understatement to state that a great deal was riding on this first one.

The Respondents loved it and so were quick to agree to the arrangement, a ruling elevating the first trial to a make-or-break test for the Secretary. They were confident of their ability to cast enough doubt on the claim that there had been tampering, no matter which case Gray had selected. A win in the first, they believed, would mean a win for all the other mines. And if they did lose, they had no intention of conceding losses in the others. Due process, they would then loudly assert, demanded that every mine have its day in court, an unassailable position.

Depending on the outcome of this case, Gray hoped that, whichever side prevailed, the other cases would melt away. He anticipated that if the results were a clear victory for the Secretary that could lead to rapid settlements with the other respondents, and if the Bobcat mine prevailed, it was expected that the Secretary would have little choice but to dismiss the charges against many, perhaps even all, of the remaining cases.

With the Respondent's quick endorsement of his decision, Gray was clueless in not realizing that they would never agree to such consequences if they lost. That would only count as the first round. They would fight on.

With the judge's opening remarks concluded and housekeeping matters resolved, opening statements were made in the time remaining before lunch.

Jake Sanford began by placing the violations in context.

"Good morning, your Honor. The government, the Mine Safety and Health Administration, more well known as MSHA, is here today because of a terrible violation, a breach of a sacred trust that this mine operator, the Bobcat Creek Colliery Mine out of Mingo County in West Virginia, owed to the health of its employees. As you are well aware, the Bobcat Mine is but one example out of more than some 800 underground coal mines entrusted with honestly taking dust samples for their miners.

Now, today, our focus is directed at Bobcat Creek's operation for which we have charged it for tampering with 78 sampling cassettes, making them appear that the amount of coal dust that miners inhaled during those 8-hour shifts was well below the maximum exposure limit. But those samples were not actually below the maximum allowable levels. Bobcat Creek Colliery didn't follow the rules, not at all. Instead, through various means, the government will establish that the mine manipulated those dust samples. And the telltale mark of that tampering was the abnormal white center. For shorthand we will be referring to those as AWCs."

Sanford continued, "But the AWCs are much more than those white centers. They represent the deception attempted to be perpetrated on the government and, more than that, they display the callous disregard for the health of their workers. Though I am sure that your Honor is well-versed on the devastating harm on miners' lungs from inhaling coal dust, for the record I need to describe the harmful effects of that exposure. The condition miners develop from exposure to excessive coal dust is the lung disease Pneumoconiosis. In common usage it's called coal workers' pneumoconiosis or CWP for short. It's also aptly named "Black Lung Disease." That may be the most appropriate name for the disease because the coal dust the miners suck into their lungs with each shift turns them from the normal and healthy pink tissue to black. Normal lung tissue, as we all know, is pink.

Early symptoms of this disease typically include coughing, chest tightness and shortness of breath. It is a progressive disease. From those early symptoms, miners will often find that they become breathless, winded is another term, with minimal activity. Climbing a flight of stairs is arduous. Eventually, many will simply suffocate. Although the body tries to fight the coal dust pollution entering the miners' lungs, it's too much to handle. White blood cells recognize the threat and those cells try to capture the dust, surround it and digest it, but they can't do it. This is because those cells can't break down the coal dust. The white cells lose the battle, then they die and when those rescuer cells die, they release enzymes that actually damage the lung tissue further. So, it's a lose-lose situation; the body tries to save itself from the invader, but the dust particles win and the dead white cells are left behind on the battlefield, leaving their remnants which include those enzymes that further damage the lungs, compounding the health damage."

When Sanford used the words "progressive disease," it struck a chord with Gray. He could not help but think of Millie's MS, *her own progressive disease*, which in time would overtake her life, too, making even minimal activity impossible.

Unaware of the health issue with the Judge's wife and oblivious to the way his description resonated with him, Sanford continued without a pause, "As I mentioned, even the things we all take for granted, like going for a walk or climbing a flight of stairs, can provoke those symptoms. As the disease progresses, as it will with each subsequent exposure to excessive coal dust, a miner may even have breathing issues when at complete rest. And the problems of inhaling the excessive dust evidences itself in different ways. If it involves large parts of the lungs, scarring occurs and that prevents oxygen from reaching the bloodstream. And, as if that wasn't enough, that low oxygen means that all the organs receive insufficient air too, resulting in stress on the heart and brain, for example."

"It's common knowledge that underground mining is one of the most dangerous occupations in the United States. Isn't it enough," Sanford posed, "with those employment risks including inhaling toxic gases, such as methane, carbon monoxide and hydrogen sulfide; being crushed by roof falls or mining equipment; drowning when tunnels fill with water; and injury from fires and explosions? Isn't that enough?" he repeated. And even if miners survive the many workplace risks and hazards, by inhaling coal dust, they may suffocate to death from those chronic exposures years later. There is no such thing as a pleasant retirement for those miners."

"Our point, your Honor," as Sanford began to wind up his opening, "of which we know you are fully aware, is that these violations are not merely about tampering with the dust collection apparatus. Not at all. They relate directly to suffering a slow death until those miners cannot even gasp for the air they need."

He then paused for dramatic effect, then stated, "And Congress commanded that this must stop."

There was only one conclusion, Sanford told the Court – the mine had intentionally tampered with the cassettes in order to present the false picture that the dust levels were in compliance. He informed that there would be testimony from experts, several of them, that the AWCs were of a different nature than hundreds of other cassettes that had been sent to the MSHA Technology Center before the scheme began.

Sanford dispensed with any polite description of what was alleged. "There was tampering, plain and simple," he asserted, adding that "there were no innocent explanations, not with the very large number of cassettes with these AWCs, not with the sudden disappearance of the AWC cassettes, once word got out that the government had discovered what was going on, and not with the admission of the very large Eagle Coal and Coke mining operation, with its multiple underground mines conceding that was exactly what they had done and for which they had paid a half-million dollar fine. Further, the government intends to have witnesses from the Eagle Coal and Coke Mine testify about the manipulating they did to produce the dishonest dust sampling results."

At that point, breaking protocol, Milo Krakovich, interrupted the government's opening. "Objection! Objection!" he bellowed. "The Respondent will be strongly objecting to any evidence regarding the Eagle Coal and Coke operations. It has no relevance to the matter before the Court. It is totally inappropriate for the Secretary to make any mention of this."

Sanford was surprised by the intrusion into his opening, but before he could respond, Gray spoke. "I need to remind the parties that the opening statements are not evidence. They represent the parties' positions and their preview of the evidence they intend to introduce, *once the testimony* begins," he emphasized. "It is generally inappropriate to interrupt an opening, unless an advocate goes far beyond the pale," he admonished Krakovich. "Certainly that hasn't happened here with Attorney Sanford's opening thus far. I would add that there is no jury here, so there is no danger of being unduly swayed by the contentions made in the opening remarks from either side." Highlighting his own importance, Gray reminded, "I am the sole determiner of the facts."

Sanford had enough sense to leave the matter where it stood. "Thank you, Judge," he said respectfully.

However, Krakovich had broken his stride and at a time near the end of his opening. He had little else to say, and was left with a brief summary of his earlier remarks, reiterating that the evidence would show that the AWCs were not the result of anything but tampering. Though Milo had taken some wind out of his sails, Sanford considered the effect of the interruption on his opening to be minimal, noting to himself, as the judge had remarked, he was in front of a judge, not a jury.

To the neutral observer, the government's opening seemed to present a strong case. Gray could not help but notice that the members of the public in attendance reacted to it that way, with some nods, nudges and whispers among them.

Malthan was then called upon for the Respondent's opening.

He began by acting wounded, expressing that the Bobcat Creek Colliery mine operation was deeply hurt by the outrageous claims, but he was simultaneously angrily indignant in response to the government's assertions.

"Nothing the government has claimed today could be further from the truth," he began. Using that time-tested technique, he then repeated the same words, this time with more emphasis, "I tell you, *nothing* could be further from the truth. The Respondent will show beyond cavil that the few cases with the claimed abnormal centers more likely than not came about due to a number of factors for which it was wholly without fault."

Malthan enjoyed the use of overstatement, a way to claim that it would be presenting more than a defense. Bobcat Creek would show beyond any doubt that the government's claim was outrageous.

He also enjoyed employing infrequently used legal phrases like "beyond cavil." It made him feel that he was better educated than opposing counsel when he invoked words like that. Though fully aware of the various explanations they would be presenting in their defense, he decided to build some drama by not offering the specifics in his opening. Of course, the Secretary also knew, through discovery, of the various excuses that would be proclaimed to show the irregularities were both innocent and out of control of the operator.

Gray listened and while he could have gleaned some of what would be coming by reading the parties' discovery exchanges before the trial began, he had not motivated himself sufficiently to make that effort. He would wait until the experts and their accompanying exhibits were presented to learn about them.

Sanford sat politely, careful not to err, as opposing counsel had done moments before, by objecting to the opening. Their defense was, as he saw it, the 'spaghetti tactic' – that old approach of throwing multiple things against the wall and hoping that something will stick.

The preliminaries ate up the morning and the judge announced that the proceeding would resume at 1:30, with the government's first witness. Gray was glad for the break, realizing that the morning had taken more of a mental toll on him than he expected. Only the first day and just half-way through it at that, he was already looking forward to the conclusion of the day, which would end at 4:30.

As expected, MSHA's case began that afternoon with the Secretary calling Donna Nelson to the witness stand, a natural chronological start, with her testimony about how she came to discover the abnormal white centers.

With a humble demeanor, she began by describing the first event, when she dropped a cassette, as resulting from her being 'all thumbs,' as she put it. It was then, she informed, that she noticed something 'peculiar,' upon seeing the filter which had split open. Then, upon direction from her supervisor, Mr.

THE CASE OF THE ABNORMAL WHITE CENTER

Balkum, she opened each of the cassettes from the batch of samples delivered by the Eagle Coal and Coke mine, all 12 of them. Each of them, she informed, had that strange white center.

Upon reporting those findings to Balkum, he directed her to start reviewing the samples from other mines to see if they also displayed white centers. Sanford then led her through all the details which followed her initial discovery of the condition and then how mine-after-mine had samples with those white centers. And, she informed, except for a very few instances within a given group of samples, nearly all had that white hole. She avoided using any of derogatory terms that miners had used to describe them, such as coal mine "bonbons."

Undeniably, she was an impressive first witness, explaining the careful attention that she, and later the other technicians who were tasked to review the dust cassettes, employed, as they examined each sample.

Winston and Milo wanted to object, asserting that, once her testimony had established the procedure the technicians had employed, there was no need for her to give the tiresome detail after detail from each review the office made of the numerous mine samples.

Sanford knew he could use this approach; it was all part of setting the stage by establishing the enormous number of suspect samples the technicians found.

As their irritation grew with Ms. Nelson's recounting of each mine they sampled and the growing total number of the samples with the white centers, Milo couldn't take it any longer.

"Objection, your honor," he began.

Gray and Sanford were surprised as the last question and the answer was nothing more than a continuation of Nelson's chapter and verse timeline recounting of one sample result after another.

And that, Krakovich then informed, was the basis for his objection. "Your honor," he began, "how much longer must we all endure this tedium. Okay, we get it, so these technicians kept finding what they thought were white centers in the dust filters. But do we have to hear about each and every sample and the claimed results?"

Derogatorily describing them, he continued, "We are ready to stipulate that these 'techs,' as they are called, found what they believed to be whitish circles in the cassette filter samples. Great! Fine! But it has nothing to do with whether, what those non-professionals thought they saw with the filters, that they were, in fact, actually white."

"I mean, with no disrespect intended," his tone making it clear that only disrespect was intended, "Ms. Nelson is merely a technician. And, with no insult intended, she possess no more than a high school diploma. She's no expert and the Secretary has not attempted, wisely we would add, to have her recognized as having any expertise on this subject. So, must we go on ad nauseam? It adds nothing."

Sanford, seriously annoyed, rose in response. "Your honor, I do believe we are entitled to put on our case as we see fit. I don't believe Mr. Krakovich would take well to our kibitzing on his presentation of their case. But, if he finds that approach acceptable, applicable to *both sides*, and that we can then direct how to present their case too, then the government is fine with that. But be advised, Mr. Krakovich and Mr. Malthan, that if those are the rules you wish to follow, we will apply them with equal vigor."

The two hadn't figured on the government's aggressive rebuttal. Uncharacteristically flatfooted for the moment, Milo and Winston looked at each other. "Your honor, may we have a moment?"

Gray simply nodded.

The two spoke in the softest voice possible. "Criminy, Milo," Winston began, "we've got to pull back on this or we'll be hearing from Sanford at every turn when it's our time."

Milo did not hesitate. "I agree. I didn't expect such a vehement blowback. We'll walk it back."

Winston replied, "Good. Agreed."

Milo then addressed the Court. "Your honor, we withdraw our objection." Trying to put an innocent spin on it, he continued. "Our intention was simply to move things along, particularly because of the cumulative nature of the testimony and in view of the fact that the trial will be of long duration."

Sanford said nothing.

Gray recognizing that the scuffle was over, simply observed, "Counsel for Respondent has withdrawn his objection. Proceed, Mr. Sanford, with your direct exam of Ms. Nelson."

His victory in hand, Sanford was not about to truncate Donna Nelson's testimony. Given the lengthy interruption, he asked the court reporter to read back the last few exchanges in the testimony. That took time and he was pleased about it. It was designed to annoy those two, punishment for their unwarranted, baseless, objection. With the previous few questions and answers read by the reporter, though Sanford didn't need it, his point was made.

He then continued, "So, Ms. Nelson, after what started with those white center filters from the Eagle Coal and Coke mine, and the other samples you and the other technicians then examined, did you keep a tally on the number of mines with cassettes showing these white centers?"

"Oh, yes," Nelson answered, her eyes widening as she looked directly at the judge with her response. "We found nearly 800 mines showing those white centers," she answered, conveying amazement that so many mines were involved.

Laying it on, Sanford acted as if he were uncertain of her answer. "I'm sorry, Ms. Nelson, did you say nearly 800 mines?"

"Yes, that's correct," she replied, not realizing that Sanford had heard her previous answer perfectly well. "797 mines to be precise."

Realizing that Sanford, and everyone else in the courtroom, had clearly heard her previous answer, that last exchange particularly maddened Milo and Winston. But given their earlier failed objection, they had to sit silently and steam over it.

Sanford had planned on truncating Nelson's testimony in a summary fashion after she had testified about a dozen of the white center incidents, but after Milo's objection he decided to add more mine sample results to the list.

Then, nearing the windup for Nelson's testimony, Sanford continued, "So, Ms. Nelson, this all began with your discovery about the white center sample from the Eagle Coal and Coke mine, correct?"

"Yes," she answered, "that's how it all started."

"And did you ever learn how Eagle Coal and Coke, responded to this?"

"Yes, they pled guilty to tampering."

The answer came so quickly that Milo could not object in time to prevent part of her answer from being made.

"Objection! Objection!" he fairly shouted. "The witness has no basis to testify about this!"

Sanford knew the question would produce an explosion and he was pleased about the objection and the vehemence that came with it.

"Your honor," he calmly replied, "I can withdraw the question, but it's going to come in later in this trial for sure. As everyone knows, it was all over the papers, and on television too, that Eagle Coal plead guilty to tampering. The Court can take judicial notice of it. And we will be asking the Court to do just that later, with newspaper clippings as exhibits recounting the mine's confession to tampering."

Gray then asked if Sanford was in fact withdrawing the question and therefore the partial answer that came with it.

Sanford responded that he was. But he was pleased that the damage had been done. If Gray hadn't already known about the mine's admission of guilt, unlikely as that was, now he had heard it directly. And, the judge would be reminded of it again when the promised exhibits were admitted later.

Feigning innocence over Ms. Nelson's answer disclosing the mine's guilty plea, he noted that "as opposing counsel is well aware, we are in front of the court, not a jury, and therefore, the response from Ms. Nelson can work no prejudice."

He concluded, "We accept the delay for now. We will enter those exhibits about Eagle Coal's admission of perfidy later. Thank you."

Malthan wasn't the only one who could throw around fancy words, like 'cavil' thought Sanford, thinking, 'hey, Winston, try perfidy on for size!'

At that point the first day of trial was nearly over with only little more than an hour remaining. While Respondent's counsel suggested that the day come to a close with cross-examination beginning in the morning, Gray rejected the idea.

THE CASE OF THE ABNORMAL WHITE CENTER

With no choice but to proceed, still smarting from what had been an unpleasant start to the hearing for them, the Respondents elected to avoid any strenuous cross-examination of Ms. Nelson. This was based upon their assessment that she presented as a gentle, unassuming witness, a conclusion they reached during the deposition they took during discovery.

Both Winston and Milo were also concerned that, especially because she was a woman, attacking the first witness could backfire. Beating up on her through an aggressive cross might risk offending the judge. Given the many times he smiled benevolently at her during her testimony on direct, it was clear that he had a favorable view of the young woman. With that assessment, they simply didn't know if Gray would take offense at a full-scale assault on her.

Besides, and more importantly, her testimony was of minimal value to the government's case. Their primary targets were to come, with MSHA facility's supervisor, Greg Balkum, and the three expert witnesses the government had lined up.

While behaving courteously, at least by his standards of litigation behavior, Malthan could not resist making two points – that Ms. Nelson was inconsequential, a mere technician and a short-timer at that. Knowing in advance the answers to his questions, he asked them as if he did not know what her responses would be.

"Now, Ms. Nelson, are you in charge of the tech center?" and then "Well, were you in charge of the review of the cassettes?"

She answered, "No" to both.

More questions along that line were presented, all designed to give the appearance of innocent ignorance on Malthan's part. "Now, how many years had you been employed at the Tech Center when you first discovered these supposed abnormal white centers?"

And then, upon informing that it was less than a year, acting surprised, he continued, "Oh, not years. Well then, how many months had you been doing that job?"

Again, feeling somewhat diminished, her eyes cast down, she answered, "Not yet a month at that time."

His stage performance continuing, reaching new levels of feigned surprise, he reacted, "Not even a month? Well, please tell us Ms. Nelson exactly how long you had been employed when you made your so-called discovery of these AWCs?"

"It was a few weeks," she said softly.

From there, having shown she was so new that she was even less than green, Malthan then turned to the circumstances when she first had the "notion," as he put it, that there was a white center on the filters and that it meant something. It began, she replied, with the cassette she dropped on the floor, a fact she had admitted during discovery.

Malthan hammered the point. "So, Ms. Nelson, you would agree that by dropping the cassette all the way down, then with it striking the hard floor and, following that, as I understand your misadventure, the thing rolled all around before ending up way under a counter, and that you then had to sweep it up to recover it, that you were butterfingered in your handling of these important cassettes?"

Acknowledging only that she had dropped it, she responded, "I agree that it slipped out of my hands, yes."

Malthan continued full steam ahead, "Now these cassettes are not to be dropped or otherwise thrown around, is that true?"

With her again conceding that she had dropped the cassette, Malthan continued, "Then would you concede that by dropping the cassette, it was clumsy on your part? A bit klutzy, would you agree?"

At that point, Sanford objected to the insulting description of the witness.

Gray, demonstrating that he had a favorable view of Nelson, admonished Winston. "Now, Mr. Malthan, we all understand that Miss Nelson dropped a cassette, one cassette to be precise, and she admitted to this without hesitation. We all get that. So, the point has been made and there is no need for the disparaging description of her error."

Smiling kindly as he turned toward her, Gray then remarked, "You may continue with your answer, Miss Nelson."

Once more, she conceded that she had dropped the cassette, and that the impact was severe enough to have resulted in it being cracked open. This time, however, very much aware that the judge had acted protectively toward her, she noted, "It was embarrassing for sure, but it was only the one cassette that I dropped."

Uncowed by the cross-examination, she was tempted to add that, if not for the incident, perhaps the investigation and the litigation would never have occurred, but she had the good sense to avoid the combative remark.

The criticism behind Malthan's questions had been spent. He had overplayed his hand. It underscored that, even during cross-examination, the first day of trial had not been a good one for the Milo, Winston and the Bobcat Creek mine.

But it was not in Malthan's nature to relent and move on, saving his insults for the more important witnesses yet to come. He could not let the young woman's testimony end on a favorable note, as he could not help but ask a series of derogatory questions, presented with artificial innocence.

"Would you agree, Ms. Nelson, that technicians are not supposed to be dropping the dust cassettes? And is it your testimony that you didn't throw around other cassettes while performing your analytical reviews?"

That last question instantly brought about another objection, something Malthan fully expected. With his smile, pleased at his clever question, without waiting for a ruling, he instantly offered, "I apologize, withdrawn. Please allow me to rephrase." The point and, he hoped, the damage having been inflicted too, he asked, "Well, Ms. Nelson have you ever dropped other cassettes in your job as a tech reviewing the condition of these cassettes?'

"It's possible," she answered politely. "I can't recall entirely, as I have reviewed hundreds of these. So, if it happened on another occasion, it was a rarity, I am sure of that," she added. "And," she continued.

Seeing that her response was about to become damaging, Malthan interrupted, "Thank you, Ms. Nelson."

Again, Sanford rose immediately. "Objection. Counsel is cutting off the witness' answer, your honor."

Gray, conveying his continuing avuncular attitude to her, ruled immediately, "Continue, please, Ms. Nelson."

Impressively calm, especially as she had never testified before, Nelson responded, with appreciation, "Thank you, your honor. I was just going to add that my dropping the cassette on that occasion stands out so clearly in my mind because that's when I discovered the white center on the filter. It was dramatic, being so white."

Her answer was far beyond what the question called for, but Malthan knew he couldn't object again, since it was the judge, not opposing counsel, that directed her to complete her answer. Still, even Gray wished he had not invited her to finish her answer.

Sanford suppressed a smile at the result and avoided even glancing at his co-counsels.

Nelson had been forewarned that she would take a beating about her short experience and that she had dropped the cassette, but it was still not pleasant to have someone describe her as sloppy and all thumbs. When the cross was finally over, the government rehabilitated her by returning to her initial testimony that, after that first mishap, she then found hundreds of those AWCs and emphasizing that not a one of those had ever been dropped.

Conveniently, it was near 4:30 when Nelson's testimony had been completed. Gray then announced that the testimony would resume the next morning. Though neither side expressed it, both were relieved by Gray's direction. Privately, the Secretary was very pleased with its solid start to the case. Gray also arrived at the same determination. He had maintained control of the proceeding; and his rulings had been sound.

By contrast, Milo and Winston were not in a good state of mind; both feeling they had taken their lumps on this first day. Used to winning nearly all the time, they were privately fuming at day's end, hoping for payback of some sort later.

With a sigh of relief that the first day was over, Gray's initial jitters over the magnitude of the case had eased as he had demonstrated his skill in presiding over the matter. In that   self-satisfied state of mind, while walking from the courthouse back to his office, he reviewed the testimony of the government's first witness, that lab technician Donna, though he could not recall her last name at that moment.

His first thought was that she was cute, an evaluation which he realized should not have been in his head at all. Gently admonishing himself for his inappropriate ideations, as he continued his walk, he moved to the substance of her testimony, recognizing that it did not have any significant impact on the outcome.

Of course, he realized that it was necessary to set the stage so to speak, the predicate for how this whole proceeding came about. But, beyond that, finding this white circle in the first filter and then in so many more, well, it proved there was a white circle, that AWC, as the government had taken to calling it, but by itself it meant nothing. He regarded the cross-examination of her as fluff, unnecessarily belittling her, as he again thought how cute she was. Feeling protective about her, though she certainly didn't need him to act as her guardian, as she withstood the cross-exam quite well, he still did not like the insulting tone of the questioning from the Respondents.

Though it was his habit to stop for a drink after work, on this first night he decided to head directly home to attend to his ailing wife. Upon arriving, he boasted to Millie about the significance of the case and how he masterfully controlled the proceeding. She smiled at him, proud and pleased that it had gone well for her husband. He had said little to her about the case up to that point, but upon offering a brief recap of the first witness' testimony, and including that one mine had already owned up to tampering, she simply nodded, occasionally adding "I see," and other neutral responses in reaction to his telling.

Privately, however, she concluded that the government had launched a strong case and she was pleased that the mines might now be held accountable. Her own significant health problems had made her sensitive to maladies suffered by others. Those poor miners, she thought, suffocating because those scoundrels put profit over their health. She hoped they would pay dearly for their corruption.

On day two, the government next called the other two technicians from the Mount Hope Tech Center who had examined the cassettes; Daniel Tucker and Tom Grasser. Sanford would have preferred to bypass their testimony, as neither was as impressive as Donna Nelson. But, for continuity, and to show that other technicians also found large numbers of cassettes with the white centers, they were necessary witnesses.

The two met Sanford's low expectations. In contrast to Nelson, as they described their review of the cassettes, both of them conveyed a detached attitude, making it clear that they viewed their work as a dry and dreary task.

Sanford was unhappy about the lack of passion they displayed, though he knew from their depositions that it would go that way. It was obvious that neither wanted to be testifying, particularly Tucker, he noted. Their poor display and especially because they were among the first witnesses for the government, worked negatively upon the case. By showing their detached attitude, approaching boredom, Sanford believed it could impact, even if only slightly, the judge's view of the case.

The defense enjoyed it. With these two witnesses treating the matter with obvious disinterest, they hoped the attitude could spill over, influencing Gray early on in the trial. With the two witnesses, in a sense on the Respondent's side, Malthan and Krakovich stretched out their testimony, employing a friendly cross-examination, consuming all of the second day.

When the day's testimony was concluded, Sanford made a point of conveying to Balkum his disappointment over the absence of any passion displayed by the two, subtly harming the importance of the case. Balkum, having the same take on their testimony, shared Sanford's irritation.

"What gives with those two?" Sanford inquired.

"I can only guess," Balkum responded, "but it may have to do with my elevating Ms. Nelson as the de facto tech in charge of the cassette reviews. They've been with the lab for years, while she was a new employee. She came aboard only a few weeks before the inadvertent discovery."

"Oh, boy," Sanford replied, "that white male privilege thing again. Well, what's done is done on that score. And, substance-wise, they didn't hurt our case, as their findings were consistent with Ms. Nelson's reviews of the cassettes."

Balkum nodded, "At least there's that," he seconded the observation. Privately, though, he was steamed. They put their resentments ahead of the miners who were sucking in the deadly coal dust. He had a long memory and would not forget their indifference to this most serious matter. Paybacks, untraceable of course, would occur whenever he could employ them. There would be things, though most would be small, when he could dispense his displeasure.

From the Respondent's point of view, as the witnesses following Nelson were males, and therefore, per their old school thinking, neither could be viewed as vulnerable, it was easier to have a more aggressive cross-examination, if they wished. But, given their lack of ardor during the testimony on direct, there was the temptation to go easy on them, as they came across as disinterested in the matter. The Respondent's attorneys already knew from their depositions that the testimony from the two would be of little consequence and that assessment was correct, with the bonus of their plain indifference to the matter. This was in stark contrast to Donna Nelson, whose testimony came with obvious passion about the issue. Given that they were unenthusiastic witnesses, their cross-exams were moderated, but they still served the purpose of tune-ups for Milo and Winston, sparring sessions in preparation for the more serious questioning of the key government witnesses to follow. As their lukewarm testimony was essentially cumulative to Nelson's, they avoided inflicting any bruises on the two.

The redirect, in recognition of the tepid effort by the Respondents, asked few follow-up questions and, as such, the testimony from the two technicians was completed by late-afternoon on the second day.

Though Sanford had no reason to know of it, Tucker felt unnerved when he learned that Bobcat Creek would be the first mine to go to trial, and worse, that Ricky Sloan would be a witness for the mine. Ruing his warning to Ricky about dust sampling at Bobcat Creek, his fear that the director of safety might spill the beans, disclosing the call, was constantly present in his head.

In a sense, the case began in earnest after that, on day three, with the presentation of Greg Balkum's testimony, the supervisor of the Mount Hope Technology Center. No mere technician, he was the government's first expert witness. His title was underwhelming, it being modestly described as the "supervisory industrial hygienist." It did not do justice to his background or experience, nor to the significance of his work.

The supervisor's humble title aside, Counsel for the Respondent recognized his importance and, from his deposition, that he would be a formidable witness, one who it would be important for them to try to take down.

Though Balkum was somewhat nervous, as he had only testified in a few other cases, and none had been of this magnitude, he steeled himself, fortified by his anger that miners were not being protected as Congress had intended. He took miners' health seriously. Adding fuel to his attitude was his resentment over Tucker and Grasser's detached testimony, an assessment shared by Sanford. Those factors animated him. He would not allow himself to be intimidated by the mine's attorneys, not when he was certain that those mines had engaged in a coordinated plan to tamper with the dust collectors, not giving a damn about the harm to miners' health. One need to look no further than the Eagle Coal and Coke mine's confession that they had done exactly what all of the other mines were charged with doing.

Taking all morning, Balkum described his credentials, covering his education and long experience running the lab, together with his years of reviewing mine dust samples, all of it occurring before discovering the suspect samples in this litigation.

When the afternoon session began, Malthan immediately challenged Balkum's qualification to testify as an expert. By that move, the Respondents made it clear that every avenue of attack would be employed. Sanford had forewarned Balkum that such a claim would be made, so he was not intimidated by the tactic.

THE CASE OF THE ABNORMAL WHITE CENTER

As Sanford had predicted, that objection was quickly denied, with Gray advising Sanford he did not have to hear his opposition to the challenge, ruling that Balkum met the standard for expertise.

In federal proceedings, as Malthan well knew, an expert is designated as such upon establishing that the witness has more knowledge about a subject than the ordinary person.

Any further challenges would have to await cross-examination, but that would be limited to assailing his background and the procedures he employed, all to diminish the conclusions he reached. Despite knowing that he would lose the challenge, it did not deter his making it. This was hardball; courtesies were not observed. If Balkum felt slighted by the claim that he was not an expert, all the better, thought Malthan. Perhaps it would shake his confidence, even if only a little.

A benefit resulted from the Respondent's challenge to the qualifications of lab center's chief, because the start of his substantive testimony did not begin until mid-afternoon. In the relative comfort of direct examination, with few objections being made, Balkum began his detailed testimony of the origin of the abnormal centers. Though largely retracing Ms. Nelson's testimony, and intentionally downplaying the roles of Tucker and Grasser, he demonstrated the professional approach to the issue when it arose. He made no assumptions that anything suspicious was going on, only directing that Nelson's review of cassettes from other mines proceed and that accurate records be maintained each step of the way. The delay in his substantive testimony about the suspect white centers meant that he was able to get his feet wet so to speak, that first day, postponing the slings that would be hurled at him once cross-examination began.

When the fourth day of trial began, now having a first-hand introduction to the aggressive nature of this litigation under his belt, with the unwarranted challenge to his credentials, Balkum was less intimidated than the previous afternoon.

THE MINE SAFETY TRILOGY PART II

Under the initial comfort provided by the direct examination, counsel for the Secretary walked him through the event that started all of this and the methodical approach he took to it. There was no rash conclusion on his part, he told the Court. To the contrary, he professed to be reluctant to conclude that anything was amiss when Ms. Nelson first brought the white center to his attention. That was a half-truth on his part; he actually didn't want those cassettes to reflect anything but an anomaly, a statistical quirk, but he had been around the coal mining industry long enough to know they were fully capable of working such an immense fraud.

His reluctance wasn't based on doubts that they had manipulated the results. Rather, it was his anticipation of the wearing war that would be lodged against MSHA, all to insist that the agency was wrong – that none of the mines had tampered with the dust tests. He knew they would be undaunted by Eagle Coal's confession.

Reiterating that he did not jump to any conclusions that corruption was involved, to the contrary, he calmly directed that Miss Nelson continue with her examination of the dust cassettes but, when the disturbing trend continued, he had no choice but to bring in two more technicians to assist in the review process. As he spoke of the two techs that were added to the review process, he was especially careful to speak respectfully about them, showing none of the contempt he privately harbored over their indifferent testimony.

It was only after, as he put it, that the three technicians had "a ton of these oddities, those white center filters," that he felt duty-bound to call in the Solicitor of Labor. In all those years, with his testimony emphasizing that he had many years of reviewing these dust cassettes, he had never seen anything remotely like this.

Even Gray, who was determined to avoid making premature conclusions, privately recognized that, at least to this early point in the trial, Balkum's testimony during direct was a blow to the defense. There were so many of these things, Balkum testified, coming in essentially at the same time and all with the signature mark of a white center.

As the Tech Center Chief forcefully made the point, one would expect the center of the filter to be the dirtiest area, not the purest. And, he added, it had always been that way over the years – the center had always been the darkest area on the filter. But then it all changed. Now, like a tidal wave, these odd cassettes were coming from mines all over Kentucky, Pennsylvania and West Virginia. It didn't matter where they came from, virtually all of them had the white centers.

Realizing the damaging cumulative effect of this testimony, the Respondents repeatedly objected, the goal being to throw Sanford's direct exam off stride and hopefully to break the force of Balkum's testimony upon the judge too.

It didn't work. Both Sanford and Balkum recognized the ploy for what it was and it only amplified their energy levels; they stayed on message.

The intensity of the trial required Gray to be on his toes every minute. Unlike most of his years of trials, there were none of the lulls, common to these hearings, allowing his attention and thoughts to wander from the testimony at hand. The few times he did have a lapse, almost as if by heavenly design, an objection would be made and he would have to scramble to understand it and make a ruling. Weary from the lack of any letup, he was relieved when the day finally ended. One bright spot was that Balkum's direct testimony was over by the end of the day.

Once in the protective bubble of his chambers, Gray packed up quickly, careful to take his trial notes with him as he left the courthouse and began the walk back to the sanctity of the Office of Administrative Law Judges. The walk did him good, not too far to be a trek, but still of sufficient distance to unwind. The activity, though minimal, was a stress reliever. To that end, he tried to put aside any thoughts of the weeks of trial that were ahead.

When he entered the Judges' Office, most employees had gone for the day, but Rich Larkin was still there, his door open, as Gray, preoccupied in thought, passed by his colleague's office.

With the office nearly empty, Larkin noted his colleague in the hallway. "Hey, Charles," he spoke out, as Gray continued to his office.

Hearing Larkin, he stopped and turned back. Their friendship had grown in the time since Gray received his unwelcome assignment for these dust cases and so he was pleased upon hearing Larkin's voice.

"One of the few still here, Richard. Such dedication," he joshed.

"It's mostly about the traffic," Larkin confessed. "I get more done after the office has emptied out and my ride home is quicker too. I'm sure you want to be home after your long day, but may I join you in your office for a moment? I'd like to hear how the trial is going."

Gray was tired but receptive to Larkin's self-invitation. It would provide a welcome respite between the demands during the hearing and the ever-present attention required by his needy wife, a situation that Larkin knew nothing about. Gray was not without compassion about his wife's disease, but he wondered if people ever took the time to consider the toll that an ill family member exacts on the care-giver? They were mostly overlooked, he believed.

"Sure, come on down, Richard," he affirmed.

Larkin gave Charles a few moments to get settled before visiting. Once he arrived, Gray welcomed him. "Come in, please," as he gestured for Larkin to take a seat on the sofa, while he came around from his desk to sit in the soft chair opposite it.

"The first few days have been demanding," he began, "but overall, it's gone well. The important thing, I don't have to tell you, is to establish that you are in control and I was able to do that early on. The respondent's counsel gave me that opportunity by interrupting the government's opening statement. Poor form on his part."

"I've never had that happen, an objection right at the start, before any testimony," Larkin reacted, "not in my trial days, nor in my brief time so far on the bench. That tactic of trying to throw opposing counsel off stride, usually it's when a witness is testifying and making some headway."

Gray nodded. "Anyway, we didn't get started with testimony until the afternoon session on the first day. The government led off with the three technicians who were reviewing the dust collection cassettes, those abnormal white centers, AWC's, as they call them. Larkin knew what the shorthand expression meant. "That finished up by the second day. "Then," Gray continued, "on the third day the fellow that runs the office, where this whole suspect dust collection business originated, began testifying."

Larkin was taken aback by his colleague's description of the case, by calling it "this whole suspect dust collection business." It sounded as if Gray was being dismissive of it. He took it more seriously, the idea that these miners, doing a taxing job as it was, were slowly killing themselves as they worked. If he were presiding, he thought, there would be none of that attitude.

Gray, unaware of his colleague's negative take on his choice of words, continued, "Name's Greg Balkum. He's the supervisor of MSHA's Mount Hope Technology Center, someplace in the hinterlands of West Virginia. Didn't bother to locate it on a map. Anyway, his testimony was passable," Gray informed, a remark that was far short of a glowing assessment, revealing that he was not overly impressed by it.

"I mean he was qualified," he added, walking back the implicit criticism, "but his credentials were pretty basic. They were sufficient, of course, for his expert opinion to be offered that he believed there was tampering with those cassettes. I don't mean to suggest otherwise. Cross-examination won't even start until tomorrow, so we'll see how he fares when that gets underway."

Another disconcerting remark, Larkin thought. It didn't seem especially neutral at this early stage, and it was hard for him to figure out the basis for his colleague's attitude. Though not in his new position as a judge for very long, he had already become aware that some judges leaned towards the mine operators, and the rationales they provided to support their findings in some of those decisions gave him serious pause. Their decisions also reflected wins for mine operators at a rate that was concerning, prevailing in more than two thirds of the cases.

In light of Gray's negative remarks, and especially with his rather dim review of Balkum's testimony, Larkin could not resist a comment. Trying to be diplomatic, he went right to Gray's mention about the supervisor for that MSHA office.

"Understood," he said, "apparently no Ivy League background, but you determined that he had the qualifications to be deemed an expert on the subject," locking him in to his acknowledgement. With that, Larkin then tried to have his friend focus on the important issue, "So, was he convincing? I mean I know it's very early in the trial, but your first impressions?" he asked.

"Well, it was pretty straightforward," Gray responded, skirting a direct answer to Larkin's question. "There were some objections as he proceeded with his testimony, but I overruled each one. I mean, at this early stage, the government got off to a respectable start, which, let's face it, they had to accomplish that. Thousands of these dust cassettes just rather suddenly start showing up with these claimed abnormal white centers, those AWCs. It hadn't happened before, so it caught their attention right away. Again, they have so many of the damn things, those cassettes. We're not talking about a handful of them by any means."

"And then," he continued, "here's the capper, once word got out somehow to the mines involved that Mine Safety had discovered this business, wouldn't you know it, they dropped down to a trickle. I mean it was a precipitous drop in these AWCs. So, again, the government got off to a respectable start."

With some relief, Larkin thought that at least Gray acknowledged that the large number of those suspect cassettes and that they suddenly dried up, were hard facts to ignore. He would have used a more favorable description than a "respectable start." But given Gray's overall tone, he had enough sense to hold back from voicing his reaction, especially because his colleague's remarks leaned towards diminishing the strength of the government's case.

He would have no such attitude, if he were presiding, he thought. Though it would be daunting, for the first time, given Gray's apparent predilection, he now wished that the case had been assigned to him. Not that he would swing the other way by presuming that the government's testimony was gospel. But no way would he be minimizing the government's case at this early stage.

Understandably, due to his near-death experience in Idaho, Larkin had a dim view of what mine operators were capable of doing. That they might engage in such illegal behavior, it was mild compared to his personal experience.

He could tell that his colleague was tired – his face plainly displayed it. Deciding it was best to avoid any direct criticism over Gray's underwhelming view of Balkum's testimony, he diplomatically determined it was time to end their talk.

"Thanks for filling me in, Charles. I'd like to keep hearing how this trial proceeds, if you don't mind. Definitely, educational for me, as a new judge. And again, for what their worth, I'll offer my thoughts, if you wish. Even a stopped clock is right twice a day a day, you know," he added with a smile.

Gray smiled. He had not interpreted Larkin's comments about his reaction to Balkum's testimony as a criticism. "No, I welcome it. You're okay in my book, Richard," he reassured.

Larkin bid him goodnight, pleased that they had the exchange and that the veteran judge remained receptive to continuing discussing the case with him as the hearing continued. Perhaps, he thought, it would be possible to nudge Gray back to the center if he began straying off course so early in the trial.

Pleased about Larkin's departure, now alone, Gray faced up that he would need to return home, as it was nearly 5:30.

Before meeting that nightly obligation, a creature of habit, he had developed an after-work routine. He realized it was not one to be celebrated because, upon leaving the office, he would regularly walk two blocks from the office to a corner drinking establishment, the G Street Grill.

Though it was not a gourmet experience, mostly appetizers with those being unremarkable too, it didn't matter to him, as he was only interested in the liquid refreshments. Routinely, it would be a Manhattan. For variety, he would opt for an Old Fashioned. Either way, a good strong whiskey was the essential ingredient. Most nights, mindful of his need to get home, he would have just one, supplemented later with another drink, his evening glass of red wine at his residence, after Millie was safely in bed.

Though an unhappy situation, it worked, keeping him going day to day, allowing him to cope with the job and then the return to his pathetic abode and to his wife's illness, which pervaded and dictated their lives.

The alcohol did not get the best of him though. He was conscious of the way liquor can creep up on the regular imbibers and then become, not just a habit, but an addiction that takes over. He had kept it in check. One and sometimes two stiff ones at the Grill, followed by a nightcap at home got him by. He did not ponder that having three drinks most nights was still a lot of alcohol. Besides, he consoled himself, some experts claimed that a drink or two might be good for one's health. If that was true, then he should be okay.

The visit with Larkin over, he wasted little time leaving his office and the building. His departure was within the range of his typical exit time, a routine that the cleaning crew and security guards had come to expect. He waved to each of them as he departed, his gesture of friendliness, and they would wave back, a wordless exchange between them. Three steps up to street level from the building's lobby, he would then turn right and make the short walk to his haunt.

Once in the establishment, upon taking a seat at the bar, his briefcase resting securely next to an ankle, he would offer a good evening to the bartender, Jerome, who, from years of Gray's regular visits, knew him well.

"What will it be tonight, judge?" he would routinely ask. Aware of his customer's occupation, he would always include Gray's title, as a show of respect for his esteemed position. Though he would ask, Jerome knew there would be no surprise order. The man knew what he liked, always a Manhattan or an Old Fashioned. As the judge always tipped him well, he would pour the premium stuff for him.

"Think I'll go with an Old-Fashioned tonight, my friend," he announced. All those years, but Gray never made the effort to remember the name of his bartender, an ill-mannered attitude, reflecting an underlying lack of respect.

"Your day went well, I hope," Jerome offered, as he slid the drink in front of his regular patron.

Gray was careful not to talk about cases outside of the office. Even on those evenings when he had two drinks, he did not slip. One could never tell who might overhear his words. He would offer a habitual response, one that Jerome was well familiar with, though he privately wished that the judge would not repeat the same reply each night. "Not bad, not bad," he would intone.

Sipping on his drink, giving himself some needed time to unwind, the respite before resuming his home responsibilities, he glanced to his left. The bar was nearly empty, but he took notice of one woman who was three stools down from his spot. He avoided staring, but upon allowing a decent time interval away from her direction, periodically he would look again in her direction, doing his best to seem casual about his observations. He was drawn in by her beauty, creating a compulsion to view her repeatedly. He estimated her to be maybe fifteen years younger than him. That was quite a bit younger, he admitted to himself, but not so much of a difference, he thought, that it was preposterous to fantasize about her. She was undeniably attractive, of a caliber that commanded taking notice.

Continuing his flight of fancy, he noted happily, that she was unaccompanied, clearly alone, so he did not have to deal with a male companion taking issue with his repeated gazes. A light blonde, whether dyed or natural, he could not tell, with its length just above her shoulders, she had what he considered to be an appealing face. Free of excessive makeup, she seemed a cross between a homespun, fresh, look, yet with a glamorous appearance too.

Never seen a woman with such star quality, he thought, not at the G Street at least. She didn't belong here, not one with her looks.

Showing his age, he thought, "she's a real dish," a description now passé by some thirty years. Maybe, he speculated, she was just in town for the night, having no clue where to go for drink.

With his subsequent glances, he took in that she was in shape for sure, possessing a fulsome figure too, a feature he appreciated. He definitely had not seen her before. Finally recognizing the need to resume his self-control, he brought his attention back to his drink, willing himself to look straight ahead. It was not easy.

"Another one for you tonight, judge?" the bartender inquired, seeing that Gray had nearly finished his order. Gray, so preoccupied, did not even hear the question.

Up to that point, the captivating woman, as far as he could tell, had not even once glanced in his direction. It was understandable, he thought, admitting that he was so much older, whatever charm he possessed in his youth, now gone.

But her understandable indifference changed upon hearing the bartender address him with that important title.

"Judge," she heard him say to the man at the bar. That title caught her attention. With that remark, she turned to take note of him for a moment before resuming looking straight ahead.

Realizing that he was preoccupied by the woman a few stools down from him, Jerome repeated his question. "Hey, judge, shall I fix you another?"

Again, she took note of the confirmation, the bartender once more addressing him as 'judge.'

This time Gray heard the bartender's inquiry for a refill.

"No, that'll be it for me tonight, thanks." He then finished the last swallow from his drink, laying down the payment along with a ten-spot, his customary tip. He ended the night with his routine remark to Jerome, "Have a good night, my friend."

"You too, your honor," he replied reverentially.

He wanted to stay, because by lingering he would have the opportunity to take in more looks her way, though he also realized that those gazes would be an ultimately unsatisfying thing to do, since nothing would ever come of it. Besides, such fantasizing would only serve to heighten the awareness of his home situation, that dreary house and his ailing wife, with her progressive malady, an unhappy contrast to the fantasy he was experiencing.

Facing up to his home responsibility, he rose from his stool.

As he did so, the woman, having heard the man's title once more, made a last glance at him as he departed. The photos she'd been given were consistent with the man at the bar. He was, without doubt, the mark.

Though Gray had not a clue, the woman who commanded his attention was not there as happenstance; her presence was in the nature of reconnaissance.

Arriving home shortly after seven, he greeted his wife with a perfunctory hug, together with inquiring, as he did routinely each night, how her day had been. She, in turn, replied with her own recurring remark that she was tired, and that the day had been difficult.

No change there, he noted, nor any expected. Cheeriness had been rare in their household for years now. Then, she added, disapprovingly, "You're late, Charles," observing that she expected him to be home by 6:30.

He took it as the complaint it was intended to be. "Millie," he offered, with a tone that conveyed kindness and patience, but in truth had neither, "remember that I told you I have this big case, the one alleging tampering with coal dust samples. I expect that things will continue this way for two months at least."

He knew his mild protestation would not stop her complaining when he was late getting home, but he did not like it. So continually burdened by her, yet she was not shy about complaining about his expected arrival time, an edict created by her, not some mutual understanding.

She had not forgotten at all about his remark that he had been assigned the most significant case in his career, that the trial would be of long duration and involve stressful days, but her illness did not prevent her from complaining, even with the big trial. He could be home earlier, she concluded, if he made the effort. No fool, she could've pressed the point by noting that his day in court would be over by five, at the latest, leaving him with an unaccounted hour and a half.

She well knew of his routine practice of having a drink before his return commute. The smell on his breath disclosed that, as usual, he had stopped for a drink on this evening too. She didn't like that either. It was an invitation for trouble if he had an accident on the drive home or if he were pulled over by the police. If he must have a drink, a habit she deplored, he could have it at home. Focused upon herself, she was oblivious that it was not just about having a drink, it was his brief chance to be away from work and her, a small amount of time for himself.

However, his late arrival did not interfere significantly with their evening, as they spent little of that time together. As her illness progressed, she would make a simple dinner, something microwavable, in the late afternoon, before he was home, even on the few days when he made no stops. When he did arrive, fending for himself was part of his routine, she not being well enough to prepare a supper. Being on his own for that task, he would scrounge around the frig, either nuking or baking some frozen item. It was only on their quiet, uneventful, weekends that they would have dinner together, an effort that he would shoulder.

None of this was to say that they no longer loved one another. They did, but it was now profoundly different, as it had been for several years. Sex was rare, to the point of being virtually nonexistent, and frankly it had become boring for him, with the same repetitious routine to their intimacy. Though he fantasized over thoughts of some more exciting unions with her, he knew it would never happen, not with her poor health and the lack of interest it produced. They accepted it to be just the way it was. It was not a happy end chapter to their long marriage.

Conversation between them was superficial as well. However, his wife did express some interest in this significant new case of his.

Having lodged her common complaint about his tardiness, she moved beyond that grievance, turning to his newsworthy case. "Charles, tell me how your case is going," she asked.

Tired and having already recounted the day's events with Larkin, he would have preferred to avoid another retelling but, out of respect and duty, he provided a summary to her.

Millie had some cognitive decline from her disease, but she could still fully appreciate his account of the day. After listening to his summary, unlike Larkin, she did not feel restrained over expressing her reaction. "Sounds like the government has a strong case," she commented.

Outwardly patient, but privately condescending of her view as she was not a lawyer, Charles told her it was like a baseball game and it was in the very early innings, a simple analogy, befitting her background, he thought. The outcome, he added, could not be foretold so soon.

She understood his response as the politely packaged put down it was, but she was not cowed by it. "I understand, Charles," she countered, "but common sense is not exclusive to lawyers," and then, pausing for a moment, added "*or judges*. What you have told me is that there are a large number of these cartridges with these white centers. I have that right, don't I?"

He recognized the rebuke. "Yes, Millie, the government alleges those large numbers." He couldn't resist correcting her though. "The term is cassettes, not cartridges," the patronizing tone of his correction plain.

Her husband's chiding did not escape her. She felt embarrassed over the mistake.

Properly informed of the accurate nomenclature, he continued, "But it's all about proof, not allegations. As I said, the trial has just begun. You wouldn't want me to jump to conclusions, now would you dear."

She realized that the "dear," at the end of his reply to mean he was patiently instructing an unschooled student. Now twice admonished, she nevertheless held her position. She could joust too, replying, "Of course not, Charles."

As there were barbs plainly being exchanged, mild though they were, she could not resist, adding "dear" in her comeback. "I was only speaking to what you have told me so far, *dear*, and those facts at this point show something significant was going on. Or am I wrong about that too, dear?" she poked back.

He recognized there was no point to continuing the friction, or worse, elevating the dispute. Instead, conciliatingly, he added, "Of course, you're right. He even dropped using "dear," recognizing that neither had employed it lovingly. "I respect your views. I'm just saying it's too soon for conclusions."

That was sufficient for them to call it a draw, as they each then proceeded to their independent nightly routines. For him, that meant, a meal of some sort, followed by showering and then his evening drink, a more than ample pour of red wine, which he would nurse while reading his non-fiction book of the moment. Once in bed, by ten, and she already there, he would present a peck on her cheek, the night coming to a close with their same dreary routine in store for the next day.

On the fifth day of the hearing cross-examination of Balkum began. As the expression goes, the gloves were off. Krakovich began by assailing the supervisor's credentials, setting up for a later comparison the stellar backgrounds of the guns they had hired to call into question every aspect of the government's case.

Balkum held his ground, remembering his counsel's warning that the questioning would not be pretty and adhering to his advice to keep his cool.

After dealing with Balkum's unremarkable educational background, and the dreary day-to-day routine of his office's work, Milo then began questioning the particulars of the government's theory that the sampling discs had been tampered. Nothing was left unchallenged.

Krakovich even challenged the idea that a white center was an abnormal feature. That claim was unexpected by the government. Milo began the assertion with an insult to Balkum's knowledge. "Mr. Balkum, sir, have you ever heard of the null hypothesis?"

Balkum, uncowed by the disparaging remark within the question, responded evenly, that indeed he had heard of it, and was familiar with it. He then then proceeded to answer, respectfully, but intentionally conveying the tone of a patient educator, "Let me explain it for you in simple terms."

Disappointed that he had failed to catch Balkum off guard, Krakovich did not miss the insult being returned to the one he had just served. Irritated at the implicit put down, he turned to the judge, interrupting the answer with an indignant complaint, "Your honor, please direct the witness to answer my questions without commentary."

But Gray was having none of it. He had paid attention to Krakovich's question, with its snide innuendo, and he informed, "Counsel, the witness has properly responded to the substance and tenor of your question. Proceed with your answer, Mr. Balkum," he said, presenting a respectful mien to the witness.

One for him, Krakovich noted unhappily to himself over being chided by the judge, while he followed the proper protocol, responding to the ruling, "Thank you, your Honor."

Balkum, feeling pleased that his return punch had landed, continued, "Well, null of course, refers to 'zero,' and the idea is that there is no difference between two things. In this matter, it would mean that AWCs appear equally in all mines; not just the ones charged with tampering. That is, there is no difference in the rate of AWCs in any mine. We have numerous reasons to knock down that theory."

Krakovich, not one to put aside being overruled in his previous objection, saw the opportunity for a quick payback. "Now, your honor, I must object again." Referring to Balkum by using a belittling title, he continued, "With that last comment this lab tech went far beyond my question. I ask that you instruct him to confine his answers to the questions posed. I didn't ask him about any theories he imagines."

This time, Gray sided with counsel. "I agree. Mr. Balkum, please keep your answer to the question asked." To make his point clear, he instructed, "Your response, sir, adding that the government has reasons to, as you put it, knock down the null hypothesis, goes beyond the question posed."

Balkum respectfully answered, "Sorry, your honor," but now he was the one annoyed, with that belittling remark from Krakovich, calling him a lab tech. The animosity between the two was palpable.

Milo was pleased with that recent ruling; it was rapid payback for what he arrogantly believed was the judge's erroneous ruling a moment earlier, in effect a referee's make-up call for that mistake, evening the score.

The responses from Balkum did not cause Krakovich to retreat from his assertion.

"With so many of these cassettes having that appearance, this claimed white center business," he boldly contended, doesn't that show that it is normal to have them!" He did not wait for an answer, brazenly continuing, "aren't they more appropriately called 'normal white centers,' or NWCs, tech Balkum?"

Balkum did not flinch. "I don't believe so, Mr. Krakovich," he replied. Trading the insult, he did not add the dignifying word 'counselor,' in his answer, a slight Milo noticed.

None of this deterred Milo, as he then continued to call them "NWCs," as an alternative description.

That provoked an objection from Sanford. "Your honor, I object," he began, "there is no evidence, none whatsoever, at this stage of these proceedings for counsel to start renaming these cassettes 'normal white centers,' nor 'NWCs,' as he has just now added. He's not a witness, much less an expert one. It might become an issue if a real expert were to testify that these filters normally would have white centers, but that hasn't happened so far."

He then looked at Milo, "Now has it Mr. Krakovich?" echoing Balkum's untitled form of address.

Gray then spoke up. He couldn't allow opposing counsels to start exchanging broadsides.

"Counsel, direct your objections to the court. It is not appropriate for you to pose questions regarding your objection to opposing counsel."

Sanford, chastised, realized he had gone too far. "I apologize, your honor and withdraw my last remark directed at opposing counsel. But it remains the fact that counsel, being neither a witness, nor an expert one, can't introduce his own evidence or create his own new terms. Further it will invite confusion in the record for any appellate review."

He continued, "If an expert does claim such conditions on the cassette filters to be 'normal' that can be resolved at that time. So, I want to emphasize there is no *testimony* to support such descriptions. Finally, your honor, we would note that during discovery no one, not one, of the individuals the Respondent intends to present as experts employed either of those terms, nor have any described the abnormal white centers as a normal occurrence."

Milo thought he might be able to slip in the fresh description without Sanford objecting, but the gambit failed. While it didn't have the same ring as "AWCs," as it did not trip off the tongue as easily, it met his "alternative facts" approach.

Gray didn't regard the use of the new term as such a big deal. There was no jury involved, he thought, so the worry that the term would influence him was not present. Still, he had no choice but to agree with the government.

"Mr. Krakovich," he said, "the objection from Mr. Sanford is sustained. You will refrain from using such descriptions unless and until there is expert testimony to support such a view. In contrast, at this point, we do have testimony from witnesses, including one expert witness, that in their experience these white centers were abnormal."

"Thank you, your honor," Krakovich smiled politely, but with no sincerity, in response to the ruling rebuking his attempt to create an alternative description. Back to a loss, he thought, unavoidably keeping score. These recent rulings on the exchanges were not pleasant; a loss, a win, but then another loss, left him smarting. Being used to winning, he was unhappy, but he had no choice other than to bury those feelings for now and get back to dismantling Balkum's testimony.

The withering adversarial examination of Balkum continued throughout the day. When it was over, both sides agreed that, with little more than an hour left in the day, it was a good point to call the first week of the trial to an end. Besides, with redirect coming up and likely more cross-examination to follow, Balkum's testimony would not be concluded until next week.

The intensity of the proceeding had taken its toll not only on the witness but on the counsels and the judge too, so the idea of calling the week to a close was privately welcomed by all. The downside for Malthan and Krakovich was that it also gave Balkum a break, affording the worn witness the weekend to recover from the long assault.

As Gray made his way back to the office, though grateful that a significant witness had largely completed his testimony, he was well aware of the parade of those yet to come, an exhausting thought. Still, the return walk to his office gave him a chance to decompress from the day's demands. There was also the welcoming anticipation of the drink he would soon be enjoying at the Grill.

When he arrived at his office, he saw no one and assumed that, being a Friday, everyone had cleared out. It was a relief, as he did not want to engage with anyone from the office. Without malice, he opted to take the longer corridor route to his office to reduce the chance of seeing his colleague, Larkin. Having a drink and then heading home were his priorities. Fortunately, except for the wave and acknowledgement to the security people, he was able to exit the office without seeing a soul.

Arriving at the Grill and taking a stool at the bar, Jerome attended to his patron without delay. Offering his customary greeting, and upon receiving the judge's drink order, he asked how things were going. Gray, in return, presented his usual, non-substantive, answer. "Fine, everything is fine, thanks," he told the barkeep, his alternative mechanical reply to "not bad, not bad."

Unable to resist, Gray scanned the others on the barstools but there was no sign of the woman who had so recently captivated him. To be sure he had not overlooked her, he awkwardly turned right and left on the stool to see if she might be at one of tavern's tables. No luck. She was not there.

When his drink arrived, disappointed that she was not present, he spent little time finishing it. With one last look after he was done, and still no sign of her, he declined a refill and perfunctorily wished Jerome a good weekend, receiving an echo of the same in reply.

Jerome could tell that his regular customer had seemed more distracted, and noticeably less content that evening, but he had no clue of the reason behind it.

When Gray arrived home, after Millie greeted him, this time without carping about his drinking habit, she immediately inquired about the day's trial developments. It had become a routine practice of hers, one which he did not enjoy. As she was his spouse, civility demanded a recounting, which he accommodated, while making it as brief as possible.

He informed that the government's first major witness, the head of the government's tech center lab, had completed his testimony on direct, the essence of which was that the lab alleged finding thousands of dust filters with abnormal white centers and further that it was also alleged that once word got out that the lab was aware of these white centered filters, the AWCs stopped abruptly. He added that the redirect would start on Monday.

Millie, not shy when dealing with her husband, the lack of a law degree not curtailing her responses, bluntly stated, "Sounds open and shut, Charles. They did it!"

He did not like her pronouncement at all. Such unhesitant certainty. What did she know! And he had already done a round with her in their previous exchange, explaining that a competent judge is not supposed to jump to early conclusions, but rather wait until all the evidence had been presented. He decided there was no point, purpose, or prospect of success dealing with his wife on the issue, as she was unburdened with any legal education, and immune from his wise tutelage. Knowing that it was hopeless to make any headway to alter her opinion, he decided it best to ignore her comment entirely, as if she had said nothing. Instead, he informed her that he was quite tired and needed to fix dinner and then take a shower.

She understood his nonresponsive comment for what it was, a rejection of her view, together with his implicit announcement that their time together was over for the evening, as he had other things to do.

The weekend was much the same. Though winter was in the offing, the weather did not take notice of the calendar. It was not unusual in Northern Virginia for the climate to remain warm. Though the mornings would often have a chill, often by midday it would be warm enough that no coat was needed. With his backyard being no more distinctive than the remainder of his residence, there were still sufficient leaf falls to require raking and, with insufficient space to pile them at the rear of the yard, he would have to perform the annoying task of bagging them. It was frustrating, too, as it was difficult to deposit the leaves in the large plastic bags for pickup by the trash removal service.

Still, it provided him with an opportunity to have some solitude, free from the needs of his wife. Most Sundays, he intentionally took the time to relax, spending several hours reviewing the newspapers. It served as another way for him to be present, the two of them together, yet functionally alone, the emptiness of their relationship on display, a byproduct of her disease.

Her illness pervaded their life. Before that befell her, they would do things together, as husband and wife. Though most would be routine matters, shopping and the like, at least the activities were done as a couple. Millie's limitations now foreclosed those once-shared activities.

CHAPTER 6

When the trial resumed, at the start of the second week of testimony, the redirect's purpose was plain: revisit the key facts avoided during the cross-examination. Just as with juries, a judge needs to be reminded of the damning facts. No, the government called to the judge's attention, those dust cassettes did not always have that appearance. Not only that, these AWCs started showing up suddenly and dramatically. In fact, there was "a flood of them," as Sanford had Balkum repeat his description of the onslaught. Nearly all the underground mines started sending dust cassettes with those white centers. In fact, thousands of them, it was underscored, showed up. And then, when the word got out to the mine operators that the government was onto it, the AWCs just as abruptly dried up. Through Balkum's testimony during redirect, and based on his many years of experience with these filters, the Respondent's bold claim of "normal white centers" was dismantled, at least for now.

Though the government considered that to be enough, wrapping up the redirect, Sanford then revisited the significant and very inconvenient fact that one of the originally named respondents, owners of several underground coal mines in West Virginia and Kentucky, admitted to doing exactly what was alleged – monkeying with the dust samples. They even admitted, Sanford made a point of reminding the judge, that reverse air flow was the primary method they employed to alter the samples.

Malthan again objected to testimony about another mine's actions, but Sanford had successfully planted the reminder in Gray's head. Pretending contrition, Sanford apologized to the Court, asserting he had forgotten that the admission of tampering by another mine would be addressed through judicial notice by entering court records of the mine's guilty plea.

A re-cross exam then followed and, as predictably as the re-direct, Malthan's first question went back to the same contentions made during their initial cross. Gray showed his exasperation when this next round of ploughing the same ground began, as the examinations simply rehashed earlier testimony, yet again. Two questions into the new cross-examination, he interrupted, commenting, "Haven't we heard this same information enough times?"

All judges have the power to curtail repeated testimony, and Gray was invoking that authority now. However, concerned that his remark, voiced during the Respondent's second round of questioning, could be used to claim that the implicit criticism was directed only to the mine operator, to protect against such a claim, Gray was quick to cover himself, adding, "And I say this to both sides. This latest round has not added new information to what I have now heard before." Expressly stating his authority, he reminded them, "As you know, I can curtail repetitious testimony. You all understand that I hope."

Malthan took the cue, not wanting to irritate the judge. He paused, asking, "May we have a moment, your honor?" He and Krakovich then briefly huddled, whereupon he addressed the Court, announcing simply, "Thank you, Judge Gray. The Respondent has no further questions of this witness."

Gray was pleased that his words had an immediate effect.

Sanford suppressed a smile, glad that the admonition did not come during his questioning. Taking the same signal from the judge, with it then being his turn, he informed, "And, your honor, the government has no further redirect examination either."

Having taken up nearly the whole day, Balkum was relieved that it was over, and all agreed that it would be best to call the next witness the following day.

As Gray made his return walk to the office, though relieved that a significant witness had completed his testimony, he was well aware of the parade of those yet to come. It was a discouraging thought, so many weeks of testimony ahead. He turned his attention to a more immediate and pleasing thought; soon he would be enjoying a stiff drink at the Grill. He did not consider that the pressing need for a drink was a problem. Instead, that anticipated pleasure prompted him to walk briskly and, with that goal in mind, he was in and out of the office in short order.

But when he sat down before Jerome for his drink, it was only partially satisfying as, to his disappointment, once again, *she* was not there. It was foolish, he knew, to dwell on it, over someone he had viewed a grand total of one time. They had neither a word exchanged, nor even an acknowledgement of each other's presence.

Though recognizing that he was acting like an old fool, his irrational side persisted, thinking, God, it would be nice to see her again!

When he finished his first drink and still with no sign of her, he declined a refill, knowing it was time to meet his responsibility at home. Again, Jerome was not oblivious to the judge's behavior. It was obvious that his regular patron was distracted, preoccupied by something, but he had no clue what it was about. With not even a thought of the woman whom the judge recently found so captivating, he made no association of her absence as the source for his customer's distracted state.

The demanding trial and the disappointment of not seeing that woman at the bar, were followed by his arrival home, where Millie, through no fault of her own, presented no uplift to his spirits. Dutifully, prompted by his wife's request, he recounted the testimony, informing that the testimony from the director of the tech center had concluded. Millie's response was irritating, as she repeated her earlier, uninvited, view that the government's case was solid. He was too tired to reply to her remark and she took note that his silence informed that he was dismissive of her commentary. Instead, as he looked at her, he imagined that the captivating woman at the bar would only express admiration for his commanding control of the proceedings.

The summary of the day completed, the two then went about their predictable and separate routines. Gray's ending with the only moment of solitude and relief – his nightly glass of red before retiring. Though he felt embarrassed

THE CASE OF THE ABNORMAL WHITE CENTER

by the thought, he was pleased to find his wife asleep when he arrived for bed as there would be no need for further talk.

The following day, with Balkum having survived the gauntlet of cross-examination, the government moved to call another significant witness for its case with the introduction of the "safety and health director" for the Eagle Coal and Coke. Sanford considered it shameful that this witness held such a title, while working so deliberately to harm miners' health. Still, he realized that where witnesses are concerned you take what you can get, including from the reprehensible, when important testimony is involved.

At least the witness, Benny Skeens, was attempting to atone for Eagle Coal and Coke's actions. Even with Skeens' warts, the government still believed the testimony to be extremely valuable to counter the Respondents' claims that there was no intentional tampering. After all, it would move the case beyond those mere experts' opinions that were yet to come about the asserted innocent causes of the white centers. Here was a large mine operator admitting that it had done the very thing the government was claiming. With that confession, the case moved beyond informed speculation about the creation of white centers. Skeens amplified his testimony, identifying the documents admitting to their dishonest actions and acceptance of the very large penalty for that.

To his credit, Skeens showed some remorse as he informed about the various steps the mine took to produce the misleading, false, results. Distorting the sampling did not require sophisticated techniques. Some sampling devices were simply placed outside the mine for the last few hours of a shift. Others were placed in a lunch bucket, sheltered from the deadly dusty coal mining environment. Simply blowing compressed air into the cassettes had the same effect. A variant on that method, reverse air flow, was another one of the methods he admitted to employing as a means to create the AWCs.

The miners, very much aware of what was going on, cooperated with the ruse. Only the naïve or stupid failed to realize that there really was no choice for them. Sure, officially speaking, miners could rebel, tell their foreman that it was illegal to tamper with the dust collections.

There would be no direct adverse action for their words, just silence and a blank stare in return. But history had taught them that it would not be long before those who foolishly spoke up found that they had committed some made-up infraction or another. A claim that there had been a late check-in for work, or some other minor transgression, would be accompanied by a warning, with the next breach resulting in a suspension. The message was received by those few who were slow on the uptake. Experienced fellow miners merely looked knowingly at those uninitiated fools who didn't understand the mine operators' unwritten rules. 'You can't run legal and make money mining coal' it was often said. There was a second message with that: 'make trouble for us and you'll soon be unemployed.'

Sanford's direct examination of Skeens ended on that high note, the aim of any skilled trial advocate, by revealing yet another trick, beyond reverse air flow, for creating abnormal white centers. It wasn't complicated, the witness explained. They found that by spraying a bit of that aerosol "No Dust" right on the cassette they could reliably block enough dust from reaching the filter, with the result of a dust-compliant sample.

This technique was well known too. Skeens disclosed that he had spoken with safety directors with other mines during the time they were tampering with the cassettes. They all knew about using the dust spray and the other dust altering techniques.

At that, both Malthan and Krakovich leapt to their feet, objecting to any hearsay about alleged conversations Skeens had with other mines and moving to have the testimony stricken from the record.

The government maintained that it was perfectly proper to testify about these conversations but Gray quickly sided with the law firm's duo. Yes, hearsay, in this instance retelling what others had said about using the dust repellants, was admissible in administrative hearings, and it was likely admissible under a few of the dozen or more exceptions to barring hearsay in any trial, but Gray sided with the argument that it was, as he expressed it, "fundamentally unfair" to allow such testimony on such a critical part of the case. The objection, he informed without elaboration, was sustained, adding as additional reassurance for the Respondent, that Skeen's answer would not be considered by him. That was unnecessary to state, but Gray said it anyway, to emphasize his rejection of Skeens' remark. The government would have to be limited to what

Skeens had to say about Eagle Coal and Coke's conduct, not his conversations with employees at other mines.

To say that Winston and Milo were relieved by the ruling was an understatement. Had the judge left it to cross-examination to attack Skeens' claim of conversations with other mine operators, all that would have accomplished would be to repeat the crippling information into the record a second time. Worse, the damning information would have been drilled into the judge's head that it was a coordinated effort by the mines to tamper with the dust sampling. Which, of course, it was.

Though their objection about the additional damaging information had been averted, Milo and Winston remained furious, as they had from the start of the litigation, that a mine operation, especially one as large as Eagle Coal and Coke, would break ranks. Even with the conversations he had alluded to being struck from the record, Skeens' words proved that at least one mine, a large one at that, and the one which employed him, had done exactly what the government was alleging that Bobcat Creek Colliery had done. The mines, they were all supposed to be in this together. A traitor, that's what Eagle Coal and Coke was, plain and simple. Once this was over, all tacitly agreed that there would be a price imposed for the mine operation's disloyalty. There was no reverence for the idea of telling the truth.

Sanford very much wanted Skeens' discussions with the other mine operations to come in, but the adverse ruling had been made, and with that, he would have to move on. Should the government lose the case, he knew that, even on appeal if Gray's ruling on the issue was found to be error, the Commission would likely rule that it was not a reversible mistake. If not reversible, then it would merely be a technical win, of no effect. There would be no order for a new trial on that basis. The only solace about the ruling was that Skeens' testimony about the remarks he shared with the other mines' safety managers and their collective understanding about the industry-wide scheme, was not a linchpin to their case. Not at all.

Good timing, the direct exam finished up just before lunch. During the lunch break, Gray always remained in the courthouse, closeting himself in the loaned chambers. He would limit himself to some light snacks, concerned that a full meal would make him sleepy during the afternoon session. He couldn't allow that, not in a case of this magnitude. The reporter from the newspaper would be sure to tell its readers if that happened. Setting the alarm on his phone, he would allow himself some brief time during the hour to close his eyes, another method to stave off drowsiness for the second half of the day. A reflection of his age, as well as the stress of the hearing, he would sometimes nod off during those lunch intervals. Though brief, the virtual nap, along with another cup of coffee during the first afternoon break, served to sustain his alertness until the end of the day.

When the afternoon session began Malthan and Krakovich treaded very carefully with their cross-examination of Skeens. Potentially, he was their most dangerous witness. They didn't want to 'open the door,' as lawyers say, by coming close to any question that would allow Skeens to mention the other mines' operations. If they did, Sanford would immediately claim that all of that testimony, earlier precluded, would now have to come in.

Creatively, but safely, they asked questions which made the point that, whatever Eagle Coal and Coke may have admitted, Skeens never worked for the other mines charged by the government, that he had never been underground in any of those mines at the time their dust sampling took place and therefore he could not even speculate about what happened at those mines. More particularly, Skeens admitted the same lack of any experience or knowledge about the present trial; the actual operations the Bobcat Creek Mine.

It was becoming a pattern. The testimony of nearly every witness was taking a full day and Skeens' was no exception. Fortunately, his testimony did wrap up at the day's end. Though he was becoming somewhat acclimated to the grind, Gray was still spent when each day was over. In his many years of presiding in cases, only a few had lasted more than a week. Most hearings were two or three days. As he trudged back to the office, he grimly thought that there were still three days of testimony left in week two.

Arriving at the judges' building and heading to his office, he noticed that Larkin was again there, one of the few remaining at that hour. This time he stopped, initiating the conversation.

"Hi there, Richard. Another day of toiling. It's exhausting I tell you."

Larkin, though never having a case of such size, could appreciate how daunting it would be, especially with the small army of attorneys involved and the anticipated complex expert testimony to assimilate.

"I don't envy you, Charles," he sympathized. "Are you up to giving me a rundown? I'm interested in hearing about it. But," he quickly added, "I understand if you just want to head home."

Though given an out, Gray didn't balk at Larkin's request. "Sure, no problem. Come down. We can talk for a few," he responded with no hint of reluctance in his voice.

Once in his office, with Larkin taking his now customary position on Gray's couch, his colleague filled him in about the events since they last spoke. As he did so, Larkin realized that it was Gray who should be on the couch and that he, in the role of a de facto psychologist, should be in the chair, listening to the judge's problems.

The elder judge began his recap by turning the tables on his colleague. "Ever hear of a null hypothesis?" he asked Larkin. Not expecting that questions would be coming his way; Larkin was caught off guard. Though he knew what the words meant individually, with null meaning zero or invalid, and hypothesis a proposed idea, he was uncertain how they meshed. "An invalid assertion?" he offered tentatively.

"Pretty close, my friend, pretty close. In this case the Respondents are asserting several null hypotheses, leading off with the idea that the rate of these AWC's was random at mines; that they occurred with the same frequency at all mines. Therefore, the occurrence of AWCs would be the same at all mines, those charged with altering the samples and those not charged. If accepted, it meant that no tampering could be alleged. These AWCs just occur randomly at all mines."

"And" Larkin asked, "what did you think of this?"

"Too early to tell," Gray answered. "It's a statistical argument and I've only heard references to the idea. The details about the claim will come later, when the experts offer their competing views. Not being strong in math and statistics, I'll be lost comprehending the technical reasons, I'm sure. I'll try to understand it, but my credibility determinations will have to come into it too."

Thinking about the claim further, Larkin then added, "I heard these AWCs suddenly stopped. If the null hypothesis were correct, that shouldn't have happened, right?"

Gray hadn't thought about that. It seemed that Larkin's observation was correct, but he didn't want to concede the point. Instead, he punted, "I don't know. I will have to give this some more thought."

The quiz he wished he had not initiated now completed, Gray then informed that, so far, MSHA's case appeared to be solid. However, he was quick to note that it was early, evidentiary wise, the many experts yet to testify for the Secretary still in the wings and the defense not even launched yet. He again brought up the testimony of the supervisor from the MSHA technology center. Though he conceded that the supervisor, Balkum, met the low standard to be deemed an expert witness, he immediately commented that his testimony was not overwhelming, adding that he would be paying close attention to the other, highly credentialed, experts the government would be presenting for its case.

As before, Larkin was surprised by Gray's renewed unimpressed take on Balkum, unsure if the supervisor's apparent lack of a stellar resume impacted his colleague's assessment of the witness or whether it was the testimony itself which was wanting. Recalling his earlier interaction with Gray, he decided, to play the role of a traditional psychotherapist, and just listen to his patient.

Privately, however, based on the brief retelling his colleague offered, he had a very different take about Balkum's testimony. Did the witness have the requisite background and was he sufficiently informed? Those were the questions he would be posing when evaluating the opinions of an expert. If Gray was unduly influenced by Balkum's modest educational pedigree, he was sorely disappointed with his colleague's perspective. Such things were, to him, largely window dressing. He had never been especially swayed by one's paper credentials. In his trial experience and now including his short judicial career, he had already been exposed to testimony from experts possessing glowing degrees who were anything but impressive.

At least Gray had admitted that there was, at this early point in the trial, some disconcerting evidence in the case, casting doubt on the defense's claim of innocence. This was due to that virtual flood of those AWCs, a staggering number of them. Nearly all the samples had them too; those white centers in the filters. They had not been present in the previous year; MSHA's lab review clearly established that. None. Zero white centers found back then.

And then, with a timing that could not be dismissed, once word about the development leaked out to the mining community that MSHA was on to it, the flow of AWCs stopped, like a faucet that had been turned off. The way they ended, virtually *en masse*, abruptly dropping to a trickle and then they disappeared altogether, it all occurred with an abruptness that could not be overlooked.

Larkin forced himself to remain quiet. Why did he call it disconcerting? That wasn't the correct adjective. It was inculpatory. That's what it was! However, by now he had come to know Gray well enough to recognize that his opining, instead of listening, would only serve to irritate his colleague.

Still, by Gray's own telling, the evidence seemed very strong, and so it was hard for him to remain silent. His concern was that if he said too much, suggesting that the onset and then the sudden stopping of the AWCs alone made the government's case, Charles might recoil at that, reclaiming ownership by reminding the younger judge that this was *his* case, and invoking his long experience on the bench, with the likely admonition that it was far too early for a judge to reach such conclusions.

Richard Larkin was learning more about Charles Gray than he had ever gleaned from their earlier social conversations and it was an unsettling revelation, this business of really getting to know the man he had known only superficially before, until this coal dust litigation.

Though he had managed to keep quiet about Gray's additional remarks concerning the MSHA technology center supervisor, when his colleague then turned to the testimony from Eagle Coal and Coke's safety and health director,

Skeens, it was too much. This was the guy who Gray revealed had fessed up to doing the very thing accused of all the named respondents, including the Bobcat Creek Mine.

Larkin could not help himself from making a remark. "Pretty significant evidence," he commented, thinking that his observation was diplomatic and understated.

But his worry about saying too much, really saying anything at all, was immediately confirmed as Gray replied, chiding his colleague, "I can't ascribe what some *other* mine did and apply that to *this* mine's conduct," emphasizing those words. "That would amount to guilt by association."

Larkin, having been put back in his place, politely nodded, but his disappointment in the senior judge's reaction reinforced his growing concern that Gray was not being objective. Sure, he understood the point, but he thought, the legal principle aside, one still shouldn't ignore common sense in the face of such evidence. Here, a significant mine operation admitted to the very thing this operator was charged with doing. Yes, every mine is owed due process, but the admission by a major mine moved the matter beyond mere speculation. It happened, making the question whether those other mines engaged in the same practices more likely. The alternative was that it was merely a coincidence.

Not for the first time, Larkin had the strong impression that Gray was listing too far to the Respondent, excessively discounting the evidence that was adverse to the mine. This tilt was especially concerning as the defense had not even begun presenting their side. He so wanted to counter Gray's comment and just say it directly – the admission of Skeens that at least his mine was doing exactly what was being charged, was damning. A major mine operation had admitted that, in fact, they did tamper with the dust sampling, revealed how they accomplished it, and then paid a huge fine, and all of that occurred during the very time period these respondents were accused of doing the same thing.

What was Gray thinking, he privately thought, that this was just a fluke? Still, he had the good sense to pull back. Though it was hard to do, he softened his reply, "I know one party's conduct doesn't establish that another engaged in the same practice, but it counts for something I would think," leaving it at that.

Gray, unhappy at his colleague's expressed views, mild as his comments were, decided that he had enough of Larkin's unsolicited perspectives. He didn't want to engage in a debate with this junior and new associate over the value of particular evidence. Larkin's role was to be a good listener; a commentator on the evidence was not welcomed. Their softly expressed disagreement prompted him to call a cease fire, remarking that he was spent and ready to go home. That mention, about heading home, made him anticipate whether he would soon be subjected to Millie's opining about the strength of the government's case. The thought of having to endure two of them kibitzing on his case this evening irritated him.

Larkin offered non-judgmental words. "Sure, Charles, it's a marathon you're in, and your week isn't yet half over."

Though Gray claimed he was ready to go home, that was a half-truth, as there would first be his routine stop at his favorite spirits dispensary. With Larkin having departed, he quickly gathered his things, and headed to that destination.

Once there, and served his much-needed refreshment from Jerome, he habitually glanced to his left and right to see if that intriguing woman was there. To his disappointment, again she was not. Unduly downcast about it, as he had only seen her that one time, he gloomily concluded that he was not likely to ever see her again. Foolishly, he thought of her as a love lost. He was conscious that there was no sensible basis for that reaction, missing her presence. He realized that he didn't even know her name, nor a single thing about her. It was nonsensical to miss seeing someone he literally did not know at all.

As he nursed his drink, a rare moment of reflection about his fantasizing came to him; plainly it was a reaction to his home situation and the allure of a very attractive woman. Any woman, he told himself, not just *that* woman, would have provoked his interest. Yet, he didn't believe his own assessment. For some reason, he believed that the attraction he felt for her would not have occurred with just anyone.

THE MINE SAFETY TRILOGY PART II

Despite the brief self-analysis, images of the woman remained in his head on his return commute. Upon arriving, while giving his wife the routine hug, he was ashamed that it was that other one who held his thoughts, even as they embraced. Millie, unaware of the conflicts in her husband's head, continued her recent practice of inquiring about the day's events. Again, he felt obliged to recount them. His gloomy anticipation that she, like Larkin, would freely express her reactions to the testimony, was met.

"I must say, Charles," Millie began, as if making an announcement, not simply a remark, "that testimony from the safety director with that Creek Mine …"

Immediately knowing where her comment was going, he interrupted her, "It's Eagle Coal and Coke. Eagle Coal and Coke," he repeated, his irritation sharply revealed, correcting her, as if she had made a major mistake, while barely holding back from adding, "damn it all, Millie." He had already been challenged, inappropriately he believed, by that Larkin fellow and now his wife was about to offer her two cents.

Uncowed, it did not stop her response. "Eagle Coal, then. The name really doesn't really matter, now does it Charles," she said dismissing his picky fault-finding. "It was a mine supervisor admitting his mine was doing the very thing the government is accusing the mine in your case, right?"

Charles was a bit of a contrarian. The accuracy of his wife's observation did not soften his resentment. Had both of them, Larkin, and now her, forgotten that *he* was in charge? This was his case; no one else was presiding. He found it exceedingly annoying when others asserted their uninvited views on a subject, his spouse being no exception. He had already heard those muted expressions from Larkin a few hours earlier with his take on the evidence and now his wife had joined more assertively and with no diplomacy. Neither one was in courtroom, he thought, and it was his case, not theirs.

"Yes, Millie," he answered, with superficial courtesy, but the name of the mine does matter, because that mine is not the mine on trial before me. What they admit to doing, I can't say that proves that this mine, or any other mine for that matter, did the same thing." Counseling her, he continued, "If two men were accused of cheating on their wives and one admitted to it, that doesn't

109

mean the other man was cheating." As he uttered the comparison, he regretted using it, given his fantasizing over that woman at the Grill, but once he was halfway through it, he couldn't very well switch to a different analogy.

Despite her ailments, Millie could still be sharp. During their many years together, she had frequently bested Charles when they were debating issues. "No, Charles," she admitted, adopting his analogy, "but if the two men were friends and they used the same motel for their rendezvous, it would count for something, wouldn't it?"

Exasperated they she did not back down and still regretting his Freudian-derived analogy, he parried, "It means something, I suppose." Then he thrust, "but not much, dear." When he used "dear" in such debates, it often meant condescension, a 'you wouldn't understand,' retort. "I just can't employ another mine's confession to find that the mine before me has done the same thing."

He had enough at that point, and he recognized that he was on the losing side of the dispute, so he put an end to it. "As I said before, Millie, this is very early on in this hearing.   I wouldn't be much of a judge if I reached my conclusions at this stage." The import was clear, while she might be that type, free of the burden of any legal education, in contrast with her,   he possessed the wisdom from his legal training and long judicial experience that she lacked. He then decided to end the dispute, announcing that he was beat and ready to call it a night.

She accepted his call to end their disagreement over the matter.

In Washington, on that same evening, Greg Balkum, residing in his temporary hotel in that city, was going about the routine he had developed for his new circumstances. At the end of each day of trial, there would be a brief courthouse huddle with the MSHA litigation team in the conference room that had been set aside for such meetings. Then he would grab some fast-food takeout and bring it to his hotel room. It was a strict, self-imposed, arrangement; the day in court, followed by the meeting with the government attorneys, a takeout dinner and then he would stay in for the night. This meant not even a nightcap at the hotel bar. He was not comfortable in the big city. It was so completely different from his quiet home and, until this event, his uncomplicated job in Mount Hope. Wandering around at night in D.C., it was only an invitation for trouble. Being in the wrong place, at the wrong time, that would be just his luck, he thought.

Once he had dinner, with the time that afforded to wind down from the tiring day, he would call home to his wife, Karen. The calls were largely uneventful. Intentionally, he did not want to recount the day's happenings. That only served to tire him more.

Intuitively, she knew that he would be drained and as such would not want him to feel obligated to report the day's events. She was a listener, letting him tell as much, or as little, as he wished.

For him, it was a relief to hear his wife's informing of the innocuous news of the day. Ordinary as it was, it still served as a welcome distraction from the 'always on' mode he had to sustain each day in court.

On this occasion however, Karen did have some attention-getting news. She informed that "the head of the nightly cleaning crew, Martina Reyes, called, asking that you call her.   I asked her what it was about," she continued, "but she only said that it involved that trial in Washington, which she had been following in the news. She felt it was best to speak directly with you. She gave me her number."

"Interesting, very interesting," Balkum said, reacting to the news as he jotted down Martina's number, but having no clue what prompted her call. He had known her for several years and considered her to be intelligent and reliable. "I'll give her a call, for sure," he informed.

Their conversation over, and as it was not yet late, he did not postpone calling Martina.

"Ms. Reyes, please," he began in response to the person answering.

"Speaking," she replied.

"Martina. Hi. It's Greg Balkum, from the office. My wife just told me you called, wanting to speak with me."

"Yes, Mr. Balkum, thanks for calling me."

"Sure thing. What's up?"

"Well, sir, I've been following that big trial of yours in D.C. It's in the news nearly every day, the one about the dust samples, and I thought maybe I should tell you about something I overheard in the office one evening, back in the summer."

Balkum was instantly intrigued. "I'm all ears Martina."

"Well, sir, I don't want you to think I was being nosy or anything like that. I mean I was just doing my usual office clean-up jobs and then I hear that Mr. Tucker fellow on the phone. Now, mind you, I don't know who he's talking to, but I remember it distinctly, cause what he said, it sounded so odd. Made my ears perk up. But I wasn't trying to be nosy," she repeated, again defending her listening to a conversation.

"I don't think you were being nosy, Martina," he reassured her. "So, just tell me, what you heard."

"Okay, thanks for that. Well, he gets my curiosity because he's tellin' that person he called, that he has to be careful about talkin' on the phone. But, see, he's doing just that, Mr. Balkum. He's talkin' on the phone to somebody, sayin' how he's got to be careful. Well, that right there gets me to notice. But I act like I'm not paying a bit of attention, dusting near his cubicle, emptying his trash and such. He notices me, but I can act like I don't understand no English, you know. So, he feels safe, and me I'm lookin' anywhere but where he's actually sitting, acting like I'm in a dream world, and then he says 'I can't say much.' I remember those exact words, that he '*can't say much*.' So now I'm really interested. I mean when someone talks that way, secret-like and all, well you're gonna pay attention. It's natural, right?"

"Sure, Martina, anyone would be curious hearing that kind of talk."

"And then he says he wants to alert, *alert* was the exact word he used too, speaking to the person on the phone, that he wants to alert that person that he should be careful with his dust samples. And then he says it again, repeating, 'be careful with them.'"

Balkum said nothing but he knew exactly what that worm Tucker was up to, the little son of a bitch!

"Martina," he told her directly, "this has been helpful information. I appreciate it a lot. Can you remember the date and approximate time?"

Martina was pleased that her information was so well-received. "In fact, I can sir, for two reasons. First, with that kind of talk, it just seemed like he was up to something, but I didn't know what he was talkin' about at the time, those dust samples. I only learned about those things when this whole trial thing began. Miners dying from breathing coal dust. I never knew that was a problem for miners. Black lung! Until this trial, I had never heard of such a thing, but just those words, they sound really awful."

She continued, "And the other reason was he made that phone call on the same day all those people from Washington visited your office. They weren't there when I came to work that afternoon but everyone was talkin' that there had been a group of people from Washington that day. And then, it was that same evening when I heard Mr. Tucker making that call about being careful and dust samples. I think he was the only worker left in the office too, least I don't remember seeing anyone else that night. That was odd too. It was rare for him to be at the office when we're doin' the cleaning. So, learning about your trial in Washington and all, I put two and two together."

Balkum was again pleased that Martina had called him, while thinking that bastard Tucker was a dumb fuck, making that call on the same day the D.C. visitors had been at the office and also calling from the office, not his home.

"Look, Martina, thanks again. You've been a big help. I really appreciate it. I need a little more help from you though. I need you to not tell anyone about this. Not a word to anyone, 'bout what you heard Tucker say and also don't tell anyone that we spoke either. Okay?"

"You bet Mr. Balkum. I can keep a secret."

"Thanks. I'm sure you can. Goodnight Martina."

The call over, Balkum, energized by the information, found it difficult to be ready for sleep. Too much adrenalin flowing. He started to consider what steps to take, but tabled those thoughts, deciding, as it was so late, it would be better to disclose the information to the MSHA litigators in the morning. Trying to get his mind off of the issue, he resorted to resuming reading some of the technical materials he had brought, a sure-fire way to bring about drowsiness. Eventually it worked.

When the trial resumed the next morning, on Wednesday of week two, MSHA began with the first of its three outside experts. Their use was not an implied admission that it had misgivings or otherwise discounted the worth of Balkum's appearance. They valued the Mount Hope supervisor's testimony and, in their end-of-the-day evaluations, the team assessed that the supervisor had done a good job. While the cross-exam had landed some blows, Balkum remained calm and was steadfast in his conclusions about the causes of the AWCs. His long experience with the dust cassettes supported those views. But now the goal was to add some gleam to Balkum's competent opinions by presenting witnesses with shinier pedigrees. Though resumes shouldn't matter, the government knew that, in the real world, they did.

First up was Dr. Victor Palmer, a specialist in aerosol particle technology, who conducted extensive studies on the dust filters. Unlike Balkum, Palmer had the educational adornments to add supposed gravitas to his testimony. He was Ivy League all the way, including his doctorate degree. Associations with the University of Pennsylvania and MIT were also among his credentials. Gray, understandably, had never heard of such a thing as aerosol particle technology. Beyond his everyday use of aerosol cans for things around the house, he knew nothing about such science, and was surprised that such expertise even existed.

Winston and Milo did not look forward to his testimony. Through a lengthy deposition of the doctor, they knew what was coming. It would not be good. Balkum was easy prey compared to this fellow who had a deadly combination; brainy and articulate.

Dr. Palmer informed that he worked with another scientist, Dr Karl Woburn who had equivalent credentials in aerosol physics. Together, they concluded that when 'normal,' a polite way of saying 'honest' dust sampling, was conducted, no white center would occur on the filters. Period. Several hundred tests running known quantities of coal dust through the sampling devices produced not one with a white center. Those tests also included varying the humidity and temperatures, as the Respondents' experts had also asserted that those variables could produce AWCs, but again the Secretary's experts could not reproduce those claimed results.

Through the Secretary's own discovery efforts, they had been alerted to the many theories that were being advanced from the Respondents to support their assertion that white centers can be created innocently. Knowing of these claims, Palmer and Woburn performed their own tests of these theories to see if AWCs resulted. They mailed cassettes with normal filter results from their laboratories to other locations, including to the Mount Hope office, but when examined after reaching those destinations, the filters looked the same as when they were sent – none developed white centers in transit. They also dropped cassettes from various heights, stomped on the hoses and dropped tool boxes on them too. None of those efforts produced white centers.

And then the hammer came down. While the experts couldn't produce white centers under any of the theories advanced by the Respondents experts, they were able to create white centers by other means and quite reliably too. From their many tests, involving more than 700 filters, they found that the dust dislodgements in the filters resulted from reverse air flow, air moving in the opposite direction than it is supposed to move. This was something that couldn't happen naturally, as the dust collection air flow was designed to move only in one direction. The devices simply didn't work that other way. Just like home vacuums capturing household dust, the dust pump intakes didn't run in reverse either. However, achieving that reverse air flow was pretty simple to accomplish. All one had to do to cause the air to flow in the reverse direction was to have air enter from the outlet side, instead of through the inlet side, as designed. The numerous reverse air flow tests created white centers every time. And they were all but indistinguishable from the AWC cassettes in this litigation.

But that was not all, as Dr. Palmer informed that there were other ways to create the white centers, and they were not complicated to produce either. One method was as basic as directing clean air into the inlet. Still another technique was to create a vacuum at the cassette inlet. Continuing with his understandable analogy, he explained that it was, in effect, no different than

THE CASE OF THE ABNORMAL WHITE CENTER

vacuuming a rug, except in these instances the 'rug' was the filter. Cruder methods worked too. Something as simple as inserting a cotton swab into the inlet, so that it contacted the filter's face, would create a white center.

All of those contrivances had the singular goal of reducing the weight of the samples and by that creating samples that would meet the dust level requirements, falsely presenting that the air being inhaled by the miners was not harmful. As long as MSHA was only weighing the cassettes, not looking at the odd condition of the filters themselves, the tampering would go undetected. But for Ms. Nelson's fortuitous accident, who knew how long the fraud would have continued?

Though Gray understood the home vacuum analogy, some of the doctor's testimony left him in the dark. He did his best to appear as if he was comprehending the testimony, though things like "particle dislodgement" produced an obvious quizzical look, his furrowed brow informing that he was lost.

Sanford, keenly watching the judge's reaction to the testimony, anticipated that there would be moments of confusion. Realizing the importance of the judge grasping the subject, he would periodically ask further questions to illuminate the testimony.

To that end, he deftly adjusted his questioning. "Now, Doctor Palmer," he asked, "just to be clear in my own mind," though he knew full well what the doctor meant, "is this dust dislodgement you describe, the same thing as the abnormal white centers, or AWCs, as we have been calling them?"

"Oh, yes," Palmer replied, "sorry about that. Yes, particle dislodgement is just the technical term to describe these AWCs."

Gray, stone faced, was privately relieved by the clarification, lifting the cloud in his comprehension by presenting the information in plain English.

As Gray listened to the expert's testimony, apart from the explanation about dust dislodgement, the technical jargon still left him bewildered. It was only the Secretary's periodically summing up his testimony, translating really, what the doctor was stating that saved him from being completely lost.

"So, Dr. Palmer," Sanford continued, "by your last answer are you saying that this reverse air flow can't occur other than by forcing the air to move in a direction that is opposite to its normal functioning?"

"That's largely correct," the doctor affirmed. "Though rare, I allowed that some other means could be used to create them, but I need to emphasize that all the methods I described can only come about through human interference. I found no natural way for the AWCs to occur and that conclusion ruled out things like rough handling or postal service mailing."

And "Doctor," Sanford persisted, "is it possible for the pump itself to malfunction and somehow cause the air to flow in a reverse direction?"

"No," Palmer responded without hesitation, "that is not possible. The pump only works in the one direction and there is no way, short of rewiring it, to alter that direction. A house vacuum could be rewired the same way. Of course," he added with a playful grin, "wouldn't be much of vacuum, if the goal was to clean your house."

Malthan and Krackovich tightened their faces, not liking the smart-alecky comment, but realized that an objection would only serve to highlight the doctor's comment.

Gray, listening to all of this confusing jargon and privately grateful for the translations, knew, from his years of experience, how to present himself as the fully comprehending sage. His manufactured facial expressions and nodding at appropriate times, all gave the impression that he was following every bit of it, though in truth he had only a rudimentary grasp of the scientific talk. Still, he understood the major points made by Palmer.

Taking the entire day, Palmer's testimony on direct was damning evidence and Milo and Winston fully understood that to be the case. The one small saving grace for them, brought about by Palmer's professionalism, was his acknowledgement that while firm in his conclusions about how the white centers were created, he left some minimal room for the idea that extreme mishandling could produce an AWC in a few instances. This minimal concession, he explained, was because he could not know of the intention behind those who engaged in such severe mishandling.

The defense would use the doctor's limited concession about the state of mind for those who could have innocently mishandled samples as far as they could, but they well knew that it could not explain away his conclusion that 70 of the 78 had AWCs. They would take the slight concession to the hilt when their own experts testified about the many 'innocent' sources for AWCs to occur, concocted as they were.

When the day came to an end, the significant testimony from Palmer during his direct examination had not concluded. Gray knew that the cross-examination would be at least equally long. Spent, he wasted no time in clearing out of the courthouse, returning to the safe harbor of his office.

As he walked the corridor to his office, Gray noticed that Larkin was again one of the few remaining at work. Pausing briefly at his colleague's office, glad to see someone who was not an adversary, he spoke up. "Evening Richard. Another long one today. Care to come down? I'll fill you in."

Larkin, pleased that this time Gray initiated the conversation, jumped at the opportunity. "Charles. Hello there. Yes, I very much want to hear how it's going. I'll be right there."

Once settled in the senior judge's office, Gray reverted to his role as the patient to the therapist, though again it was Larkin who took the couch.

"Went through a full day of testimony from the government's second expert witness, and the direct isn't even finished," he began. "An impressive fellow, I must say. Smart as they come. Strictly between you and me, the scientific jargon and much of his testimony left me in a haze, but at least I grasped his bottom line. That's really all I have to know, thank God for that. No way these abnormal white centers could develop in their normal operation, this doctor said. Just couldn't happen. Of course, he couldn't say that the mine operator actually tampered with them. He couldn't know that for sure, so he allowed that maybe rough handling of the dust collection devices could possibly account for some of it."

Larkin was instantly skeptical of Gray's remark, as well as the judge's tone, suggesting that he placed emphasis on the rough handling excuse, but he understood that the expert could only go so far. One would need an employee of the mine operator to fess up that they were tampering to have no doubt that their conduct was intentional. Fat chance of that.

He tried to nudge his friend to consider what he believed to be the obvious conclusion.

"How many of these filters had this issue?" he asked, knowing full well the answer.

"It was seventy-five or so, I think," Gray answered, unable to recall the exact number correctly, then adding, "but apart from the actual number, it was most, but not every one of the samples that had those AWCs."

"And they could *all* be subject to rough handling?" Larkin asked, the skepticism clear in his tone, as he tried to steer his colleague to the only reasonable conclusion, without explicitly conveying that such a claim would be totally unbelievable.

Gray did not miss the obvious implication. "I know, I know," he responded, this time not taking offense. Falling back on his senior status, he opted to chide his friend gently, reminding him, "there is the other side to hear from yet. I try to avoid making conclusions prematurely."

Larkin was wise enough to take the cue, leaving matters where they were. He changed the topic. "So, what's in store for the rest of the week?"

"Two more experts for the government are yet to come. If they continue as this one did, at a minimum I'm probably looking at all of next week for that testimony to be concluded. Hoping the Secretary will rest at that point."

Larkin nodded. Realizing that the trial would continue for at least two more weeks beyond this one, he was again glad that this wasn't his case. Concerned about wearing out his welcome and wanting to continue learning about the trial's developments, he decided it was best to end their session. At least this time, he had been sufficiently diplomatic to avoid irritating Gray. "Thanks Charles. I appreciate learning about how this thing is developing," he added, wanting to keep the door open for future updates.

Gray, tired from the day, was pleased that their conversation had been brief. Freed, he could head over to his spot for a drink before moving to his other, draining, responsibility, tending to Millie's continuous needs.

To his disappointment, again the blonde was not there.

THE CASE OF THE ABNORMAL WHITE CENTER

Dejected over her no show, though he still realized that it was irrational to feel that way, he then considered that he might never see the woman again, a gloomy thought. Hopeful that she still might make an entrance, he extended the time he would normally use to finish his drink, and with that additional time, he was taking in the other patrons in the bar, scanning to see if she might be there.

Again, there was no sign of her.

Though disappointed, he soberly realized that if he had spotted her, there was little he could do in reaction to her presence. He was no smooth operator. And even if he ever had such a skill, it had evaporated with his age.

Jerome took note of Gray's surveillance of the customers. In his years of serving the judge his liquid refreshments, he'd never seen such unusual behavior by the man. In the past, his customer had been reliably steady, almost always looking straight ahead, with his focus on the drink before him, oblivious to the other customers. This was different behavior, clearly, this divided attention between his beverage and repeatedly scanning the patrons. It was as if he was anticipating the arrival of someone.

Though he hesitated, worried that the judge might take offense, he inquired gently, "Judge, you seem like you have a lot on your mind. Everything okay?"

Roused from his preoccupation, Gray did not act annoyed by the question. "No, I'm fine," he insisted, "thanks …" as he paused, awkwardly, unable to finish his answer, at a loss for the bartender's name.

Picking up on Gray's struggling to recall his name, but unaware that Gray simply hadn't made the effort to store it in his head, aided the judge. "It's Jerome, Judge. You must be really distracted to have my name slip your mind. Sure there's nothing you want unload? It's part of a bartender's job you know. And I never repeat things people tell me," he assured.

His distractions put aside for the moment, Gray seized upon the dispensation for being unable to utter the barkeep's name. "No, I'm good," he insisted, this time adding "Jerome," to his answer. By repeating the bartender's name, he hoped it would help him remember it. "Sorry your name slipped my memory for a second." Unable to reveal his actual thoughts, a fantasy far too intimate to disclose to anyone, let alone to the bartender who was no more than an acquaintance, he continued, "Must be my age or just being tired from the case I'm hearing," his voice trailing off as he offered the excuse.

Jerome, unoffended, was very much aware, from reading the newspapers, that his patron was presiding in the well-covered case involving those miner dust samples.

"I can well understand that, judge. Just reading about the case, I can see how it must be wearing. Still," he continued, careful to show respect for their very different occupations, "I hope you don't think I'm stepping out of line. Just saying I'm glad to listen, sir, if it might help."

"No, no," Gray insisted. "I'm fine, Jerome," repeating his name out loud again.

Must not forget the guy's name, he silently admonished himself.

"Really," he insisted, "Just tired after a long day," adding, "but thanks, Jerome" including yet again the bartender's name, in the hope it would become imprinted in his head. "It's a kind offer and I take no offense. You mean well, I know."

The exchange between them over, with Gray left to himself again, and now aware that his behavior had been noted by Jerome, he returned his attention to his drink. Yet, occasionally, he was compelled to look around. No luck. When it became clear to him that the blonde was not there and with no reason to think she might yet appear, disappointed, he decided against a refill.

He bid Jerome good evening and walked out, the bartender knowing that his customer left with no cheer. Even his walk as he exited the bar, a slow and hesitant departure, signaled that whatever unadmitted purpose was behind his visit to the bar that evening, it was not satisfied by the drink.

His glum state followed him to the garage, and continued all the way during his drive home. Upon his arrival, and then the brief subdued embrace with Millie, his attention was minimally directed toward her. The disappointment at not seeing the woman who so captivated him was still fresh in his head. Feeling guilt over his preoccupation with that other woman, he then felt obliged to provide his wife with his now customary recap of the day's hearing.

As with Larkin, she too was aware that Charles did not want to be challenged about his summary, nor was he receptive to even mild commentary. On this occasion, though she took his retelling as more confirmation that the mine was up to no good, concluding that they surely had done something to tamper with those samples, she decided to avoid expressing her critique.

The spousal duty to report fulfilled, he excused himself to microwave his dinner, after which he poured a generous glass of red wine and then plopped in front of the TV to listen to the cable news take on the day's events.

Though apart for the entire day, the two had settled in to a practice of brief interaction, which was then followed by their separate evening routines.

Not wanting great attention to his trial – he had never dealt with such coverage of his cases in all his years – he was pleased that reporting of it had been largely limited to the papers. The local news, at least for now, gave it minimal and infrequent attention.

While each trial day seemed to move slowly, the same could not be said for the free time between each session. Those intervals flew by. It felt, even on those days when he stopped by the G Street, that he was no sooner in bed before the morning alarm would sound and he would be on the road again, facing another long day.

Now, entering the fourth day of the second week, Palmer's testimony on direct wrapped up by mid-morning. Given the doctor's testimony, so damaging to the defense, it came as no surprise to Gray that the initial cross-examination of the doctor and the redirect following that, with several recross and redirect exams ensuing, that the testimony ate up the remainder of the week, but at least by Friday afternoon his testimony had been completed and would not bleed over to the following week.

As for his take following the cross-exam of Palmer, the judge was left confused about the details in support of the doctor's conclusions. The expert's opinion had been assailed in every possible manner. But, he more than held his ground, to the frustration of Milo and Winston. To their dismay, they realized that, far from scoring points, they actually lost ground in their questioning. Perhaps, they hoped, the Secretary's subsequent experts would not fare as well. Barring that, the pressure would then shift to them and their own experts, all in the attempt to sow doubt in Gray's head.

Many of the questions were highly technical, but while the parties and the witness understood the import of what was being asked, Gray, not wanting to be the only participant who was confused, did not want to interject by asking questions of his own, as it would put on full display that he was lost. He thought of the expression that it was better to remain silent, making it uncertain if one was confused, than to speak up and remove all doubt.

What he did realize was that, bottom line, this Dr. Palmer fellow did not retreat in the face of the many attacks to his methodology and the conclusions he reached from his studies of the dust cassettes and how those white centers were created. However those AWCs came about, the witness remained confident and adamant – that they were abnormal, and that it took some affirmative action for them to occur. The mechanisms designed to capture the dust particulates just wouldn't produce those white centers. The conclusion was unavoidable – something, not happenstance, intervened to create them.

Little new information came out in the ensuing rounds of redirect and further cross-examination. In that sense, Gray realized that even for this case, big as it was, the subsequent rounds of questions were no different from his many years of hearing experiences. They accomplished next to nothing, being mostly rehashes of the testimony that had been given during the first rounds. He knew the game. It was all about repeating the key points from each side, the idea being that repetition would make it stick in the judge's head.

The sides could not help themselves – having the last word, as in most arguments, even those outside of a courtroom, was an urge neither side could resist. However, given the significance of Palmer's testimony he decided against any words aimed at curtailing the subsequent rounds. Let them continue, he thought, until they had tired themselves out, like two fighters eventually clinching one another to the point of exhaustion. Finally, Sanford was able to draw the protracted battle to a close, simply by announcing he had no further questions on redirect. That meant Milo and Winston had no basis for further questioning.

It was a relief when Friday's proceedings ended. With the weekend ahead, Gray would have that respite, though it was a meager one, what with all of his unrelenting duties at home, Millie's needs being the most pressing of them. Looking ahead, Gray knew that there would be two more government experts, one of them a statistical expert. He was no better equipped to understand the intricacies of the statistical analysis, nor the competing analysis that the defense had announced it would be offering, than with the testimony about aerosol particulates. In college he had struggled with math generally and the statistics course he took earned him only a passing grade, an embarrassing result given the lax grading practices of that time.

Although the pace would ease for the attorneys, at least compared to the demands of the trial days, their weekends were still certainly burdensome. Assessments of the testimony from the week, preparation for upcoming witnesses, checking exhibits to be introduced, and strategies to be employed, were all part of weekend. Each day, with weekends providing no exception, was all a part of the work required for this marathon hearing.

Though tired, Milo and Winston were perturbed with the timing of the week's end, as they considered Palmer's cocksure testimony. His opinions about the origin of the AWCs had been largely undented by their cross-examination. They knew, even allowing for some innocent creations of those damn white centers, they couldn't all be swept aside on that ground. Not so many, no way. That was bad enough, but with that doctor's views being the last testimony of the week, they feared it would linger in the judge's mind over the whole weekend. Better if they could've at least had the chance to move his mind away from that testimony and direct his honor's attention to a new, hopefully less formidable, witness. It was not to be.

While the two were packing up Milo looked around to be sure others were not nearby and then drew close to his partner, whispering, "I think the time has arrived. That expert's testimony, I just don't know how it impacted Gray, but I am greatly concerned. We should convene tonight, back at the office."

Winston knew exactly what his colleague had in mind.

"I agree wholeheartedly," he replied, matching with a barely audible voice to his colleague. "Delay would be unwise. This is the time for action."

The nature of the subject, undisclosed in the courtroom, had been discussed long before, but now it was time for that further discussion, moving it from a hypothetical plan to one of implementation and rapid action.

The two hailed a cab back to their potent law firm. The discussion was held in Malthan's office, as his partnership status was senior to that of Krakovich. Before beginning, Malthan brought out two crystal glasses and an expensive single malt from his credenza.

"Ice, Milo?"

"Yes, thanks Winston. My usual," he instructed. He then held up two fingers, to make sure Winston applied the correct amount. There was no need for him to signal the dosage; his friend knew that Milo always had a double shot.

Winston made the same for himself.

"So," Winston began, "you concur, the time has arrived?"

"I do," Milo confirmed. "I most certainly do. It's become urgent, in my view. That testimony from Palmer; he's been killing us."

"I share your position, definitely," his cohort quickly agreed. "We still have two in place?"

"We do," Milo affirmed. For the Honorable Charles Gray, we have the alluring Marla. We've never met her but you've seen her file. Mid-forties. But she could pass for ten years younger. That's a fact. Undeniably, she's a real looker. Were I not so happily married, she would be a temptress to me." The last part was true. He'd seen her photos. The woman was stunning. Describing her as alluring was an understatement.

But Milo's claim about being happily married was a lie, as Winston very well knew. His buddy had long been shagging his secretary and it was no secret. Everyone in the office knew about it. It was joyous union for a time, but when his 'personal assistant' as he called her, a term which made all the employees discretely chuckle when he invoked it, told him she wanted marriage, he ended it abruptly. As he saw it, there was no choice. He deemed her wish and later when it became a demand, as entirely unreasonable. What could she have been thinking? He was married after all!

When she realized it would not happen, it was not without cost. She did not take his decision graciously and when she spoke in terms of sexual harassment and otherwise making it a hullabaloo, a monetary settlement was rapidly arranged, along with her departure and an elaborate nondisclosure agreement.

Other partners in the firm were displeased. It was not about being unfaithful to his wife; too many others at the firm had dalliances on their unofficial resumes. It was that he would do it in his "own backyard" an unwritten rule not to be ignored.

Somehow his wife never learned of his transgression and Milo, feeling that God had intervened, giving him a pass, decided to make an ostentatious religious conversion to Catholicism. Before that, he had been a non-practicing protestant, but with the close call, he chose a new denomination. Aided by his large donations, he was quickly adopted by the parish priest and, in time, became a church official, a status he announced to all with the deacon pin he prominently wore on his lapel.

His wife never figured out the impetus for the change. She assumed it was a mid-life crisis thing but whatever the reason, her dear Milo had changed for the better, noticeably more respectful and even doting on her.

Malthan, with full knowledge of his colleague's lengthy transgression, laughed, "Can't say I'd blame you." Taking the diplomatic approach, he made no mention of his friend's prior, extended, fling, only mentioning, "Course you'd have to be willing to lose more than half your wealth if you went down that road," he soberly reminded his colleague.

That was a gentle warning, as a second tryst could also jeopardize his employment. Being a partner did not insure against being removed from a firm. The prestigious firm would not tolerate such scandalous publicity.

In contrast, Winston had never breached his marriage vows. Though he considered Milo to be a friend, he felt morally superior to him, being free of such sin. His waning libido made faithfulness easier to achieve. With no need to change his denomination, Catholicism had always been his brand and he, being that good soul, accepted his colleague into the Church, though privately held some doubts about the depth of Milo's change.

Milo smiled, as he thought how close he came to such a disastrous result with the firm and his home life. Acknowledging the friendly advice, and the warning that was attached to it, he was still mildly offended that his cohort implied he might let his little head do the thinking once again. He felt compelled to defend himself, remarking "I said tempted, but I'm no fool, my friend. And don't think I would let her beauty obscure my recognition of her line of work. You could never trust a woman like that."

Fortunately, their high standards did not stop the two from employing her.

Malthan smiled back, reassured that his friend was keeping his feet on the ground. Still, they were human and therefore the allure of a woman like that and the bedroom skills they imagined she possessed remained in their heads.

Keeping them strong, away from the temptations she possessed, the duo inoculated themselves by regularly attending church, even occasionally during the week, not just Sundays, when their personal resistance to sin waivered.

Updating Malthan, Milo informed that Marty Tranter, their 'investigator' as they respectfully called him, had begun laying the groundwork, he paused, laughing at his choice of words, "laying the groundwork in more than one sense," he repeated, amused with his cleverness. "This was done several weeks ago. He had this beauty already set up what was presented as a happenstance meeting at Gray's usual watering hole and she reported that he looked her way several times. The hook was set, as she put it to Tranter."

Milo, despite his assurances that he would not go beyond his fantasies of what that temptress could do for him, still found himself getting a little excited himself, mentally transporting himself to the bar and his thoughts of hooking up with her.

Malthan picked up that Milo's recounting was not a sober, nor sterile, report. His friend seemed a bit too engaged with his update. Still, he continued the conversation. "So, we give him the go-ahead for her then. She understands the plan?"

"To a T," Milo responded. "As you know Gray is very susceptible. Tranter did a terrific job. Gray is old, nearing retirement and he is fundamentally unhappy. Poor devil has a sick wife, multiple sclerosis or myasthenia gravis, one or the other." Displaying his ignorance, he added, "I can't remember which condition she has, I get the two things mixed up, but it's serious and will only get worse."

Malthan, having a cousin with the same affliction, had not forgotten the name of the disease Gray's wife suffered from. Diplomatically he offered, "I think I recall reading in his report that she suffers from MS and that it is in an advanced stage too."

"Anyway," Milo continued, unconcerned about the correct identification of the name of the disease, "on top of that, he lives in a hovel of a place. A ranch, split-level thing, in a neighborhood full of similar unremarkable houses. Somehow, Marty learned that Gray longed to retire to a place on the Florida West Coast, but his finances make that impossible. Where he lives now, with retirement nearby, that's where he will end up, stuck in his sorry Virginia suburb."

"Which is where we can help," Malthan added, both aware of the grand plan they had devised. Of course, none of the other law firms' attorneys knew of this. This was an 'executive action' as Malthan had dubbed it. Disclosure of it to any of those firms would have provoked rancor, at least with some of them, not to mention the risk of losing their law licenses. And if the plan was revealed to others, inevitably someone would spill the beans. But, in this game, with the table stakes so high, money-wise, and the reputation of the entire underground coal industry at risk, the two determined that it called for winning at all costs. A victory simply couldn't rest solely on the hope of winning in the courtroom.

"Then," Milo continued, "there's the other prong. We hope to snare Balkum too. Essentially the same arrangement. Sex matters. Tempt that sanctimonious son of a bitch, he who is so mightily offended by a few inaccurate dust samples," deliberately miscasting the extent of the fraud by so many coal mines.

"For him, the girl's out of Beckley, right next door to Mount Hope. Much younger than Marla, only in her mid-twenties. From her pictures she has a bit of a truck stop look about her. Hope she dresses appropriately for our mark."

Ruby's her name. A West Virginy name if I ever heard one," he scoffed, belittling her given name. "She's worked for Marty before too, just like Marla. All divorce matters, but it's the same thing, get the guy in a compromised position." Milo laughed again at the words he chose, "In a compromised *position*," he laughed, "complete with HD color video," unable to contain laughter at his own jokes.

"Ruby," Winston remarked, agreeing with his colleague's put down, "awfully stereotypical name for a West Virginia girl. Guess it's better than Dreama or Opal. You'd think the folks out there would stay away from names like that anymore."

"Well, I'm sure she won't be using her real name anyway," Milo replied.

His arrogance in full display, crudely demeaning all the people in that state, he added, "Sure, something more West Virginian cosmopolitan style, like Wilma or Loretta," amused at his display of prejudice.

"Hope ol' Ruby creates a nightmare for that self-righteous Balkum! Big defender of miners. The man's got no understanding of what it takes to run a coal mining business."

Winston thought it was time to wrap up the discussion. "So, it's agreed, we'll have Marty get these plans rolling against those two. Definitely time to put them into action."

Satisfied with their two-pronged plan, Milo reached across to Winston, extending his glass towards him. The two clinked their glasses, content at their skills both in and outside of the courtroom.

Employing a brisk pace, Gray had returned to his office and spent only a few minutes gathering the materials he would want to have at hand during the weekend, should he feel industrious, though it was an unlikely prospect. Being a Friday, everyone had cleared out of the office, a condition he enjoyed, as it meant there would be no need to exchange greetings and no need to recap the day with Larkin either.

Mindful of Millie's carping about his late times in returning home, he decided to forego the visit to the G Street. She would routinely complain about his tavern stops. And, *she*, that blond that preoccupied his thoughts each day, would likely not be there anyway.

And if she were, he then considered, what would he do about it? It was not his style to boldly approach a woman he did not know and start up a conversation. The odds were that he would be summarily rebuffed, and he considered, nowadays, who could tell what might happen? For all he knew she could create a scene right there in the bar for making any sort of advance, accusing him of accosting her! Such a risky move, that was for smoother operators, not him.

With no stopover for a drink, as he made the return commute, his thoughts grew away from the blonde, back to reality of his homelife with Millie. Frowning at the thought of another joyless upcoming weekend, he engaged in self-pity. Wouldn't one in her utterly dependent position realize, with all the neediness she required, that she should just shut up and let the caregiver have a moment's respite for a drink at the end of the work day before turning to what was in effect, his second, equally taxing, job at home?

With those dismal thoughts occupying his return ride home, he then regretted not stopping for a drink first. *She* could have been there, he thought. Working from that completely speculative view, he rued his too-prompt decision, foreclosing the chance to see if she might have been there. Especially, he thought, but again without any real basis, she could have been there, because it was a Friday. More people stop for drinks on a Friday. He knew this to be true from his own regular visits to the G Street.

So, it was with more gloom than usual, the thoughts swimming around in his head of having wasted the chance of seeing that alluring woman again, coupled with the weekend reality of his dreary home life, that he pulled into his driveway, an unhappy man.

The weekend itself was, as every weekend had been for a very long time, uneventful. But Millie made it worse, starting it off by insisting upon hearing about the day's testimony. Dutifully, he provided it.

That was bad enough, but his wife could not resist adding her two-cents' worth of her take on the testimony of that Dr. Palmer. Gray, again did not appreciate his wife's unhesitant conclusions about the impact of the expert's opinion, but he was too tired to debate or rebuke her views, and he knew that nothing he could say would change her opinion anyway.

As with the other, largely indistinguishable weekends, he soldiered through it, filling it up with tasks, some invented, just to have some time for himself. It was hardly a relief, boring as it was, when the weekend came to a close, as it marked the advent of the third week of his presiding in this draining hearing of all hearings. Oh, how he missed the routine hearings he used to have; those two, or at most, three-day affairs, with a peaceful travel day to begin and end each such event. Here, it was a five-day, full-throttle, experience and no travel days at the start and finish to unwind.

CHAPTER 7

Monday, marking the start of the third week of trial, arrived too soon. It hardly felt like there had been two days off for Gray, as his home life offered no genuine respite. As usual, his commute to the office at the start of the work week was nearly double the usual time, this time made worse, the result of a minor accident on I-395. Even a fender bender, which this one appeared to be, as he eventually inched by it, caused significant disruption for hundreds of commuters. Given the minimal damage from the accident, it hardly seemed worth it to screw up the commute of so many. Just get the damn cars over to breakdown lane and let the rest of us get to work, he thought. Already in a sour mood from the weekend, the traffic delay meant that he had to rush from the office to the courthouse, arriving nearly a half-hour late, an unpleasant, stressful way to start the week.

Upon making his entrance, the counsel knew how to behave, acting as if the proceeding was starting on time. As Gray took the bench, he recalled there were those few occasions before he became a judge when he was unavoidably late for some reason or another. Then, he was met with frowns. Not now, in his presiding judge position.

He decided to acknowledge his tardiness. "I want to apologize for the late start. A minor accident on the interstate turned my commute into a crawl. Nothing I could do about it, but I am amenable to a shortened lunch or having the day last a bit longer if the parties wish."

Neither side expressed interest in the option. The intensity of the trial wore on them too. A shorter day, even at the start of the week, was welcomed.

The government then called its next expert, Dr. Robert Braun. As with Dr. Palmer, the details of Braun's background and the meticulous steps he took in evaluating the filters took a full day. Like Palmer, he too explained that just as a vacuum is designed to flow in one direction, so too the dust pump and assembly functioned in the same fashion. He added that the pump mechanism was sealed so that one could not rewire it to run in the opposite direction. That was a new point, not mentioned by Palmer. Even if one could accomplish a rewiring, it would not make sense to do that, he explained, as there were simpler methods to achieve the same effect; just disconnect the exit hose and send a reverse current of air through the opening.

All that preliminary information had to be laid out and although it was cumulative, Gray recognized that the government was allowed to present a second witness on the same issues. The defense would be permitted to do the same.

More important than the foundational evidence was the conclusion the second expert reached. That part, at least, was something Gray could grasp. To no surprise for the defense, when it came time for the doctor to express his expert opinion, he reached the same conclusion as Palmer – the AWCs came about primarily by reverse air flow. Leaving no doubt, he informed that such results could only come about by intentional conduct. In that respect, his testimony was stronger than his fellow expert's. Though he didn't say it outright, he did not accept that mishandling could explain the AWCs.

There had been no cross-examination yet, but Milo and Winston had become increasingly pessimistic over last week's testimony from Palmer and now they had to contend with this expert, Braun, who was every bit as sure of himself as the previous expert. The deposition of Braun presaged that he would be a strong witness, but his testimony on the stand was compelling and, as such, more than they had anticipated.

Now, they realized, the government had hit two home runs with these experts. The only immediate consolation was the wisdom of their decision to launch Tranter into the mix. Sure, the plan was to win the case on the basis of their own evidence, on the merits, so to speak. But, at bottom, that strategy was really about throwing enough dirt on the Secretary's case to cast sufficient doubt for Gray to conclude that the preponderance of the evidence test had not been met. But their ability to persuade Gray that the Secretary's case had holes in it was not certain, and they knew that only a fool would place the expectation of a win on that one strategy – winning on the merits. Not for a case of this magnitude. No way.

As for the second front of their attack, the set ups, there was reason to be enthused. The two had learned during the lunch break that Tranter already had the plans in motion. He advised that, beginning tonight, the first trap, the one for his Honor, would be set, with Balkum's snare to follow.

To cover himself, as he coldly knew that the two attorneys who hired him were cobras, Tranter cautioned them that both schemes were unpredictable. Those two, he thought, needed such reminders. Sometimes a fish does not take the bait, as he put it to them. In such cases, the line needs to be set again.

And, he emphasized, sometimes no fish is ever caught. Tranter knew the nature of these clients. For them, success was the only news they wanted to hear. Still, it was important to repeatedly warn them that success was never guaranteed. The nature of his work involved dealing with unsavory people, but he had become accustomed to that reality. The enticement for him, the reason he took this job, despite dealing with those vipers, was simple: they were paying him a ton of money.

To no one's surprise, Braun's testimony on direct took the entire day. Milo and Winston fully realized that Braun's testimony had been as solid as Palmer's, and so the two left the courthouse filled with irritation over the awful start to the new week. And though cross-examination would start the next day, they knew it would not offer the prospect of relief because there was little hope of damaging the second expert's work and the conclusions he reached. Still, failing to examine the witness would produce an outcome which would be worse. The judge, they knew, would certainly take note of such silence and the Secretary would make hay of it too.

With no choice, the following morning the two proceeded as the circumstances required, presenting an aura of skepticism and outright disbelief in reaction to Braun's answers to their questions. Since the two experts had now independently reached the same conclusion about the cause of the AWC's, their examination could do little more than repeat the same lines of attack, hoping for a slip up with this witness.

Wasn't it possible, the doctor was asked, that a number of innocent actions could have produced those white centers?

Braun, was less diplomatic than Palmer, fairly scoffing at the suggestions that rough handling, dropping tool boxes on hoses, and that mailing the cassettes could explain the results away.

"Maybe a few of the cassettes, and I emphasize, maybe," he added, "a few of those events could perhaps produce those white centers," he said dismissively, "but 70 out of 78, do you really believe that counselor?"

Malthan reacted immediately to the sassy answer. "Objection!" "Objection!" he repeated, more forcefully. "Your honor I ask that the witness' improper and impertinent answer be stricken! The witness doesn't get to ask the questions!"

Sanford enjoyed the comment from Braun. Put the defense back on its heels, he thought. But, knowing how the judge would rule, he did not respond to the objection.

Gray, recognizing that Sanford didn't want a dispute over the remark, responded, "Yes, the answer will be stricken." He continued, "Dr." he said evenhandedly, "Respondent's counsel is correct. A witness is to respond to questions, but may not counter with questions of his own. Opposing counsel will determine if follow-up questions are warranted on re-direct examination."

Upon hearing the judge's gentle admonition, Braun had the good sense to pull back. "I understand, your Honor," he said respectfully. "I apologize."

When the cross was completed, Sanford could not resist revisiting the confrontation. "Dr. Braun, you'll recall that your response was stricken when counsel asked you if the AWCs could be explained by rough handling and things of that sort. Do you recall that exchange?"

"I do," Braun answered.

"Why sir do you believe that the AWCs could not be so explained?"

Malthan, knowing what was coming, objected. "Your honor, you have already ruled on this."

This time Sanford did not remain silent. "Your honor, as I understood your ruling, it was that the witness may not pose questions to the examining attorney. But, certainly, he must have the opportunity to explain the basis for his conclusion that rough handling and the like cannot produce the AWC's."

Gray wished the dispute had not been revisited, but he knew Sanford was correct. It was entirely proper to give the witness the opportunity to explain the basis for his opinion when on re-direct.

"The witness may answer," Gray said simply.

Sanford acknowledged the ruling, "Thank you, your Honor."

Then, nodding at Braun, he said, "So tell us Doctor, why did you reject that the handling and the various other reasons counsel for the mine operator suggested could be causes for the AWCs?"

Braun seized the moment, pleased to have an opportunity to shoot back. "There are several reasons. As I explained, the pump and cassette simply don't work in reverse, just as in the vacuum cleaner example. These things are designed to flow only in one direction, not two. Also, it just seems impossible that with all these AWCs that rough handling could create that many white centers."

Sanford looked back at his co-counsels, unable to hold back a slight grin.

Anxious to move to their defense, Malthan and Krakovich decided that further cross-examination would not advance their case. Their attempts had been ineffective, as the doctor's testimony remained intact, undented by their attempts to assail his methodology and findings. That guy, Braun, he was a contentious little son of a bitch in their estimation. It was unlikely that further questioning would yield any gains. They would have to rely upon their own experts to cast doubts on the Secretary's claims.

The Secretary, fully aware of impressive testimony presented by Palmer and Braun, engaged in a minimal redirect exam.

When recross began and Milo tried to raise matters outside of the Secretary's redirect, Sanford objected, asserting that, per the practice rules, such questions were not permitted. Gray, ever mindful of the enormity of the case, exercised caution, advising that while the Secretary was correct, in the spirit of fairness, he would exercise his discretion and allow further questions, though raising new material. With that, he added, as notice to the Respondents, that he would afford the same leeway to the Secretary when it came time for his recross examinations of the Respondent's witnesses.

That satisfied Sanford, as he leaned over to his co-counsel, whispering that they must remember to remind the judge of his ruling when the inevitable objections were made by the Respondents. Sanford, knowing the nature of his opponents, was aware that they would vehemently object to any recross questions that brought up new matters. The two were not the type to be inhibited by the grace afforded to them earlier by the judge's ruling. They didn't play that way.

Sanford largely remained silent after Gray had given his opponents license to go beyond the subjects of redirect, but on two occasions when Milo was again raising new topics, he diplomatically called the subjects to the Court's attention, stating, "Objection, your honor. Our objection is of a technical nature. The Secretary understands and respects the Court's ruling permitting an expansive arena for the scope of recross examination, but our purpose is to simply remind the Respondents that the same rules will apply to them when we are conducting our recross examinations."

Sanford framed his objection as a reminder to the Respondents about the ground rules the Court had set, but clearly his purpose was to remind the Court of its own ruling in that regard. For that reason, he strategically reiterated the objection. He would then be able to cite from the transcript, pointing to the instances when the wide open recross exam rules were approved by the Court.

Trying to convince themselves that the tide would change once their own experts took the stand, the two hoped that, with the weeks of testimony ahead, perhaps the damaging effects of the Secretary's experts would fade in Gray's mind and that he would focus on the Respondent's experts who would challenge every claim made so far.

Now with two formidable experts damaging the mine's assertion that the white centers all came about as a result of accidents, and nothing more than that, their claims looked very weak. These unhappy events, at least for the moment dimming the prospects of prevailing in court, served to reaffirm Milo and Winston's wisdom, really the necessity, of launching their backup plan.

It had been another satisfying day for the Secretary. The foundation had been well-established by Balkum and his technicians with the enormous number of suspect cassettes, a bountiful supply of AWCs. And then, more broadsides, with two solid experts concluding that tampering was the only rational explanation for the AWCs. A good score, now at two weeks and two days into the trial, there had been no serious blows landed by the Respondent so far and that was especially true for the two recent experts. And though this trial was confined to the number of AWCs found for this mine only, Gray knew that the AWCs were in the thousands, occurring mine-wide in the coal fields. And the Secretary's next witness, a statistical expert, was yet to come, presenting damaging numbers to refute the claim that the white centers were random occurrences.

Glumly, Milo and Winston, were keenly aware that, at least for the courtroom part of its defense, their hopes would depend upon the effectiveness of their own experts to create enough doubt for the judge to conclude that the Secretary failed to meet the preponderance of the evidence standard to which it was held.

But just how the testimony from their experts would play out, that could be a roll of the dice, a disconcerting prospect. It underscored the importance of the other part of the plan, that extra-judicial strategy.

That part of the defense had now become more essential, though both soberly realized that it had no certain outcome to it. There was the risk that Gray and Balkum could each reject the enticements that would be offered. With the legitimate part of the defense, at least for now, looking dim, they hoped that the temptations of the flesh would carry the day.

Buoyed by the thought that tomorrow would mark the mid-week, Gray packed up quickly, readying for his head-clearing walk back to the office. It offered a respite, a chance for a brief interval from his courtroom role before assuming his home responsibilities. Were it not for his lack of overall fitness, a longer walk would've been in his best interest. The brisk late fall air felt good too, stimulating his level of alertness.

Unavoidably, his thoughts turned once again to that woman at the G Street.

In what was his day's-end ritual, upon arriving at the office, Larkin was once-again there, his door open as Gray passed his colleague's office. He was not thrilled that these briefings were becoming routine. He was tired enough as it was and discussing the day was an unwelcomed task. He anticipated that even a brief summary of the expert's testimony to his colleague would support his earlier kibitzing.

From his prior unsolicited comments, Gray fully realized where Larkin stood on the case and the obligated recounting about today would continue to support his view, there being no way to discount Braun's testimony. Even if Larkin kept quiet about it, free of commentary, Gray knew his colleague would leave their meeting with a self-satisfied attitude. That would be irritating enough, but then he would have to give another summary to his wife. No doubt, she would pile on after receiving his mandatory retelling.

Unhappy over the twin summaries he would be required to tell, he still felt compelled to say hello, summoning himself to present faux friendliness, by remarking, "I see you're hard at it, as usual, Richard."

With the office being so quiet at the end of the day, Larkin was aware of his colleague's approaching, figuring it could only be him. However, he didn't want to initiate the greeting in case Gray preferred not to socialize. So, it was heartening that Gray made the first remark.

"It's not that I'm a workaholic," he demurred, "I'm just more efficient at the end of the day."

"Come on down and I'll fill you in, if you're interested," Gray felt obliged to offer.

"I do want to hear how it's going," Larkin confirmed buoyantly. "Be right down, Charles."

Too bad, thought Gray, that he had not declined his insincere invite.

THE CASE OF THE ABNORMAL WHITE CENTER

Moments later, the two had assumed their now customary arrangement in Gray's office, with the 'patient' in his tall back chair and the therapist on his office's couch.

"Well," Gray began, "the government presented its second expert today, Dr. Braun. He echoed the sum and substance of their prior expert, that Dr. Palmer fellow I told you about."

Larkin, without thinking, replied, "I thought this would have been the third expert. Have I mixed it up?" he inquired, feigning confusion.

"Okay, it's the third," Gray conceded, fully aware that his junior colleague was correcting his retelling. Grudgingly, he added, "If you count that lab tech out of Mount Hope."

Larkin was disappointed with his colleague's repeated diminishment of the first expert, the fellow from MSHA's lab. It seemed shallow to be swayed against him by virtue of his modest educational background. Shouldn't the substance of his testimony carry the day? he thought. After all, Balkum did know what he was talking about.

Still, he wished he had not made the correction, as it was plain Gray that was irritated by it. He should have kept the focus on the latest expert's testimony, knowing full well that the Secretary would not have given the witness such prominence, the second of its prized retained experts, had his testimony been anything other than impressive.

Annoyed, but moving past Larkin's editorial comment, Gray continued as if he had not been corrected, admitting, "I have to say this doctor was also compelling, both from his background and his review of the cause of those white centers on the dust cassettes."

Again, Larkin thought, the background of the witness seemed to unduly capture his colleague's evaluation of the worth of his testimony. It was disappointing, but he knew that noting his colleague's predilection to be enthralled with one's curriculum vitae would only cause him to become more entrenched with that view. His first comment had already landed with a thud, forcing Gray to admit his expert witness count was off by one. Attempting further persuasion would backfire; saying something salutary about the first expert would do more harm than good.

Gray informed, "These AWC's, as they call them, this doctor also concluded, just as Palmer had testified, there was no way they could just appear without intentional behavior. Something affirmative had to have happened for those to result. And he dismissed the ideas that mailing the cassettes back to MSHA, nor humidity, nor rough handling, nor any of the many other grounds the defense is asserting, could be the cause. The defense made no headway under cross-examination; the witness was unshakable."

Larkin, in his de facto therapist role, avoided any further comment. It was clear that his remarks only had the opposite effect. Still, he could not help but consider that Gray, from the start really, seemed to have a tilt against the government's case.

But why? The defense had not even started and by Gray's own account its cross-exams had done little damage to the government's case. It did not make sense to him. Especially as there were so many of these AWCs and with that one large mine having admitted to doing the very thing being charged in this trial.

He then decided to end the discussion on a neutral, even upbeat, tenor, the idea being to keep the lines of communication open. If he went too far with comments, Gray might just shut down further discussions as the trial continued.

With those considerations in mind, he closed their conversation. "Thanks, Charles, for the update. It's an interesting and challenging case for sure." Then, throwing a bone to his colleague, he added "and as you have correctly noted, the defense has not even begun."

The last comment was insincere. Larkin brought his own predilections to cases. He was not oblivious to this but he tried to stay balanced and his brief time as a judge showed it – the government prevailed in some of his cases, as did the mine operators in others.

Gray seemed to appreciate Larkin's last observation. "That's right, Richard, a lot of testimony yet to come," he smiled, believing that the two of them were on the same page.

Upon Larkin's departure, Gray's thoughts turned to his first stop for the evening, a repeat of his usual routine – a drink, or maybe two, at the Grill. Then, when his respite was over, the commute to home and Millie, neither of which brought a smile. Ah, Florida and retirement, he thought, if only he had not been so burdened by his wife's disease, perhaps they would be planning that relocation, far away from the damn cold temps he was presently tolerating in D.C.

Though Gray knew his plans, with the next stop in his schedule being a visit to his favorite bar, he had no idea that others had set up plans of their own for him, as they were ready for the judge's departure. Tranter had met with Marla twice to be sure she had the arrangement clear in her head. Happily, Gray was a reliable creature of habit. He would predictably leave his office around 5:15, immediately heading over to the G Street Grill.

With some mild anxiety, a condition she always experienced before beginning one of her setup roles, Marla was ready to begin her new assignment. Sometimes things worked perfectly, but not always. There was always a dicey aspect to her line of work and it was an ever-present source for her nervousness. Over the five years in her role as a femme fatale, there had only been two dangerous incidents. In one, a little more than a year ago, the subject immediately suspected he was being set up. She thought he was ready for a romp at her hotel. But once outside the bar, he grabbed her and started shaking her violently. Luckily a stranger came upon the scene and she took flight.

The other incident was more unsettling because there had been no divine intervenor to rescue her. She had bedded the fellow and he had no clue that he was being played. What she did not count on was that he had a sexual abuse fetish. During the act he began slapping her and, enjoying his sicko practice, he increased the intensity of his blows. One smack, she did not like it, but when another followed and much harder than the first, she then knew it had become a very dangerous situation. Panic coursed through her and, though he was bigger and stronger by far, aided by a surge of adrenalin pumping through her, she somehow wrested herself free, running to the hotel room's door. With the door wide open and she completely naked, the assaulter immediately realized that the tables had turned and now he was the one in a fix. Instantly, he grabbed his clothes, pulling on his pants in seconds and fleeing out the door with his shirt and shoes in hand.

She forced those scary memories out of her head. This guy, Gray, he was a judge. It was unlikely that he would act like those two dangerous types. The challenge was not about dangers; it was about seducing him and having it all recorded on video. Having worked with Tranter before, she knew him to be meticulous, providing her with all the important details about the mark. This included providing her with a folder which included several photos. There would be no mistaking someone else for him. And she had already confirmed his identity at the bar, an event at which she was well-aware that he had taken repeated notice of her.

The folder from Tranter summarized the judge's career, and his wife's serious ailment, along with his home address and financial situation. Although that information was technically not needed, and though she would never reveal her knowledge about him, it would help her understand his vulnerabilities.

Per Marty's instructions, the week before she had watched him exit his office for a few evenings, and those observations confirmed what she had been told. The man's routine was like clockwork; very predictable. He'd exit his building shortly after five each evening. That regularity made her job easier, that he had such a trait. It meant that there would be no tedious waiting around for her 'accidental' encounter.

And on this evening, there he was, like a train dependably running on time, leaving his building at 5:10. She was ready, carrying two packages in hand, stuff she didn't want or need, purchased thirty minutes earlier at the low-end department store on the same block.

As he opened the glass exit door from the building, she timed it perfectly, bumping into him and simultaneously dropping both handled bags, the contents of one spilling out on the sidewalk.

"Oh, I am so sorry, sir!" she exclaimed. "I was distracted and wasn't paying any attention to where I was going. Forgive me, sir." She knelt down to grab the emptied contents strewn over the immediate area of the staged accident.

Though startled by the collision, Gray reacted without hesitation, "Don't apologize, please," he gallantly responded, while wishing she hadn't addressed him as "sir" twice, the term applied as a statement about his age. Do I look that ancient? he thought.

Taking the blame, he continued, "I wasn't paying sufficient attention either," completely unaware that he'd just been set up.

He knelt beside her as he attempted to collect the completely emptied contents of one of the bags, a result she adroitly accomplished. As he did so he could not avoid noting that she was attractive. And, even though they were outside, some compelling perfume was emanating from her. To bump into a woman of such beauty would be a delight on any evening. Accidents like that were welcome anytime.

The bag's contents restored, the two stood up, affording the first opportunity for an extended look at one another. So caught up with the mishap, he still had not looked at her closely.

Expressing her thanks for his assistance, Marla could tell he had not placed her yet and so she seized the moment with feigned innocence, saying, "I feel that we've met before. I know that sounds odd, but is it possible?"

Gray thought about it, her remark following the collision raising the possibility that they would not necessarily simply say good evening, departing, never to see one another again. He wanted to believe they had met before, but it was night and his age let him down, as he could not immediately place her.

Astute, she knew her prey would need some assistance, so she continued with her ruse.

"Hmm," she said, "let me think." She paused, as if searching her memory. "Could it have been at that taproom a while back?" she posited, not wanting to diminish the location by calling it a bar.

Seeing that he needed yet another clue, she offered, "I occasionally have a refreshment at the G Street Grill."

Finally, now with the benefit of a longer look of the woman before him, it dawned on him that he *had indeed* met her before. Well, he silently realized, 'met' was too strong a word. More correctly, he had viewed her before, just short of ogling, a few weeks back.

"I do remember you," he then announced. "How could I forget?" he admitted, fairly confessing that she had captured his attention on that occasion. The woman he had repeatedly dreamed about was before him!

Seeing her opening, she smiled approvingly. "I'd say this calls for us to have a drink at the G Street," she quickly responded, seizing the moment. "For old times' sake," she continued, a playful lilt accompanying her coquettish words.

Gray was thrilled, not pausing to consider that, unless he was very wealthy, a woman of her beauty would not give him a moment's glance. Obviously, he thought, she had zero knowledge whatsoever about his financial position. On that supposition, he was wrong and on a grand scale.

Elated over the good fortune of their accidental encounter, and better yet her thinking that they were not complete strangers, though wrong on both counts, he seized the moment.

"That sounds like a grand idea, and please, the drinks are on me."

Cheerfully, she accepted. And, she attentively noted, he said 'drinks,' meaning there would be more than a single serving before a parting. The man was now on the hook, she knew. Reeling him in, now that was always tricky.

In short order they took a cozy booth at the G Street. The bartender, Jerome, expecting his patron's usual solo act at the bar, saw the judge enter but immediately noted that he was accompanied by a woman of uncommon beauty, and that the two went to a secluded booth.

This was a distinctly new arrangement for his long-time customer. All this time, the judge had come in by himself, quietly consumed one to two drinks and then been on his way.

Couldn't be his wife, he thought, far too young for the guy. Nor a daughter, if he even had one; she was too old for that. He was certainly intrigued by the event and his curiosity about it could not be sated, neither presently nor in the future, unless the jurist were to bring it up himself on some future visit when he resumed his usual spot on a barstool.

She ordered a gin and tonic and he went with his usual, a Manhattan. Marla could hold her liquor quite well, but she was careful to sip her serving. This was no time to lose any sharpness.

"What are the chances," she began with faux innocence, "that we would bump into each other and then learn we had met before! I'm embarrassed. I forgot to tell you my name. It's Nicole." Then adding her full name, "Nicole Wilson."

She had used the alias before, so she was comfortable with it. That familiarity would mean there would be no chance of confusion, mixing up names.

"Nicole. That's a nice name," Gray responded. Unlike his forgetfulness over remembering Jerome's name, her name was instantly imprinted in his brain.

"Every Nicole I've known has been a kind soul," he added, ignorant that he was about to connect with one who would be a distinct exception to his experience with Nicoles.

"I'm Charles Gray," he reciprocated with the exchange of identities.

"Charles," she said, admiringly, "a distinguished first name."

He ate up the compliment. 'Distinguished,' he thought, lapping up the characterization.

Attempting to put on some charm, he noted, "What are the chances that bumping into someone would result in such a pleasant outcome. I mean there I am coming out of my building, not paying sufficient attention, and my lack of care produces a collision. I'm sorry for my clumsiness."

"Oh, please," she replied. "It was just as much my fault, watching my packages more than where I was going."

Reaching for words that would avoid the issue of blame, she adroitly continued, "Let's just say that it was good fortune at work, and then to learn we've met before!" she added with a smile.

Charles accepted her description, returning a smile, while ignoring the liberties she had taken by describing the prior occasion as having met before, which was far more than a stretch of that encounter. Glances, bordering on stares, all on his part, was all it was, that wordless earlier moment at the bar.

Being skilled at small talk, Nicole proceeded to put her subject at ease, talking first about her occupation, an approach relieving him of disclosing information about himself, unless he volunteered it.

"I'm in real estate," she informed. "Mostly high-income clients looking for housing to match their station in life. It's financially rewarding, but as you might imagine such people are quite demanding. It comes with the territory. I'm based downtown and I work alone. That's more work, operating solo, but it's easier too, with no personnel conflicts to address."

She continued easily with her fabrication, foregoing the natural sequence to then inquire just what his occupation was in connection with the building he had exited, though she was well-aware of his post.

"The people I deal with expect a certain presentation," she added, "so my office has to convey a high-end atmosphere."

Gray took note of her remark, noting with regret that he did not fit within such clientele. Well, he thought, no need to let such negative thoughts spoil this. She seemed pleased to be in his company, so enjoy the moment.

Feeling the need to respond, he struggled for a reply. Lamely, all he could come up with was "it sounds interesting."

In truth, he considered her occupation, even if focused on the well-to-do, to be at once both tedious and exhausting. While presumably lucrative, it would be, he believed, a perpetual headache.

It was then that he felt compelled to reciprocate with some information about his livelihood. "I'm a lower-tier judge," he informed, in a self-deprecating manner. "My position is administrative law judge." Feeling that description to be inadequate, he then elevated himself, adding "but I am a federal administrative judge."

"Doesn't sound lower tier, as you put it, at all," she answered, contesting his description.

"And federal," she added. "You're the first federal judge I've met in person," she said glowingly.

He sopped up the compliment. "Thanks. I admit, while I said lower-tier, it's true that on occasion I do encounter some cases of importance," he responded, retreating from his critical description a moment ago. "I hear mine safety and health cases now, but I have presided in cases brought by other federal agencies too," as he shifted from being humble to boasting about his work.

"Mine safety?" she asked, as if she was not quite clear what that term entailed. "You mean like underground mineral mines?"

In truth, she never paid attention to mine safety issues. Until now, she thought, why should she? She had no family ever associated with mining. But now, as part of her assignment for Tranter, she read up on coal dust and the devastating effects inhaling that stuff had on miners. She was not uncaring about their plight, but this was work and she wasn't involved in protecting miners' health. That she was now involved in protecting those mine operators, effectively facilitating their escape from accountability by tampering with the dust sampling, escaped her conscience. She needed the work. She needed the money, giving it no further thought.

"Exactly," he affirmed, "but it's all manner of mining cases that come before me, from coal to everything else, which are broadly called 'metal-nonmetal.' And it can be underground or surface. If it comes from the ground, all such cases can come before me. It also covers all the processing of those ores." he added, now bragging about the scope of his cases.

"Sounds complex," she said admiringly, though she had little interest in the details. It involved mining; that was enough for her to know or care about it. She really didn't care whether the cases were complicated or simple.

Not recognizing that her admiration was all fluff, he smiled at her remark. "Well, it can be, but one develops expertise over time," now pumping up his work without hesitation, hoping that he was impressing her. "Much like your line of work, I would imagine," returning the compliment.

Continuing with his desire to wow her, he could not resist touting his ongoing case. He began with apparent modestly. "I don't know if you heard about it. It has been mentioned now and then in the newspapers. I am the judge hearing the claim that hundreds of mine operators tampered with the Mine Safety Administration's coal dust sampling."

She knew about all that, courtesy of Tranter, but she put on a good face, her eyes widening at the information, conveying the impression that this was the first time she learned of the matter.

Gray didn't treat her professed ignorance with doubt, though anyone who watched the local news stations or picked up the newspaper would have been aware of it.

"Now that really is interesting," she responded, employing her best acting skills, "unlike the tedium in my line of work. I'm here with a judge and one who's hearing a big case! It's sounds like such a very important matter."

She avoided, and he did not bring up, his marital status. Good fortune, he hadn't worn his wedding ring in years. As it was so long ago, he no longer had any of the tell-tale signs that he once wore one.

Aside from the brief exchanges of their lines of work, the conversation remained light and she was careful not to delve into any areas that he could interpret as prying. The best part for Marla was that the talk remained cheerful and, even better, that the good judge seemed to be in no hurry to part. With the time having passed quickly and the conversation easy, not forced, Gray then ordered a third drink for himself, signaling that he wanted their interaction to continue, which had now lasted nearly an hour. Millie was completely absent from his mind.

For her part, ever mindful that she was working, she had nursed the first drink and was barely into her second over that time. By her calculation, after the judge had consumed half of his present drink, the moment seemed right. The alcohol had done its work but not so much that he was soused. Too much booze in him would interfere, not help, with the rising possibilities for the evening. She had not anticipated that their first interaction would go so well. Her thoughts were that it would take a second or third such meeting before the idea of sex would arise. But she could tell, the old guy had a strong case of the hots. Things could happen this evening.

Though her next remark suggested that it was time for their evening together to come to an end, her plans were for anything but such a conclusion. "You know," she said, "I've had a wonderful time in your company, but I best be calling it a night. I have a full slate of clients for tomorrow, so I need to get to bed."

He was unduly excited by her even saying of her need to "get to bed," but he was flatfooted how to respond to her words suggesting it was time to say goodnight. Had he been a skilled roué, he would have had the words available to keep the night going.

She recognized that his amorous skills were subpar for the moment, so it was up to her to provide the next step, by ostensibly offering an innocent suggestion. "I'm staying at the Regal," she informed. "It's temporary, as I am having the wood flooring in my house redone."

Employing her forte, smoothness, she then gently implored, "Since it's dark now and I'm in temporary quarters, would you mind escorting me to my hotel? Sometimes I get a bit nervous at this time of night."

Gray, ignorant that he was being played, didn't hesitate. He saw it only as a continuation of his lucky streak. He certainly knew of The Regal; it was literally just a few blocks from his office. There was no effort involved, as there would have been if her hotel were some distance from the bar.

"Glad to," he chivalrously responded, without hesitation.

"I appreciate it so much," she smiled at his willingness to afford her safe passage to her hotel.

Jerome took notice that the two left together, an oddity for sure. In all those years, he'd never seen the judge accompanied. Seemed like he had a bounce to his step too.

They took the short walk respectfully, no physical contact occurring, nor, heaven forbid, any hand holding, such a show being entirely out of place. Upon arriving and then inside the hotel lobby, she short-circuited any chance that he would say good evening and be on his way. "Please come up for a thank-you drink."

He hesitated for a moment. It was the first time since the fortunate collision that Millie had entered his mind. Although at this time he was already late for home, an excuse came immediately to mind. His wife was fully aware of the complex, and lengthy, hearing that was underway, what with her daily questions about it, and, as he had told her, it would continue that way for several weeks. I'll just tell her, he thought, that his delay was due to the litigation, though he had not yet invented the details for his excuse.

She noted his brief pause to her invitation. Being this close, she didn't want to lose him now. Presenting a hopeful smile was the best she could do.

Saying more might have the opposite effect on him. Don't overplay this, she thought. Confident of her effect on him, she realized that if he decides to leave there will be another meeting.

Her smile, and the anticipation on her face was too much to decline the offer. He accepted. "Sure. Just a quick one though." Lying, and resolutely avoiding disclosure of his very-marital status, he informed, "I need to prepare for the next day of trial before I turn in."

"Of course, I completely understand," she sympathized. "We'll make it a quick one and then you'll be on your way," avoiding the using the phrase "on your way *home*" so as not to provoke any discomfort or guilt in his head.

Once inside her hotel room, Gray could not help but notice that it was a suite, not simply a one-room arrangement. There was a separate area with a couch, two chairs and a coffee table, much like a mini-living room. In fact, he noted gloomily, this arrangement looked better than his own living room. Off to the side was a separate bedroom area, and not one that was open to the living room either, a privacy door dividing the two zones. The décor was consistent with the story of her prosperous real estate career. She must be well-off, he thought, to afford an accommodation like this.

Nicole excused herself for a moment, retreating to the bedroom. "Charles, please make yourself comfortable," as she gestured for him to use the sofa. "I'll just be a minute, then we'll have our drink." Once inside the bedroom, she turned on the hidden video camera, checking to make sure the tiny red light on the back was on.

Gray felt a little uncomfortable. He was not the type to put himself in these situations. He had no history of playing around. This was not due to any rectitude on his part. Instead, it was in large measure because he had not had many opportunities like this present themselves, nor had he actively cultivated such arrangements. Seizing the moment while he was by himself, he then had the presence of mind to silence the ringer on his phone.

True to her word, Nicole reappeared in a moment, this time wearing a satiny colorful print top, almost as if it could qualify as sleepwear, he thought. He noticed that it fit her curves too, accenting her well-endowed shape. She presented a distracting appearance though he tried not to stare, a hard task.

Behaving as if there had been no change of her clothes, Nicole went immediately over to the wet bar, asking, "Same as before, Charles?"

"Sure, that'll be fine, Nicole," his earlier drinks placing him at ease.

With no pretense of shyness, upon bringing their drinks she sat next to him on the sofa, her legs just slightly coming in contact with his.

"To a wonderful meeting, Charles," she proclaimed their toast.

Then, putting her hand on his knee, she reassured, "now let's just relax and enjoy our drink before you're on your way."

Had she not offered those calming words, noting that he would soon be on his way, sitting so close to him and then placing her hand on his knee, would have been worrisome. Yet, he fully enjoyed the closeness, and the physical contact. That was undeniable. Part of him thought that he should head home. A stronger impulse, the urge to stay, won out decisively.

As this was now his fourth drink of the evening, he felt its effect. Marla had been careful to water it down. If he fell asleep now, the evening, so close to success, would have been for naught. Though more than his usual dosage, he was able to hold his liquor. As he continued to imbibe, the feeling of relaxation overtook his fading apprehension. Millie was a hundred miles from his mind.

His comfort level increased as they enjoyed more of the small talk they experienced earlier at the bar. She was an expert at idle chat. Nearly done with his drink, the alcohol at full effect, she looked at him affectionately and he returned her expression with a similar gaze, free of any inhibition. Utilizing her experience, assessing his state, Marla knew the time was right. With no hesitation she leaned over, planting a deep kiss on him. He reacted instantly to it with a passionate response. It had been years, literally years, since he'd had such a strong sexual reaction.

Now, knowing she had the play in hand, she did not hesitate to make a more aggressively passionate act, moving a leg across him and, as he did not reject her action, a moment later she had both legs then straddling his waist, as she pressed another penetrating kiss on him. He responded in kind.

For her, it was all pretend but, through practice in such circumstances, it seemed genuine.

A few more moments of uninhibited passion continued, and applying her playbook, she then arose, her legs still outside his, as she took his hand, helping him arise, now erect in both senses of the word. Making sure he was steady, with no risk that he might fall, she led him to the bedroom.

To her surprise, minutes away from the fait accompli, for a second, he hesitated. "I think," Gray began.

"Don't think, dear. There are no ties here. Just come with me."

His scant hesitation soothed; he did not fight it further.

Making sure he was safely on the bed, a goofy smile fixed on his face, awaiting the main event, she smiled back at him presenting a faux presentation of affection.

Then, wasting no time, in seconds she was entirely disrobed, her naked body there for him to take in her undeniably spectacular form. There had been a few, a very few, women before Millie, but none of them, his wife certainly included, had a body like Nicole. Hers was like a centerfold's.

While for her it was all about the business at hand, and though she had zero affection for any of her subjects, his honorable included, it was still satisfying to know that she still had it, the pleasure of seeing men so hypnotized by her body.

He then started to sit up from the bed, about to stand and take off his trousers. Seeing this and wasting no time to intervene, she gently placed him down on his back, unbuckling his belt and then attending to his zipper, with no resistance to either of her actions.

He was blissfully happy for her to be in charge.

Moments later, she had his trousers off, and then his boxers, with him presenting a full erection.

Wonderful, she thought, there would be no need for further stimulation, the alcohol having been just the right dosage to remove any inhibitions, but not so much as to make sex impossible.

Attentive to her objective, she was careful to then stand back, allowing the DVD recorder to explicitly capture it all.

With her momentarily out of the scene, there would be no doubt that Gray was the co-star in this movie. She then made her reappearance, briefly turning to face the camera, and by that assuring that the device unmistakably captured her image too.

Completely taken with her, he was also aware and pleased that his equipment was fully working. Though his member didn't need extra stimulation, she then considered it prudent to apply her hand and mouth, to keep him in the state of full arousal.

Smiling at him, presenting an affectionate mien, she then promptly unbuttoned his shirt. At that point, with him sufficiently naked, she then straddled him. A second later, deftly using her hand, she inserted him, gliding his member all the way into her.

It would be a lie for her to claim that his presence in her was devoid of pleasure. Sex, at least this part, still felt good, even under such circumstances. It was about his equipment, not him. So sensitized, there was a moment of mutual enjoyment. Now she was moving in a manner to pleasure both of them. To that end, she slowed down when sensing that he was near the end. Then, when confident that his peak had been postponed, she resumed. No harm in a girl achieving her own orgasm, she thought.

It was clear that she could not postpone him again and the eruption then arrived. With little time left, her attention turned to her own need of the moment, as she worked hard to achieve her own climax. For him, her animated ending was elating, as he was aware that she also came. Old as he was, he fancied himself a lady-killer.

Done, the two then lay there, both in a full state of nature, side by side, as the camera faithfully recorded, the before, during, and now, the after state.

He had enjoyed the romp, but now his head began throbbing, the price paid for too much liquor and his rapid heart rate. From experience, he knew it would be a killer of a headache that would last for most of the next day.

After his time of ignoring his husbandly obligations, thoughts about Millie emerged. He looked at his watch. Though he should not have been surprised, he saw that it was now after nine. Couldn't think of a time when he'd been so late to returning home. He realized it would be near ten before he was back. At that late time, there would be significant explaining required for Millie, meaning a lengthy, and hopefully believable, lie to present to her.

THE MINE SAFETY TRILOGY PART II

While all these worries were now front and center, there was also the distraction of Nicole, as she lay next to him, together in their stark and complete nakedness. She was still in her role, presenting her act of continuing contentment, as she gently stroked his abdomen, all of it being duly recorded on the video camera.

It was still pleasant for him, her soothing touch, but with each minute, thoughts of his need to return home as soon as possible took over his attention. The only lie he could invent was the most obvious. He would have to say it was all about the big case, that it had overtaken him to the point of exhaustion, that he'd been asleep on his office couch for all that time. Though he knew that his mendacity would be skeptically received by Millie, it was the best he could concoct. She could not completely dismiss that this was the biggest, most complicated administrative case in his long career. He'd been telling her about that for weeks now, so the predicate for the lie was established. Working late, he would insist, was an unavoidable consequence of this one-of-a-kind case.

Mentally fortified by the only excuse he could present, he then recognized a potential benefit from the fabrication – if Nicole would have him again, he would be able to employ the same excuse, having established it on this occasion.

Still, he realized that its believability would be diminished when used a second time. How many times could he claim the same excuse? Though ailing, his wife's condition did not impair her capacity to be skeptical. This first time, he thought, maybe she would accept it, but to use it again, that was a steeper order. Against Millie's natural reaction to doubt the claim if he employed it again, was the pull of wanting to be in Nicole's arms a second time.

There was, even at this moment, no question which impulse would win out. Inventiveness was not his strong suit. If she did not buy it, well, he would stick with it anyway. How could she prove his late returns were due to something else? A sad statement on how low he had sunk, that thought was supported because her illness precluded her from driving to his office to check on his whereabouts.

Still calculating, he began to consider whether a once-a-week dalliance would be possible, an exciting thought. His fanciful thoughts did not consider whether Nicole would be similarly interested, an arrogant assumption on his part to think that a woman some twenty or so years younger than he would have similar enthusiasm.

Juggling his future interest in having continued sex with Nicole with his husbandly duties and the pounding headache that was only growing, he turned to tell her, "I'd best be going."

With that brief remark, itself unusual in any normal sense following sex, he arose from her bed. After such a coupling, typically, a parting would not occur until morning arrived. It was an unwritten custom. He still had enough of his senses operating to realize he could not say more. He did not stop to consider that it was itself unusual that she voiced no objection to his words. Just as he was blind to this gorgeous woman's willingness to bed such an older man, who was no more than a stranger, he continued to ignore that her silence was also out of place, so atypical that one should be accepting of his departure so soon after intimacy. All the warning signs were being ignored. Even had they come to mind, it was now too late to do anything about them, the die having been cast.

Marla knew that her line in the script was now due. "Wish you could stay," she responded with feigned sincerity, while knowing full well that it was out of the question for him to remain. Relieved that he would not be able to accept the insincere wish, she could hardly wait for his departure.

A new concern then came to mind for her, this time a genuine one. "Charles, we both had more than a few. Are you sure you're okay to drive?"

She had a stake in his safe return home. If something bad were to happen, a car accident or even being arrested for DWI, and as a consequence he had to be replaced as the presiding judge, all of her efforts and the immense success that resulted this evening, would be for naught. Then it would be back to square one. And, thinking of such a dark scenario, one could not predict who his replacement would be. Perhaps one not so susceptible to blackmail.

Sitting on the side of the bed, he paused a moment to assess his condition. Aside from the continuing pounder of a headache, he determined that he was okay. On his feet as he walked to retrieve his clothes, he was steady. He did not feel drunk, a condition through long experience he could assess. His balance and self-assessment affirmed his conclusion that he was sober enough to drive.

Maybe, he considered, it was not sufficient to pass a sobriety test, but he would stay focused on his trip home so as not to attract the attention of a stray police car he might encounter along the way. While it was late, at least in terms of his normal time to be home, it was still before ten, not something like one or two in the morning, when the police would be on the lookout for drunk drivers.

When he was ready to leave, she escorted him to the room's door. Before she opened it, there was one more detail to address, per Tranter's directions. "I hope we can see each other again, Charles," she said softly, giving him a hug as she said the words. She had no desire for a reunion. None. It was strictly business, and the arrangement required a second serving of sex.

Though guilt over his unfaithfulness had been with him shortly after he climaxed, her words of a future interest in him displaced that remorse for the moment. How could he say no? It was not even a close call. He was thrilled that she brought it up, relieving him of the fear that if he raised the subject, he would appear to be pleading, and worse, that she might be noncommittal or even announce that there would be no encore for them.

"I want that too, Nicole," he replied, without delay.

Ahead of him, she had the presence of mind to initiate the means for their next meeting. "Just a second," she said, as she retreated from the door. She came back a moment later, her cell phone number jotted on a piece of paper. She knew enough to provide her number only, no name.

"Thanks," he said, pocketing the paper.

Seeing that he needed a prompt, perhaps, she thought, due to dullness from the alcohol, she said, "And yours, Charles?"

Brought up to speed, Gray, who was focused on the prized paper she gave him, answered, "Gosh, I forgot. Sorry," as he then proceeded to provide his cell number.

"Let me get another piece of paper," she said.

In a moment, their exchanges completed, she bid him goodnight.

As he walked down the hotel hallway to the elevators, Gray considered that, over his many years, the evening had been unlike any other experience he'd ever had. How could such good fortune come his way? Emotions tumbled within him, as he thought about her beauty, her charm and the grand pleasure of their intimacy. Such unexpected immense luck. What were the chances? It was almost as if a dream. He had just had sex, great sex in fact, with this woman, a woman much younger than he, and yet neither of them knew anything of substance about one another. Or so he presumed, blindly believing, without a moment's thought, that she knew nothing about him.

Working under those very incorrect assumptions, he considered how neither knew where the other lived, what their personal lives were like, or anything else for that matter. That was so out of order, he realized. In all his experience, all of it before his marriage, intimacy only developed after several dates. Each time, he and those few sexual partners knew at least something about one another.

There had never been a one-night stand for him. Until now.

Yet, it aroused no suspicions in him about what was a first in a lifetime experience.

When he was very young, barely past his teens, he had that one experience in a brothel, but that made sense – there was not supposed to be any disclosure about personal information in those arrangements. You pay your money, the service is provided, and then you're on your way.

For her part, now back to being Marla, she closed the door to her suite, feeling great relief that, for tonight, it was done. Pausing for a moment, she leaned back against the door. She was more than tired from maintaining the evening's prolonged performance, a state exacerbated by the consumption of alcohol beyond her usual number of drinks.

Momentarily, she considered feeling some pity for the guy. He was pleasant enough and she knew that he did have the significant burden of a wife with a longstanding, and debilitating, illness.

Still, on the other side of the equation, he had been unfaithful to that wife, and this violation of his vows occurred within the span of four hours or so. The night was not the result of some weeks or months-long relationship that accidently elevated into unexpected intimacy. At least that development would have some respectability to it.

Thinking of the rapidness, drinks to fucking, all in a matter of hours, she discarded those thoughts of sympathy for him. The judge was not to be excused for his unfaithfulness, she decided, a conclusion omitting her role in bringing it about.

Having collected herself, she knew there were a few tasks to complete before turning in for the night. First was to check the video. It was perfect; in color, and clear with no graininess. Though she'd done this work many times before, it was still embarrassing to watch her performance. Much easier to watch an 'adult film' as they politely call it, than to see yourself doing the fucking.

But this was work, not a time to reflect. Focusing on that, like a director reviewing a scene, there was also that, most skillful, revealing moment, where she displayed her heartlessness as, when they were done, she turned very clearly to the camera. There would be no mistaken identity that she was the co-star in the vignette, nor that he was the other participant.

Tomorrow, there would be three copies made of the recording. One of the copies would be undisclosed; her personal copy. She trusted Marty, but not that much. Girl can't be too careful.

Next, there was the obligation to report to Tranter. It was expected promptly. Recognizing her number, he picked up the phone immediately.

"It's done," she informed.

He was unsure exactly what that meant, as his expectation was that, at best, tonight would be a first encounter, the setup for a second meeting, but with that one planned, not contrived.

"Meaning?" he asked simply.

"Much more than anticipated," she informed. "The 'accidental' meeting had resulted in drinks at his usual haunt," she continued, "and not many hours after that we were in bed at the hotel. All of it recorded. I just checked. Nice and clear. Anyone viewing it would know immediately it's the judge."

Tranter was ecstatic. Such quick results were rare. He was fond of saying that, for these traps, some cultivation was required before the crop could be harvested, his attempt at a clever remark.

The two briefly discussed the follow-ups to be completed the next day – delivery of the recordings and the strategy for the next event with his Honor.

A second meeting would be extremely helpful, as it would serve to dismiss any claim that the first time was a forgivable mistake, a product of the weakness of human nature, but not one that was repeated. A subsequent taping, that would clinch the issue. She was quite sure that could be arranged. In fact, she informed, it was very likely that the judge would be initiating a second rendezvous.

Her work done for the night; Marla avoided looking at herself in the mirror as she prepared to bathe. She wanted to wash away all of Charles Gray before bed. Personal hygiene steps, followed by a long shower accomplished that, at least physically. The psychological cleansing, that was not so easy to wash away. She knew from personal experience that it would take some time for that, but told herself it would be worse if she could instantly dismiss her behavior. Comforting her conscience, she thought that at least she had not become so hardened to be soulless. Everyone has to make a living.

As Gray now reached the underground parking garage, along the way he had routinely checked his sobriety. Reassurance of his state was provided as his gait was steady, with no trace of wobbling. If there was any lingering concern, he determined that he would remain in his car until it was safe to drive. A further delay in returning home would not make matters worse than they already were. Aside from the throbbing headache, which he knew would remain with him even by morning, he was passably clear-headed, the cool evening temps aiding his alertness.

Reaching his car, as there were only a few cars remaining at this hour, he had the presence of mind to look around to make sure no danger lurked.

Though seeing no activity, he still felt uncomfortable, unaccustomed to being there so late and in its deserted state.

Making another rapid review of his surroundings, he quickly entered his car, but as he made the maneuver so fast, he struck the top side of his forehead on the door frame in the process. It hurt like hell and with it there was a gash, a significant one too, as confirmed by the blood which instantly started to flow. Grabbing a tissue, he held it tightly against the wound.

"Fuck!" he exclaimed, a bad ending to what he had considered a joyous evening.

Then he realized that the mishap had distracted him from locking the car door. Instantly he pressed the lock button, while continuing to press the tissue against the cut. After making another check of his surroundings for reassurance that no danger was present, he then lifted the tissue, peering into his rearview mirror in order to examine the extent of the injury. He saw it was much more than a cut, a laceration really.

If it needed a stitch that was out of the question. He couldn't show up at an emergency room. They would know immediately that he'd been drinking, a fact that would be duly noted in the hospital record of his visit. And if his alcohol level was too high, they wouldn't let him go! Besides, Millie would likely be frantic if he arrived several hours later than his already very late return time. There was no choice but to sit in his car for a time, applying pressure to injury.

Before long, upon checking his condition again in the mirror, he saw that the bleeding had stopped. Time to start the trip home, he thought. All that adrenalin coursing through him helped to lessen the effects of the alcohol. No more damn mistakes, he admonished himself, as he checked twice before backing his car out of the space. Seeing that it was all clear, he then slowly left the garage. Once on the streets, he continued to be ultra-careful. The last thing he needed on this sour note ending to what he had considered to have been a perfect evening, would be a police-stop. Even though he felt alert enough to drive, he had serious doubts that he could pass a breathalyzer test.

A small blessing, given his still inebriated state, and the bloody gash on his forehead, he made it home without incident. On the way, periodically, he would open the driver's side window to boost his alertness.

It was nearly 10 p.m. when he arrived. This was enormously late. While remaining attentive to the road, he had used the time during the trip to prepare for the accounting Millie would require for his very overdue arrival.

Once in the garage, he checked the wound again. Fortunately, the bleeding had not resumed, a crusty line of blood having formed over the injury. He knew the injury was due to the clumsiness brought about by all that drinking, an accurate conclusion since he was rarely so uncoordinated. Appropriate punishment, he thought, his inculcated Christian guilt emerging involuntarily, a price to be paid for being unfaithful.

To his surprise, and great relief, Millie was asleep when he entered. She mumbled that he was so late, but was apparently too tired to make an issue of it, perhaps not fully aware of the hour. Though from time to time she would worry if Charles might stray, particularly as her disease progressed, that concern ebbed as the years passed. Now, she concluded with contentment, he was simply too old for such adventures, so the issue ceased to preoccupy her.

Out of necessity he had to shower before bed. He was thorough about it too, wanting to be sure no scent from Nicole lingered on him. He detected nothing with his many sniff tests. He also realized that most of his contact with her had been with his clothes off, so he had no deep worries on that score.

What he did not know was whether he could have picked up anything communicable from her, an untimely thought given what had happened and without any protection. A salve of sorts, he did not have any great worries that, if he had caught something, he could transmit it to his wife. With intimacy so rare between them, it brought about an unusual benefit, as he could simply avoid any sex with her until he was sure that he was clean. That worry solved, he doubted that a woman like Nicole would be a carrier of any STD.

Once clean, neurotically smelling himself, he detected no perfumes, but just to be sure he applied an ample spray of his deodorant to mask anything he might have missed. When about to enter their bed, he was again relieved that she did not stir. He slipped into the sheets as quietly as possible. Again, she displayed no awareness of his presence.

Now on his back, careful not to move, he lay there, his thoughts then returning to his evening with Nicole and the hope that he would be able to see her again.

In bed, of course.

Much earlier that evening, during his commute home, Larkin remained deeply troubled by Gray's attitude toward the case. It seemed to him, well, he then reconsidered, it was much more than 'seemed,' that the man decidedly leaned away from the government's position from the very start. But why? Especially since at this point all the testimony had been from the witnesses MSHA called.

Except for his criticism of Balkum and that was over his pedigree, not his testimony, his colleague had admitted that the experts that followed him were impressive. And though the first two experts that Gray recognized as such had been cross-examined, he made no adverse remarks about those examinations, a silence implicitly admitting that the Respondent had not scored points against them.

So, in spite of the evidence thus far, which should have dictated his take of the case at this point, inexplicably, Gray had a dim view of the Secretary's presentation. Instead, his focus seemed to be presumptively critical of the contention that the filters had been tampered. It didn't add up.

When he arrived home, still preoccupied over Gray's behavior, he spent considerable time telling Sandy about his misgivings, in part to unload his consternation, but also to use her as a sounding board to see if he was missing something. This was not the first time he expressed his dim view about Gray's remarks to her. Her earlier reactions had been primarily noncommittal, listening without opining. But the latest information now prompted her to agree that, given the stage of the case, the judge's uniformly negative remarks about the Secretary's case were troublesome.

Though the two were in agreement that something was very much askew, she then raised an uncomfortable point – was there anything Richard could do about his serious misgivings? Unhappily, he conceded there was nothing to be done.

Although it was late, Tranter decided that his clients would appreciate a call, updating them to the significant development. Recognizing the number, Milo picked up without delay, leaving the room where he and his wife had been watching TV, retreating to his den. It was his practice that no call from Tranter would ever be conducted in the presence of anyone, including his wife, Bessie. The one exception of course was his teammate, Malthan.

"You must have some news of importance, I take it," he answered, keeping his voice low and partially covering the mouthpiece to further reduce his spouse overhearing his words.

"I do indeed," Tranter responded, with recognizable enthusiasm in this voice. "The good judge literally bumped into Marla this evening, a planned event, just outside his office. From there, she adroitly had him enjoying some of that liquid refreshment at his haunt, the G Street Grill. I considered that alone a success, having him enjoying drinks with her. But there was much more. Far more, than I ever expected," he continued.

"The suspense is killing me," Milo interjected, happily anticipating what was coming from Tranter.

He got right to the point. "She bedded him is what! Can you believe it? The same evening!"

Milo anticipated that was the news, but it was hard to imagine that it could all come down so triumphantly in a single evening. He was elated, knowing that they had just won the case, the evidence be damned, though Gray did not know it yet.

In full control, even with the momentous news, his training curtailed the emotional high he was then experiencing. Needing to make sure that his wife remained in the dark, Milo responded only with a single word.

"And?"

Tranter knew what was being asked, needing no prompts to comprehend Milo's question.

"Yes," he informed, "it's all recorded, on a hard disc, in full color. Marla looked at the recording before she called me. Crystal clear, of cinematic quality," he boasted. "There's no mistaking the two of them. She even positioned herself and him during the event so that the good judge's face and hers are unambiguously displayed multiple times."

"Couldn't be more pleased," Milo reacted. "Nice job."

"I'm glad that you're delighted," he responded to the compliment. "I'll have several copies delivered to you promptly."

He then added, "my girl understands that we want an encore performance of the two of them. She's ready to do that. She fully expects that he will initiate a call to her soon, for a second helping. If he doesn't call within the week, she will call him. Based on tonight, she's confident he will be unable to resist contacting her."

"Good, good," he replied. Breaking his caution, he could not resist adding, "If she is able to have a second tape of them *in flagrante delicto*, Gray will truly be sunk. One would be enough, clearly, but two, that would make for an unescapable situation for him."

Bessie then called out from the other room. "Milo, whatever are you talking about at this late hour?"

Should've made the call briefer, he thought.

Covering the phone, he responded, "Oh, nothing, my sweet, just an update from this most-important trial. Be right with you, dearest."

Realizing that he had to wind up the call, lest his wife take it a step further and come into the den, and though the eventful and celebratory news had been disclosed, he could not resist moving the conversation to the other part of the plan. It was his nature, a greedy streak he'd displayed even as a child, to never be satisfied.

"And how about that smug guy, Balkum?" he asked. Anything on that score?"

Tranter wasn't surprised. It was never enough for the prick, he thought, the thrill of a major accomplishment already behind him, now he wanted to hear about the other part of their plan.

"Working on it. Working on it," he repeated. "Planning a launch on that very soon."

"Good, good," Milo answered with the same response. "Can't have too much, you know. Snaring two, beats one," though in truth he realized that Gray was the prize catch, Balkum being just gravy.

"Appreciate the news, keep me updated," he told him, which was his way of ending the call.

Translating the remark, Tranter knew Milo had decided to close their conversation.

"Will do. Have a good evening," he replied, thinking as he hung up, that the man was an ungrateful little bastard. A pat on the head is really all he got from the attorney. The salve was his services did not come cheap. A big payday was coming. He would "forget" to send the disc copies of Gray and Marla fucking until he received and cashed that check.

The call over, Milo then returned from the den. Bessie, still curious, asked, "Who was that Milo, calling at such a late hour?"

A professional at lying, he breezily dismissed her inquiry. "Oh nothing, honeybun, nothing at all. Just Winston letting me know that some new documents arrived." It was an empty answer, but he had made it a point to keep his spouse in the dark about the case from the start, so much so that her knowledge about it had come from the papers and local news, not her spouse. She didn't like it, but accepted it, as Milo had always operated that way for his cases.

Milo, now aware that the outcome of the trial was no longer in doubt, had been tempted to call Winston, but with Bessie's intrusion he decided against it. Besides, it was late and making a call would only further arouse his wife's curiosity. She would know that something was up, though left in the dark about its nature. As there was no urgency to impart the news, he would wait until morning to reveal it.

Though Winston was co-counsel in this litigation, Milo's innately competitive side brought him pleasure that he was the first to learn of the huge development about the judge. He would be the one telling the story, not the other way around.

CHAPTER 8

Though he had arrived home without any incident, other than that gash on his forehead, his unfaithfulness and far too many drinks made for a fitful sleep for Charles Gray that evening. When sleep finally arrived that night, if not for his alarm, which had been preset for 6 a.m., he easily could have overslept, with the resulting late arrival for that day's hearing.

Millie woke with his alarm, her first words inquiring about his very late arrival. "Charles, what is going on?" she asked. "I tried to stay awake, but eventually feel asleep. You were so late last night. It had to be after ten, which was the last time I looked at the clock. I tried calling too, but you never picked up."

He knew an answer was required but he hadn't formulated a convincing lie or really, lies, for his responses.

Lamely, summoning the best story he could fashion, he told her, "Millie, after such a long, stressful, day I admit that I went for a drink, and then I had a second one," he confessed.

At least the start of his story was true.

"Then," he continued, moving to his fabrications, "I forgot some papers, so I returned to the office."

Trying to create some undue sympathy, he continued his tale. "I was at the point of exhaustion, so to be safe and not risk an accident from my drinking, I decided to rest my eyes for a few moments before driving home and before I knew it, I had fallen asleep. When I awoke, it was two hours later. I couldn't call you. It was so late then. As for my phone, I shut the ringer off during the trial and simply forgot to turn it back on. I'm so sorry dear."

She listened, while noting that he had avoided direct eye contact with her during his explanation. Though his answer did not revive her past worries about whether he might have a dalliance, she did not believe that he was telling the whole story. There was no point in challenging him. With so many years of marriage, she knew he would stick to his account. He'd always done it that way. More likely, she thought, he had too many drinks, perhaps even more than the two he admitted having, and needed to sleep it off before driving.

This was not a pleasant conclusion by any means. For several years now, she had expressed her concerns about his drinking habits. At home, she knew first-hand that he'd been drinking more. When not home, she could not know, but surmised that, if anything, his alcohol consumption was likely worse, as he would have no one monitoring his drinking.

Sensing she needed more from him, he continued, offering a contrition, "Dear, I'm so embarrassed about this. I'm truly sorry. It won't happen again. But now, I've got to move fast. Hit the shower and be on my way. Can't be late for the hearing. Already had one late arrival a few days ago due to a fender bender on the interstate."

As he made his promise to her that it wouldn't happen again, he was immediately aware that created a problem for him if he were to hook up a second time with Nicole. There was no ambivalence about that wish. He desperately wanted to see her again. But fashioning an excuse for another late arrival home, he had no idea what he could invent.

One blessing, somehow, she had missed seeing the cut on his forehead, perhaps due to the dim light in their bedroom. It would not escape her attention later that evening, and she would question him about it, for sure. For that mishap, at least he could be truthful about how it came about, though not about the circumstances precipitating it.

As he hurried about in preparation for the commute to the hearing, and as there was no time for further words between them about last night, the press of time allowed an interval to extract himself from her further questioning. He knew she might revisit the subject that evening but hoped she would weigh the point of doing that. Their history together had informed her that no additional information, only more apologies, would be presented by him.

It was a relief to leave the house. As he crept along in the stop-and-go traffic along the I-395 route to the office, the worry over whether Millie would pursue the topic further when he came home preoccupied his trip to D.C. One thing was certain, there would be no stop at the Grill Street after today's trial session. No way. Continuing to consider his return home that evening, he plotted that he couldn't arrive home too soon either, as that would only make her think that there was more to his story. Resolving his plan, he decided that he would time it, stay for a while at the office after the day in court was over, and only then begin the return commute.

Consumed with the tension between his exploit and the successive lies he had to create to pacify his wife, the traffic was particularly maddening to him on this morning. The flow would pick up, unhindered, at 35 miles per hour, then suddenly become a crawl, inching forward and none of it with any apparent causes for the changes.

On top of that, he felt like hell, his head still pounding. Too much booze and too little sleep. It would be difficult to stay sharp all day but he had to do it, just like every day in this marathon of a trial. Careful not to make matters worse by a lapse of attention to the stop and go traffic, risking a fender bender, he still looked at himself in his rearview mirror when the travel would come to a momentary stop. In those glimpses, he knew that he looked terrible, made worse by the obvious gash on his forehead. The blood had dried, and he tried to dab some of it away, but no one could miss it, and applying a bandage would only accent it.

Back home, Millie, unable to fall back to sleep, made a bathroom visit. She felt unsettled. Instinctively she knew her Charles had not been forthcoming. There was more to his story, of that, she was sure. Unable to imagine other causes, for now she concluded it was about his drinking. When finished in the bathroom, while drying her hands, she then noticed that there were two wet bath towels on Charles' side of the towel bar. That's very odd, she thought, recognizing that he had bathed twice – last night and again this morning. The observation left her perplexed. What would bring that about? she wondered.

When Gray arrived at the office there was little time to spare before he had to head to court. After grabbing his notes and stuffing a fresh legal pad in his briefcase, he made a quick check of his appearance in the restroom before leaving. Still looking ragged, he correctly assessed his condition, but nothing could be done about that.

Upon arriving at the courthouse, and donning his robe, he made another appearance check in the private bathroom for his chambers. This time he took a closer look at that gash on his forehead from last night. It was noticeable, but at least not dramatically so. He applied a little water on his hair, trying to have it cover up some of the bruise. That and a check to make sure his tie was straight, was all he could do. Conflicted about last night, he felt some shame as he gazed at his reflection. But, that woman, God help him, she was so alluring. The need to see her again overwhelmed his remorse.

When he entered the courtroom, per usual, all stood, though no bailiff was there to direct that respectful display. He fully knew that he was a lower-tier judge, a product of Article I of the Constitution, not from the far more revered Article III derivations. Still, it was undeniable that he enjoyed the reverential behavior exhibited before him. In that setting, his position commanded respect from all. And, on top of that show of veneration, he'd become an unbelievably lucky guy, having had great sex with a beautiful woman. The gash on his head, the hangover pounder, neither mattered, because there was Nicole. He felt on top of the world.

As he took his seat he looked out at the attorneys, now seated, at the counsel tables. They looked no different than any day over the past two plus weeks of this proceeding. Still, he could not help but wonder, did any of them know, could any of them know, of his extra activities of last night? Of course not, he reassured himself. How could they? Among those now assembled before him, he saw not a soul he recognized during the prior night. Of course, he had not been looking for such familiar faces then either, being preoccupied with Nicole and his attention to those who might spot him diminished by the alcohol. Reassuring himself, he concluded that such thoughts were nothing more than that Christian guilt at work, ingrained since childhood, when he made 'transgressions,' sins they were called. How foolish and neurotic to entertain such irrational thoughts.

From a rational perspective, the judge's fears were strictly neurotic, except that, unknown to him, one side, specifically the two lead attorneys for the litigants did know quite well about the judge's activities of the prior evening. Facially, neither Winston nor Milo displayed any telling look, presenting perfect poker faces before him. They were practiced in displaying such unreadable expressions.

If only he knew, they thought with great satisfaction, the sorry son of a bitch would soon be in much more of a fix than he was aware of at the moment. He was now solidly on the hook and there was no way to get off of it that wouldn't produce disastrous personal and career ending consequences.

Now, in a very real sense, it didn't matter if the defense prevailed on the merits; they would prevail on the demerits – the jurist's ill-advised behavior had sunk him.

Both also noticed the wound on Gray's right forehead. It was very obvious, though how it happened they could not know. Tranter made no mention of that, so it must have occurred after his tryst, perhaps even this morning, they guessed.

Gray, clueless about what he had stepped into, began. "Good morning to all. We are on the record. Are counsel ready to proceed?"

They affirmed that they were. The defense wrapped up its largely ineffective cross-examination of Braun, but now and from this point forward, Milo and Winston were privately upbeat, buoyed by knowing that the outcome of the matter had been determined. It also provided a sense of devilish satisfaction that, except for them, neither the Secretary nor the judge knew of the immense development brought about by the good judge's moral failing. That fact provided a salve for their unproductive attempts to wound the testimony of this second expert.

Though he forced himself to appear attentive, it was a struggle for Gray. There were moments, especially during the afternoon session, when he could feel sleep coming upon him.

Employing an old technique of his, he pinched his thigh hard to get him past it. At each break he also refilled his coffee. The two methods got him through the day. When not fighting off sleep, his mind toggled between the testimony of the expert witness and his frequent thoughts of that captivating woman, Nicole.

Mercifully, when the day finally came to a close, the cross-exam of the Secretary's second expert having concluded, not even the walk back to the office reawakened him. His age showing, nights like the last one, with the drinks and insufficient sleep, had a toll on him. There would be no stopover at the Grill tonight. Just get home, he thought, deal with Millie and get to bed as early as possible.

Once home, though preoccupied over Charles' very late return last night and without answers as to the real explanation for it, Millie elected not to interrogate him further. Relieved that she did bring up the matter again, Gray took the opportunity to tell her how exhausted he was. She could tell that at least that was no lie. He looked spent. And, she wondered, how did he get that gash on his forehead. Maybe, she thought, the real story was that he was so wasted last evening that he took a spill. Thank God, he didn't drive home in that condition. Feeling some sympathy, she agreed with his assessment. Sleep was a necessity for him, especially because there were still two more days of trial ahead for the week.

Gray did not take long to be in bed. So drained from the last two days, he had only one glass of wine before retiring. By morning he was recharged sufficiently that he was ready to face the day.

With the trial now past the mid-week mark, the government called its last expert, another impressively credentialed witness holding an Ivy League doctorate, James Limler. He was the Secretary's numbers guy. It did not take long for

Gray to get lost in the expert's explanation of his statistical analyses and this was true of both sides' attorneys. No one in the room completely followed his mathematical explanations, though all acted as if they did. It was tedious, but absolutely necessary, stuff, with the doctor laboriously explaining the foundation for his numbers and just that introduction took the entire morning.

Lunch was a welcome break from the numbness they experienced with the doctor's presentation, though the doctor himself was unaware that no one else found the information interesting.

When the afternoon session began, the mathematical basis having been set for the expert's conclusions, he was free to move to the heart of the matter – his conclusions from all the data. These AWCs, he stated authoritatively, were not random across all coal mines. Further, shortly after the date that the mining industry learned that MSHA had discovered the AWCs and began a void code for the dubious dust samples, the AWCs had a marked decline which was not otherwise explainable.

As with the experts that preceded him, Malthan didn't like the cocksure certainty that accompanied Limler's testimony. Seemed to draw from the same highfalutin playbook as those other guys, Palmer and Braun. Acted like he was reading from stone tablets and not just expressing his opinions, he thought. And some of his expressions were especially annoying, like his use of the phrase that once it became known that the government was on to the AWC's that "the cat was out of the bag."

Though Winston objected to that expression, Gray overruled it, advising that it was within the realm of reasonable description. That only served to highlight the expert's expression, a tactical error reinforcing the words in Gray's head.

Sanford suppressed a smile.

From a purely evidentiary basis, the defense had taken three solid hits with the parade of the Secretary's experts. That would have been greatly worrisome for them but for the ultimate card they held – Gray's objectivity had evaporated, though even he did not know it yet.

Ironically, the defense did not know what Larkin was all too aware of – Gray was already listing heavily in their direction. But, even if they had been privy to the judge's leanings, they were not about to let the outcome of the case turn on his predilection. Not on a case of this industry-wide magnitude.

Unable to go toe-to-toe with the doctor's math expertise, the defense was left with the usual cross-examination repertoire, noting that he had been hired by the Secretary to do his numbers analysis. Sanford took note of it, but he did not mind it. He considered it as another strategical error by the Respondent, thinking of that 'what's good for the goose is good for the gander' expression. Go ahead, he thought, impugn the witness by noting that he had paid for his work. Those two, Winston and Milo, had not thought sufficiently ahead, as they could not prevail in an objection to Secretary posing the same question to each of their experts. If viewed as a chess move by them, it was dumb, he thought, a momentary point scored by them but soon to be cancelled during the government's cross-exams of the Respondent's own experts.

Other than the short-term gain, the best the defense could do was to have the expert repeat the grounds for his determinations, hardly an effective strategy. Though they did not like that approach, as it meant that the judge would be hearing the basis for his views again, they believed it was necessary to set the stage for their own math expert who would dispute everything this Limler guy was spouting.

It took all of that day for Limler to complete his testimony on redirect. Seeing no advantage, the defense announced they had no more questions for the witness.

For Gray, having had a decent night's sleep, it was quite manageable compared with the day before. Again, he knew better than to visit the Grill. Foregoing it served two purposes. He still needed another solid night of sleep to be fully restored and returning directly home would allay any lingering concerns Millie might still be harboring.

When he did arrive home, she was visibly pleased about it. Though he could not know, it did work to lessen her speculative concerns. Their recent routine had returned and, on this night, he provided an unprompted review of the day's trial testimony. Though far from the truth, his retelling further served to reassure her that all was as it had been. With their quietude ostensibly restored, he was able to prepare dinner, have his wine, and go to bed, all as before that recent night.

By midday on Friday, the Secretary's presentation had been completed. Taking three weeks, the team assured themselves that they had made a first-rate case. Other than Tucker and Grasser's mundane testimony, all the other witnesses, including Benny Skeens, had been solid.

Timing wise, Malthan and Krakovich wanted to stall. Starting the defense on a Friday afternoon was anything but propitious. Ending the week at noon would give them a fresh start for the upcoming week in addition to providing them the opportunity to have the weekend to review and polish their defense.

Malthan approached Sanford to see if he was willing to jointly ask the Court that the proceedings adjourn after returning from lunch. Sanford was in no mood to be accommodating. As he saw it, those two had not been particularly cordial, repeatedly launching specious objections, and otherwise trying to throw the government's witnesses off stride. Why give them any unearned concessions?

Winston and Milo discussed the issue over lunch.

"That prick Sanford," Milo began, "We certainly would have consented to adjourn with only a half-day left in the week."

That was a lie. The two of them would have objected strenuously if the Secretary were making the request.

Winston nodded in agreement, though also knowing that was untrue. "Well, then," he continued, "what do you want to do?"

"We could eat up some time, when we resume," Milo answered. "I know we could spend nearly an hour in moving for a directed verdict. And I'll slow my tempo. Not too slow, of course, that would annoy Gray, but enough to irritate Sanford. I'll enjoy that. Then, Sanford would need to spend a like amount of time to defend against it."

Continuing, he added, "We will lose the motion, of course. I've only had two cases in my career where I prevailed on such a motion and this one won't be my third. Then, with so few hours left, I will ask the judge if we could end the day and start fresh next week. I can talk about the benefit for everyone by having continuity with the witness's testimony, making it much easier for everyone to follow if it is not broken up, especially with two days off before resuming on Monday."

"Throw in that you asked the government if they would agree to call it a day, but that they refused. Might as well suggest that they're acting unreasonably," Milo added, a crooked grin accompanying his remark.

When the trial resumed following lunch, the government announced that, subject to testimony it might offer in rebuttal to whatever the respondents presented, it rested.

To no one's surprise, the Respondents immediately moved for a directed verdict. It went as predicted and planned. Deliberately slowing the pace of his oration, Milo ate up more than an hour presenting his motion.

As predictable as sunrise, the Respondents spent considerable time asserting that, especially when considering the "unassailable" points they made during cross-examination, the government had utterly failed to make out their case. Overstating the strength of their cross-examinations, a trademark of the two, they maintained no reliable evidence had been presented to show that the respondents had tampered with the cassettes. Why the government itself, they smartly maintained, could not even handle their own cassettes without dropping them, a reminder that Miss Nelson's clumsiness started this whole "adventure" as Milo called it.

Sanford knew that the directed verdict motion would be coming, with those motions appearing in nearly every Mine Act case that went to a hearing. As such, he treated it as the routine maneuver it was. While not threatened by it, he also knew that it was important and not something to be presumed to fail. Not in a case like this. That would be foolish. With the risk of losing his opposition to the motion being very remote, it was still a worry, and so he presented a full-throated, point-by-point, rebuttal to the Respondent's arguments.

Though his opposition in response to the motion was shorter, it was approaching 3 o'clock when he had finished.

The Respondent then called for the matter to pause until Monday, ostensibly to give the Court time to ponder the arguments presented in the motion. They then added an additional benefit to a pause. Now, as they had planned, with less than two hours left in the day, they asserted that the continuity of the Respondent's first witness would be broken and if that happened, Milo suggested that it would take almost as much time to review that testimony on Monday, to refresh everyone about Friday's testimony, before moving on with new matter from that witness. In short, he informed that there would be no real time saved by launching the testimony from the first witness so late in the day, and just before the weekend.

Gray knew full well how he would rule on the motion for a directed verdict. It would be foolish, and rapidly reversed, if he were to grant the motion in a case of this magnitude. Applying the test for such a motion in favor of the Respondent would require him to find that there was no legally sufficient evidentiary basis to find that the cassettes had been tampered.

Based on the testimony presented by the Secretary, a directed verdict could not stand appellate review. It would be thrown back for sure. And, he would look foolish too, holding that the evidence presented was so lacking that no reasonable judge could find for the Secretary. The only gain, if one could call it that, would be a delay in the hearing for a few weeks, at most.

Then, it would be back to it, the result being the time for the thing to be over had been extended. Who would opt for that, prolonging the matter! There was also the consideration that when it inevitably did resume, he would be in the posture of having been reversed. No judge wants that, especially before a decision on the merits had even been issued. Though technically only a mild slap, it still meant he had been corrected, wounded in a sense.

While he was instantly amenable to calling the week to an earlier end, he had to hear from Sanford before ruling. The government noted that it had not sought breaks in the presentation of its case, and that both sides had sufficient time to prepare well before the hearing began, now virtually three weeks ago. The case, Sanford responded, should proceed apace.

Gray paused for only a moment, then spoke. "I endorse the Respondent's suggestion. It makes sense, as I believe that it will assist me in assimilating the testimony if we start promptly on Monday." Remembering his late arrival, he continued, "and I assure all of you that I will leave for court even earlier next week to avoid any delay due to traffic, like the one that occurred before."

He then continued, "I also want to fully consider the Respondent's motion for a directed verdict. I certainly don't want to be rushed for such an important decision. The weekend will afford me with the opportunity to fully consider it." He then paused, adding a word of criticism. "In the future, I urge both sides to work together in accommodating one another on issues like this."

It was, Sanford understood, an implicit criticism of the government's unwillingness to end the week early, but he didn't care. The other side had not been the model of cooperation.

Though Gray asserted that he would be contemplating the directed verdict motion over the weekend, Milo and Winston believed he was pretending.

Sanford took Gray's words seriously, even as he reassured himself that it was very unlikely that he would rule against MSHA. Still, as the government was the only side at risk, he could not help but worry.

Gray believed that his assertion for adjourning came across as genuine but, his acting abilities aside, his mind was made up. In his long years of trying these cases, only once had he ever ruled in favor of a directed verdict and that was because the government had rested after relying on the wrong enforcement regulation. Still, from a theatrics point of view and given all the publicity that had attended this case, he advised that he would take the motion under advisement, a dishonest suggestion that he would need to give it the weighty consideration it deserved. Affording himself an early end to the day with the small time remaining, under the pretense that he would be deeply considering the merits of the motion, he concluded the day's proceeding.

Unavoidably, it continued to worry Sanford that no immediate ruling would be announced by Gray. Typically, such rulings were made with no delay, so it was an unusual and unexpected development, not one to be brushed off. There was nothing more he could do.   He had made his forceful objections to the motion and now he and the team would have to wait. Though he still believed the motion would be rejected, he could not help but think of the hailstorm of condemnation that would follow if it were granted. Worrying further, though he believed such an adverse decision would be overruled on appeal, the critics of the MSHA litigation team would be lined up for several blocks, he thought to himself. The expression that victory has a thousand fathers, but defeat is an orphan, came immediately to mind.

As for the Respondent, Milo thought there was only a slim chance that the delay in the ruling could mean an early victory, but it was an outcome that he did not want. Just as Gray recognized, he knew the win would quickly turn into a loss, the standard for rejecting a directed verdict being so low. And it would have achieved nothing. A delay of several weeks offered no advantage. Christ, he thought, Gray, old as he was, he could kick the bucket, topple over from a cardiac arrest. Then where would they be! The whole triumph from Marla's services for naught! Too late now, as he thought maybe they should have passed on the directed verdict motion entirely.

Winston had no such pipe dreams. Gray was too careful to grant the motion. Denying it presented no risk. As a matter entirely within the trial court's discretion, he knew that the judge would never be reversed by denying their motion. Heck, it wasn't even appealable!

Upon adjourning the proceeding, Gray promptly returned to his office. With the remainder of his afternoon ostensibly burdened, he knew in fact that he would not need to spend any time at all considering the motion. Better yet, he would not even have to make a statement in support of his ruling. The terse, "upon consideration, the Respondent's motion is denied," was all that he would need to say and that was exactly what he would do, but not until Monday. The downside was that he could not literally have the remainder of the afternoon off. He would have to stay at the office until the day's end. That's the way it was for administrative law judges. Article III judges had no such constraints – they could just leave for the day, any day, with no questions asked.

The thought of next Monday's predetermined and perfunctory ruling required no more of his time. Even if it had, only one thought occupied his mind now. Nicole. Nicole. Nicole. What a joyous trouble-free life she would provide for him, he fantasized, his thoughts unburdened from any of the realities such a relationship would bring.

Enthralled, wanting so much to be with her again, he gave in to his urges, calling her on his cell from his office, his door firmly closed. Still, careful about the risk that someone might overhear him, he scooted his chair over to the office window, with the added precaution of speaking in a soft voice.

She recognized his number immediately. Her experience in these matters made her confident that he would be calling, so it was no surprise, except perhaps that it was so soon, only a few days later, and he was already wanting to drop his pants again.

"Nicole," he began, "it's Charles. Wondering how you've been," a lie of sorts, because it hid the real reason for his call.

Just wondering how I've been, she smiled over his opening remark. Right. She knew full well why he was calling; there was no misconception on her part.

"Hi Charles," she responded. "How nice to hear from you. In fact, I've been thinking of calling you," she informed. That part was true, but not for the reason Gray presumed. If the good judge needed a nudge, it was planned that she would call him, but not until the following week.

'Nicole,' Marla to most, had already discussed the plan with Tranter. Bed him one more time, then she would be done, her mission completed. That way, by having a repeat performance, on a video disc again of course, there could be no claim that the sex was a one-off terrible mistake, an error of judgment that was never repeated.

A person, perhaps even a judge, the Winston-Milo team considered, could be forgiven for one mistake.

But not two.

She didn't mind a second linking. He was old, and a bit crusty due to that advanced age, but he was presentable and clean, so it was okay by her. She'd slept with worse, sad to say. Besides, she was being paid handsomely for this assignment.

The preliminary niceties out of the way, it did not take long for Charles to bring up the real purpose behind his call.

"I was asking myself if we might see each other again," he asked with uncertainty apparent in his tone.

"I'd like that, Charles," she said, with no hesitation, feigning enthusiasm for the suggestion to shore up his lack of confidence.

He smiled at the news. "Glad you feel the same," he replied, clueless that it was contrived. "I know this is short notice but is it possible we could meet say mid-afternoon Monday?" He added immediately, "I understand it's so soon and afternoons may be ill-timed, with your work and all. It's just that Monday's proceeding will be ending early."

It would end early, something that only he knew, because he would proclaim that it would end early, such decisions being a benefit of his presiding in the case.

Marla figured it all out. If this weren't business, and she had a legitimate conflict in her schedule, she would have sought a different day and time. But this *was* business, marking her second payday for it and part of her job was to accommodate the 'old fool.' It was the first time that description entered her head.

'Old fool,' she thought, well, that's what he was! So many men, she thought, let the little head make the decisions. Anyone who read the newspapers would know this. Every year, the papers routinely reported of new, prominent, men who would fall hard to the lure of the flesh, discarding their existing relationships, their vows, and their obligations, in pursuit of what was, in truth, unattainable, but for which they were blind.

And Marla didn't have to read the papers to know of this. She knew it firsthand, with this assignment only being the latest example.

"I can adjust my schedule, Charles, no problem," she said pleasantly.

"Say, around 1:30. Is that too early?"

"Not at all," she responded without pausing. In truth, any time would have worked, because it had to work.

"Shall we meet at the G Street?" he asked.

"Well, if it's all the same to you, Charles, and you don't think I'm being too forward, let's meet at my hotel."

'Too forward,' she thought, as if anything she could say in that regard could be too audacious. They'd already fucked once. There was no need to start from square one again.

Nor was the Grill in any sense someplace special. This was merely a follow-up assignation of sorts, but certainly not one between lovers, no matter what Charles' imagination may have created. No, this was between an old fool and an employee of Marty Tranter, nothing more.

If she ever were to have a genuine relationship, something she had not had in several years, it certainly would not be with someone as ancient and financially unsuccessful as Gray. She knew she still had the looks and could do better based on that alone.

He was joyous at the suggestion. It meant there would be no risk that someone would see him at the Grill. And what would Jerome think, he thought, arriving in the early afternoon, several hours before his routine time, and in the company of a stunning woman, so much younger than he.

Other risks were present too. There were regulars at the place, though he did not know if they frequented the place so early in the day. But if they were present, he could be spotted and everyone would take note of the attention-grabbing woman in his company. Given those risks of being identified, he realized that his suggestion to meet at the Grill was boneheaded.

What a relief with Nicole's suggestion to go straight to her hotel suite, the two of them secreted away with no prying eyes to observe, he thought. She had saved him from those risks. It was perfect. Seeing her again and so soon. Better yet, he would be home by his regular time on Monday. He couldn't risk another late return so soon after the recent one.

"That sounds like a wonderful idea," he answered with enthusiasm. And especially because it meant there would be no need to convince her to go from the G Street to her hotel. She made the suggestion and the invitation. It also meant, plainly, that they would be making love for sure, he thought, avoiding any crass description of the upcoming activity as fucking.

The thought of being with her, and with only the weekend intervening, left him stimulated. He noted the arousal it produced, silently complimenting himself, a smile appearing with it. At his age and still able to get excited just thinking about what was ahead. No blue pills needed for this guy, he thought to himself, proud of his still strong virility.

"Do you remember my room number?"

"Of course," he reassured. "So, I'll see you at 1:30 then."

"I'll be waiting for you, Charles," she said warmly, as if they'd been seeing one another for a long time, not just once before.

He hung up the phone a happy man. Given the anticipation, and the excitement that would launch on Monday, there was no purpose for a stopover at the G Street on this night. Besides, with the planned rendezvous, his other, and new, purpose for visiting the Grill was no longer needed. *She* would be seeing him in three days.

A bonus, arriving home on time this evening would please Millie. His conscience momentarily tabled; he would be presenting himself as her dutiful husband. Perhaps she would view it as making up for his late arrival at the start of the week.

On his return commute, putting aside his upcoming infidelity, he boldly praised himself for his conduct, driving directly home, with no stopover at the bar. She would notice the absence of alcohol on his breath when they exchanged their asexual kiss. Hopefully his improved return time home would cause her to drop further interrogation about his late arrival earlier that week.

Scheming, he shamelessly considered how the upcoming Monday rendezvous, with the bonus of it being an afternoon delight, would also mean another early return home, albeit with the scent of alcohol present. He hoped she would not wonder how he could be home without delay, yet still have the odor of booze. That wouldn't add up, so he would need to invent a story.

He knew it was important to think about things like that ahead of time, so that he would not be flatfooted if she commented about it. Simple, he thought, I will just tell her that the hearing ended early. At least that part would be true.

Then he would leave the truth behind, informing that he decided to take a break by having a single drink before his commute home. A plus, he would have explained away the alcohol on his breath, and she could not tell where he had the booze nor how many he had consumed. One drink or three on his breath, she could not tell the number he consumed. No one could.

Still plotting over Monday's rendezvous, he then thought it was important that he limit his drinks with Nicole. No more than two, he thought, to avoid any driving under the influence issue.

Millie was in fact pleased that her Charles was not late, with three days having passed since that very late arrival home, her concerns began to ebb and her belief that his story was true grew.

Thoughts of Monday remained on the forefront of Gray's mind the entire weekend. Unlike most weekends, he was visibly upbeat this time, a state that Millie observed and took note of. "You seem rather bouncy, Charles. I must say I haven't seen you with such a cheery attitude in a very long time. Something good happen?" she asked.

"Nope," he reassured, offering a plausible excuse, "just pleased that the government's side of the case is over. At the half-way mark, so to speak."

If she knew, Charles thought, if she knew. He was unflustered by his wife's intuition. He had to be, fully realizing that disaster that would ensue for the marriage and her health, if she learned of his cheating. Though aware of the great harm he was risking, the pull to see Nicole was too strong for him to reverse course. He would not miss their meeting.

His story was believable, so Millie, ignorant of the truth, smiled back at him, proud of her husband and happy that the end would soon be in sight for the long and demanding trial.

CHAPTER 9

Mount Hope, the sleepy little town where Greg Balkum lived and worked had a population of barely more than a thousand. Balkum favored it, despite its shopping shortcomings, as it was a quiet, peaceful community. Its size meant that nearly everyone had at least a passing familiarity with fellow citizens. Lots of waving to one another in various local settings. With few drawbacks, he viewed the location as a plus. Traffic jams, those were for the unlucky souls in the big cities.

As for those supposedly better places to live, the ones with all those big-name stores and multiple shopping malls, he did not consider the stress and havoc at those more metropolitan areas to be worth it. He knew whereof he spoke, as for several years he worked in the greater Pittsburgh area at MSHA's Approval and Certification Center. The daily commute would cause his stomach to churn. It seemed there was a road problem every week. And, even when there was no traffic accident or construction work to impede the trip, on those so-called smooth days, the commute was still a slog, the sheer volume being the culprit. Cycles of speeding up, and rapidly slowing down, with no discernable source for it, were all part of the inescapable routine.

He had grown up in the small West Virginia town of Hurricane, an odd name since there had not been any storms of that force during his childhood and adolescence. Mount Hope, only 80 miles away from the residence of his youth, brought back that familiarity, the towns being similar in size and slow-paced.

He admitted to his wife that their location wasn't perfect. Of course, no place was idyllic. But the unhurried atmosphere, the quiet if offered, all easier on one's nerves, those were the things that counted in his mind. His wife would've preferred something busier, more upscale.

A drive through the small community bespoke of people of very modest means. Their house, one of the better residences, still was tired looking. As it stood, not updated, it was a reminder of much earlier times, well before they moved there, when those houses, as initially built, must have been impressive. There had been more industry there, back in the day, but when it left, slowly, one business after another, the community sagged from the departures.

Now, even among those houses remaining from that past heyday, they were so dated that no real reclamation was possible. It would cost a fortune. Razing was the only realistic option but, if that happened, why begin anew there? One wouldn't need to travel far to find better surroundings. Why, Beckley and Fayetteville, both less than twenty miles away, were far superior, and that was objectively speaking, not a mere personal evaluation. But, Greg, well, he still liked where he was, along with the ten-minute, hassle-free, commute to work. He would mention, too often, Karen thought, how much money they were saving on gasoline. It wasn't as if they couldn't afford the cost of a longer commute. But, as he was the primary income earner, his vote on where they lived carried greater weight. Her job, a clerical position at the logging supply business in town brought in less than a third of his salary.

Faithfully, each Friday, Greg would make the six plus hour drive from the Washington trial location to his home. The traffic on Friday evenings was a frustrating slow trek, reminiscent of his Pittsburgh days. And it would not lighten until he reached Manassas. Though that part of the journey was only thirty-five miles, it was a time-consuming leg which could eat up an hour and half or more, a weekly reminder of how much he hated the congested drive lifestyle. How could people endure it, he thought, week after week, driving from the surrounding suburbs of Virginia and Maryland into the Capitol?

Usually, after reaching Manassas, the pace would steadily pick up, as he continued along I-66 and then to I-81, at Strasburg. At that point, by speeding, but only ten above the limit, he could make up for some of the lost time. By the time he reached Lexington, then on I-64, his last leg, and still on the interstates, he had two hours left, no small distance. But at least the tumultuous world was then behind him and he would be home, usually by eleven. Once home, he tried to avoid thinking about the Monday return trip to D.C. which involved the same wretched commute. With each trip, he longed for the time when the trial would end, his former hectic-free routine again in place.

Though spent from the long drive between home and D.C., the twice-a-week affair, Greg still did the family grocery shopping. It involved his routine jaunt to the major chain in Beckley, a reminder that Mount Hope had its drawbacks. He dismissed his town's shopping shortcoming, though his wife would periodically remind him of that fact, as the store was only some twenty, no-hassle, miles away from his home. Before the start of the 'dust tampering' trial, as he insisted on calling the ongoing litigation whenever the subject came up, he would shop on Thursday evenings after work. The choice of that night was not random. It was another way to avoid the weekend shopping crowds. For the time being he had to alter that routine, the grocery shopping now done on late Saturday afternoons, a less busy time of the day.

Nearby Beckley, West Virginia, was Ruby Mae Stone's home town. She'd grown up there, at least chronologically, though her mother, Emma, would keep imploring her trouble-prone daughter, "Ruby Mae, when are you going to grow up and do right?'

Trouble had been a trait of her youngest, even before her teens, the difference being that the trouble she got herself into grew more serious as her age advanced. It didn't help that there was no Mr. Stone to help corral the wild-minded teen. As Emma told her neighbors about her spouse, he just 'up and left' one day. Not that he was any kind of a proper father figure when he was present. He would routinely come home late, after an evening of carousing. Quiet was not his style. Given his loutish behavior, he was not missed by anyone in the family.

All of that meant, even before that sorry excuse of a husband actually left for good, that it fell upon Emma to mind the two daughters on her own.

Now, with Ruby in her mid-twenties, she had not yet heeded her mother's pleas. "Why can't you do like your older sister?" she would ask, more of a plea than a command.

Ruby had no use for her oh-so-perfect sister, Laura, or her ways. Never seeing her as a model, she resented her big sister. A licensed practical nurse, her sibling was, but the younger Stone was not impressed at all. Being around sick people all day, who would want that! Laura, Miss goodie two shoes, always with the top grades and on the student council too, those achievements were simply beyond the younger sibling's capabilities.

Ruby, to her mother's heartbreak and continual dismay, had taken a starkly different road from Laura. Drugs, they were a part of it, along with two arrests for prostitution, both eventually dropped, thank God, through that 'continued without a finding' business her mother learned of during the court proceedings. Set her back financially quite a bit too, with those burdensome lawyer and court fees, as if she could afford them. Despite her younger daughter's promises that she would pay her back, Emma was not fooled. Never got a nickel from her.

It was in connection with those arrests that Tranter, through his contacts, had learned about Ruby Mae. In her court appearances, there are observers who see potential value in girls like her. There was no denying that she was hot, a real looker as they say, and not burdened with things like right and wrong, just the kind of girl who could be brought aboard with money for jobs employing her promiscuous ways. She was the perfect lure to catch a straying husband for a wife who had enough of the cheating.

People like Tranter were known to the divorce lawyers, and they spotted girls like Ruby, in court for other problems, as useful to ensure that a soon to be ex-husband would settle on very favorable terms to his spouse. And if the straying husband had any kind of public face in his occupation, so much the better for the terms of the settlement.

Tranter had reached out to Ruby weeks ago and to his satisfaction, the girl had done her homework. While she had never been diligent in her formal schooling, careless in fact, managing to frequently have failing grades, even in the lenient times for education performance, when it came to assignments to ensnare an unfaithful husband, she got A's.

But this job was distinctly atypical for her, as the setups usually occurred in bars. Drinks always made the subjects easier to entrap.

However, Balkum was no drinker and his home life was stable, so a different approach was required – beginning with a staged fender bender incident. It was the best Tranter could improvise for this subject. He had tried to dissuade Milo and Winston from it, advising that the Technology Center director wasn't burdened with the judge's weaknesses, but those two wouldn't take no for an answer. That Gray had succumbed didn't lessen their zeal to catch a second one. Two hooked fish would turn the focus of the whole litigation to government miscreants, the coal dust case taking a back seat.

So, ordered to do it, Tranter had equipped Ruby with a junker car for this assignment, along with a phony driver's license, providing a new name and address. Given photos of Balkum and the make, model and color of his car, together with his license plate, Ruby could easily identify her mark. Tranter had also learned that, like the good Judge Gray, the supervisor of the Mt. Hope office was also a creature of habit. Since the onset of the trial, he would dependably show up at the Super Foods Market, customarily on Saturdays, around dusk.

Ruby had been given her instructions for this Saturday and she was ready to set the plan in motion. Though an unfamiliar routine, a parking lot, instead of a bar, Ruby immediately spotted his car as Balkum showed up at his usual time, watching him as he entered the store.   It was better to position her car so that the 'mishap' would occur after Balkum finished his shopping when backing out of his parking location. That meant, if possible, having her car in the row immediately behind Balkum's space. It still would have worked had she been positioned a space or two opposite his car, but directly in line with his spot was the best location for the planned accident.

As she idled in the row behind where Balkum had parked, she waited, patiently, hoping that the driver of the car directly in back of Balkum's space would leave. Although she knew it was not essential to claim that space, with shoppers frequently coming and going, there would likely be sufficient time for that prized space to open up.

Luck prevailed as, before long, the targeted space freed up and Ruby, posed to take it, immediately moved for it, beating a late comer who tried to overtake her for the same space. Securing the spot was not so easy, as the interloper aggressively wanted the space too, and the two cars nearly collided. If the competition had occurred at a time when she had been there simply to shop, she would have stayed in her car, afraid that winning the duel for the opening would exact payback by the loser, slashing a tire or keying her car. Things like that could happen. Having no reason to leave her car this time, she looked straight ahead but watched the other driver eye her car as he walked past it on his way to the store.

Securely in the optimum space, she now had only to wait for her prey to exit the store.

Before long, she observed him leaving the store, pushing a cart full of grocery bags to his parking spot and then loading up his car with the week's needs. Patiently waiting for the moment, her car idling, Ruby was stationed right where she needed to be, in the row and space directly opposite the unwitting supervisor's spot.

She waited for the moment when Balkum got behind the wheel, watching him as he secured his seat belt and then observed him checking his rearview mirror, readying to leave.

He had only backed out a few feet when she went into action. In seconds, the two cars collided.

She had to be careful, ensuring that the impact did not seriously dent his car. Such a development would upend the plan. If his car were to become disabled, requiring a tow truck, and worse, meaning there would be police involvement, she would have to abort the scheme immediately. The goal was a dent, taking along a tail light if possible; meaning damage that could not simply be waived off, but with both drivers deciding it was unnecessary to summon the police.

Her effort worked. She was pleased with her skill, producing a modest dent on the car's rear fender and shattering that side's tail light. Perfect, she thought, he could still drive his car but the damage meant that an insurance claim and a body shop visit would be needed.

With no delay after the collision, she sprung out of her car. "You smacked me pretty good!" she asserted, acting upset and tearful as she pointed to the damage to her car's left front fender. "I lost a headlight too and now it's dark," informing him of her plight.

Balkum was caught completely off-guard. He was sure he checked before backing up, as he always did. No car was approaching, nor did he see any car leaving a space. His driving record had been impeccable. As he further considered the development, he recalled there was no car with its headlights on, a necessity at this time of the evening. In that respect, he was correct. To carry out the surprise crash, Ruby knew she would need to keep her lights off until the impact, then switch them on.

Regaining his composure from the startling event, Balkum asserted his side of it.

"Now wait just a minute," he answered with authority in his tone of voice, "I believe it was *you* who struck my car."

Ruby, practiced as she was in confrontations, would have none of it.

With certainty in her reply she informed, "That's not so. You were backing up. You're supposed to check before you back up!" she said critically.

Though in the middle of their opposing contentions, Balkum's hormones were simultaneously at work, as he couldn't help but notice the driver's attention-grabbing appearance. She was undeniably attractive and quite young, in her twenties he guessed. And what a figure, voluptuous was the description that came to his mind. He'd always had a weakness for that.

And his assessment did not require guesswork. Even though it was chilly that evening, her fluffy faux-fur coat was, quite deliberately, partially open, displaying a revealing and seductive top, which had some kind of sparkling dots all over it, her breasts incompletely covered. Very odd, he thought, to be dressed like that in a grocery center parking lot, more like a dancer's outfit at a gentlemen's club.

None of this should been going on in his head, but Balkum was human. He still had eyes and was not oblivious to provocatively dressed women.

His claim, Ruby knew, would be difficult to establish. Both cars were in the middle of the travel lane, about equidistant in it at the collision point.

"Respectfully sir," as she purposely toned down her response, "it was your mistake," she said authoritatively.

Using a term like 'respectfully' was not part of her usual lexicon. 'That's a bunch of bullshit' would be her typical response, but this was business and the plan was to reach an accommodation, not to elevate the dispute.

But Balkum could tell this dispute was going nowhere and with their cars blocking the travel lane, they couldn't remain there, arguing about it. A few cars, impatient about the holdup, had already started honking.

"Look," Balkum told her, "We're going to need to move our cars out of the travel lane and exchange our insurance information and all that stuff."

Now appearing civil, Ruby agreed.

After the two moved their cars out of the roadway, Balkum retrieved his information from his glovebox and walked to her car.

She produced her information too, but held onto it.

It was at that moment that she presented a starkly different tone.

"Look," she said, going for maximum sympathy, "I just got laid off. I don't need this grief. Is there any way we could resolve this informally? I mean, you see my car. Not exactly a gem."

"I don't know what you're suggesting," he told her. "Are you saying, just forget the circumstances and just file our own claims, as if we didn't know how this came about?"

That was not his style, one lie begets another, he would often say.

"Well, that's one way to deal with this," she responded, now smiling and reaching towards him, placing a hand on his wrist. "See, I don't have insurance right now. Came upon hard times. My registration is about to expire too."

He was momentarily dumbfounded by her remark.

She went for it. "What I'm saying is I can make it worth both our while to solve this another way, more friendly like," she said, now adding a coquettish smile, along with a light squeeze to his hand.

He recoiled. Maybe when he was very young, before his marriage, the little head would have considered her proposal. Not now. Temptations had come along a few times in his years, but he had stopped short of violating his vows. He'd remained faithful to his wife and wasn't about to go down that road now.

Responding to her proposal, a firm look came over his face.

"Look, I don't know what you mean or what you're up to, but I'll tell you what, this calls for the police to be brought in, that's what. So, I'm going to do that right now," as he reached for his phone.

Ruby panicked. She'd been turned down before, but not often, and never like this. The police! she thought, this would all unravel in minutes if that happened. They would know in short order just who she was. Handcuffs would follow.

"You're just a hick jerk!" she told him, as she abruptly turned, and moved quickly to her car.

"Wait, you can't leave. There's been an accident here," he yelled.

"Screw you!" she answered, falling back on her usual vocabulary, saying nothing more as she then jumped inside her car.

Stunned by the development, he still had the good sense to take a picture of her car with his phone but, as for her, he could only take shots of her backside, hardly helpful for identification.

In less than a minute, she had taken off, having the presence of mind to keep her car lights off as she left.

Balkum took a few more photos but it was dark now and the parking lot lighting was spotty. Examining the photos, he could not be sure her license plate would be detectible, even when enlarged. As he increased the image, he saw that the plate number was obscure.

Tranter took care of such things; the plates were old and faded. Also, Ruby, per his instructions, had muddied them up.

He would only have the car make and color to offer the police. Not much help.

The police arrived in a short time, but Ruby was long gone. Balkum explained the incident to them, informing that that they had not exchanged their registrations when she made the proposal, which he asserted was an offer of sex for dropping the whole fender bender incident.

THE MINE SAFETY TRILOGY PART II

When he showed the officers the photos from his phone, as he feared, while the make of the car was clear, the color and the license plate were not. Provided with the officers' contact information, he then emailed the photos to one of them.

Although, they advised that they would try to enhance and enlarge the images, they told him frankly that the prospects for better resolution were not good. They wrote up a report on the spot, reading it back to him to see if he agreed with it and he confirmed that it was accurate.

They didn't doubt his story and they had seen a few crash scams like this in their experience, but those were about insurance claims. This was the first time that sex was claimed to be part of the story.

While they didn't come right out and say it, it was clear that the officers held out little prospect that anything would come of their investigation. Though he was upset by the event, the officers' tone conveyed that they didn't share Balkum's reaction; it simply was not an event commanding significant investigative resources. Scams happen all the time.

With no more that could be done at the time, and with the prospect that nothing would come of it either, Balkum remembered his manners, thanking the police for their efforts. They responded in kind, politely informing that they would be in touch if anything developed, but everyone knew, it was the end of the matter.

Upon returning to his car, and now neurotically careful as he again backed out of the space, he remained irritated that such a thing would ever occur and on the only two days he had off. Some way to enjoy his weekend, while this whole stressful trial was going on!

As he drove home, his thoughts shifted from the need to contact his insurance carrier about the damage to his car, and concern whether the frozen items from his shopping would need to be tossed, but he kept returning to the weird event of that evening. And just what could he tell his insurance company? That some woman intentionally hit his car and then propositioned him?

He couldn't lie about what occurred, making up a story that after he finished shopping, he then saw the damage to his car. That's not how he behaved. And he knew, insurance companies being in the business of denying claims where possible, wouldn't just pay up for the damages. No, he was sure they would say further investigation was needed. Contemplating that headache, he realized making a claim would be more trouble than it was worth. He would just have to eat the repair costs.

It then belatedly dawned on him that perhaps it was not a fluke occurrence with the promiscuous young woman. He had never experienced anything like that in all his years. The possibility that it was a setup began to grow in his mind. He couldn't be sure, of course, but it started to make more sense than what it appeared to be on the surface. Who would make such sexual overtures in that setting, a grocery store parking lot of all places. It was absurd. And then she flees?

By the time he reached home he had concluded that the only logical answer was that it was connected with the trial. This had to have been a scheme, and he did not have to ponder long who was behind it. Just had to be those disreputable attorneys for the mine.

Once home, he immediately recounted the bizarre event to his wife. Her first reaction was astonishment that such a thing could occur, but she did not hesitate in agreeing that there had to be something more at work. Things like that were too abnormal; they just didn't happen. Something had to be up and it was only logical to conclude that it was very likely connected with her husband's central role in the big case. It defied logic to accept the event on its face.

Reassured by her affirming that he was not being paranoid about the likely source for the event and that it was logical to associate it with his testimony in the ongoing trial, he told her that he would be calling Sanford later the next day. Though he realized that the government attorney would not be able to do anything about the news, and that tomorrow would be Sunday, he could not wait to until he was back in D.C. to inform him about the strange development. He just had to know if Sanford had the same take on it.

While Balkum had the comfort of telling his wife about the strange occurrence, Ruby Mae Stone had no one to confide with about her own disastrous experience. She felt in a near panic state over the turn of events. Nothing like this had ever happened to her, and she shuddered to think about how it could have developed, if cops had been nearby. A patrol car in the shopping center was not unusual. The whole thing could have unraveled if one had come upon the scene, and that asshole, Balkum, he would've raised holy hell to the police about it. She would've been arrested for Christ's sake! she thought.

After fleeing the scene of the failed mission, not having any idea where to go, except far away, she had no destination in her head. Her only thought was to get the hell out of Beckley.

She avoided the interstate, as it had tolls and she wanted to avoid any state cameras taking pictures of her car on that road. Confined as she was to Route 19, her stomach tightened as she passed the sign for Mount Hope, which she had been informed was the town where Balkum, her supposed prey, lived. Now, she was the prey.

Upon reaching Oak Hill, where she knew there were a number of small strip malls, she pulled into one with a number of nondescript stores. At least it was a place to lie low for the moment. As she sat in her car, the ignition off, she tried to tamp down her apprehensive state.

Consistent with her behavior since adolescence, she blamed others, never herself, for the current mess. This time, she put the blame squarely on Tranter for things going wrong. Why the hell did he think that such a scheme could be pulled off in a grocery parking lot? Bars and booze, those were the reliable settings to trap someone.

She remained worried that, if that Balkum jerk gave sufficient identifying information the police would come calling before long. What then? she thought. She saw Balkum pointing his phone at her car, unaware that the photos would be too vague to track her down. She did not know that Tranter had considered that a bad ending was possible, and because of that, even if the car could be ID'd, the police would find out that the car was unregistered, a dead end for them.

Trying to compose herself, her heart still beating rapidly and her anxiety level undiminished, she simply sat there. With her fears of being arrested still dominating her thoughts, she could not help but look around the parking lot periodically to make sure no patrol car was prowling around in search of her. If she saw one, she had decided to slink down low, so that it would appear that no one was in her car. As time continued, she began to think that the danger had passed and with that her breathing slowed down, returning to near normal.

Though she dreaded it, she knew a call would have to be placed to Tranter.

Seeing her number, he picked up without delay. Knowing it was she, but unsure what prompted her call, he protectively answered with only "Hello."

"It's me," she responded, surprised that he did not seem to know who it was. "Things are not good! Not fuckin' good at all!" she responded shrilly, her rapid respirations and high anxiety level returning immediately, displaying themselves as she howled.

The tone of voice accompanying her words also made it instantly clear to Tranter that the planned trap had turned into a mess. How big a one was his only concern.

"I'm not sure I understand," he said coolly, carefully avoiding using her name in his response, wanting to avoid any suggestion that he knew the identity of the caller by speaking her name. Christ almighty! he thought, for all he knew, she could be calling from a police station right at this moment with her conversation being recorded!

Too upset and by that distraught state oblivious to Tranter's vague responses, she continued, "The guy was a real a-hole."

From her description and tone, one would think that Balkum had initiated the whole scheme and she was the victim.

"I mean he gets all fucking huffy just because I suggested to him that there's a fun way to resolve the car smack up. Most guys, they'd jump at the idea. Especially with someone like me," she added, having an inflated view of her beauty. "But no, this guy thinks he's a saint or something and says he's calling the cops!"

Tranter didn't like the way this retelling was going, but now he could tell that she wasn't at a police station, a relief. He then felt confident enough to respond, though cautiously.

"And, then what" he said, keeping his end of the conversation to a minimum.

"And I got the fuck outta there. What'd you think I'd do! I'm parked in a strip mall right now, far away from the place where this went down. No cops, so I'm in the clear."

Tranter was displeased. Though he was used to dealing with crass types – it was common in his line of work – it still irked him when people like Ruby continually used 'fuck' when speaking. Such a limited vocabulary, an indication of a simple mind, he thought.

For sure, she was no class act, nothing like Marla. She was more like a trailer park tramp. This was the end of the line for his business dealings with her. Should've stayed away from the type that didn't finish high school, he rued. For any future assignments, he'd have to find a classier woman for that area of West Virginia. He was done with her.

Confident that now he could speak without worry, he told her, "Ruby, you screwed up big time with this one," putting all the blame squarely on her. "Just park the car where I told you before. It's done, girl."

She was immediately pissed. He was the one who gave her the stupid setup plan! Her comfort spot was a bar, where she could get her mark liquored up. She never thought Tranter's idea was so smart.

Privately, Tranter didn't like the plan either. He never thought it had a high chance of success, but those two shysters insisted that he go after both the judge and Balkum. Should've held his ground and just said no.

Ruby, knowing her employment with him was finished forever, turned to business. Her earlier fears were now replaced with anger.

"When will I get my money? she asked, irritation and impatience clear in her question.

"You'll get your money," he answered, with an even tone.

Now, more aggressively, she persisted, "I said *when* will I get my pay?"

"I heard you Ruby," he said simply. "You'll be paid."

Ruby was not the type to be taken lightly. She knew how to fight. "You'd better, Marty, you'd better, or else! I know what this setup was about. I read the papers you know."

Tranter knew a threat when he heard one. And though he was confident that others were not on the call, he decided it best to end the call promptly. He'd rarely reacted with force in dealing with rambunctious employees, but on occasion there would be a need to send a message if one got out of line, forgetting who was the boss.

Ruby, he knew, had a strong unpredictable streak and he couldn't afford to have her shooting her mouth off. This wasn't one of his run-of-the-mill set up the philandering husband routines, his usual staple. Far too much was riding on this one. Stately D.C. law firm or not, he knew if the shit hit the fan, who would take the fall. Not the lawyers, that was for damn sure. In a matter this big, there was a real potential danger for him.

This required some contemplation on his part. He didn't want to overreact, but insufficient action could be worse. He'd call her tomorrow, he thought, see if she'd cooled down.

Acting as if her threat meant nothing to him, he informed, "I have other things to attend to at the moment. I will be in touch. Don't worry, you'll get your money. Goodbye."

The call having ended, she did not know how to respond to Tranter's nonchalant reaction to her alarming news. Feeling she was without any recourse, and contacting the police being completely out of the question, as that would only make matters worse, she drove to her apartment, a safe place to hole up.

Tranter considered the awful development, comforted only by knowing that it could've been worse if the cops had become involved. The situation presented only a momentary lull for him. He'd have to watch that ol' Ruby closely. Sure, he'd pay her. He'd never tried to stiff his setup women. But if she tried to extort him, well there would have to be something done about that and rapidly if she had any designs along those lines.

While he pondered the unhappy development, he knew that Winston and Marlo would be expecting a call, reporting to them how it went. Telling the truth, and worse, voicing his concerns about this wildcat, those subjects were out of the question. He would just downplay it, say that nothing happened and that this Balkum guy simply turned her down. He'd remind them he advised that success was unlikely. They'd have no reason to doubt his tale. Besides, Ruby's attempted ploy was gravy. They already had won the game with Marla seducing Gray. They didn't need Ruby. Course, when the plans were hatched, no one knew if either would hit the jackpot.

There was no sense in avoiding or delaying the call. That would only heighten their concerns. Both, he knew, were ruthless men, but he decided to call Krakovich, thinking he could allay his concerns more effectively than if he were dealing with Malthan.

Unless he had good news to report, he knew that making the call that evening would prompt concerns with the attorney, so he decided to wait until the following day and to frame it as an event that simply did not work out, along with a reminder of the success they achieved with the key figure, the no longer so honorable Judge Gray.

Although the timing of his call was settled, Tranter remained uneasy for the balance of the evening, as he considered the best way to handle this eruption from Ruby. The problem was serious enough that he slept fitfully that night, the unsuccessful conclusion to her task being enough to cause unabated concern. It wasn't so much that her mission failed as it was her rambunctious reaction to it. She was a wild one, that girl; it was unpredictable how she might behave.

When he placed the call that Sunday afternoon, Krakovich picked up immediately, instantly recognizing who it was. He and his wife had just returned from church and fortunately she was occupied making plans for their customary late afternoon dinner.

"Hello," he answered simply.

However, she did hear the phone, asking "Who's that Milo? It's Sunday," she added, weekend calls being rare. Sunday, she firmly believed, was for God, not work.

Milo, covering the handset, responded, "Just the office, dear," he said easily. "You know this is such a significant case. Calls are to be expected, even on the weekend, honeybunch." He then added, "I'm sure this call won't be long," his attempt to tamp down future inquiries from her.

Given her interjection, he left the room for privacy, affording no opportunity for his wife to eavesdrop.

Tranter spoke calmly, conveying a matter-of-fact tone. "Well, we were unable to take down the other guy," he informed.

"I see," Milo answered. "No complications?"

"None," Tranter lied. "He just wasn't interested, unlike our friend, the judge," reminding him again of the earlier great success.

Wanting deniability about the plan, but suspecting that there was a lot more to the retelling, he decided to avoid any queries, especially with the missus nearby.

"Well, thank you for the update. Have a good afternoon," he answered, ending the call.

Upon returning to the living room, his wife could not resist asking, "What was that all about?"

"Nothing. Nothing at all, my sweetheart. It could have waited until tomorrow. Some people call about the most innocuous matters."

To his relief, she left it at that.

CHAPTER 10

Excited over Monday's upcoming afternoon event, Gray had trouble falling asleep that Sunday evening and he awoke well before his alarm. Millie stayed in bed, mumbling only 'have a good day,' after he was dressed and ready to go.

He winced at her unwitting goodbye wish to 'have a good day.' Well, he thought, except for the twinge of guilt that well-meaning remark brought on, he was sure to have a good day, a great day in fact.

Yet, during the commute, his upbringing reminded him that his afternoon adventure ran against his, now lost, moral code, not to mention his marital vows. Continuing to think about that was a downer, maybe even to the point of ruining his time with Nicole.

To combat it, he rationalized his behavior. The salve applied to his conscience was that, up until now, he'd been a good and faithful husband, while besieged by years of her progressive illness and all the additional burdens that placed upon him. Was he not entitled to some pleasures? Wouldn't most mortals succumb to such temptations?

He would keep those thoughts front and center for the remainder of the day.

When the trial resumed that morning, Gray was preoccupied with excitement over the soon to come afternoon link with Nicole. Like a child filled with anticipation over a pleasant upcoming event, he had difficulty thinking of the business before him.

As he looked out at the counsels then standing respectfully before him, he informed that they may be seated. For a moment, he was about to ask the parties if they were ready to resume the testimony of the witness, absentmindedly trying to remember who that witness was, and entirely forgetting that the government had rested on Friday.

Now there was that matter of the motion for a directed verdict requiring his ruling – that important ruling, the one he had soberly informed the parties on Friday that he needed time to consider over the weekend. An eerie quiet filled the courtroom, the parties, but not the judge, anticipating his ruling.

Saving himself from what would have been a noteworthy embarrassment, somehow, he caught himself as the issue of the moment came back to him in the nick of time. Presenting his most solemn demeanor, with a presentation worthy of an actor, he began by reminding the parties of the issue to be decided, the motion for a directed verdict, which was entirely off his radar minutes earlier.

Gray solemnly announced his decision, the one he had privately made as soon as the motion for directed verdict had been presented on Friday.

He began, "At the conclusion of last week's proceedings, the Respondent made a motion for directed verdict. I considered the motion upon adjourning that day, and frankly," he lied, "I gave it further thought over the weekend." It had not been on his mind for a minute over those two days. That the issue was far from his thoughts was clear by his momentary lapse, forgetting that the important decision was the first order of business that morning.

Milo and Winston knew full well that Gray's remarks were untruthful. All this pretend deliberation over the motion was not believable. Winning a motion for directed verdict was as rare as hens' teeth.

Sanford too knew that such motions were almost never successful but, as he was on the receiving end of a potentially disastrous ruling, he could not afford to be as relaxed as the Respondent's attorneys about the outcome. Oh, how the big shots at MSHA would howl if Gray ruled for the respondents! Even if overturned on appeal, an adverse ruling from Gray would be viewed as a failure on Sanford's part. He literally held his breath, fearful that the ultimate disaster could be announced.

The expected loss was of no consequence to the Respondents. In fact, they wanted the motion to be denied, so that their defense could be presented.

Besides, winning the motion would only delay, not wind up, the hearing. An interruption, while awaiting the judge's decision to be reversed on appeal, would be no victory at all. They knew no review body would support such a ruling for a case of this magnitude.

Gray continued, "As the parties are well aware, to prevail on such a motion it must be shown that no genuine issue of material fact is present and in making that determination the Court is duty-bound to view all the evidence in the light most favorable to the movant's opponent."

Hearing those words, Sanford was able to breathe again, his fear then abating.

"Upon consideration, I deny the Respondents' motion. The Secretary has met the minimal burden to withstand the motion."

In making the remark, Gray put emphasis on the word "minimal," signaling to both sides that he likely considered the Secretary's case to be weak. All that anticipation, the "need" for Gray to supposedly deliberate over it during the weekend, and he disposed of it in two short sentences.

While relieved over the determination, for Sanford, and the other members of MSHA's litigation team, Gray's words unmistakably informed that the road ahead would be rough. It meant that they would need to not simply call into question, but to destroy, the Respondent's evidence.

Neither Winston nor Milo was disappointed by the ruling. Especially now, with the trap having snared Gray, they didn't want a favorable outcome. Full speed ahead, they thought. They now had two roads to victory; present a legitimate defense, creating doubt on the experts' opinions offered by the Secretary, and the more certain road, force the compromised Gray to rule in their favor.

The ruling from the Bench issued, Gray then announced that the day's testimony would end at the noon hour, as he had to attend to other matters which, he added, could not be postponed.

The government was surprised about the announcement of a short day, especially as the week had just begun, but it was fine with the defense and of no surprise to it at all. In fact, it was good news, confirming what Tranter had advised them over the weekend – that the judge indeed had other matters, as he had a new appointment with Marla that very afternoon, less than a week after his first fall from grace.

Though he didn't know it yet, the good jurist was already in up to his neck after his first time with her and now he was digging himself into a deeper hole. If the first event could somehow be explained as a one-time forgivable mistake, their second time together offered no such excuse. His repeated poor judgment, causing a delay in the proceeding, so that he could have an afternoon romp no less, only made matters worse.

Apart from winning on the merits, an effort directed solely at disparaging the government's case as a mere hypothesis about the AWCs, the outcome would be preordained in the Respondent's favor for the second reason: Gray's poor decision to commit adultery, soon to be described as 'multiple' transgressions. The odds that he would rebel against the Respondent, when presented with his grievous moral failings were nil.

With the motion disposed of, the Respondent then called its first witness, Ricky Slone, Bobcat Creek Colliery's director of safety. Apparently, no one had thought to advise him that appearing in court called for, if not one's Sunday's best, at least a jacket and tie. Instead, Slone presented himself much as one would've anticipated if visiting him at the mine's office – wearing a checkered flannel shirt and jeans, and not bothering to shave that morning, a dark stubble across his face. At least his appearance presented authenticity, being in line with the public's image of what a miner would look like. Yet, when Milo and Winston met him before the proceedings began that morning, they were unhappy about his appearance, though they said nothing to him about it, there being no time to spruce him up.

A shirt and tie showed respect and, better yet, miners in such outfits always looked out of place when so dressed. This was because the shirt and tie had an unusual benefit, conveying to a Court that it was not customary for the witness to wear such clothing. An ill-fitting, low-end shirt and a cheap tie sent that message; it simultaneously displayed respect while making it clear that it was unusual for the witness to be so dressed, a sympathetic combination to present to the Court. There would be stern words from both attorneys to the errant paralegal who made the arrangements for Slone's travel and lodging by forgetting to inform the witness about the appropriate clothing for his testimony in court. Making the best of it, they consoled one another that at least he brought genuineness. No one would mistake him for some white-collar worker.

Certainly Slone, quite oblivious to his sartorial error when he took the stand, had no thoughts that the situation called for better dress. He had testified in other Mine Act cases and his dress was no different on those occasions. Those prior experiences in testifying also gave him confidence. He had lied before and today he was prepared to lie again and to do so with an unwavering, rock solid, presentation that it was, as he had just sworn before God, to be, "the truth, the whole truth, and nothing but the truth."

Slone knew how the game was played. He hadn't risen to become the director of safety by strictly insisting on complying with those foolish MSHA rules.

With a practiced, but false, presentation of conviction in his speech, Slone firmly denied that anyone had tampered with any of the many cassettes. He was mightily offended that anyone would even think that he would do such a thing. Of course, he acknowledged that after the charges were filed, he had heard about those "white center claims" as he called them.

All he could state was that he oversaw the dust sampling and that in every instance it was done properly. Each miner's sampling was performed just as required for a full shift. And no, he said firmly, there was none of that business he'd heard about, that samples were taken outside the mine for some of the time, or placed at intake air locations, or the like. And yes, he had heard, but only after the charges had been brought, of the claim that some reverse air flow had been done with the sampling, but no one had done such a thing at this mine, that was for sure.

He professed, touting his ignorance, that he didn't even know exactly what 'reverse air flow' meant, telling the Court, "I don't know nothing about this whatchamacallit reverse air business." He asserted, adamantly, that each miner tested did his normal work shift. Then, at the shift's conclusion, the cassettes were packed up and sent directly to MSHA, exactly as required. Everything seemed normal to him. As the cassettes were sealed, he would have no idea what the filters looked like inside and therefore he had no clue about this white center thing.

Winston and Milo were pleased with Slone's resolute testimony. In short, he lied convincingly.

During the pre-trial interview sessions, the two were careful to explain and emphasize, well before they started interviewing him, that they were speaking purely hypothetically about the dust sampling charges. They believed that this insulated them from any ethical violations. Then they made it clear to Slone that if a person were to admit to any tampering with the cassettes, as attorneys, they would be in an ethical bind. They could not then offer his testimony denying tampering. But, having made it clear even to the densest person, if a person were to deny doing any such thing, never telling the attorneys of such chicanery, there would be no such quandary, as there would be no basis to challenge his statements.

Slone understood perfectly, as he proceeded to tell the attorneys that no tampering had ever occurred. From that good start, the rules of the game having been imparted by the attorneys and fully comprehended by Slone, the two were confident that the director of safety was a reliable player. They communicated the good news to mine management too, couched in appropriate terms of course.

Slone's loyal responses to the attorneys were reinforced when he received a bonus with his next paycheck. Everyone played along, the bonus was described simply as the mine's appreciation for his hard work of late. Slone could not recall anything extra he had recently done work-wise and that being the case, he understood the unstated basis for the reward.

Malthan and Krakovich were sufficiently satisfied with their direct examination and they used up the entire morning, an intentional strategy. Though the witness's testimony could have likely wrapped up that morning with an hour to spare, the two intentionally slowed the process down, requesting several pauses during the morning session. Those recesses were all designed so that the judge would be left with the witness' unassailed testimony.

This was a two-edged sword however, a consideration the two had weighed. Sure, on the plus side, the judge would have the day end having heard a one-sided account of the dust collection practices at the mine, the idea being that the testimony would sink in deeper than if it were immediately subject to cross-examination.

Balanced against that, the Secretary would have the entire afternoon to better prepare for its turn. Both sides had requested same day transcripts. Though expensive, given the stakes, it was well worth it and, in the big picture, the cost was negligible. Possessing that day's testimony, the Secretary could pour over every word the safety director had uttered.

An additional benefit of having his testimony at hand, if the witness inevitably denied some of his testimony, uttered less than 24 hours earlier, the Secretary could pounce on the inconsistency. Armed with such conflicts, the Secretary could smugly point out, "Mr. Safety Director, isn't it true that just yesterday you said…" A denial that the words were spoken would be even better because it allowed the Secretary to drag it out with a flourish. It was always great fun when, in the face of a clear denial, the Secretary would first politely show the transcript pages he was relying upon to opposing counsel. Then he would show the witness his testimony from the day before.

Respondent's attempt to defuse a harmful conflicting statement, showing that he had spoken out of both sides of his mouth, would include a congenial offer from them to stipulate that the witness's earlier testimony was inconsistent. The amiable suggestion would be met with an equally friendly expression of appreciation in response, but declined. The government was entitled to point out witness inconsistencies, they would note. Just stipulating to them would diminish the impact of the inconsistent testimony.

The tension associated with the start of the defense left Milo and Winston tired. Tomorrow that first witness would face cross-examination. At least he would be fresh to start the day. They would meet with the safety director at seven, prepping him for the cross-exam and reminding him of the important rules: don't lose your temper; don't answer a question you don't understand; and don't respond with more information than the question asked.

Slone had been in the game for nearly 30 years. He didn't rise to become the Director of Safety by being stupid. Without any coaching he had enough sense to deny the government's claims from the get-go. He knew how it was played. He did not need to have it spelled out.

He also knew that his continued employment depended upon denying any complicity. And worse, such a mortal sin, the effect of admitting to tampering, would extend to any future mining job, not just with his present employer. If he were disloyal, he would be out, and permanently, branded as a turncoat. His livelihood would be cut-off. Given those unacceptable results, he would be a good soldier.

Involuntarily, Gray could not help but to repeatedly look at his watch during Slone's testimony. Though he tried to make those time checks casually, glancing at his wrist, both Milo and Winston observed the judge's behavior. They knew what was on the good judge's mind and it had nothing to do with the testimony being presented on this morning. But they were careful to suppress the smiles they felt each time the judge made those checks. It was obvious that he was not giving close attention to the witness. He was too preoccupied to afford any critical assessment of Slone's testimony.

Not by accident, the defense timed their questioning so that it wound up with only a quarter hour before noon, an undisclosed plan of theirs, extending courtesy to the judge's busy afternoon schedule. The timing gave Gray extra time to close the day's proceeding and he would not have to rush with his return to the office, possibly working up a sweat, if hurried.

Gray wasted no time getting out of the courthouse. As the hotel was nearly next door, he had no need to depart until just before the set time. In recognition of his age, he intentionally napped briefly, some insurance that he would be in good form for the anticipated sex. Worried that the nap could accidentally last too long, he had the foresight to set the alarm on his phone so as not to oversleep. His door firmly shut during this time, no one interrupted his rest period.

On this one occasion, when it was time to step out for his meeting with Nicole, he did not seek leave. No way would he want a record that he was off work for a portion, perhaps all, of the afternoon. Given the nature of the trial, no one would be questioning his unaccounted afternoon absence.

Shortly before the rendezvous, he made one last restroom check and then immediately exited the building. With relief, he saw no office employees during his departure. Minutes later he was upon the hotel, but out of caution he made a full look around to make sure no one from the office was around as he made his entrance. Seeing no one, that worry was put at ease.

He strode through the lobby, avoiding even a glance at the front desk clerks, acting as if he were a registered guest at the hotel. Aiding his pretense, he had remembered the elevators' location. The gods were looking down with favor upon him, he thought, smiling, as no one was aboard the elevator with him.

The imagined gauntlet passed, with no recognition or other issues, he knocked on her unit's door. Immediately, Nicole opened the door, welcoming him in with a practiced warm smile.

"Right on time," she noted, "I like punctuality."

"I as well," Gray replied, happy over the warm greeting. "My line of work requires it," he remarked, an obvious brag about his judicial position.

She smiled, but given the circumstances of their meeting, was not impressed.

"I know a judge is a dependable person and because of that I anticipated that you would be on time. I fixed us our drinks. Hope mid-afternoon is not too early."

"I've been known to have a drink before dusk on occasion," he smiled, "but usually it's on the weekend."

With that remark, he wished he could take it back. It was too close a reference to his whereabouts when not at work. Of course, he had made no mention of his after-work life, and for whatever reason she had not gone there, much to his relief. He had not thought ahead to the answer he would provide if she had asked, though he should have had a story ready.

"Let me take your coat, Charles. Make yourself comfortable on the sofa. I'll bring our drinks in a jiff."

With him comfortably waiting on the sofa, just sitting there caused him to become aroused, thinking back to their time before. Embarrassed at the moderate bulge those thoughts brought about, and thinking that it would be noticeable to her and perhaps even not well-received, he made himself turn to thoughts of the hearing, thinking about the upcoming witnesses. It always worked for him to quiet an erection, thinking of a topic completely apart from the source of his stimulation at that moment.

The method was effective; his condition quieted down considerably before she arrived with their drinks.

Upon her return she had a cheerful remark. "To our new friendship, Charles," she saluted as they clinked their glasses.

He smiled. A friendship, he thought, pleased at her description. It was the best of both worlds. Nothing to upset the home situation. At least not for now.

Realizing they couldn't begin lovemaking immediately; Nicole avoided any awkward moment of silence, filling the void by initiating small talk. "Been a busy week for me. I imagine it's been more so for you, with your trial each day. Tomorrow, I have a full schedule, so I'm glad to have this afternoon for a break."

"Yes, me too," he replied, somewhat clumsily. Recovering from his lack of eloquence, he added some detail about the hearing. "Today the defense began its presentation. Their director of safety testified first. They have a host of witnesses, many employees of the mine and their own array of expert witnesses to challenge the experts the government presented. They will be a critical part of the hearing, their scientific testimony in defense of the charges."

Unlike his recounting of the hearing to Larkin, he abstained from expressing his views about the testimony or the strength of the Secretary's case.

For her part, Nicole carefully avoided straying into any uncomfortable subjects, such as anything personal about his life, though it would have been a natural topic for any friends, even new ones, to inquire about.

Acting impressed, she responded, "The case sounds very interesting."

It was the best she could offer. In truth, she did not care either way about the whole dust collection tampering charge. Wasn't her problem.

When they had nearly finished their first drinks, she, observing his nearly empty glass, simply stood up, announcing she would be right back. By design, she did not inquire if he wanted a refill, taking away the choice. In a few moments she returned with fresh drinks for both.

As she handed him his drink, she cheerfully proclaimed again, "To us and our new friendship." She wanted to be sure there would be no possibility that Gray might have a fit of conscience, and back off from a second union. A second drink would help wash away such pangs, if they existed.

Though he was not sure if he wanted or was even ready for a refill, he had little choice but to accept the new offering. It felt rude to decline.

She again clinked her glass to his, and with that both took a large swallow. She had made his a strong one, while hers was mild.

With more artful small talk, by the time Charles was half done with his second drink, it was obvious to her that the alcohol had taken effect. She noticed that his smile was a little different now, his initial timidness gone.

Seeing the moment, she put her leg astride him, just as she had last week. Though her behavior was manifestly forward, aided by the alcohol, he welcomed it. It turned him on last time and the effect was again the same.

Noticing his arousal, and as they had been intimate before, she did not hesitate to place her hand on his member.

As he welcomed the move, offering a silly grin in his semi-intoxicated smitten state, she then began lightly rubbing the zone. After a moment of stroking, she then moved completely astride him, planting a deep kiss on his lips.

In her role as a de facto actress, which was how she viewed herself, it was part of the job. But in truth she did not enjoy it, massaging that old guy's stale pubes.

Marty had promised that, assuming the video captured it all, there would be no call for a third recording. She was relieved this would be the final performance.

Wanting to get to the finish line as fast as possible, and knowing he was ready, she then arose, extending her hand to lead him to the bedroom. The camera was set and had been running before he even arrived, a sentinel to capture their second coupling.

As he wanted it, she went along with some preliminary fondling, while she played the role of a woman enthralled with his lovemaking.

But accomplishing the act was the key, so after a few minutes it was time to pull down his trousers, unbutton his shirt and get those articles off the bed, so as not to interfere with the filming.

It was, in effect, a porno film, but with Gray unwittingly playing a costarring role. In their scene, as it were, of their coupling, upon entering her, it did not take long before he was spent. The final footage required her practiced presentation that she too had arrived at orgasm, a state to which she was nowhere near this time and did not want to be.

When they were done, she arranged things so that the camera could faithfully record the two of them lying in bed. Damning himself further, he continued to stroke her thigh after they were finished. There he was, as clear as day, fully enjoying the afterglow.

In time he excused himself to wash up, thinking of the importance of bathing away the scents from Nicole. As soon as he closed the bathroom door, she used the moment of privacy to check the camera. Once she heard the sink water running, she moved quickly, in case he opened the door unexpectedly soon. It would be a disaster and possibly a threat to her health if had emerged, seeing her near the bureau.

Good news, the device's red light remained on, reassuring that it had all been recorded and there would be no requirement for another meeting.

Immediately, she returned to the bed. Though she was not discovered by him, it was foolish, she thought, to have acted so impulsively. She could've waited until he was gone. This time, she thought, relief in site, gone for good.

As she waited for his emergence from the bathroom, she assumed a pose of luxuriating from their sex.

Despite her act, she could not avoid thinking of her history of dispassionate couplings, of which now there had been too many of them. The money was there and it paid handsomely, but at a significant cost, as it had reduced sex for her to a function, devoid of emotion. It was a high price she had paid for this source of income, so much so that legitimate sexual attraction had withered for her. Dating was rare and she would routinely end those instances well before any relationship could develop. It was true, she realized, that money, the reason she began these arrangements, wasn't everything.

When Gray returned, she continued her required role of a woman still elated over their encounter, smiling affectionately at him, while her anxiety grew, wanting this final scene to be completed.

He smiled back, inflated with his presumption that he was her Romeo.

Unlike her, for him the sex had been another thrilling event, so much so that, as he dressed, he then expressed his desire to get together again. Guilt did not enter his head as he told her of his wish.

Christ, she thought, so damn soon! Who does that, bringing up the next tryst right away! This guy's idea of a relationship was so empty. Didn't he realize they knew nothing about one another? His idea of a relationship was only about getting laid.

The only balm was knowing that it would never happen again with him, thank God. Though put off by his behavior, she remembered that there was a role to play and so she made herself display feigned enthusiasm over the prospect, as required. Able to do that, under these circumstances, she thought perhaps she should've been an actress. The scene would end soon but the time to let down her act would not occur until after he had departed.

Though it felt like a very long time, eventually she got him to the door. Smitten, as he was, saying his fond goodbye, and repeating the wish for another meeting soon, only she was aware that it would be their last time.

Her hotel room door shut, she leaned against the door, relieved that it was over. If the amorous one were to come back for another adieu, she had already determined that she would not answer any knocks.

She waited, peering out the door's peephole. Nothing. The corridor remained empty. Relieved that he did not return, there was work to do before she could relax. First up was to check the video. It was fine, the sex scenes even better than the first recording. The Judge was in a major fix, though he was clueless about it. Then, for her own purposes, as before she downloaded it to her laptop. Tranter would not be informed that she made her own copy. Can't trust anybody, she thought, best to protect oneself.

That done, she turned to her next duty, calling Tranter.

"Marty it's me," she informed.

He was expecting the call and knew immediately it was her, but he was edgy, given the mess with Ruby. What would he do if Marla's second event with Gray went south?

"And?" was all he said in response.

No 'Hi Marla,' no greeting of any sort, she thought. That's a fine how-do-you-do for her work! She was pleased to have made a copy of the sex for herself. Might need it someday, she thought.

Putting aside the absence of any courtesy from him, she answered that the second 'visit,' as she called it, from the judge went off without a hitch and the video was sharp. There will be no question identifying that it was Gray, she informed.

"Good, that's very good," he responded, instantly relieved that there was no Ruby-like disaster, the pleasure in his tone of voice unmistakable.

She picked up the change in his tone. Must have been apprehensive, she thought. Still, that was no excuse for his lack of civility.

His brief compliment over, he immediately turned to business. There was the high cost of the hotel suite to address. "You'll be checking out by tomorrow morning, right?"

That was especially annoying to her. She just finished the second sex session with the judge, and immediately Marty was worried about another day's charge at the hotel. No appreciation, she thought. She was, for now, dispensable to him.

"Yes," she said simply, now adopting his business attitude, without any pleasant tone added.

It prompted her to add that she was not on call whenever he beckoned.

"Marty, I want you to know I'm stepping away from this work for a time."

Obtusely, he did not recognize that his 'all business' approach angered her. He simply never considered that Marla's line of work was not easy on the conscience for some women. He set these events up, he pulled the strings, but he never had to carry out the intimate side of the job, oblivious to its toll.

"Yeah, sure, Marla," was all he could say. At least then he recognized that the vibes from her voice alerted him that she was displeased about something, though he didn't know what was bugging her. She did her job, she's getting paid quite well for it, he thought, what's the problem?

Though he could not see any reason for her to be unhappy, he was sufficiently wary to leave his response at that, and not open a potential hornet's nest by asking 'if anything was wrong.'

In his dealings with women in these roles and in his twice failed marriages, he had learned that it was better to remain quiet. If they're angry, they'll tell you, he thought, no need to prompt them.

As Gray entered the lobby and exited the hotel, he remained in his euphoric state. A bonus, as he checked his watch, he would be home on time, so there would be no inquisition from Millie. He had thoroughly washed after they were done so there would be no tell-tale odors lingering from Nicole but out of extra caution he returned to his office, changing into a fresh outfit, which he kept in his office locked dresser cabinet. Later, he would take the clothes from his afternoon adventure to a dry cleaner near the office. There was nothing he could do about the odor of alcohol on his breath. Though it was dissipating, he knew it would remain detectable, even mints did not hide it. At least it was nothing new; Millie had come to expect it, though she didn't like his unsavory habit.

His arrival home went as expected. Having granted himself dispensation for his adultery due to the burdens of an ill wife, he entered the house free of guilt. He smiled at her as always, hesitating for a second before giving his usual peck on the cheek, a lingering concern whether any of Nicole's fragrances remained on him.

Happily, Millie displayed no recognition of any unusual odors about him, and her intuition failed to signal that anything was out of the ordinary. To her, it had just been another normal day for her Charles at work. In what had now become a routine for her, she did inquire about the day's trial events and Charles recounted them, omitting of course that it had only lasted until noon. This time he didn't mind the review, as it reinforced his determination that she had no suspicions and it gave him the opportunity to fill up some conversation with his wife, presenting a misleading semblance of normality.

The evening continued to go well, with his carrying out his usual bedtime routine of showering, affording a second chance to wash off any lingering scents from his afternoon adventure.

It was almost a perfect ending except that, on this of all nights, Millie had one of her rare urges for romance. Twenty years ago, if he had an afternoon dalliance like today, he could have pulled it off, having sex for a second time, but he was no longer capable of accomplishing a repeat performance on the same day.

He declined, contending the marathon trial has sapped his vitality.

She was hurt at his turndown, especially because they were intimate so infrequently, a state of affairs for which she shouldered responsibility. Up to that point, the evening had gone so well that he completely ignored his faithless afternoon, but now, with his turndown, his secret infidelity was front and center.

Rejected, his declining hurting more because she had initiated the idea, Millie rolled over, her back to him, a statement of her bruised feelings. Unable to dismiss his adultery, the pleasurable night's sleep he was looking forward to was spoiled. He then rolled on his side, facing away from her, both apart, as if in separate beds. Forcing himself to remain motionless, he feigned sleep, but he would remain awake for several hours, his breach of their marriage vows no longer so easily dismissed for the remainder of the night.

CHAPTER 11

Gray woke before his alarm sounded. That was a relief, turning it off in advance, in case Millie was still asleep. She seemed to be, not moving and in the same position as last night, her back facing his side of the bed. He showered and, when ready to leave, she remained in bed with no acknowledgment that he was up and no sign that she was awake. He doubted that his wife remained asleep, what with all the unavoidable noise as he prepared to leave, but thought it best to avoid saying goodbye, playing along with her presentation.

As soon as she heard the garage door open, she turned, resting on her back, staring up at the ceiling, her act of sleeping over. She tried to put last night's rejection in perspective. Maybe it's true, she thought, Charles was no longer young, his retirement on the horizon. Perhaps it was unreasonable to expect him to be interested in sex given all that was going on with that trial. Still, something inside her insisted that all was not quite right. She couldn't identify it, but she felt it. It was an additional unpleasant thought to start her day, her disease already making each day a challenge.

For Charles, once he was out of the house and on the way for his commute, his conscience easing, the elation he felt over his second time with Nicole again dominated his thoughts. What did he do to find himself such a prize! God's blessing bestowed upon him. Maybe it was part of HIS plan, he considered, a reward for his long burden of caring for his spouse. Such concoctions were a way to assuage any guilt.

THE CASE OF THE ABNORMAL WHITE CENTER

When he arrived at the courthouse that Tuesday morning, upon entering the courtroom he displayed a jaunty appearance. Still, as the parties rose upon his entrance, just as with his first romp with Nicole, he could not help but examine those before him for any sign of awareness about his extracurricular activities. His conscience forced him to peer into the faces before him, as if, by engaging in mind reading, somehow, he could look into their thoughts.

Did they know anything? Could they know anything?

It was completely irrational, he reassured himself, to entertain such notions. Only two people knew about yesterday's afternoon delight, the heavenly Nicole and him. And, his cautious side at work, he reminded himself that he was careful to see if anyone noted his departure from the office yesterday afternoon. He saw not a soul. And, prudently, he kept up that vigilance as he walked to the hotel which was conveniently on the next block from his office. Again, he saw no familiar face. And finally, perhaps the most important location to be sure he was undetected for his excursion, he scanned the lobby of the hotel, a watch he kept up until he safely entered the elevator to Nicole's floor. No one, not a single person, recognized him. Upon exiting the floor, the same was true, there was not even a housekeeper present, their day's duties apparently completed by the early afternoon. He left the hotel as he entered it, in complete anonymity.

Satisfied that his secret about yesterday was intact, his thoughts turned to his twin fortunes. There he was, presiding in the biggest case of his career, with widespread impact on the underground coal mining industry, a case receiving nationwide notice, and with him at the center of it all. It meant his retirement would end with noteworthy fame, as his decision would be prominently discussed. And, on top of that newsworthy role, there was the icing on the cake, an unexpected huge bonus, that alluring woman, Nicole. Just the thought of being with her again made it difficult to focus on the business at hand.

Thrilled that he was riding the apex of his life, and having reassured himself that all was well, he brought his attention to bear upon the day's business. But two attorneys, Milo and Winston, knew that despite Gray's upbeat demeanor, the judge would soon learn that the game was over. For now, though they knew everything about his twin dalliances, their poker faces offered no hint of their awareness. The two were pleased and titillated by the fact and details of the good judge's damning behavior, all as reported to them earlier that morning by Marty. Nice clear shots, he related, every bit a porno film, he bragged to them, not merely clear images of the judge in bed with his entrapper. If, as likely, Gray thought of his prominence in presiding in this significant trial, the action shots of him fucking would eclipse that fame many times over. The subject of the trial would be, they joked, lost in the dust. And there could be no denials coming from Gray about his behavior, not with two explicit videos to refute them.

"I believe," Gray said with practiced gravamen in his tone, "that the direct examination of Mr. Slone was completed before we adjourned yesterday. Are we ready to begin cross-examination?"

Winston spoke up first. "Good morning, your Honor. That's correct. We did complete our questioning of Mr. Slone."

"Is the government ready to cross-examine?" Gray then inquired.

"Good morning, your honor," Sanford began, echoing Winston's respectful address. "Thank you. Yes, we are ready."

Slone was unshakeable during his cross-examination, maintaining that he was personally offended at even the suggestion that he could do such a thing as tamper with the dust cassettes. The notion was unthinkable. He was hurt, wounded, by the allegations.

As he testified, during direct and now during the cross exam, both sides noticed that Gray was making notations of some sort. Oh, for the chance to see what he was writing! There wasn't much Sanford could do with the witness. There would be no Perry Mason moment when this witness would breakdown and admit that all his earlier testimony had been fabricated. Only on TV did that happen.

The best Sanford could do was to suggest that Slone was lying, without of course directly asserting it.

"Didn't you find it remarkable, Mr. Slone," he would ask, "that your mine suddenly had so many of these cassettes with white centers?"

Unphased, the safety director, replied, "I can't tell you why those things had them so-called white centers. Alls I know is none of my miners touched 'em and I certainly didn't either. And I've never, even yet, seen one of those white centers filters y'all been talkin' bout."

Sanford, not surprised by the denial, in plain disbelief of his answer, continued without hesitation, "Well, Mr. Slone, and how do you explain that your mine suddenly stopped having those filters with the white centers, then?"

Unflappable, Slone smoothly brushed aside the implication. "Again, I tell you, I don't know why they stopped, as you claim and that's if those things really had those white centers things from the get go. Like I just told you, I've never seen a one of them things yet."

Slone did know the playbook as he added one of the mine's defenses with his answer. "I did hear tell much later that maybe some miners could've accidentally done some rough handling of the dust sampling equipment, dropping them and stepping on hoses and things like that, and that at some point later on they were told to be more careful with those things, but whether those accidents, if they happened at all, maybe could have caused those things, I couldn't rightly say. Things like that," he concluded, "I leave that to them scientists."

He then added, pretending to be humble, "Me, I only got a high school education. I'm just telling you that we didn't never fool with those things, like you've been suggestin." Though he knew otherwise, he denied knowledge about any of experts' claims that the white filters could come about by accidents, such as mishandling. By remarking about the possibility of accidental causes for the white centers, he was adeptly laying the groundwork for the experts who would testify later exactly to that claim – the white centers could be explained away as accidents.

Milo and Winston, their faces emotionless, were extremely pleased with his performance.

With redirect following the cross-examination, it took the whole day to complete the safety director's testimony. Though the Secretary tried to instill doubts in Gray's mind over Slone's claims, his testimony was largely unscathed. The critical concern was whether the Judge found him to be credible. Of that, neither side could know. Gray, unreadable, gave no facial expressions from which one could draw such conclusions.

During a break, in the sanctuary of their counsel room, Winston and Milo exchanged mild self-congratulatory nods at the conclusion of the testimony for the defense's first witness. Slone had held up well. No once did he seem hesitant or shaky. He did a good job and, in their estimation, they were off to a solid start. They would inform mine management of his superior testimony, even suggesting that, in appreciation, a bonus to the Director of Safety was deserved, adding, for his truthful testimony.

Not that it mattered anymore with the hole Gray had dug for himself.

As the day's testimony came to a close, it was not just the defense that was feeling good, Gray too felt contentment. Walking back to his office, yesterday's rendezvous with Nicole and the great sex he imagined they both had, occupied his mind, bringing a smile to his face. It was so noticeable that a few of those who passed by him wondered why the guy was so obviously elated.

How fortunate he was. Here he was, presiding in the biggest case of his career, making him feel so important, and on top of that, a woman of such beauty and bedroom prowess had entered his life, finding him so appealing. It could not get any better, he cluelessly mused.

Arriving at the office, he decided against taking the circuitous, colleague-avoiding, route, his understandable anti-social behavior from yesterday gone. Contact with those in his office was fine by him today. And Larkin did notice that, as Gray passed his office, his colleague gave a wave accompanied with a cordial "good afternoon, Richard."

Larkin responded immediately. "Charles. Good to see you. Am I invited for a recap or would you prefer that for another day?" he asked evenly, trying to provide an easy opportunity for his friend to decline, if he wished.

As Gray did not consider it to have been a particularly taxing day, especially in view of the fact that the testimony from the mine's safety director did not require him to constantly be on his toes, he was receptive to a visit from Larkin. Slone had been a simple fact witness, and as such there were no knotty questions over expertise or hearsay involved.

Whether he had testified truthfully, Gray had not reached a final conclusion on that, but he did jot down on his legal pad that the fellow seemed to speak with earnestness and certitude, a favorable assessment of his credibility.

Whether it was all a bluff, '*testilying*,' as they call it, he was not quite sure. That final determination about what to make of the safety director's testimony would have to await his close evaluation of the other employees who would be testifying, starting tomorrow. In view of what was a very good day, he welcomed Richard's request.

When Larkin arrived, minutes after the invitation, they assumed their respective seats, once again in their de facto roles as virtual patient and therapist. This time, learning from his prior "sessions" with Charles, Larkin resolved to avoid judgmental comments, recalling that even his soft remarks had landed with a thud. This was, he found, difficult to do, as he brought to mind his own skepticism when Gray informed that the past two days had involved testimony from the mine's safety and health director. Gray's recounting omitted mention that this took up a day and a half, not two days, with his other activity on Monday afternoon carefully undisclosed.

Listening to his colleague's recounting, Larkin continued to feel disappointed over the version being presented. Did Charles really expect anything other than a complete denial of any tampering from this witness? With all his years of experience he could not be so naïve. Besides, there was no way the defense would have offered him up, as their first witness no less, had they entertained a sliver of doubt over the version he would swear to be the telling of the truth. Still, though the urge to make a comment was strong, he managed to quietly listen, presenting his best inscrutable appearance.

For his part, Gray, as the unwitting patient, tried to read Larkin's reaction to the recounting, but he was unable to discern whether his colleague entertained doubts about the safety director's testimony. Didn't matter anyway, he thought, as Richard wasn't at the hearing to observe the man, and the credibility determinations were his province alone. There was comfort in that for him, being very much aware that a judge's credibility determinations are sacrosanct, untouchable except in situations where no reasonable judge could find a witness credible.

When Gray informed what was in store for the rest of the week, a dozen miners employed by Bobcat Creek, each testifying about their actions when wearing the dust measurement devices, Larkin blanched in his gut. Sure, he knew it was the way the game was played, but my God, twelve of them! Hell, he thought, wouldn't matter if they paraded up twice as many employees to say the same thing – that nothing improper was done. The determination of truth is not so crass as simple addition. One witness's version of events could outweigh many contradicting it. While listening to Gray without expression, he transported himself to the moment, imagining if he were presiding in the case, thinking that it would be a high bar for him to accept a word from any of them.

Yet he did not view such likely contrived testimony with moral disgust because he knew what those employees were up against. All it stood for was the sad statement about what a man will do to keep his job. For each of them, it would be a matter of survival, especially in the state where the Bobcat Creek mine operated. West Virginia, even more so than its adjoining states, was facing a steady decline in coal mine production year after year, as wind and solar persistently crept into the business of supplying energy. Coal, with its intractable emissions, continued to be viewed as an undesirable source of energy. Understandably, uppermost in the minds of those employees was the need to put food on the table. Complicating the equation for them, it could not be ignored that, black lung or not, it was pretty damn good pay they were receiving. They weren't rich, but they lived well in their community. Who would want to put that at risk?

With Gray having finished with his summary of the day's testimony and provided a look ahead to the witnesses coming for the remainder of the week, Larkin graciously expressed his thanks for the recounting, adding that he knew his friend must be anxious to return home and he did not want to hold him up any further. He had managed to keep his views to himself, knowing that any such comments would not be received favorably.

Gray was glad to be released from additional conversation, ending it by merely agreeing that he was ready to call it a day. As he made the remark, he omitted mention that the commute home would not be next on his schedule, a stop at his G Street haunt intervening. Once Larkin had left, he wasted no time in gathering up the few things he needed to carry in his briefcase, this time exiting the office using the less traveled route, reducing the chances of encounters with others from the office.

Knowing Judge Gray to be a dependable creature of habit, as confirmed by Marla's recent experience in her first encounter, Marty Tranter waited patiently, confident that his mark would be exiting the building soon. What he could not know was that his honor's normally dependable schedule had been delayed by his discussion with another judge from the office. Tranter grew antsy when Gray failed to appear at his normally predictable time, but the meeting with the good judge had to occur on this evening. He had promised those two attorneys that it would. They would accept nothing less.

Keeping an eye out, as missing the judge's exit would be an unpardonable failure, he waited nearby, appearing to look in the display window of the adjacent clothing store. While he did so, his fretting increasing, he could not resist lighting up a cigarette. He'd been trying to kick the habit for months. A period of success would be followed by reverting to the things. Tried that nicotine patch too. None of the tactics worked. Those intervals when he stopped smoking were always broken when he was under high stress, and this was one of those times, for sure. Though he had Gray by the short hairs, thanks to Marla, it was still stressful. And working for those two, he knew, they didn't take well to failures. So, feeling the pressure, he was back on the smokes. Finishing one and still no sign of Gray, he immediately lit up another.

Finally, halfway through his second one, Gray exited the building. Tranter moved quickly, immediately tossing his cigarette. He did not hesitate, approaching Gray seconds after he had hit the sidewalk. "Judge," he called out. With no introduction, he added, "I need to speak with you for a moment."

Calling him by his title, Gray immediately stopped, turning to the direction where the person had called his name. But Gray did not recognize him at all. This was simply a stranger before him. Perhaps, he thought immediately, the individual had mistaken him for another judge from his office.

Dismissively, he informed the caller, "You must have mixed me up with someone else," respectfully adding. "I don't know you, sir."

Tranter fully expected that, but he had never been shy and being put off was not easily achieved with him.

"I need to speak with you judge," Tranter, undeterred, informed, this time more deliberately.

Gray, seeing that his attempt to dismiss the stranger had not worked, looked at the individual more closely this time. Nope, he thought, there was no recognition of this person. Trying to remain polite, but now also feeling some anxiety over the nature of this exchange, he warily informed the unfamiliar face, "I'm afraid I have no time for conversation now. If it's official business, you'll need to contact my office and then a call can be arranged. Good evening," he concluded, firmness in his voice, signaling that the conversation had concluded.

Well accustomed to such rebuffs, Tranter was undeterred. "It's not about official business," he informed, "well, not exactly." Then, allowing but a moment to pass, he added, "Judge Gray," with an ominous tone.

Gray was alarmed by the unsettling response and in particular that this unrecognizable person knew his name. Not about official business, and with that 'not exactly' remark, it was very disquieting. He was determined to avoid becoming entangled with this stranger, so he responded with the most authoritative judicial tone he could present. He looked briefly at the man, informing, "As I told you, contact my office for any business."

Immediately he turned and headed away, deciding apprehensively on the spot that there would be no stopping at the G Street Grill on this evening. Go straight to the garage, he thought, and make sure the stranger was not following him.

Tranter, totally unimpressed by Gray's bravado, informed, "This won't wait. We need to talk now," he spoke commandingly.

Gray, fearful that the guy could just be a nut, continued to walk away toward the garage, hoping that a policeman might be nearby.

"It's about Nicole Wilson," he then announced.

Stunned by those words, he stopped abruptly in his tracks. Panic ran through him. Speechless, he turned around, facing the man, the color quickly draining from his face.

"I don't know who you are talking about," he claimed, but his voice was shaky, revealing he knew the name exactly.

"Look, Judge, I don't have time for games, okay?" Tranter bluntly informed. In control of the situation, and knowing it, he repeated, "No games, your honor," employing the dignified title with plain derision. "Could I make myself any clearer?"

Gray, realizing his ruse was a flop, nervously looked around, worried if someone from his office was observing this. Seeing no one and relieved for the moment, he relented. "What is it you want?"

Tranter, confident of his upper hand, answered, "We can't talk here, not out here on the sidewalk. We need to go to your usual spot, the G Street," he said, conveyed in what was in effect an order and designed to make it even more clear that this was no bluff.

Gray grimaced. Fuck, he thought, his stomach in a terrible knot, this is serious trouble. Whoever this guy is, he's informed. Too well informed at that. First, he knows the woman's name and he also knows the place I frequent. What the hell had he gotten himself into?

A feeling of dread came upon him and now he felt light-headed, realizing this was a major problem. The imaginings of his fortunate relationship with 'Nicole' were now instantly and thoroughly doused.

A hushed "Yes," was all he could muster to say, the word difficult to get out.

"Follow me," Tranter instructed.

Relenting, now without a choice, he and the stranger proceeded to the bar. Upon arriving, as usual, Jerome took notice of his routine customer's entrance. And again, he observed, the judge was accompanied. This visit was also so very distinct from the customer he had known for years. His stops had always been a solo act.

This time that woman was not with him; instead, as best he could recollect, it was a guy he'd never seen before.

The way the two entered, it felt to him as if his familiar customer was a prisoner this time. Something about the way he walked in, in tow with that stranger, like he was under control or following orders.

Whatever it was, Jerome, from his years of knowing this regular customer and his experience in reading customers generally, knew that something was up. This was no convivial event.

Moreover, as the two entered, Gray, his head down, didn't even acknowledge the barkeep's presence, an oddity for sure. Then they proceeded directly to a booth, again with the judge behaving as a follower, subservient, not someone leading the procession. Keen in his observations, Jerome could tell, there were no emanations that this was a sociable association. Viscerally, he felt concern for his friendly, long-time, customer. He'd clearly been different ever since he started visiting with these newcomers, first with that considerably younger woman and now with this guy who dressed like he was a shady character out of some mystery movie.

The two, once seated in a remote booth, were approached by a waitress. Still making it clear that he was running the show, Tranter ordered a screwdriver. "And for you, Charles," he expressed with a tone of unwarranted familiarity, "will it be a Manhattan or an Old Fashioned?" an undisguised statement of the depth of his knowledge about his trapped companion.

In a barely audible voice, Gray, who had no interest in having a drink, obediently replied, "an Old Fashioned." Still stunned, somehow, he remembered his manners, adding belatedly to the waitress, "thank you."

Tranter waited, deciding to say no more until the drinks were served. He looked at him, with no expression, and Gray in fear, looked down, avoiding eye contact. Though he hoped it was not noticeable, he was trembling slightly, and his heart was racing, symptoms he could not stop.

From the bar, Jerome kept an eye on them.

Then, after what seemed like a long wait, the drinks arrived. Tranter again took command, starting the conversation with the audacity to announce, "To us, Judge Gray. You have nothing to fear, my friend."

Gray felt sickened. This total stranger, who patently brought no glad tidings, had the nerve to describe him as a friend. Though Tranter attempted to toast by offering to clink his glass with Gray's, the judge would have no part of it. He had been knocked off-guard, but now he began to right himself. There was no choice but to learn what this character will be demanding, he thought.

"Enough," he told Tranter. "No more niceties. You might as well tell me what your gambit is."

Tranter recognized that the judge had stopped his subservient posture. An attempt to rebut the judge's effort to gain the upper hand, he calmly responded, "There's no need for hostility. Since you want to be direct, here it is. We know about the whole thing with Miss Wilson," he informed.

"Allow me to introduce myself. I am Marty Tranter," he said with no other information offered. "You sir, are in a serious predicament. A crude person would say you are fucked," he said firmly, a reaction to Gray's sudden boldness. "You're in the biggest trial of your life, and The Sentinel is covering it every day, as you know. The last thing you need is to become the story, that you're fucking a woman who is not your wife. You know the case will be immediately reassigned to another judge. A horrible final note to what had been for you, that is up till now, an unblemished career."

Back on his heels again, Gray's stomach knotted anew, as he waited for the announcement of the extortion terms that were about to come. He said nothing, as he looked closely at the adversary before him. Involuntarily, beads of sweat now formed on his brow. Gray was aware of it, but it was not as if he could will the display of fear away. He hated that his anxiety was so recognizable. There was no choice but to mop it up, as he reached for his hankie to wipe the moisture away. Tranter noticed. Though he remained expressionless, he was pleased that Gray was intimidated, knowing that he had him.

"So," Tranter continued, now almost breezily, "you're going to need to find that this AWC business was not at all intentional. That the government simply didn't prove its case. You legal folks call it preponderance of evidence, I believe. That's what I've been told is the standard. You're going to find they didn't meet that burden."

It was clear that he had just given the judge his orders.

Having just landed the hammer, Tranter immediately continued. "But, there's something good in this for you. We know of your financial situation. We know of the very unfortunate situation with your ailing wife. And, we know where you'd like to be when you retire, a date that is on the near horizon. To that end, my people will be depositing $300,000 to accounts in your name.

And, as a show of good faith, once you give your assurance that you will cooperate, deposits will be happening, starting in a few days, and they will continue and be completed well before you issue your decision. That, we have calculated should put you in the position to acquire that Gulf Coast residence you've wanted for so long, but which had been totally out of your reach."

Gray could not believe what he had just heard. He was dumbfounded. First the stick and then the carrot, a very sizeable carrot. His dream being offered as part of the package. It wasn't hard to do the calculation. When combined with the promised bribe money, even his dumpy house would fetch enough to make the Florida prize a reality.

Housing in the suburban D.C. area still commanded a sizeable price. It was just that way, proximity to Washington being a key determination in home sales. His house had proximity, though not much else. Then there would be the bonus that while he couldn't afford a palatial place in Florida, the housing was considerably less expensive down there. A nice, perhaps even new, house would be attainable. With all this being presented, the sweat ebbed, his mind distracted by the deal he was being offered.

It could be worse, he realized, they could've just extorted him over his sex with that Nicole *bitch*, his revised view of her now in his mind. They didn't need to offer any benefit at all.

Tranter recognized that it was all overwhelming. He then tried to soothe his catch.

"This is for real. We know you are capable of writing a convincing opinion. You've been around long enough to know how to craft a decision which will be incapable of being overturned. You don't need any instructions about that. So, it's a win-win."

Gray had never been corrupted before. Of course, he'd never had a case of this order, one that would present itself as a subject for corruption, so there was that.

Realizing that the man was flattened, Tranter offered a balm. "Look, what's done is done. The mines charged with this, well they're not fooling with these dust cassettes anymore. That is, if they ever did," he was quick to add. "And if we assume it did happen, well no decision of yours can undo the dust those miners were exposed to."

Going too far, sounding like an uber-advocate, Tranter argued outrageously that "fines like the government seeks, that can only impair those mines from running safe operations."

Not even Malthan or Krakovich would make that claim.

Gray recoiled at that last claim. He knew better than that; such an argument mixed up mutually exclusive matters. Given his serious predicament though, he decided it was wiser to say nothing.

The threat, and the pitch, having been made, Tranter knew it was time to stop the session. He decided to end it, as much as a meeting of this nature could conclude that way, on an postive note.

"Judge," he said imparting a faux tone of respect for his title, "think this over. No real harm will be done. As I said, any hypothetical harm to miners, that can't be repaired. This dust issue is now in the past," he repeated. "If they ever did it, those mines aren't going to be fooling around with those dust samples anymore."

Bringing it back to Gray's interests, he continued, "And for you, it's the dignified retirement you deserve. A quiet time in a Gulf Coast Eden."

Pausing, he then continued with the business at hand. "But, I'll need you to affirm that you're onboard in order for this to move forward. As people in your profession say, time is of the essence. You'll need to confirm this by tomorrow."

He waited a moment, then, to remove any doubt or hesitancy the good judge might entertain, continued "and if you can't buy into this mutually beneficial arrangement, well I don't have to tell you, we'll have no choice but to move to Plan B, if you will."

This person could not have been clearer. There was no misunderstanding. Plan B was clear. Gray somberly nodded that he understood. As if he had any choice, he thought. Say 'no' and the whole Nicole Wilson thing explodes. He wouldn't have to resign for such a transgression, but there would be pressure for him to do so. Highly unprofessional conduct for a judge, the office would announce. Highly unprofessional.

And though it made no sense logically, the government's case would be indirectly damaged. It would be a setback, though through no fault of their own. Then, the whole dust tampering case would have to be restarted with a new judge assigned. Every judge would dread that the assignment would come their way and he would become a permanent pariah in the office.

Beyond that, none of those awful results even took into account the devastating effect on his unwell wife, and the permanent and deep damage to their marriage. She would carry the wounds from it every day until her last breath.

He didn't need to ponder the decision and the idea of contacting this guy tomorrow was a nauseating thought.

"I will do what you ask," he said tersely, thinking that 'do what he demanded' was more accurate. "I'm confirming it now," he added to avoid any uncertainty.

The arrangement was on.

Tranter uncharacteristically shut up. "Okay," he said simply. "Thank you, Judge. Saves both of us a call tomorrow. The first installment of our appreciation will occur within a day or two," he reaffirmed. The rapidness of a payment was not based on good faith, it was to entrench the jurist deeper into this immediately, foreclosing any chance for him to reverse course.

Gray then arose from the booth, without a concluding goodbye. Jerome again took notice, observing that the guy the judge arrived with remained in the booth. Though he could not know what was going on, he had enough experience to realize that the judge left with a heavy look on his face and a walk that matched it. He worried for his patron friend.

As Gray drove home, understandably, there were no good thoughts in his head. He was nauseous too; reflux caused some food to rise near his mouth. He thought about pulling over to wretch, but he was able to keep it down. That Nicole thing, he thought, now considering for the first time that it was unlikely her real name, that thing was over. He'd been had. Big time.

What an old fool he had been, entertaining the idea that a woman of her beauty and much younger years too boot would be interested in him. Such nonsense.

At the same time, anger arose about her. That bitch, he thought. Such a tramp. What kind of woman would be involved in such duplicitous and immoral conduct? His condemnation did not extend to himself. It was all directed at her.

And now, because of the bargain with the devil made moments ago, his career would end in shame. There was no fixing that. The most he could hope for was that it would be limited to his private disgrace, one he would carry inside until the end. All those years of being upstanding and then to conclude that long career on such a note.

Soberly, he realized that shameful ending was a best-case scenario; that he would retire to Florida and privately harbor his compromised behavior, carrying it to his grave. He then added to that thought, that such an ending was only if it all went 'well,' so to speak. He was no fool, as he realized that if it unraveled, if somehow the whole arrangement were exposed, criminal liability, namely felonies, would be brought. He would have to hope that the multiple parties involved, parties for whom moral standards would not be of concern for them, would honor the agreement. Honor among thieves, he thought, was all he had to rely upon.

Upon arriving home, still terribly shaken by the earlier events, he learned that Millie had experienced a tough day with her condition. Each day was unpredictable for her, and today there had been a flare-up. His conscience spiked, ruing the unforgivable potential harm he had created for his ailing wife. Seeing her, he now felt deep shame over the breach of his marital vows, a shame that was absent until Tranter confronted him.

Before tonight, he had tabled the few moments of remorse, focusing on what had been his thrill over Nicole. Now, when he thought of her, that jezebel, it was with phrases like, 'that lying bitch,' and cruder descriptions of her that he tagged in place of her name. His violation to Millie, it was made far worse because of her illness. She, so burdened with the unrelenting disease and yet he could not remain faithful until her time came. He was not thinking rationally about the whole matter, his thoughts shifting from self-loathing to self-pity.

Oddly, with his defense mechanisms then kicking in, he tried to see the mess as a benefit to her, telling himself that with a Florida retirement now reachable, it would be a joy for her, the warmer climes, a fresh place, perhaps it would reduce her symptoms and extend her life. But he knew it was a dishonest mental game, nothing more than contrivances, trying to justify his behavior and the deal he had just struck, by presenting it as a benefit to his wife.

As best he could, he doted on Millie that evening, until he finally had her safely in bed. Then he retreated to the living room with his companion glass of wine, as he considered the mess again. It was no use. There was no escape, no way to undo the trouble he had created. He could sit there all evening and nothing would change. An hour later, with no way out, he realized he had to get some sleep.

Once in bed, Millie was by then sound asleep, thankfully oblivious to all the turmoil he'd brought. As he lay there, no peace existed. Tomorrow would be an ugly day. When he faced those devils for the defense, the two who had known of the trap in which he'd been snared, he would feel hate, but he would have to keep it contained, unable to display it. It sickened him that his thoughts had used the term "the defense." Those two did not employ a 'defense.' They used an offense, one completely apart from any legitimate legal practice.

Yet, he knew, there was no way to get even.

They had won.

CHAPTER 12

When morning arrived, Charles prepared to leave the house without dawdling, as he wanted to avoid any prolonged time with Millie. The haste was brought about by his guilt, which she brought to the fore with her rare amorous invitation for love-making the night before. He especially wanted to avoid eye contact with her. He knew his wife could employ that method to see through his words, assessing whether his excuses were made-up or genuine.

To his relief, he was able to make his exit without giving her the opportunity to apply that assessment, her malady leaving her too tired for any meaningful exchange between them.

He left their bedroom with his usual goodbye, the short, "see you tonight," but dropping his customary "dear," from the end of his words, replacing it with "Millie." After his afternoon rendezvous with 'Nicole' and then his recent turndown of Millie's offer of intimacy, and now captured by Tranter for his wrongs, he couldn't bring himself to punctuate his goodbye to her with 'dear.'

Could he, legitimately, ever call her 'Dear' again?

Though she was half-awake, Millie picked up on his formal use of her name, replacing the ostensibly caring expression of 'dear.'

Relieved to be on the road, away from the direct contact with his wife for now, and though he would normally be fussing over the traffic volume of the morning commute, the conflict between home and his extracurricular activity dominated his attention.

A welcome relief, upon arriving at the office, of necessity, his attention turned to the day's courtroom proceedings, though that simply substituted one set of problems for the other. There was little time available before it was time to start the walk to the hearing site.

On his way to court, the distraction he hoped for during the walk to the courthouse, did not happen. Unavoidably, his thoughts shifted rapidly between the transgressions against his wife, and that he was now trapped because of them. Worse, he had agreed to the financial arrangement with Tranter. There was no way out. Why, he considered, that son of a bitch probably recorded their conversation at the G Street last evening. He gave no thought to the day's upcoming testimony. He knew that none of it mattered anymore.

His trips to and from the courthouse used to provide a chance to clear his head before the day began. Now it was a jumbled and unpleasant way to make the morning walk. So completely occupied, he started to cross a street, though the light warned not to walk. A horn blast from an oncoming car saved him from being struck. It was a near miss as he fled back to the sidewalk, shaken, his heart racing. Would have deserved it, dying on the spot, he thought, so ashamed of his fall from the prestige he once held. Now ultra-wary, he continued his way to court.

When the Court's morning session began, as Gray looked out at the defense counsel standing before him, he could not help but examine their faces again, just as he did after the prior instances of his infidelity, a vain attempt to discern if any of them looked at him differently on this day.

Their faces looked the same as all previous days, both sides respectfully looking back at him, completely unreadable, as they awaited his word that they be seated. But this time he grimly realized that one side, despite their stoic faces giving no hint of what they knew, had all the details, his two acts of unfaithfulness, and now his acceptance of the bribe.

As he now recognized, both lead counsel for the mine knew all about it. Winston and Milo had been fully briefed by Tranter in the early evening the day before. They were delighted. Though one event would have been totally sufficient, now the jurist had been snared twice. They knew that, even if Gray didn't buy into the string of experts the Respondents were about to present, with his sexual entanglements, and the bribe, he would have no choice but to dismiss all the charges.

The trial had now shifted dramatically, though only Milo, Winston and the judge knew it. The Secretary was clueless. From here on out, the purpose of the testimony would be to provide a record sufficient so that any appellate court would have no choice but to affirm Gray's ruling. This was easily achievable because the experts, as well as the mine personnel witnesses who had earlier testified, would provide the 'substantial evidence' to uphold his decision. Also in their favor would be Gray's expected credibility determinations. Such rulings were almost never reversed, a fact of which the judge was well aware. With rare exceptions, Courts routinely honored those conclusions, the idea being that no transcript can trump a judge's firsthand observations of the credibility to be given to the testimony of a witness.

In the predicament he had placed himself, he could neither fight nor flee. On the verge of losing it, he willed the appearance of composure, though barely, as he got a grip on himself.

"Good morning," he began, his voice cracking as he spoke those words, exposing the fix he was in.

Milo and Winston immediately recognized the fear in the judge's voice. Neither of them wanted the judge to come undone in public. That would cause the whole scheme to collapse.

Gray continued, "Please be seated. Is the Respondent ready to call its next witness?"

Must maintain composure, hold steady, he told himself over and over, hoping that by repeating that mantra he would avoid a meltdown.

Winston responded, calmly, evenly, acting as if there had been no new developments at all.

"Good morning, again, your Honor. Yes," he announced, "We are ready. The Respondent calls Virgil Cobb."

Both sides were aware that a lot was riding on the judge's take of the multiple witnesses about to come. Though the Secretary tried to diminish the effect of so many employees testifying that nothing untoward had occurred by offering to stipulate that they would all testify there was no tampering, the defense would have none of it. All twelve must be allowed to testify Milo and Winston demanded, especially in a case of this enormity.

Cobb was the first of twelve miners to take the witness stand. The twelve apostles, thought Sanford, hoping that there could be a mine employee Judas among them, but knowing it was a mere flight of fancy. Milo and Winston would never run such a risk.

The witness approached the stand and Gray began by swearing him in, but Cobb announced that his religious beliefs only allowed him to make an affirmation. This was not new to Gray; occasionally witnesses would invoke this and it was not objectionable. Affirming was permissible and it had the same effect, the witness promising to testify truthfully. The problem was, in all his years, Gray had found that the "affirmers" tended to be untruthful.

As with Slone, Cobb had not spiffed up for his court appearance. His clothes were similar to those he would wear when arriving for his shift; a brown flannel shirt and jeans, but at least both witnesses had washed up for the occasion.

It was not his first time testifying in a Mine Act proceeding, though he had never traveled to Washington for testimony or for any other reason. Though he had only seen images of the Nation's Capital on TV, he was not the least bit intimidated by the location, nor by the prestigious courtroom where the proceeding was being held.

He had also stayed up quite late the night before, hanging out with his fellow workers, all of whom were there to testify for their mine employer. They were all told that everything was on the mine; travel, hotel, food and drinks. They would not have to spend a cent, and they should have whatever they wanted, no scrimping was expected. And if there was an expense not covered up front, they should simply fill out a voucher when they returned home. There would be none of that business requiring a receipt in order to be reimbursed.

The nature of the bargain was all well understood, though not a word of the terms was ever spoken. Winston and Milo had interviewed each of them and during the course of those interviews the nature of their testimony was politely explained. Knowing that each witness had to be completely trustworthy, with no risk that any of them would acknowledge any dishonest behavior by the mines in collecting the dust samples, Milo and Winston carefully vetted each prospective miner.

Careful as always, in evaluating the potential miner witnesses, neither attorney ever made a hint that any of them should testify untruthfully, but the goal was to make sure that they would dependably lie. This objective was accomplished through a benign description explaining what the government was claiming with this dust collection case.

But the miners, all of them, knew exactly what was going on. The miners talked with one another and they all had eyes. There was no confusion over the dust sampling at the mine. Doing things with the sampling, they'd all seen it and, when required, assisted with the manipulation of the devices.

Their stories were kept simple. Complicated explanations could invite dangers when it came time for cross-examination. The word perjury never came up when preparing the witnesses but, to a man, they knew that was exactly what they would be doing on the stand.

"You may have heard," Milo would patiently explain to each miner, as if they were clueless about the matter, "the government is asserting that your employer, Bobcat Creek, tampered with the dust collection samples." Just beginning that way, calling the other side, "the government," and also by reminding the witness that Bobcat was his employer, set the tone.

Throughout the mining community, that term, 'the government,' was an odious word. Miners and their families alike bought into it. It was the government, not the mine, who was the bad guy. This view held, even though it was mine operators, for over a century, who were the cause behind mine disasters.

Miners knew who was responsible for the deaths, as the stories had been told from generation to generation. It was not the government. They did not need to read history books to be aware of major death events in mines, like the Monongah disaster at Fairmont Coal's Number 6 and 8 mines, where 367 miners died in 1907. That led to the government's creation of the Bureau of Mines. Following Fairmont, mine disasters continued, regularly, and the miners knew of each one. Yet, most simply considered the dangers as part of the job, thinking it was just the way things were.

And never mind that far more federal dollars flowed into West Virginia and Kentucky, than went out in tax dollars. The families in those states would be much worse off if not for that federal spending, but most did not make the connection.

The mines reinforced those negative words. "The damn government," they would repeatedly call it, "all the time, always trying to hurt your ability to make a living," they would tell them, with their "unnecessary interference" and "needless regulation."

For good measure, foremen and others with management would suggest that all of this business of inspecting mines also placed a burden on the operation, threatening their jobs, either by reducing the workforce or shutting down entirely.

Those threats, in particular. always caught the miners' attention. "The government," they would frequently say among themselves, "they're gonna kill our jobs, that's what!" The approach, effectively used, was that a lie, repeated often enough, becomes the accepted truth. For a majority, the tactic worked.

Knowing that each witness had to be trustworthy, with no hint that they would acknowledge any dishonest behavior by the mines in collecting the dust samples, Milo and Winston carefully questioned each prospective miner. A few, displaying some hesitance during the interviews, were quickly discarded from the witness list. To make sure the message got out, the two would alert mine management to pay close attention to those potential turncoats.

In setting the stage before each interview, with each one done separately, no other miner in the room, the two would explain the dust tampering case in a tone unmistakably conveying the outrageousness of the claim. They artfully made it personal too. "So, the government is asserting that people *like you* did awful things such as taking the dust monitors outside during the testing period, or placing the devices in the intake air, or putting them in a lunch pail, and nasty things like that. Now if *you* did something like that, then we would want you to tell us about that. Course, we'd be obligated to disclose that to the government and they might take action against *you* for doing such a thing, but we can't help that. But understand we just want to hear the truth from you."

Even the dimmest bulb understood what the attorneys were telling them, and the obvious threat that came with it, all under the guise of just innocently explaining the reason for the interview. The words from the attorneys were all said before the tape recorder was turned on and the interview began.

Few of them believed the operators' line, and those who knew the truth had enough sense to keep their mouths shut, talking only with those miners who shared their skepticism.

After Cobb had been 'affirmed' for his testimony, Milo began by reviewing his long work history at the mine, some seventeen years underground at various jobs, roof bolter, continuous miner operator, belt examiner being among them. Cobb then explained the procedure he used on those occasions when he was fitted with the dust sampling unit, maintaining that he followed the instructions "to a T" as he put it. He asserted that he was careful with the unit during the entire sampling period and that he never interfered with the sampling. Presented with a laundry list of all the things that had been alleged as tampering, he denied each one.

"And, Virgil," Milo asked, using his first name in addressing him to present a folksy atmosphere, "did you ever intentionally step on a dust collection tube?" and "did you ever take the dust collection unit to the intake air during your shift," and "did you force air into the unit, or see anyone do such a thing to the unit?"

For each question, Cobb answered firmly that he had never done any of those things, and improvising, he added, with a predictable triple negative, "and I never did nothing else neither to the equipment."

Milo was unhappy that Virgil went off script as it were, because it had been hammered into each of them that they were only to answer the question asked. Period. Staying away from using terms that could be viewed as looking down on the miners, the two litigators avoided pompous terms like 'extemporize."

They were told not to go beyond the questions presented, no "winging it," as Winston put it with a half-smile, but accompanied with firm instructions.

Virgil had gone off the reservation with his extra comment, but fortunately with no harm resulting. Still, Milo wrote on his legal pad, pushing the paper over to Winston, "need to review again with the other witnesses the rules for testifying. No improvising!" Out of caution, he then scribbled over the remark and was careful to tear off the page during the next break, depositing the scraps in his pocket.

Next up was Billy Tanner. Predictably, his testimony was clone-like to that of Cobb's. They were, as it's said, singing from the same hymnbook.

Gray had heard enough by Wednesday's close. It was tedious and he knew it would be more of the same from the parade of miners yet to come. But it was not his place to comment on the repetitiveness of miner witnesses. Not in a case this big and especially not now, with his ship sunk. Had he not been irreparably compromised, he likely would have discarded their too-uniform testimony when it came time to decide the case. The few blows landed by the Secretary on the subject during cross-examination were to no avail.

Besides, the case was now over in terms of the outcome. Being skilled in writing decisions, initially he would have to note the too similar consistency in the miners' testimony, a show that he was objective, but he would then conclude that it was of no great moment because the critical issue was whether there was tampering. It was a sideshow, not outcome determinative.

In addition, he had always taken a more forgiving attitude toward witness preparation. Coaching, done artfully or clumsily, was always done. The legal profession was not without its warts. It was simply more pronounced when so many witnesses spoke to the same subject – did they tamper with the dust collection process when they were being sampled? Heaven forbid, no!

But now, with the developments compromising him beyond any repair, he knew better. Of course the mine had tampered with the sampling!

And, so informed, what could he do about it now?

The answer was clear. Nothing!

Though he held himself together the whole day, his thoughts continually returned to the fix he was in. There was no way out. If he were to confess to all of it, his career, though retirement was near anyway, was over, with disastrous results. No one would deem him a hero. He would be viewed as simply a louse, a violator of his marital vows, and then, confronted with it, he made it worse, becoming a bribe-taker. They might find a way to cancel his retirement benefits too.

Criminal charges would be inevitable, as would the certainty of a conviction. Sure, he'd get some leniency for fessing up to all of it, but there would be some jail time. Even given his age, it would be for some number of years. And Millie, he thought, would give him no credit for all the years he had been encumbered with her disease. She would leave and stay with a friend.

Given all that, the only chance was to stick with the corrupt arrangement he had made with Tranter. That, and pray that it would not unravel in some unpredictable manner. Then, his thoughts continued, if it went that way, he would retire the same day he issued that damn decision and, as the expression goes, get the hell out of Dodge.

Trying to think about the bright side, he considered that, if the payments started flowing in, as promised, he could start the process of selling that crappy house of his. Millie would just have to accept that Florida would be their next residence. She really had no choice in the matter, no cards to play. He would finagle a story that they could afford the move and besides, he would insist that the warmer climes would benefit her health. He could sell her on the move, he believed.

With all this weighing on him, the walk back to the office offered no breather from his problems. He especially wanted to avoid seeing anyone from the office, but his poor luck continuing, Larkin was right there in the foyer when he arrived at the office.

Given his problems, Larkin's buoyant greeting was particularly unwelcome. Receptive to talking or not, just as he had to keep himself together all day in court, he was again called upon to maintain the pretense in front of Richard.

"Hey there, Charles," Larkin began, "Hope you can spare of few minutes to fill me in on today's developments," he continued, inviting himself for a new visit to learn about the hearing developments.

Gray, seeing no alternative but to grant the visit, forced himself to bring up a smile of sorts. "Of course, Richard. Just give me a few to get squared away."

With all his trouble Gray wanted the session to be as brief as possible. It had already been exhausting, maintaining the façade of calmness all day during the hearing. Now he would have to keep up the act. At least it would brief. He could get through it. He must.

When Larkin arrived at his office, he began with an innocuous remark. "So, how's it going?"

"Not bad, not bad," came Gray's response, thinking as he uttered the words, the gross overstatement it conveyed. 'It could not be worse,' would be more like it, he thought. If his colleague knew the truth. If only there was someone to confess his sins without fear. He could not even rely upon a priest. He knew this personal disaster could not be revealed to anyone, not a one, though he wished it were otherwise just to lessen the burden on his soul.

His adversaries knew, of course; that Tranter guy and those two scoundrel attorneys for the mine. They all knew. He was not so dense as to fail to appreciate that Malthan and Krakovich were the bastard orchestrators behind the set up. Someone like Tranter doesn't come out of the blue. With those thoughts clouding his head, it was difficult to simultaneously keep up his conversation with Larkin.

Willing himself to stay on message in the exchange with Larkin, lest he breakdown and spill out his irreparable fix, he continued, "The day was taken up with the testimony of two miners who were involved with the dust sampling. As expected, they swore there was no monkey business with it. Neither wilted upon cross-examination either. Their testimony was consistent, a little too consistent in fact, as they used some of the same phrases in describing the testing. Clearly, they had been prepped to give the same account, but it went a bit too far at times when it felt like their testimony had been scripted."

Larkin was relieved upon hearing his colleague's account. So much of their prior sessions had reflected Gray's seeming tilt toward the defense, a perspective that Larkin felt was unwarranted. He decided to avoid any comment which might provoke Gray to answer defensively. Instead, he simply nodded, acknowledging the recounting. "So, the whole day with those two miners' testimony. What's up for tomorrow?"

"Tomorrow, it's more of the same. The Respondent's lawyers are calling up twelve miner witnesses." He couldn't bring himself to refer to them as "counsels," too dignified a term to apply to those scoundrels.

He continued, "So, ten of them to go. It'll be cumulative of course, but with such big stakes, I can't comment about it being overdone. The Respondent's attorneys would never agree to the government's willingness to stipulating that the next ten witnesses, or any number less, would testify along the same lines. They want the parade of miners to each testify that there was no tampering going on. Stipulating diminishes the impact, so I would accept the defense's objection to it. Respondent is building a record and in a case of this enormity, I would never impose such a limitation."

"I get it," Larkin answered, nodding as he replied. "With this matter applying to so many mines, all the stops have to be pulled out."

Gray was relieved that Larkin didn't criticize his take, as he had done so occasionally in their previous discussions about the trial. With no need for more detail about the day's testimony, he just had to hold on a little longer. Following his hostage status of the previous evening, today had been the toughest in his career. A whole day of trial, all the while knowing that those two attorneys had captured his former independence. It was exhausting. And then, the necessity to speak with Larkin, even brief as it was, made him feel near collapse.

Larkin gave him the out he needed to end the conversation. "Well, I know this is so taxing, Charles. I don't want to hold you up from getting home."

"Thanks, Richard," he said appreciatively. Almost done with this conversation, he thought.

"Yes, I'm pretty well spent, that's true."

Once Larkin departed, Gray closed his door, the first moment of the day to take a breather from his public persona. Privacy finally, but his problems would not let go. The developments in the testimony today were of no moment. Hell, even if one of those miners had admitted to tampering, it wouldn't change his decision. Not now. In that unlikely event, he would just have to create some reason to discount such testimony. He could do that. Just conclude that the witness was an outlier, if not an outright liar! A malcontent with some axe to grind.

With so many years of deciding cases, he knew how to craft a decision that would reach the result he wanted, even if there were warts in it. He dismissed the idle thought. Those two attorneys for the mine, they wouldn't let a gaff like that occur. If it did, they'd have the witness recanting before he was done. Not to mention that the misbehaving miner would be out of work.

The ironic part was he was leaning toward the mine winning anyway. If the trial continued as it had thus far, the trap they laid for him might have been unnecessary. There would have been no need to set him up. Wouldn't it have been so nice, if he had just met Nicole and she was interested in him without being part of a scheme. His moment of unrealistic fantasy then evaporated immediately, anger taking its place; he could not ignore that it was all an act on her part. The nerve of her! The nerve of those scoundrels!

Then, as he continued this moment of conflicted thoughts, he tried again to put a positive spin on it all. There was, after all, that chance to rid himself of that awful house and retire to Florida, with its friendlier climes. It would be better for Millie's health too, he rationalized again. Soberly, he knew it depended upon that Tranter guy making good on his promises and, beyond that, no one exposing him. Those lawyers, unscrupulous as they were, they had their own very big interest in the outcome. If this scheme unraveled, they could suffer just as much, he reassured himself.

His thoughts then shifted back towards that bitch, that so-called Nicole, whatever her real name was. Though the lawyers and Tranter would likely stick by the bargain made, that trollop could be the wild card in this arrangement. She could leak it all or just blabber about it to someone in a bar and from there it could go to the press, the whole arrangement then tumbling out. Unlikely that she would do that, he thought. It would not be good for her health to err that way. With people of this ilk and so much money involved, she would become, as they say, expendable.

The brief time to sort out his tumbled thoughts provided little solace and he knew that no peace would be in the offing. Only much later, in fact after years had elapsed from this mess, could he then begin to stop obsessing over the whole thing. It was the price to be paid. The alternatives were worse, he reminded himself; disgrace, a conviction, some time in prison certain, those would be the only things everyone would think of when it came to the subject of the formerly Honorable Charles Gray.

He looked at his watch; time to head home, his obligations calling; his existence moving from one weary event to another. As he left the office it was a relief to exit without seeing any co-worker. Exiting the building, he made his customary goodnights to the building security personnel.

It was then, as soon as he hit the sidewalk, that Tranter appeared.

Gray recognized him immediately, thinking, Shit, now what?

Tranter knew that his presence would not be welcomed. He got to the point without delay. "Judge, sorry to intrude. There's been a change to our arrangement."

Gray was fearful. Now what, he thought? They're reneging on the money, he anticipated, figuring they wouldn't need to pay him a cent.

"It's not a big deal," he began, trying to allay the worry that Gray's face plainly displayed, his color turning pale. "The payments will now be in cash. We determined that it would be too much of a hassle for us to create bank accounts, with signatures and all that stuff required. Leaves a trail too. Cash has no trail. That's it, we're done. Told you it was no big deal," he finished, and with that he thrust an overstuffed manilla envelope to the judge.

As it happened, Larkin was exiting the building at that moment. He immediately spotted Gray with a stranger, who was speaking to him. The individual was no one he recognized, certainly no one from the office.

Of immediate concern, Larkin did see an envelope being passed from the stranger to Gray. So very odd. What was that about?

Not wanting his colleague to spot him, he immediately turned away, heading towards his parking lot. He didn't know what was going on, but he was troubled by it. It was unsettling.

Gray, though floored by the openness of the encounter, still reflexively accepted the envelope. This was highly dangerous, he thought, this cloak-and-dagger business. Unaware that Larkin had just witnessed the two, he worried that if anyone were to recognize him, it would prompt questions, or at least curiosity, about what was going on.

With those great concerns in mind, he spoke up. "Look, this can't be repeated. If you're to pass anything to me, do it at the Grill, not outside the goddam place I work!"

Tranter, not in the business of being intimidated, told Gray, "That's fine. Had no choice this first time. Just showing we're acting in good faith, holding up our end. You need to give me your cell number, so I can alert you to meet me for the future installments."

'Acting in good faith,' 'future installments,' thought Gray, such neutral words, for what he was engaged in – there was no other way to describe it; those words 'good faith,' and 'installments,' they had no place in this scheme.

It was nothing less than bribery, plain and simple, that's what it was. Still, he complied, providing his cell number.

Wishing the encounter had never occurred, he decided to end it. "Now, we're done. Good bye," he told Tranter, as he pivoted away.

Larkin, though he decided to move some distance from the scene, could not resist another glance back. The two of them, standing there, Gray holding the envelope the stranger had passed to him and then observing words exchanged between them, but he was unable to make out what was being said. A moment later, now standing far enough away not to be recognized, he saw the meeting end, each moving in a different direction. No handshake or mutual wave, nothing to indicate that the encounter was congenial. It was clear something was very much awry.

Fortunately, as Gray left his meeting, he was headed away from Larkin's position. The other guy, whoever he was, was moving directly towards him. He had no worries, each a total stranger to one another. So, knowing he was safe, Larkin stood still, pretending to be occupied, holding his cell phone to his ear, seemingly in conversation. Tranter walked by him, oblivious to Larkin taking a good look at him. He had no recognition of him but tried to hold the man's appearance in his memory.

Tranter, having long played in the arenas of the corrupt, could not fathom Gray's lack of cordiality. Who did Gray think he was? An angel? Someone whose own conduct was above his? Gray was no better than him. As he saw it, they had an arrangement, one that was mutually beneficial. No, he knew they wouldn't become friends, but there was no need for the judge to act huffy, implying moral superiority.

Even as Gray began to leave, Tranter undeterred, got in the last word. "We'll be in touch," he informed, loudly enough, that the judge heard the unwelcome remark.

Larkin, more intrigued, heard it too.

Neurotically, as he briskly walked to his garage, Gray held the envelope tightly. Once in his car, locking its doors and looking around to make sure no one was nearby, he opened the envelope. He had never seen so much cash in his life. Ten thousand friggin' dollars! Checks of large amounts, sure, he'd seen many of those, but not cash. All hundreds. Fearful, not thrilled, he looked around again, to make sure no one else was near his parking spot.

Reassured he was alone, he counted them, a hundred of the bills. Stuffing the money back in the envelope, he thought, time to get the hell out of here! He leaned over, stuffing the envelope under the passenger seat. Careful, careful, he reminded himself, get home with no incidents.

Following his own admonition, his return drive home was ultra-cautious and without incident. Occupying his thoughts on the way, a new worry presented itself – how would he go about depositing this cash and all that was yet to come? Once in his garage, he leaned over to stuff the envelope further under the passenger side seat.

He then took a moment to compose himself before seeing Millie.

Disturbed by the unusual meeting he observed between his colleague and the stranger, the event reinforced by that puffy envelope being handed over to Gray, Larkin instinctively knew that something foul was afoot. He could not help but dwell on it, as he reviewed the scene he'd just witnessed. There was no innocuous explanation to it. The only logical conclusion was that it had to be associated with Gray's ultra-significant case. Nothing else made sense.

What he could do about it, that was a very different matter.

Once dinner was over and Sophia was in bed, Larkin told Sandy about the disconcerting development with Gray. Upon his describing the scene, she had no ambivalence in her reaction to it, agreeing that it could not be dismissed as a harmless encounter which should not to be read into. Quite the contrary, she also had a dark take on the event, especially with that business of the envelope being exchanged.

How to react to it, as with Richard, for that she had no answer. Part of her reaction was a hesitancy for Richard to become involved. Hadn't he already had a full plate of danger in his life with that Idaho mine business?

Besides, at this point, his concerns were merely in the realm of suspicion. He could hardly raise his observation with anyone else and expect action to result.

Okay, so he sees two people meet and he knows one of them, but not the other, and he witnesses an envelope being transferred.

So what! Not exactly the kind of stuff to make a federal case out of it. Such concerns would likely be viewed as none of his business, mere meddling on his part, to what might be an utterly harmless act. And what good would come of it?

This was an invitation for trouble. Do nothing, she urged.

Entering his house through the garage side door, Gray greeted Millie with as much calmness as he could project. Uncharacteristically, he initiated the recounting of the day's trial events, not waiting for her to prompt him about it. This took some of the pressure off him.

She was surprised that Charles started the subject. Most times, she would have to bring up the trial. Only then, with varying degrees of obvious disinterest, he would oblige, and provide a summary. Not this time, as he offered more detail than usual, though the testimony he recounted seemed less noteworthy than the briefer summaries he gave of more important past witnesses.

The retelling met his objective, capturing her attention and diverting her ability to size up her husband's behavior. It also calmed him, if only for the time being, by focusing on the miner witnesses, instead of the tumultuous mess he had created for himself.

The summary completed, he was able to conveniently excuse himself to prepare his dinner and, later, when alone, for the much-needed drink he would need to calm his nerves.

The time for dinner and, following his routine, showering, freed him from further exchanges with his wife. When those things were done, Millie had already retired to bed, per her own dependable schedule.

This left the beleaguered Charles the moment of solitude he desperately needed. His circumstance was so overwhelming, but the alternative was demonstrably worse and not just for him but for Millie too, perhaps more so for her, he considered. The problem was not going to go away but at least the hour plus he gave himself to have a glass of wine, and then a refill, was, by comparison, a respite from the exhausting day. When he did come to bed his wife was already snoring, a noise he did not mind, as it meant peace, not conversation, would bring his night to a close.

Somehow, he slept well, the alarm waking him. Surprised that his night had not been fitful, he attributed it to sheer exhaustion from the day's tumult. It would have been almost too much if he had to drag himself through another full day of trial on minimal sleep.

CHAPTER 13

Tranter was thoroughly burdened with the Ruby mess. Lying in bed that evening, he worried about how to contend with her. At least Marla, discrete and trustworthy, presented no problems, but that Ruby, she was a wild card for sure.

His phone rang. A late evening call too often meant a problem.

As if his thoughts about his West Virginia troublemaker prompted the call, it was her.

"Yes, Ruby, what can I do for you?" he answered.

She brought no congeniality in her response.

"You can pay me, that's what!" she said flatly.

The trouble he feared she would bring was front and center.

"Ruby," he answered, holding back conveying the irritation he felt, "it's only been a few days. You'll be paid very soon."

Overplaying her hand, she asserted, "A few days too many! Just when will very soon be?" she barked, her demand, and the underlying threat with it, plain.

"I'll arrange to meet you this week with your money. Cash, of course," he reassured, maintaining an even pitch, though he was more than irked by her combative tone. "Don't forget, you've always been paid," he reminded her.

"I think a bonus is due me," she added, making a new claim to her compensation. "I know what this was all about, you know. I read the papers. I know exactly who that Balkum guy is and why you wanted me to fuck him. I'm no fool. I'd hate to start talking with others about this," she said sarcastically, her warning clear.

Tranter knew there was no mistaking her intention. Keeping his cool, he pretended to caste the demand as a reasonable request. It was important to mislead her, showing no anger.

"I get it Ruby and I agree," adopting her term, "a bonus is due. Does twenty-five percent extra seem fair?"

Thinking she had him with no choice, she answered, "I think more like another fifty percent is due me, given the situation."

"Sounds fair, sounds fair," he immediately relented. As he reassured her, his fear about her was affirmed. She was a loose cannon. Like most extortionists, he knew her demand wouldn't end with this one. They didn't operate that way. Meeting a demand only prompted them to follow it with another. She would be making a new one before long. No doubt about that. Greedy little slut, he thought, absolving himself of his own conduct.

Calling upon his ability to mislead her, he advanced his best soothing tone, informing, "I want you to be happy, Ruby. I'll be out there by the end of the week with your cash. I'll call you tomorrow to arrange our meeting place."

It almost seemed too easy, his meeting her demands without objection. She had expected some resistance. It felt empowering. His quick agreement to her new terms, left her feeling that she was in a position of strength.

Still, a side of her was wary. "No funny business," she warned, thinking he might short her on the bonus. "Fifty percent more," she repeated, "nothing less."

Glad to hear that her worry was misfocused on the money, he said soothingly, "Why Ruby, I'm hurt that you would say such a thing! You've always been paid in the past, every cent you were due and the same will be true this time," he reassured.

But, he knew, now with certainty, that this wild thing would not be satisfied, even when meeting her new demand for a sizeable bonus. No, there would inevitably be another demand for more. She was the greedy type. Grimly, he realized that she had left him with no choice about how to deal with her.

Gleeful over her presumed win, a sizable bonus without haggling, she accepted his words, "Okay then, I'll be a-waitin' your call. Don't stall on me."

Tranter, relieved that he had mollified her, but only for the moment, rued once again that he had ever got involved with this whole thing. Too big a matter, too many players, too much money, and far too serious with the federal government involved.

His usual staple, setting up philandering husbands, was comparatively low risk. But tangling with the feds, the risk of criminal exposure, those were not part of his resume.

Only once before did he have to resort to extreme measures. A CEO out of Charleston threatened to push back, big time, when Tranter had one of his girls bed the executive. Though he didn't want to use such extreme measures, a serious beating was used on the fellow, one he would remember, along with a warning that anything further from him would bring about the ultimate price. The CEO, his face swollen from the assault, along a seriously broken pinkie finger, the digit damaged so severely that it would never look normal again, a symbolic act of what would follow if didn't relent, were sufficient for him to heed the warning.

No fool, Tranter didn't employ the force himself, but he was well-acquainted with those who would perform such services. It was expensive, but necessary for that guy and worth it.

Now, extreme measures were called for again. The problem was that, for one like Ruby, a beating with a warning was too risky. Clearly, she was a powder keg. Unlike the CEO, Tranter's take was that she might very well decide to go right to the authorities, and then it would all explode. He was very much attuned that such a development would put his own health at risk.

With no "Plan B" available, acting without delay, he placed the call. The individual on the line picked up, answering only, "Yes." He recognized the caller's number, no identification needed.

Tranter got right to business. Careful to avoid any of the underlying details, he informed that he needed some work done, the kind that did not involve any warning of what would follow in the future if the person didn't comply.

"I see," the individual responded. "You're sure that's what you need?"

"Unfortunately, I am sure. Anything less won't work in this case."

"Understood," he simply responded, adding, "This will be expensive, you know."

Tranter did know.

"I'm aware," he answered simply.

He also knew it would come out of his pocket. Couldn't exactly bill those crooked lawyers for this expense. Trying to extort them for the cost, that was a crazy idea. They were big league. He was not. It was another reminder that he never should have gotten involved.

"When, will you need this?"

"ASAP," Tranter informed. "Delay could be a big problem."

"Okay," he answered, "understood."

The two then exchanged the necessary information, including the cost.

"I'll let you know when it's is done," he informed Tranter, closing the call.

Tranter contemplated the arrangement he had just completed. It was so drastic, but unavoidable. She was not one who could be reasoned with. Nor trusted. A sense of honor was not part of her makeup. That unfortunate trait would be her undoing. Once this is over, he swore to himself, never again would he become involved in such high stakes matters. With consequences like the one he had just set in motion, he was way out of his league. Stick with cheating husbands, he resolved.

The following day Delbert Rollins set about his new assignment without delay. He did not flinch on the task. Done it before. That first time, it was a bit difficult, but with each subsequent job of that order, this one making it the fourth, it became easier. Killing someone, it can be viewed as a task, impersonal, something in need of being done. He'd done some time, but for other, relatively small things, a few convenience store holdups and small quantities of drug sales. He'd been out now for five years, without even an arrest. Though well-known by law enforcement, for some time he had been off the police active radar.

He called Ruby's number. When she picked up, by habit wary of any call, she offered only a simple 'hello.' Rollins presumed from the female voice that it was her.

Cheerfully, he began, "Why hello there, Ruby," as if they were old friends. "I'm a friend of Marty's. He asked me to deliver the payment you're due. I can bring that to you today."

Though she was instinctively on guard about any call, now heightened because it was from a stranger yet, her desire for the money overtook caution.

Her first words were, "When you say the payment, it had better include the bonus," she told him with an aggressive tone.

Only a minute into speaking with this woman and Rollins appreciated what Tranter was dealing with, a real wild one, not civil from the get-go.

"Sure," he said putting forth his best calming voice, I've got it all, the $2,000 as originally promised and the $1,000 bonus, right here with me. Just need to meet you, deliver your money and then both of us are on our way. A done deal."

She remained cautious. Never even heard of this guy, let alone met him.

As she was quiet, Rollins sensed the need to continue. He didn't want her insisting that Tranter had to bring the cash.

"So, we need a place with some privacy, but still very public and all," he said reassuringly. Can't be giving you the money in front of a crowd."

Careful not to demand the meeting place, he offered, "I have a suggestion for us. There's that God's Grace Baptist Church, right there in Lochgelly, right off of Route 19. Just take the Route 38 exit. It's like a mile going west from the exit. Can't miss it, right off of 38. Can't miss it," he repeated.

It seemed safe enough to her. A church, for god's sake, she thought. She jotted down the name of the church and the exit. "Okay, but no funny business," she added as a warning.

Privately, he sneered at her bombastic threat. "Of course not. Sweetheart, I'm just doing this as a favor to Marty. He's busy in D.C. these days. I hand over the money to you and we'll both be on our way," he answered soothingly.

In a sense, he was being truthful. He was doing it as a favor for Tranter, though not for free. And once he'd taken care of things, they would be on their way, except together, not separately, with her very much dead.

Another move designed to lull her, Rollins added, "We'll meet in the church parking lot at 4:00, so it'll still be light outside." More important to him, he knew the church would be desolate on a weekday evening.

Satisfied that the meeting would not pose danger, she agreed. He then informed, without giving any concrete identifying information, that he would be driving a gray SUV and wearing a blue baseball cap. He would flash his lights when she arrived.

Something instinctual, primal, deep in her gut told her, 'No Ruby, don't go. Forget about the money.'

But she couldn't resist the lure of the payoff. She really needed the money. Times had been lean of late. Girl's gotta eat and live, she told herself. And this gal knows how to take care of herself too, she added, a confidence boosting reassurance.

It was agreed and though it was not far from her apartment, she left early, just to scope out the meeting place. Once there, though no cars were in the lot, it seemed safe enough and there was outdoor lighting there too, although it was not dark enough for them to have lit yet.

She could hardly wait to have all that cash in her hands, a big payday, at least in her view.

When he arrived, hers was the only other car in the lot. He drove past it and turned around so that his driver's side faced hers. Putting forth his best, practiced, warm smile, he lowered his window and a moment later she did the same. "Hi there. I sure hope you're Ruby," he said, innocuously.

Well, she thought, this stranger certainly didn't seem threatening. Still, her caution remained intact.

"I have your compensation," Rollins informed, displaying an envelope.

"Pass it over," she replied.

Breezily, he answered, "Now Miss Ruby, you know I can't do that. Just let me sit in your car or you can sit in mine, if you prefer, so you can count it. Your choice. Then, once you confirm it's all there, we'll each be on our way."

Something in her head again warned her, 'No, Ruby, don't do it,' but another side, the side wanting the money, countered that it would be okay. I'm in a church parking lot for Christ's sake, she told herself.

"I'll come around to your side," she informed. "I'm leaving my car running," she added, somehow thinking that her warning provided some security if she had to flee.

He simply nodded, then adding, reassuringly, "Whatever you say. You're the boss."

But only for a few more minutes, he thought, his disarming smile intact.

With hesitation, she opened the passenger side door of his car. As she sidled into the seat, he knew it was over for her, an ending she had no clue was imminent.

Though he knew her termination was seconds away, he kept up the folksy pretense to allay her trepidation, comfortably adding, "This will just take a sec," as he handed over the envelope to her.

A serious lapse, now her attention had shifted, focusing with anticipation upon the money. She quickly opened the envelope and began counting, as if she were a bank teller. Though reflexively, and repeatedly, glancing at the guy, her primary attention was with the cash.

To further lull her, for his part, he put on the appearance of disinterest, looking out the windshield.

All hundreds, she noted and not too new. That was good. Easier to use them. Those too-crisp ones, they made people look at them more closely.

He let her continue her count, as she spoke aloud, "five hundred, six hundred."

It was then that, in a flash, he tased her in the neck, repeatedly. If it killed her, a heart attack, well so much the better, he thought.

Stunned, she was instantly and completely immobilized, her eyes so widely opened. Then, she slumped, apparently knocked out.

Acting without a moment of delay, wearing driving gloves, he held her neck tightly until it was clear respirations had stopped. He waited to be sure. Nothing. She was gone for sure. Her eyes remained open, starkly registering the shock when she realized her time was over.

Rollins was unnerved by it, seeing those eyes still looking at him in shock that he would murder her. Unable to bear the frozen startled look from her, he moved her head away.

This was no time to pause. It was critical for him to regain his senses quickly. Had to get away without delay. Panic began to fill his head and his heart rate accelerated, as he realized that he had no plan if someone were to suddenly enter the parking lot. Checking around, he had a measure of relief, as again no cars appeared.

Back to business, he then he pushed her body down on the seat so that it was below the window line. At least then, if someone were to drive into the lot, absent looking directly into the car, she would not be visible. Out of unnecessary caution he shut off his car, and walked briskly over to hers. He couldn't leave with her car still running. That would alert anyone, especially the police, that something bad occurred.

Turning off the ignition of her car, he then took a moment to grab anything that might identify her. Rapidly, he checked the back seat, and under the driver's and passenger side front seats. Nothing. Then, he examined the glove box and both visors. Again, nothing. Marty had told him the car was untraceable. Still, it was critical to be careful. Satisfied that there was nothing in the interior, with the keys and her purse in hand, he popped the trunk. It too was empty. His search was thorough, but necessarily fast. It was time to leave, pronto.

Once back in his car, it was reassuring upon viewing her again. Yep, he thought, she was definitely dead. Remorse, pity, guilt, none of those thoughts entered his head. It was a job.

But those eyes of hers, still wide open, as if staring at him, he couldn't take that. He reached over, closing each lid, ending her accusing look for what he'd done. Even taking that moment, delaying his escape, that was stupid, he thought, the police or a church security driver could appear, checking the parking lot and church.

Get the fuck outta here now, he thought.

Forcing himself to stay calm and cool, he began slowly exiting the church parking lot, careful not to behave in any attention attracting manner. As he had no plan if someone were to appear in the lot, he would just keep going, but if it were the police or a security guard service, he would be in a mess. Those risks were out of his control, but at least the timing was perfect, with dusk was coming on.

Anyone who arrived later, yes, they would see that sorry excuse of a car in the lot. Its presence would raise questions for sure but, as the car was a junker, and finding nothing inside to connect it with anyone, the likely conclusion would be that it had simply been abandoned. Sure, there were license plates, but Marty was no fool, the cops would find they were stolen. It would be a dead end in more senses than they would realize at the time.

To Rollins' great relief, not a soul was around as he left the parking lot, unnoticed, and from there, he returned to Route 38, before heading to Route 19. Once there, again with no incident, he took the northbound entrance ramp, heading towards the New River Gorge Bridge, an area he knew well. Upon arriving there, a winding road off state road 19 took him to the river's bottom. Again, not a soul in sight.

Too early for smoochers, too late for anyone curious to see the river up close. Assured that no one was around, he deposited Ruby in some brush some yards away from the turnaround spot.

Time to get home, he thought. A job well done and a large payday coming.

As he returned to the main road, retracing his earlier route, it was not long before he was on Interstate 77, which would take him back to his Bluefield residence. As it was some 75 miles from the New River Bridge, it felt good to be such a distance away from there. Once home, he entered his double wide, carrying the envelope along with Ruby's purse and the car keys. The money was a bonus. No way would Tranter assert that it was a partial payment for him. Except for one thing, he would deposit all the other stuff in a dumpster, all wrapped up and a good distance away. Mission accomplished.

Against his better judgement, he kept one of Ruby's items. It was a small white leather purse, a clutch he thought it was called. It was of obvious value. Small pearls were around its perimeter and it had a sterling silver snap closure. He could tell that the lining was silk and there was a small tag identifying it as "Ziffany." He'd heard of that name. He knew they sold expensive jewelry. It was another confirmation that the item was of value, not to be tossed in a dumpster.

He then called Tranter.

"It's done," he said.

Tranter grimaced upon hearing the words. This was a first. Threats, even a beating when it was determined that a threat would not do the job, those were of a different order. He didn't like it, going down that road, a life ended upon his direction. If her death were ever solved, he'd be charged with murder. Despite that worrisome speculation, he still saw it as the correct decision, the only option really. That girl, she just wouldn't follow good sense. It was tragic, but unavoidable.

"No problems?" he responded cryptically, employing words that conveyed no details.

"Nope," came the response. "None."

Understandably curious about the details, but not so foolish to inquire, he replied, "Thank you for your assistance," as if Rollins had performed a routine, completely innocuous task. "I'll send your payment right away. Appreciate your help," he added.

With the call ended, Tranter hoped that it was true, that the task had been completed without any problems. This was no time to further reflect upon the life that had been ended upon his direction. He rationalized that Ruby gave him no choice. There was no reasoning with her. My god, he thought, if he had risked that she would not open her yap, but then she did, his own life would be at great risk. Exposing the whole thing, creating an enormous national story, involving the coal industry and that powerful law firm, the thought of crossing them made him quake.

In way over his head, again he thought it was either Ruby or himself, a choice that required no deliberation. An odd source for reassurance, he knew that half of all murders are never solved. Still, if due to something that Rollins overlooked, the police were somehow to have reason to question him and then to have suspicions based on his answers, it could unravel quickly. To save his own neck, he knew Delbert would give him up in a heartbeat.

With nothing he could do about that possibility, he could only hope that Delbert would not be a target of any inquiry. He consoled himself that, if

Ruby's body were found, given her troublesome background with the law, it was unlikely that any serious investigation would result from her death.

The car was discovered the next day when a church elder dropped by to check on the place. Immediately mystified about the car's presence, and finding no one in it, he promptly called the police. Two officers arrived without delay. Finding nothing inside the car to identify ownership, they immediately considered that its presence could be nothing more than an abandonment.

Still, that idea was not the only rational conclusion. Sure, it was a wreck of a car, that was obvious, but it made no sense to leave the valueless thing at a church lot. One could simply drive to a strip mall and walk away, though there could be a risk of surveillance cameras recording it at those places. Maybe that's why, they thought, whoever left the heap here decided on this location, as there were no cameras at the small church.

They conferred away from the church official, both considering that something might be afoul. It certainly had some suspicious elements. But, in these parts, they also knew that some people just abandon worthless cars. While some locals just left useless cars to rust away in their yards, many preferred to leave them elsewhere. Because there would be a recycling cost involved; the idea of responsibly disposing of a worthless car was not an option for some.

The officers decided to simply tell the church official that they would arrange for the car to be towed. He was satisfied with the result; his main concern was that the eyesore not be in the lot come Sunday.

The police quickly found that the car was untraceable, a factor that raised the possibility that something bad had gone down. Because it was so prevalent, they also considered that drugs could be involved. But it was all conjecture. This matter, an abandoned, untraceable car, would not produce an investigation of any significance. With no leads, they were left with towing it to the police car storage lot.

However, several days later, Ruby's body was found by a local hunter. It did not take long for the police to make the connection between the car and the victim; a hair sample and some latent prints from the car determined it to be a match with her. From there, however, neither the nearby Oak Hill Police, the authorities close to the Gorge Bridge, nor a State Police office, located not far from there, had any leads.

Given her record, it did not take the police long to identify the woman. Her past arrests, and the fingerprints associated with them confirmed that it was Ruby Mae Stone.

There was then the unpleasant task of informing Ruby's mother about the loss of her daughter. When a car stopped in front of her house, Emma heard it and she then peeked out behind a window curtain, seeing it was the police.

As it was early in the day, an instinctual feeling swept over her that this was something more than reporting some trouble involving her daughter. She hadn't heard from her errant one in several days. That was not unusual, but the police arriving meant something else had happened.

In jail again, she first thought. What trouble had she gotten into now? she worried. But her antennae told her that this time it was something different, something of a larger order. The cautious, almost hesitant way, the two officers walked up to her door told her that. It wasn't purposeful. It was slow and steady, their heads looking down. She opened the door as they came up the steps, a grimace planted on her face.

"Ma'am," one began, "are you the mother of Ruby Mae Stone?" he inquired.

She confirmed, with a barely audible, "Yes."

"May we come in ma'am?" one of them asked.

Again, she answered, simply, "Yes." That introduction, she instantly knew, confirmed that the worst was about to be announced.

Without delay, one informed, "Mrs. Stone, we're very sorry to inform you that your daughter Ruby has died."

Drugs, a car accident, immediately entered her thoughts but when they informed that she had been murdered, the shock caused her to lose her balance, a collapse imminent. The officers seeing her reaction moved to hold her from falling, guiding her to a chair.

Recovering from the near faint, she began to sob.

"How? Why?" she moaned.

Solicitous, but without answers, one of them responded, "We just don't know, ma'am. We're looking into it."

It was an empty promise. Unstated was that a murder like this, involving an ordinary citizen, and, in Ruby's case, less than that, with her criminal history, however small, it all meant that little time could be devoted to the matter. The investigative resources available to the police were limited and in cases like these, that meant only a perfunctory investigation would occur. More would happen only if evidence fell in their lap.

Hardened by a mostly-sad life, only one daughter doing her proud, she willed herself to regain her composure. There was no point in asking questions about the circumstances, nor if they had any clues. Even if they had responses, nothing would bring her back.

She thought, compassionately, yes, Ruby was 'troubled,' but she never deserved an ending like this.

"When you're able, we need you to identify her, to confirm that it's your daughter. We can drive you to the morgue."

Now feeling embarrassed, she thought that the neighbors had surely taken note of the police car out front. If they then watched her enter the police car, that would heighten their curiosity.

Soon enough, she realized, they would all know what happened, even if it didn't make the local paper. Word gets around.

"No," she answered softly, maintaining her decorum, "Thank you. I will drive myself. I'll be there shortly."

After confirming the morgue address, the officers again expressed their sympathy for her loss.

CHAPTER 14

Gray, now far more burdened than when he only had to deal with his unfaithfulness, realized there was no exit strategy to the mess he had created. All he could attempt was to keep a lid on the disaster. And, irrespective of controlling his own behavior, he was painfully aware that it was not just up to him – others could complicate things. That Nicole and now this slime, Tranter; he was at risk to whatever they might do.

Following the commute, he was relieved to be able to enter and leave the office without meeting colleagues and enduring the empty exchanges, which routinely occurred. Even before this trouble, he hated those encounters – 'Good morning,' followed by the obligatory, 'Good morning to you,' in reply. Then, the frequent continuation, 'How's it going?' The predictable, 'Very well, thanks.' followed by the required, 'And for you?' Though brief, a further reply was mandated for the polite, but superficial, word dance, answering 'yes, good here too.' All of it would then move to the worst, the vacuous closing wish to 'have a good day!' To which, the formulaic, 'And the same to you!' would finally bring it to an end.

On a bad day, there would be several of these. The only relief was that sometimes, a nod, wave and smile with only a 'morning' or 'evening' added could be employed, as long as it didn't seem too brusque. It wasn't just his quirk, he told himself, believing it was equally empty for those on the other end of the tiresome exchanges.

The walk to the courthouse, free of any recognition of anyone he knew, was welcomed. Nothing was solved, nor would it be, but at least it did give him an opportunity to begin contemplating how to stow all the cash that would be coming. Though the odds were remote that someone would break into his car at the office parking garage, the idea of all that money sitting there, right under the passenger seat, remained greatly worrisome. This was a problem in need of prompt attention. Uncomfortable with opening too many savings accounts, he considered safe deposit boxes as another avenue. But, upon reflection, that seemed risky too, what with curious bank employees perhaps seeing him stuff cash in one of those boxes. Probably there was a camera in the deposit box room too, recording the customers' activities.

As he considered the options, he arrived at the idea that some of it, maybe all of it, he thought further, should be stored right at home. Buying one of those fire-safe containers seemed like a good option. There'd be no prying bank employees watching him.

Plotting further, that a home storage safe was the way to go, he realized that it would be easy to accomplish. He could pick one of those things up on the way home or during a weekend trip for groceries.

But where to put it? He certainly didn't want to tell Millie about it. There'd be no believable explanation to offer her. Why, she would ask, after all these years, was there a sudden need for such a thing?

And even if he could create a reason, once he brought it home, inevitably she would open it. Then what! Once she viewed all that cash, a new and unexplainable problem would exist. Even if she were not ill, Millie was not capable of being a co-conspirator. Unlike he, she never would have made the choices he had, not the first sin, adultery, nor the second, bribery.

Certain of his wife's solid values, he knew that any firesafe box would have to brought in and stored without her knowledge.

Carrying his scheme further, he thought that, with her malady, Millie rarely ventured into the basement. That, he determined, would be the place where he could store the safe, so she would never learn of it. He knew just the spot to secrete it too. Just under the stairs would be ideal. Feeling more comfortable about the decision and how to carry it out, he was sure it made a hell of lot more sense than any safe deposit box. It would be his own home safe deposit box, free from any snoopy bank worker and with only one soul knowing about it. Having the money at home, with the total privacy it afforded, it would also be protected if there was a fire or water in the basement. And the chance of a burglary was nil. Sad as his house was, the neighborhood had always been safe. Not a single break-in during all those years; the area had always been crime-free. Pleased that he developed the plan to store the cash and all before the trial day started, he could concentrate on the proceedings.

Despite the satisfaction over solving how to store all the cash, both that at hand and the payments yet to come, when he took the bench that morning, his stomach clenched anew. Looking out at those two unethical bastards, Malthan and Krakovich, both of them knowing exactly the inextricable situation he had put himself, sickened him. But he was locked in now and the two knew all about it; his fucking that tramp followed by taking the bribe. Knew about it, hell, those two orchestrated it! No way out now. It particularly annoyed him – that the two ably presented the façade of total innocence – as they exchanged looks with him.

"Are we ready to resume," he began with the pro-forma inquiry made to the sides. Both affirmed they were, one side clueless about the state of affairs, not knowing that their loss was ensured.

"The Respondent calls Roger Sayre," Malthan announced. There wasn't much for the Secretary could do with testimony from the miners. None of these employee witnesses would be reversing themselves during cross-examination. Knowing the score, the Secretary did not take depositions of any of them. There was no point to it. Their testimony would be very limited, covering only the subjects of whether they engaged in or observed any tampering. It was deemed a waste of resources to conduct that discovery.

The only genuine tactic for cross-examination was to make it clear to the judge that, whether it was Virgil Cobb, or any of them, not a one would dare cross their employer. This was accomplished by questioning the witnesses about the number of years they had been employed by Bobcat Creek Colliery, the unsubtle and obvious conclusion that they were beholden to the mine. To drive home the point, the Secretary would ask each miner if he was the sole breadwinner and even if others in the household had employment, if the miner's income was the main source. Invariably the answers made it clear; these people depended upon the mine for their livelihood.

The Respondent stuck to its plan of marching up all twelve of the miner witnesses, each one solemnly swearing that there had been no tampering with the dust collections. It worked out well. Presenting several each day, it was intentionally stretched out to have the week close with a few to go. That meant the testimony of their experts would begin early next week.

As rehearsed, each of the miners agreed that "things" could happen during the course of sampling. Unavoidable things, like "rough handling," occasionally occurred. Of such events the miners were not apologetic, describing such instances as "accidents." As brought out by Winston in the direct examinations, they were working in the challenging environment of mining. Their occupation was not carried out at a hospital, nor for that matter, a courtroom. And so, they acknowledged that, on occasion, they could accidentally step on the hose for the dust collection unit, or drop something, like a tool box, for example, on the collection hose.

As the Secretary well knew this was setting the stage for what was to come. Discovery had informed them that the Respondents had experts who would be asserting all manner of 'accidents' can occur in mines and that such events could create these AWCs.

Despite the uniform nature of the testimony from the miners, a few small inroads were achieved. As the number of miner witnesses grew, each sequestered so that they would not hear their fellow workers' testimony, it became clear that they had rehearsed their answers collectively, an overplay on Milo's part.

The first eight each spoke of dropping tool boxes on the tubing and they all used Cobb's phrase that they had followed the procedures for the dust testing "to a T" a stark oddity that the expression was uniformly uttered. Surely, they had been to rehearsals before their testimony.

It was an obvious pattern and Sanford was making note of it through his innocently sounding questions. "So, as I understand your testimony, there were occasions when you accidentally dropped your tool box on the dust collection tubing. Is that right?"

Unaware of what was going on, each witness affirmed that was true. If so, they were a clumsy lot, Sanford thought. In fact, unbelievably clumsy, to the point of being unbelievable.

He made some additional scores, upon noting that all but one of the miners used the term "to at T."

"Now, it's your testimony that when you were being sampled, you absolutely followed the sampling procedures? Did I get that right?"

"Yes," or "absolutely" were the nearly uniform responses.

"That's fine. And you're sure of that, sir?" he would ask, locking them into their answers.

Again, the answers confirmed the sampling procedures were followed.

"And, in fact," Sanford continued, sounding as if he were supporting their testimony, "you described following those procedures 'to a T.' That was the expression you used in your earlier testimony; you followed the procedures 'to a T.' Am I right?"

Each witness, remembering using the expression in their initial testimony, agreed that was the expression they had used.

Having them where he wanted them, Sanford then innocently asked if they had heard any of their fellow miners use that 'to a T' expression. Happily ignorant of what the prior miners had said during their testimony, each denied hearing anyone of their fellow miners use that term.

Each professed not only that they had not heard other miners use those words, they added that using the description was entirely their own. Sanford could not have been more pleased.

Gray understood the Secretary's point.

Milo and Winston shuddered. Christ, Winston thought, seeing the repetitive damage unfold with each miner witness, is there some way we can get to the others to stop this bleeding? Practiced at the game, both exhibited stone faces, as the miners' testimony sounded like echoes of one another. They were risk takers, had been routinely during their careers, coming right up to the ethical lines, and crossing them more times than they would acknowledge, but not this time. Trying to coach the remaining miners would likely be exposed and if the Secretary was aggressive enough, it was possible that one of them might confess that they'd been told to nix the 'to a T' references. The potential for harm outweighed the risk.

So, they were committed to the parade, and knew that if they tried to shorten the list, the Secretary would call them as adverse witnesses and demand that they continued to be sequestered until called.

Milo grimaced when he heard those questions from the Secretary but there was no way for him to get word directly to those who would follow that they were to avoid using that phrase, nor the repeated excuse of dropping tool boxes on the devices' tubing. They ignored that the blame was upon them for their over-rehearsing the witnesses.

The best Milo could do was to complain to the mine manager, Lowell Tanner, who was there each day of the hearing, that the uniform nature of the miners' testimony was damaging. Nothing was said directly, Milo could not take such a risk to his law license.

But Tanner was no dope, he knew the attorney's complaints were not idle remarks, so he told a story to the remaining four about the earlier witnesses who sounded like they were reading from a prepared script and as such were not believable. So as to awaken even the dullest of the remaining four, he even gave an example of witnesses who all used the phrase "to a T." Each of them had heard it and they were planning to employ it too, but Tanner's 'story' wised them up.

Repairing some of the damage created by the first eight, none of the last four miner witnesses spoke of dropped tool boxes nor did they utter the "to a T" phrase. Clearly someone had gotten to them, but it was not Winston nor Milo, at least not directly. That would be a third rail thing and neither lawyer was so foolish as to try it. Still, they were pleased that the message had been conveyed.

Sanford was pissed. It was plain that coaching had occurred after the damaging remarks of the first eight, a serious breach of ethics. Though it was obvious, there was nothing he could say about it. A witness for the mine would have had to turn against his employer. That was not going to happen. And, not even Sanford's asking about the subjects brought out the repeated words from the last two. The essence of their testimony was strictly that they knew nothing about any tampering and not one, god forbid, had ever engaged in such behavior.

When, by Thursday's end, several more had finished, Gray was relieved that there would only be Friday to contend with and that it would be uneventful, as it would simply be more of the same – denials that anything untoward was done. Even better, upon his return to the office that Thursday evening, he was not met by any fellow employees and he was especially pleased that there was no sign of Larkin.

No surprise, Friday was a virtual repeat of Thursday's testimony; different faces and names, but all of them reading from the same missal. Gray considered that, had he not been compromised, he might have afforded some weight to such a large number of miners, each swearing solemnly under oath that they had never tampered with the dust sampling devices or the procedures.

But now, given his entrapment, he knew better. Each of them was lying, impervious to the oath they had taken before testifying. And worse, he thought, they did it breezily. There was no stuttering, no hesitation, no display of nervousness, even in the austere courtroom setting in which they gave their testimony. Perhaps, he considered, if one worked in the ultra-hazardous business of mining, where one could without warning be crushed by a roof or rib fall, lying under oath was child's play.

Each of the employees, the worker-bees, had uniformly denied any such illegal behavior. The Bobcat Creek supervisors, seated in the back of the courtroom, were pleased. It worked well all around. The mine received the testimony they desired from their employees, each one denying any tampering occurred and for those employees in return they were put up in a first-rate D.C. hotel, an experience none had known before, and they were fed well, at restaurants they would never visit if they had to foot the bill. Their testimony also meant four days of avoiding work in the mine, two days for travel, with a mileage allowance and a no-limit per diem and the two nights' stay in D.C.

All of them had worn the dust devices and to a man each solemnly denied that there had been anything improper done. Each denied that the devices had been taken away from them for a time during a shift. They never observed anyone doing anything untoward either, like blowing air from the reverse direction into the devices. These presentations were brief, by design, but the defense hoped the large number would have a cumulative effect, persuading the judge that whatever the government claimed, no employees participated in tampering with the sampling process. Each employee's testimony, even including the cross-examination, did not take long. As orchestrated, by Friday's close there would only be two miners remaining.

The misgiving, the two lawyers fretted, was that while they each denied such conduct, they had done so a little too uniformly. They realized that a judge could view the testimony, collectively, as rehearsed. Which, of course, was exactly what occurred. That ten did so, the number being so large, could work against them. Too late now, but the two would remember for future Mine Act litigation to make sure employee witnesses for mines varied their words as they told the gospel truth in court.

The significantly comforting consideration was that Gray being painfully aware that, if he had entertained any misgivings about the stark similarity in the testimony from the employees, now he would have no choice but to conclude in his decision that they were all quite credible, downplaying any suggestion that they had collaborated. He was quite aware that a judge's credibility determinations for witnesses were rarely challenged and successful challenges were rarer still.

The difference between Thursday's uneventful close of the day and Friday's completion, was a mid-afternoon text message from Tranter, directing that they meet at 5 p.m. at the Grill. There was no pretense of inquiring if that day and time worked for the judge, the text might as well have said he was "commanded" to appear there, as if he had been subpoenaed. Civilities aside, Tranter was correct; they were to meet, period. With no choice, Gray complied.

Upon entering the Grill, Jerome saw his familiar patron. Though he extended his customary, 'Good evening, your Honor,' to him, Gray barely acknowledged the greeting, presenting a half-hearted wave, barely raising his hand, while quickly turning his attention to others in the bar.

Jerome was certain that the judge looked distraught. The slight, it did not escape him. All those years of serving his drinks and now treating him with disregard. He watched as the judge moved directly to the lone person sitting in a booth. He recognized that guy. Seen him before with the judge in the place, with Gray again looking more like a prisoner with that guy, not some companion. No question, something was up.

In a moment, Gray spotted Tranter, waiting in a remote booth. Recognizing his entry, he nodded to the judge.

As the judge moved into the opposite side of the booth from Tranter, he said nothing, not even an acknowledgement of him. Jerome noted that too. Gray definitely did not want to be in the company of that guy.

Tranter, fully aware that he owned this judge, dropped any pretense of respect. Why show respect, he thought. Just because of his title? He screwed around, twice, and now he'd been bribed; he was not due anything.

His acknowledgement to the judge's arrival made his view of the man plain. "Good evening, Mr. Gray," he said.

It did not escape the judge, the demeaning salutation of 'Mr. Gray' being no accident. With his straying and now the bribe, humiliation accompanied those acts. Powerless, Gray only nodded, barely, in response. Tranter, knowing that the judge would not be late, had ordered drinks.

Speaking in a low voice, Tranter informed, "Twenty G's," as he passed an envelope to Gray's side of the table.

Gray said nothing but acted quickly to remove it from its position of plain site. He placed it next to his thigh, while quickly opening his briefcase. The thing could barely fit in it. At least he had the foresight to have emptied out the case before going to the Grill.

During the brief time the two were in the booth, Jerome could not resist continuing to observe them. He watched closely, just short of staring. He knew that people, perhaps from some primitive survival trait, could sense a stare, so he avoided too long a look but he was taking it all in.

In the many years of serving the judge, he was obviously behaving oddly, so different from the customer he knew.

He also took a longer look at that other guy; he'd seen him with Gray that one time before. There was something sleazy about him. No good vibes, everything he projected was disreputable; his posture, no smiles, a perpetually somber expression.

He recalled that previous instance, when the two came in together, that Gray was ill at ease that time too. He could tell, plainly, this was no pleasant meeting going on between them. He liked his long-time customer and so hoped that nothing was seriously wrong. While he tended to the customers at the bar, he kept glancing at the two in the booth. Their speaking to one another, the exchanges were more like utterances than conversation, and there was no good cheer between them. Gray seemed to act like he was a hostage, Jerome thought.

His concerns were heightened upon observing the stranger hand over a bulging brown envelope to Gray, which his patron accepted, and then furtively removed it from the table, placing it next to his side, out of sight.

What the hell? thought Jerome, not liking what he observed. His street-sense informed that the exchange was anything but innocent.

He noticed that, following the transfer of the envelope, the two said virtually nothing. There was not a single indication of friendliness between them – no smiles, their meeting was devoid of any pleasantness.

Drugs? he thought for a moment, but then immediately dismissed the idea. Not with the judge. For one thing, he was too old. Whiskey was his thing, and in moderation, but not drugs.

Still, everything he observed told him something corrupt was going on for sure. A puffy envelope like that, it could only be cash, he concluded. What else?

Their meeting ended not long after the exchange. There was little to say and small talk would be absurd, given the nature of the meeting and their mutual distaste for one another. They did not delay in finishing their drinks, both wanting to be on their way.

Arising from his seat, Tranter informed Gray, "I'll be in touch with the next installment. We'll continue to meet here," he instructed.

Gray just looked at him. His defense mechanism kicked in. Sure, he silently admitted to himself, I'm a rat. But what is this guy? Far worse, he comforted himself. I made one mistake. Then, he allowed, two mistakes, with the second resulting from the first. I'm only human, he pled to himself, burdened with an ill wife for years. His self-assessment ignored being bribed.

In contrast, this weasel, he thought, it's his occupation to prey upon, and trap, otherwise good people.

Confirming that, whatever was going on between them, Jerome then noted that when the stranger arose from the booth, there was no parting handshake between them; just a few more brief words, again with no pleasantry.

He then watched the judge sitting there, now alone. Clearly, he was a troubled man, as he remained there, with a vacant, far-off look, frozen on his face. Then, when he came out of his stupor, he immediately checked to his side, where he had earlier placed that envelope. He looked at it twice too, a neurotic check, the way one checks a second time to make sure a door is locked. Whatever it was, his behavior informed Jerome that it was something of importance that the judge was watching over. There was nothing innocent about his whole behavior.

A man under pressure, a guilty man, that's what Jerome was seeing.

His observations continuing, he next saw Gray slide out of the booth, tightly grabbing the handle of his briefcase. Once standing, he placed it on the table, checking to make sure it was securely closed. As he left, he looked down at it again, an indication that, whatever was within inside, it was something of value. The bartender also saw that the briefcase bulged.

The judge left with a deliberate, almost hurried, pace, looking straight ahead, but with his head looking downward, as if purposefully careful to avoid any interaction with a soul as he departed, and with not even a glance in Jerome's direction, another oddity noted by the bartender. Rare was the time when Gray would omit saying good evening to Jerome.

His heart racing the whole way in the short walk from the bar to his parking garage, Gray was relieved once in the sanctuary of his car. He took a deep breath and then made sure the car doors were locked. He then nervously scanned the area around his car to make sure he was alone.

Feeling secure, he could not delay unsnapping the briefcase, starring at the money in the envelope. As before, it was all cash, and it did look to be twice the size of the first payment.

But, unable to help himself, he felt compelled to count it. As he did so, periodically, he nervously looked around, checking to make sure that he was still alone.

While then reassured of his privacy, the interruption caused him to lapse in his count and so he had to begin counting again.

This act, he thought, was a stupid thing to do. Like these people would miscount or short him. And, if it was short, what could he do about it? Complain? All he accomplished with this foolish counting business was staying in the damn garage too long, a potentially risky place to remain, given the large amount of money in his possession.

Looking around yet again to make sure he continued to be alone, he closed the envelope, this time stuffing it under the passenger seat, now tucked next to the other envelope.

Christ, he thought, I've got thirty thousand dollars in my car! I can't let that amount of cash remain where it is!

With his departure delayed by his mandatory meeting with Tranter, he would be having another late arrival home and with that Millie's predictable complaint over his tardiness. Still, he decided that all that cash demanded a stop on the way at that office supply chain store near his home. That further delay wouldn't make her complain longer.

Besides, he thought, it would be foolish to continue leaving all that cash in his car. Who knew what could develop? It was true that a theft was unlikely in that garage. Never happened before. But, apart from the garage concern, if he were to have an accident while driving and his car had to be towed, then what?

A big mess is what! Exactly what innocent story could he concoct to explain away the presence of two bulging envelopes with all that money?

Nobody, nobody, drives around with that kind of cash in their car.

Except a criminal.

THE CASE OF THE ABNORMAL WHITE CENTER

With the thought of that word, 'criminal,' he realized the term now properly applied to him. Those packages would naturally provoke questions and who knew what would happen if the police got involved? And if the envelopes were opened, as they surely would be, all that cash would prompt serious questions.

What response could he invent to satisfy them? If they had reasonable suspicion, based on his behavior, if his voice or other obvious signs of nervousness alerted them that all was not right, they would act. No, to avoid such a risk, this had to be attended to promptly. The cash, it just had to be stored at his home and without further delay. Millie's complaining, even if it was longer than her usual carping because of his later arrival, was not enough to postpone the matter.

A small detour from his home route, he was relieved that the office supply store didn't close early. Nervous to leave his car with all that loot in it, he waited until a parking spot opened right near the store's entrance. The envelopes were stuffed under that front seat, protruding only a few inches from it. They were not noticeable unless someone were to peer in the car windows, an unlikely event.

After neurotically checking the car door locks twice, he then entered the store. A salesperson immediately appeared, offering help. Knowing the corrupt purpose behind his much-needed purchase, Gray felt uncomfortable. It made no sense for him to behave as if he had just robbed a bank, though he considered that his 'arrangement' with Tranter was not so very different from that.

He brought himself under control. "Need a fire-proof safe for my home," he informed. Unable to leave it at that, his guilty state of mind at work, he offered a justification for the purchase, though the sales clerk did not inquire as to the reason. "I have things like passports, social security cards and the like. It would be a real problem if they were destroyed in a fire," he explained.

The clerk, not caring why the guy wanted to buy a safe, barely listened, as he thought that the offered reason for the purchase was not exactly novel. That's why everyone buys them, he thought. "Sure," he responded, as he led the way, "They're over here."

Gray looked at the assortment on display. Don't need a Fort Knox safe, he thought. Just big enough to hold all that cash. Considering its purpose, and the amount of money he'd be stuffing in it, price was not a concern. He pointed to one that listed a capacity of two cubic feet. "Tell me about this one," he inquired.

"Well," the clerk answered, "Each tag gives the critical info. Tells you how long it can withstand a fire at listed temperatures. Watertight too, he added."

Viewing the tag, Gray remarked, "Seems like a good one."

Noticing his age, the clerk responded, "It will do the job, but you need to consider the weight too. This one is 80 pounds."

Gray hadn't considered that aspect at all. Couldn't carry the thing to the basement, he thought. "Probably should consider some lighter ones," he responded, grateful that the clerk noted the issue. He had no idea how much space $300,000 would take up, but perhaps later he would need to buy a second one. That decision could wait. The important thing was to buy one for now.

"This one," the clerk informed, "is close to the rating of the one you just mentioned, but it's half the weight. And it has the same capacity. Just a slightly lower fire capacity. Otherwise, it's the same."

"I'll take it," he responded without hesitation. Forty pounds, he could handle that, but eighty, no way.

In short order, his new purchase was loaded in the trunk of his car, and with the stop taking less than a half-hour, he would not be much later arriving home than if he had made no stop. Certainly not much later than those times when he would linger at the Grill, ordering a second drink.

In simpler times, it had been a place of refuge, a welcomed break between the end of the work day and the return home with the unending responsibilities attending to his ailing wife. Now, the bar only brought up unpleasant thoughts. Suckered right there by that Nicole tramp and now this Tranter character using the location to hand over the payments.

When he reached home, he entered from the garage carrying only his briefcase, as usual. Bringing the safe and the cash to the basement would have to wait. Though feeling some shame over his latest deception, he still began calculating a plan for accomplishing the task of placing the safe and the loot in the basement. His mind employed the word 'loot,' an involuntary thought revealing that he knew exactly what it was – bribe money, as crooked as it could be.

But this was no time for a new guilt trip, so he resumed thinking about delivering the safe and the cash to the basement. Refocused, he realized that his wife's disease worked to his advantage, as she would be in bed by around eight. Then he could retrieve the safe and the cash from his car, relocating all of it to the basement.

This had to be done tonight. He was not about to cart all that money back to D.C. next week. That would just be asking for trouble.

Putting aside his purchase and the plan to stow it and the cash in the basement, he entered, greeting his wife with his usual remark, asking about her day. Then, as he had recently done, he initiated the recap of the day's hearing, distracting her from complaining about his late arrival.

"Uneventful day, again, very uneventful," he began. Consciously, he did not add 'dear' at the end of his sentence, his perfidy blocking him from uttering the loving term.

"More of the parade of miners who wore or facilitated sampling the dust measuring devices. Each of them steadfastly denying that there was any tampering going on. The respondent has now presented testimony from most of them. The last two are scheduled for Monday. Then, it's on to the array of the Respondent's expert witnesses."

Millie had already been told about the other miner witnesses who had testified on the same subject, so this was not news. Still, uncomfortable with his earlier summaries in which he seemed unduly critical of the government's evidence, she inquired about her husband's reaction to the testimony of those miners.

Given all that had happened, Gray was now squeamish about his response. Before all hell had broken loose, he would have given a professorial answer to his wife, telling her that, of course their testimony would be, as expected, denial of any such tampering but that, as the fair-minded judge he was, he would still need to make credibility determinations for each witness.

Just as it would be inappropriate to blindly accept their testimony, it would be equally unfair to dismiss it all as rehearsed, he would have lectured her, as if he were speaking to a complete naivete. Though his tone of voice implied it, he would not be so condescending to his wife by expressly adding that the wisdom from all his years on the bench would enable him to make those determinations. A remark like that would be insulting. Now, knowing that the respondent's attorneys had set him up, simultaneously extorting and bribing him, he knew that the lecture he would have given to his wife was entirely empty.

In its place, he improvised. "It's troubling," he admitted. "Marching up twelve or even more witnesses saying the same thing can't automatically carry the day. These determinations, they're not simply a numbers game. I haven't made any final decisions about the impact of their testimony."

That approach seemed to satisfy Millie. She would have spoken up in opposition if Charles had suggested that the testimony dictated a favorable outcome for the Respondent. At least this time his response seemed balanced. Perhaps he was not leaning against the government so much now, she hoped.

He was relieved that his words avoided sparking a harangue from her. His duty to recount the day's testimony completed, he took the opportunity to excuse himself with the remark that he was "famished," and needed to prepare his dinner. He used that time and his nightly shower to fill up the time before his wife's usual time to retire arrived. Unwittingly, she cooperated with his plan to take care of the safe and the cash, being in bed at her typical time.

Following his nighttime routine, he then announced, to her, "Going down for a glass of wine before bed," this time closing the remark with "goodnight, dear," his unmistakable signal that he would not be returning to their bedroom soon. As there was nothing unusual about his nightly wine routine, she accepted it without question, though she wished he was not so wedded to the stuff.

And, in fact, he did begin his evening with a glass of red. As he sat there, reviewing the uncorrectable mess he was in, he listened carefully for any stirrings from his wife. After a time of continued quiet, satisfied that she was asleep, he returned his wine glass to the kitchen and made his way quietly to the garage.

THE CASE OF THE ABNORMAL WHITE CENTER

With as much stealth as he could muster, he opened the kitchen door entrance to the garage. Annoyed at himself, he then realized that he should have pulled his car in further as the space between the garage door and the trunk was narrow. In that tight space, lifting the 40-pound safe was an effort, but he managed, thinking that there would have been no way to do it had he purchased that eighty-pound thing. Even at half that weight, it was difficult to lift it out of the trunk and he then had to rest it on the step from the garage to the kitchen. Uppermost on his mind was not to wake Millie, a minimal risk as she was usually a deep sleeper. Then it was back to the car's trunk, but it would not close firmly without a slam, creating some noise. It was a risk he decided to avoid, while making a mental note to close it tight Saturday morning.

Once in the kitchen, he first rested it on the stone island and then, ever so quietly, opened the door to the basement, flicking on the light. From there, after lifting it off the island, he was cautious not to fall down the damn stairs, a calamity he could not afford. Taking his time, he made it safely down the steps, setting the safe in the space directly under those stairs. Then, removing the box, he took a moment to learn how to open and close the thing, giving it a test using a four-digit code he could remember. For now, it would be 1, 2, 3, 4. Yes, it was a blockhead choice, but at least he would remember it. Within a day or two, he would reset it with a less obvious code.

So far, so good, he thought, satisfied with how quietly he had completed the task. It hadn't been so easy. His age showing, the weight of the thing, even at only forty pounds, and its awkward size, made it a challenge. The toughest part accomplished; it was back to the car with the now-empty carton. Quietly, ever so quietly, the job nearly finished, he placed the box in the trunk and again closed it gently. Good thing the trunk hadn't been completely closed, he thought, as he would've had to open it again. Later he would tear up the box into small pieces for next week's trash pickup. That accomplished, he went around to the front passenger side, retrieving the two envelopes of cash. Here too, maintaining silence, he only partially closed the car door.

Pausing for a moment, holding the two envelopes, he marveled at all that money. Christ, he thought, both elated and fearful to have that much cash in his hands. Then, the criminality of his act took over his thoughts. But he stopped himself; this was no time to dwell on what he'd done, he thought, and so he willed himself to return to the business at hand. This final trip was the easy part, the safe already tucked under the basement stairs.

A good feature, there was no easy access to the basement except through the kitchen. Yes, there was a bulkhead entrance, but Millie could never use that, what with its heavy and awkward steel doors.

It only took a few minutes to complete the last step, but he was mindful to remain ultra-careful, the mission nearly completed. The money in place and the safe's lock secured, he placed a few items in front and on top of the safe, a quick and sufficient method to hide it for now.

Done! he thought.

It had been a taxing effort. With the stress of not making any noise and the trips up and down the basement stairs, he had broken a sweat, but he was relieved that the cash was out of his car and that he now had a secure place for it. Fireproof and waterproof too! he delighted in his accomplishment.

He had just ascended the basement stairs for the final time, ready to make his way upstairs to bed, when Millie called down to him from the second floor.

"Charles, whatever were you doing? I heard this noise. Sounded like you were in the garage or the basement."

Oh crap! he thought, he had been sure she slept through his efforts. She had been right on both counts.

Normally, the sounds he would make when she retired for the night would go undetected. Not this time. And how the hell did she become aware of his garage and basement visits?

Well, he thought, at least she didn't come downstairs when he was carrying the safe, or worse, with the envelopes of cash in hand. What a disaster that would've been, caught red-handed!

The circumstances called for an assertive lie and he was up to the task.

"Your right sweetheart. I was in the garage and then the basement." The best lies have some truth in them, he thought. "I heard something, maybe a rodent. Just some kind of noise. So, for peace of mind, I looked around in both places. Found nothing though. Maybe my imagination. But everything is good. No worries. You can go back to sleep, dear," adding, "I'll be up in a minute."

"Okay," she answered, but then, seeking reassurance, asked, "everything is secure?"

"You bet. All locked up. Nothing to worry about."

She wanted to accept his answer but her intuition told her that Charles was up to something. Millie could play cards too, not just Charles. Nothing sinister, of course. That was not her Charles. Maybe some more alcohol purchases he didn't want her to know of, she considered. Perhaps, she thought, on Monday, while he was at work, she would scout around, just to satisfy her curiosity.

Now under compulsion of a sort, Charles came up to bed shortly after their exchange. With tomorrow being Saturday, he decided to forego the nightly shower. The sweat he had developed during his exploit was diminishing and at least on this occasion of deception it was simply that, with no need to first wash off scents as he did from his acts of unfaithfulness.

When morning arrived, Millie opted not to raise the subject of Charles' stirrings from the previous night. He wouldn't be changing his story in any event, she realized, so there was no point to making any further inquiry. Though he would be out for some Saturday errands, there was no urgency to engage in a reconnaissance. Monday would come soon enough. Then, with him gone all day, she could explore without concerns about whether he might return from shopping before she had checked things out.

For his part, Charles, noting that Millie did not pursue the issue of last evening, grew confident that his excuse had put the matter to rest, though he wished she had not stirred in reaction to his activities. With winter's presence, aside from a brief jaunt to the grocery store, he was homebound for the weekend. The other seasons, at least they offered the chance to piddle around the yard, but now the weekend otherwise consisted of TV, some reading, and a nap.

Especially for this weekend, there would be no basement visits. None.

CHAPTER 15

With a mixture of relief and dread, Gray made an early start to Monday's commute. Relief, because Millie never raised the issue of the sounds she heard, but dread over the resumption of the trial, which had become meaningless, the outcome decided. Even a modicum of evidence from the Respondent would put his decision in an irreversible position. With his long experience, he knew that, upon making a finding that all those miner employees were credible, even apart from the remaining two miner witnesses due to testify today, that alone would be sufficient to sustain his decision. He just wished it was over, this empty show, like reading the last page of a novel first, the preceding chapters then having no impact.

On the other hand, with the trial continuing, there would be more payments, a form of insurance that the money would keep flowing, at least until his decision was issued. He worried that the valve could be shut off upon issuing the decision. If that were to happen, he would have no leverage if the payments stopped. One can't very well complain to the authorities that bribes have stopped.

No surprise, the last two miners paraded up for their testimony did not veer from the ten who preceded them. Even if he had not been entrapped, Gray knew all the stories would mesh. No skilled trial attorney sends up witnesses in situations like this without near certainty that the testimony will toe the line being presented. With the judge and the Respondent's attorneys fully knowing the score, only the unwitting attorneys for the Secretary thought that justice was being played out. By mid-afternoon, the Respondent had completed the testimony of the twelve, with no renegade upsetting the story line.

The Respondent's attorneys knew that their presentation had to continue with the same solemnity as if the outcome were not certain. To that end, Milo asked if the Court would be willing to end the afternoon session early, explaining that its first expert witness was next up and it would be easier for the Court to digest his testimony if it could be presented in an uninterrupted initial presentation. The Secretary objected, noting that it had not sought such indulgences.

Though he maintained an emotionless façade, Gray was irritated with the request, playing their case to the hilt, he thought, as if it remained a legitimate dispute. The Respondent's counsels knew that their expert witnesses could border on incoherent technical testimony, but that none of it would matter, the outcome of the decision foregone.

"Your request is denied," he said simply.

"Thank you, your honor," Milo responded, invoking the formal politeness used in litigation, even when a request is rejected. Privately, his twisted logic at work, he thought Gray was ungrateful by denying it.

The Respondent then called its first expert, Dr. Peter Kim. The expert witnesses, each of them, beginning with Kim, were there to refute the analytical methods and the conclusions of the experts for the Secretary.

Although the jurist's extracurricular activities, now recorded, twice yet, and in vibrant color, would command the outcome, Milo and Winston still hoped that Gray could intellectually conclude that the Secretary's experts had been undone by the Respondent's experts, or at least that he was left so confused by the technical testimony he had no choice but to reach that conclusion, though he could never admit to being flummoxed by it.

That the two attorneys could entertain such a hope made no sense. It was completely unrealistic to think that somehow, Gray, caught as he was, could somehow still conclude that the defense's experts were believable. Given their destruction of Gray's objectivity, the thought that he could separately conclude they had presented a legitimate defense was foolish. They had no shortage of hubris.

The only conclusion for Gray was that the whole lot of them, witnesses and experts alike, for the defense were fabricators.

Over two hours were spent detailing Kim's superb credentials. They were undeniably impressive, a fact which, in the view of the Secretary's legal team, only proved that, for the right price, most people, with experts being no exception, can be bought.

After presenting them, it marked the end of testimony for the day. In a practical sense, Milo and Winston had prevailed on their request to have the doctor's testimony delayed. They had engineered it so that no useful information had been presented beyond Kim's gleaming CV. As they packed up to leave, the two exchanged smirks. They had prevailed, despite Gray's ruling, as the substance of the doctor's testimony would not start until the next day.

The trial day over, as Gray made his walk back to the office, he was still nursing his annoyance over the Respondent's request to delay the start of its first expert's testimony. Why, why go through these pretenses? he thought. He realized the testimony of all their experts had to come in, but they were overplaying their hand to make such requests. Perhaps, he considered, it was calculated to present the façade to outsiders that the outcome was very much in doubt. Still, it was galling.

Though he gave no thought about his wife during his return trip to the office, Millie's day had been eventful.

It was to be her last.

She had waited patiently all weekend, foregoing the opportunity to snoop around when Charles left for some Saturday grocery shopping. It could wait, she thought. He would be away all day on Monday. Then there would be plenty of time to investigate.

She had not slept well the entire weekend. Something inside told her that Charles was up to something that Friday night.

Not long after Charles was on his way that morning, she made her way down to the kitchen. Although she felt a little unsteady, a frequent symptom at the start of her day, it did not cause her to postpone her plan to see just what her husband had been up to so recently. In part because she had not slept well and in part because of her illness, she also felt lightheaded. That symptom was not unknown to her; it would make its appearance from time to time and she managed to navigate around the house despite it.

THE CASE OF THE ABNORMAL WHITE CENTER

She began by checking kitchen cabinets, of which there were many, but she found nothing unusual. However, when she arose from kneeling after checking the cabinets under the breakfast island, she was again momentarily woozy. She steadied herself and when it passed, determined to complete her mission, she resumed her search.

The garage was next and there too she saw nothing out of the ordinary. Perhaps, she thought, Charles' explanation was accurate. Maybe he really did hear a noise and simply investigated its source.

Still, there was the basement to examine. At the entrance to the basement, she turned on the light switch and began her descent but her dizziness then suddenly returned and she grabbed for the railing as she started to lurch towards a fall down the stairs. In that effort she missed the railing and the tumbling began from the top, and quickly, as she literally fell head over heels. Upon reaching the bottom, she struck her head on the concrete floor with force. Though momentarily half conscious, she quickly lapsed into a stupor.

Realizing she might not recover as darkness filled her head, her last thought was regret that she had not been more trusting of her Charles.

Although Gray, perpetually burdened at home and now at work too, had hoped to be able to enter the office at the day's end without meeting any staff or colleagues, that wish was not fulfilled. He passed by a few members of the staff, which was not an issue, as he was able to offer up the minimal polite exchanges with them.

Unfortunately, Larkin was still present and he could not be dismissed so easily. More would be required than a wave.

For his part, Larkin had an additional reason to stay late beyond his customary practice of a late departure for the benefit of reduced traffic in his return commute. He remained troubled by that scene he had recently observed; Gray with that stranger and the passing of that envelope. Of course, he couldn't broach the subject, probing for answers to what he saw.

True, he couldn't be solidly sure that what he witnessed was nefarious, but it was undeniably very peculiar. It just didn't smell right. Any reasonable observer would have had his curiosity piqued by it.

Not risking Charles just passing by his office as if he did not notice his colleague was there, Larkin, alert that Gray would be arriving around this time of the day, spoke up as he walked by.

"Charles," he said, with faux enthusiasm, "Good to see you. Do you have time for a quick recap of your day?"

Of course, Gray had time, but he was in no mood for conversation. The circumstances demanded it however. Grudgingly, but with a tone that did not fully convey his attitude, he offered, "Yes, Richard. But it will have to be brief. I need to head home."

Larkin accepted the terms. "Sure, I understand, Charles," he responded diplomatically, realizing that he would be a listener only, avoiding follow-up questions.

On this occasion Larkin had little genuine interest in Gray's recounting of the testimony. Instead, though the prospects were unlikely, he hoped to glean something from his colleague's tone of voice and body language that might inform whether something dark was going on or, hopefully, gain some reassurance that his concerns were unfounded.

But Gray's behavior was not reassuring at all. This was a different Charles Gray before him.

All Larkin's instincts told him something was going on with his colleague. The tone of his recounting the day's testimony was markedly different. It was as if he had no interest in it, a peculiar attitude given that it was his case and of such enormity. He seemed tense too, and distracted, even as he spoke. Substantively, the unremarkable testimony from the day could not explain his demeanor.

No, Larkin concluded, something was up with the guy. It only served to reinforce his view that the stranger, and especially seeing that envelope being passed to Gray, that this was not a harmless event.

Within a few minutes, Gray called the session to an end, the shortest discussion ever with his colleague.

"That's about it," he abruptly concluded his summary. "Pretty uneventful. Only the credentials for their first expert were laid out this afternoon. Tomorrow, the expert will begin speaking about his findings about these alleged AWCs."

Gray was right about one thing, thought Larkin, the day's testimony was uneventful. It was all so predictable for the miners who testified for the respondent. As for the expert, the lengthy testimony about his glowing background was standard procedure.

Even so, Larkin could tell that his colleague was clearly not himself; something was seriously wrong. He wanted to believe that Charles was free of sin. Maybe, he considered, those attorneys for the respondent dug up something from his distant past, something embarrassing that he did not want made public.

Certainly, the passing of that fat envelope to him, that didn't support the notion of his colleague being innocent. No way.

Larkin, aware of the importance of not overstaying his welcome, arose immediately upon Gray's announcement that his retelling had concluded, and bid him a brief goodnight, summoning a forced smile, as he attempted to hide his concerns.

"Hopefully the traffic won't be too bad tonight for you, Charles," then adding, "Tomorrow's testimony sounds eventful. If you have time, I would be interested in your take on the views from the Respondent's first expert."

"Yes," he responded, "well, not much I can do about the traffic," but his answer was intentionally unresponsive to Larkin's request about the upcoming testimony, the absence noted by Larkin.

Gray wasted no time packing up the few things he needed to take home. When the elevator reached the lobby he left the building briskly, reducing the chance of encounters with anyone else leaving his office. Once outside, he was relieved that Tranter guy was not waiting for him. His aversion was so strong that he crossed the street immediately from his building, though there was no crosswalk at that location.

He remained tense until he was safely in the garage and within the protection of his car. Even then, he could not resist looking around to make sure no one was around. Satisfied that he was alone, he sighed in relief, doubly glad that the damn envelopes of money were no longer under the front seat. Following an uneventful ride home, with the traffic congestion minimal, as he pulled into the garage he thought his arrival time, being earlier than usual, would mean no carping from his wife.

When he entered the house from the garage, a peculiar feeling swept through him, as Millie did not immediately appear to meet him, or at least to call out to him, her usual practices.

"Millie, I'm home," he announced, thinking she could be in the bathroom. He proceeded to the foyer to find her, but the bathroom door was open.

"Millie," he repeated, "I'm home," using a louder voice.

As he began moving about the first-floor level, not finding her, he was about to go upstairs when he noticed the door to the basement was open and the light was on.

"Damn," he immediately thought, did she go exploring because of the noise from last week?

The answer came immediately. From the top of the stairs, he saw her. There was his wife, his wife of so many years, sprawled and motionless at the concrete floor bottom of the basement stairs.

"My God! Oh my God!" he cried, as he rushed down to her.

He tried to rouse her, but she remained motionless and he could see no sign of breathing. He turned her over onto her back. Still no respirations. As he attempted to get a response from her, there was nothing.

Now frantic, he then put his ear to her chest, but heard nothing. Holding a wrist, no pulse was there.

He then began to weep. She was gone.

This was his fault. Had he done the right thing, not getting entangled with that tramp, none of these spiraling events would've resulted. Had he just done his job, as he had all those years as an administrative law judge, until that Nicole woman had set him up, his wife would be alive.

And he did not have the excuse that his transgression was a one-time incident. He had gone back for seconds, eliminating that excuse.

And even then, a third romp with the woman was constantly on his mind. The truth was, it was only the revelation from Tranter that he'd been had, which extinguished his future treachery.

Digging himself only deeper, there was then the bribery. Shame upon shame, upon shame. None of this had to occur. He could've finished his career unblemished.

After a time, he regained his presence of mind, realizing that he would have to call the police. He tried to compose himself. He had to compose himself, he realized. There was too much else at stake now.

His self-protection, his survival really, kicked in. He arose from Millie's side and slowly ascended the stairs, not looking back at her.

Once in the kitchen, he gathered himself again and made the call. Forcing himself to stay calm, he called 911, informing that he had arrived home from work a short time ago, and found his wife dead at the bottom of the basement stairs. Instinctively now protecting himself, he added, "She had multiple sclerosis."

The police official responded, "Are you sure your wife is dead, sir? Perhaps she is unconscious."

"No," he responded, "I have taken first aid courses several times. She has no pulse. I listened to her chest. There was no heartbeat."

In the moment, he had forgotten that these emergency calls were recorded. His effort to stay so calm was not such a good idea.

"We will still send a rescue truck. It's on its way now," the responder informed. Your address came up with your phone." It seemed odd that the husband was so calm, she thought. For most calls like this, the person is frantic, nearly out of control. Not this one, she noted. The recording made that plain, he told the event without any emotion.

Gray confirmed the address. Again, he was steady, strictly matter of fact, in his response.

Within fifteen minutes, the police and a rescue truck arrived. Charles met them at the front door, escorting them to the top of the basement stairs. The rescue personnel, three individuals, rushed down to evaluate her, but within a minute they confirmed no revival was possible; she had passed away.

A uniformed officer and a plainclothesman then approached Gray.

Only the man in a suit spoke. "I'm detective John Spalding," he announced, "I'll be investigating this death."

A detective! thought Gray, instantly alarmed.

"What is there to investigate?" he responded with a challenging tone.

"Anytime, there is a death and the circumstances are unclear, we are obligated to investigate," he answered matter-of-factly.

With years of experience, his antennae went up upon hearing the challenge. Not always, but too often, when one asked that question defensively, there was something behind it. Somehow, Gray's challenge didn't sit well with him.

Unable to suppress his surprise, Gray reacted oversensitively.

"Well, I don't see what there is to investigate. I was at work all day and arrived home around six and then found my wife, just as you have seen her."

"I understand," Spalding answered, his initial negative reaction to Gray affirmed, "still we have our job to do."

Gray backed off from his unhappy demeanor, seeing it would only provoke the detective. He did not need to arouse any suspicion on this investigator's part, not with the baggage he was carrying around, figuratively, and literally too, what with the safe holding $30,000 only feet away from where the two were standing. It was all he could do to avoid looking in the direction under the stairs where the safe had been secreted.

"It's standard procedure in cases like this,' Spalding continued, "for an autopsy to be performed. So, any funeral arrangements you make will have to wait until that is completed."

Autopsy! thought Gray. This was pure bureaucratic excess. No wonder conservatives get upset with government!

Suppressing his grimace, and aware that he could not alter the procedures, he answered only, "Do what you have to do."

With that response, the aggressive 'do what you have to do,' a begrudging remark, only reinforced Spalding's instincts that something was amiss. He had learned over his years that most people wanted to know the cause of death. Not this Mr. Gray though.

That fall, it didn't necessarily mean it was the cause of death. She could have fainted first or had a stroke, or any number of other events could have preceded her tumble down the stairs. A few of his cases had involved medications given to a victim. It was not beyond the pale that the guy's wife could've been pushed. Gray didn't have to be present for that. One can be hired to complete such a task. He had seen it all.

Of course, he reached no conclusions, but he expected more grieving than this guy displayed. It could be nothing, no more than what it appeared to be, he thought, but viscerally something still nagged at him. There had been times that his intuition was later confirmed, but not always. Before this guy, Gray, he just didn't know.

Takes all kinds, he knew from his decade of these cause of death investigations.

"As soon as the autopsy is completed," he informed, "I will be in touch, so then you'll be able to make the plans for your wife."

As he spoke, the rescue personnel had placed Millie on a stretcher and were taking her up the stairs.

Gray, his attention preoccupied with the investigator, noticed her removal, but he did so without emotion, another odd reaction in Spalding's view. No tears from this guy.

Without prompting, Gray felt it necessary to explain his situation, an attempt to justify his behavior.

"My wife, she had MS," he offered. "It's a progressive disease, you probably know, and of late her condition had worsened. Asked her to avoid stairs. She had fallen recently too," he added.

Spalding just listened. I suppose, he thought, having an invalid wife lessens the grieving. Still, he thought, the guy's a cold son of a bitch, given that his wife had just died.

"You're employed, you said. I'll need a number to reach you."

Gray provided his cell.

"What is it you do for work?" Spalding asked.

Gray was always glad to answer such inquiries. Now, he felt on top of things. "I am a federal judge," he informed.

"Oh, what court?" Spalding inquired.

That was a bit of a letdown for Gray. He had oversold his first portrayal of the position he held. Now it was time to retreat from that high-sounding initial description.

Keeping the word 'federal,' he answered, "I'm a federal administrative law judge."

Spalding was not awed. He knew the difference. "What agency do you work for?"

"Mine Safety and Health," Gray answered.

"Well, your agency has been in the news. I read there's a big case going on about mines tampering with dust collection equipment. That's right, isn't it?"

"Yes, you're correct," Gray only answered.

"Not your case, though?"

"In fact, it is my case, detective. I am the presiding judge in that matter," he said, the boast clear by using the "presiding judge" description.

Spalding was not impressed by the revelation. Still an administrative law matter, he thought.

Nor did it impact his view of the cause of death investigation he was presently handling. He made no connection or conclusions either way about that disclosure and his wife's passing. There was no logical reason to associate the two.

He tried to sound solicitous, offering, "Tough time, with a case like that on your hands and then your wife's death."

Gray was unsure if the detective's remark implied anything, the guilt over his adultery and then the bribery, both at work feeding that worry.

"We do what we have to do. Responsibilities don't evaporate when an accident occurs," he tartly responded.

The less said the better, he thought.

The response only served to confirm for Spalding that, at a minimum, this guy was a cold character.

His business completed for now, the detective prepared to leave.

"Well, Mr. Gray," he informed, "that wraps up my responsibilities for tonight. "As I mentioned, in a few days, I'll be in touch with the autopsy results, so that you can then make the arrangements for your wife."

As he spoke, he looked around the basement. Nothing unusual, though he did notice the partially covered fire safe under the basement stairs. It looked new, he thought. Struck him as an odd location for such a thing. Those things are usually in a bedroom or office.

Gray noticed the detective nosily scanning the basement as he spoke, his words about the autopsy uttered as if Gray was not present, an unusual way to communicate, not looking directly at him. He said it as if the remark was an aside, as if he was distracted, looking around the basement surroundings like a bloodhound, not expressed to a judge who had just lost his wife.

What the hell was he looking for, he thought, a murder weapon?

And that was not all that was offensive. He did not care for the investigator's attitude.

Mr. Gray! he thought, why he clearly told him he was a judge. Not respectful at all.

So, he's a detective for a suburban community. If Gray was a lower tier judge, who was he? No one with bragging rights for sure. He was tempted to call the detective *Mr.* Spalding, but he held his irritation over the slight in check.

"Good evening then," was all that he said to the investigator. No closing 'thank you,' was added, that respectful familiar expression he regularly heard in court from litigators when before him.

When they finally had gone, Gray could not resist returning to the basement, the scene of his wife's death. Her curiosity came at the ultimate cost, he thought, now coldly absolving himself for any role in what happened. Neurotically, with that nosy detective looking around like it was a goddam crime scene, he checked to make sure the firesafe was locked and undisturbed. It was, thank God.

Once upstairs again, he tentatively pulled back a curtain on a front window, making sure the police and rescue trucks had gone. Assured that they had left, he walked down the driveway to retrieve the mail. As he did so, he thought if that detective were to see that, he would view it suspiciously, a supposedly bereaved husband still composed enough to check his mail.

It could have waited, he thought. He could have checked the mail the next morning. It wasn't going anywhere. Too late now, his crazy thoughts continuing. If he was being observed, it would seem strange for someone to see him walk down the driveway and then retreat, the trip pointless.

Arriving at the box, again he looked around. Upon opening it, the contents made him feel guilty too – one bill but a bunch of brochures about the joys of living in Florida. His imagination in full tilt, he considered that if Spalding saw that, he'd be wondering if there was a girlfriend in the picture.

He looked around again at his surroundings. Not a soul. Careful not to drop any of the incriminating brochures, he held them tight as he made his way back to the house, this time forcing himself to look straight ahead. Once inside and checking the door twice to make sure it was locked, he made a last furtive look out the window. As before, no one was around. Entering the kitchen, he tucked the brochures in a cabinet, leaving only the one bill on the island.

His stomach churning, he could not consider eating that evening. A drink was very much in order though. Though he denied it to himself, for years the alcohol had been a requirement. Tonight, it was a necessity. As he sat in the living room, where he would often sit with Millie in the evening, telling her about his day, he then recalled, with some guilt arising, that he viewed the recap as a chore.

As if that weren't enough, the place now felt a bit haunted to him, his wife so suddenly gone. He could not entirely dismiss the part he played in her death. Of course, it wasn't as if he pushed her down those stairs, but he could not completely exonerate himself either, his covert activities of last week prompting her to see what he was doing. Couldn't he have been quieter? He admonished himself for the noise he made, minimal as it was, but not for his actions.

Then, thinking about that obnoxious detective, he realized there were no real concerns. The law may call upon me one day, charging me with bribery, he thought, but it would not be about Millie's death. Hell, he noted, defending himself at least from that, he'd been in the trial all day, with many witnesses who could attest to his presence. Her time of death would establish that she died at a time he was in court. He was in the clear on that.

He paused over that imagined defense, shuddering for a moment over the thought that if Millie's death had happened during that second time he was with that Nicole-bitch, he was not in court that afternoon, nor even in his office. With no solid alibi that he could voice, he would have been a suspect. That Spalding guy would hound him for sure. Continuing with his wacky thoughts, he told himself that he could just say he went for a walk and a late lunch that afternoon. No one could place him at home that day. His imagined defense continued, necessarily free of any disclosure about that tramp. He could show that his wife was not a well person, with her documented, progressive, MS and medical records showing her balance and steadiness had been deteriorating. No way, he thought, could it be established beyond a reasonable doubt that he had pushed his wife down those stairs.

Satisfied that he could defend himself against a murder charge, if Millie had died on the afternoon he was with that strumpet, he forced himself to think of something brighter – Florida and the future it could hold. This was shameful, he realized, thinking of Florida with his wife's death only hours earlier, but he had to have some escape from the deranged thoughts of being charged with a crime. He just had to think of something positive if he was to have any sleep tonight.

Despite the mess he was in, if the secret arrangement remained as such, it would still produce that dream location he had in mind. And, though the embarrassing thought now entered his mind, he would be there free of the burdens of Millie's constant care. He was ashamed at the thoughts of retiring there at a moment like this, but they unavoidably entered his mind.

Icily, he then considered that now there would be no debate from Millie about whether to sell his house, nor where or what house to buy in the Sunshine State. Guilt swept through him for such shameful thoughts. His wife dead for less than a day and he was calculating the advantages from it!

And then, mixed in with all these thoughts, was the ever-present fear that his perfidy would all come out, exposing him as the immoral, unfaithful spouse to his disabled wife and on top of that, he was a bribe taker too! If that were exposed, the bribery, he would do some serious prison time and it would be the only thing people would ever remember from his entire judicial career. One transgression, just one, he thought, over the span of his long period on the bench.

Yet, not completely blind to his actions, he knew they were monumental failures, the adultery and taking a bribe, and that together they would be his true epitaph, even if they remained a secret to the end.

Considering all those clashing thoughts left him addled. That two more drinks followed the first did not aid matters. With nothing clear and by then fairly inebriated, he made his way up the stairs for bed. For a moment, with so much alcohol consumed too quickly, he lost his balance as he neared the top step. He teetered backwards, lurching, but he was able to grab the handrail just in time to avoid tumbling down. Those stairs, he thought, had the same number of steps as those that took his wife's life and, if he had fallen, he would've hit the stone foyer hard, the results of such a fall impossible to predict.

Adrenalin flowing from the near accident, he ascended the last two steps, in a child-like fashion, on all fours, so afraid of a fall. He continued to crawl until he was clear of the stairs and safely in their bedroom. Shaken from the near-accident, he decided to sit on the bed, their former marital bed, where he took off his shoes and, still seated, pulled off his pants and unbuttoned his shirt. Lacking confidence in his balance, he concluded there would be nothing more in the way of his usual bedtime routine, no shower, no attention to his teeth. They all seemed too risky now. Better to just move from his semi-wobbly seated position to the security of lying down.

Now safe from injury, that was the only protection the bed offered. It provided no refuge from his thoughts, as he lay there, alone in their bed for the first time in all those years of marriage. The same ghostly feeling he experienced downstairs had followed him to their bedroom. If this persists, he thought, he could not move to Florida quick enough. Multiplying his fears, he considered whether she would haunt him down there too, following him forever. Eventually, he did fall asleep, a combination of exhaustion from the day and the alcohol.

The alarm, fortunately preset, woke him at his usual time. Immediately afraid, he looked to the other side of the bed, hoping that he'd experienced a frightening nightmare. But it was empty. His Millie now gone forever. Tears began, thinking about what his sins had wrought.

The clock's snooze feature sounded again, bringing him back to the dark reality he'd created. It could have been otherwise. Had he just stayed in his lane, focusing solely on fairly deciding the biggest case in his life, and obeying his marriage vows, none of this self-inflicted mess would have occurred. He could have retired at the apex of his judicial career, deciding such a significant case. Yes, he would have then retired relatively poor with no Florida residence but his integrity would have been intact.

Of necessity, he had to think about the day ahead. The trial would resume in only a few hours. He willed himself to get his act together. There really was no other choice.

Facing that reality, he then thought there would be no point in having an interruption to the trial because of Millie's death. And what would he accomplish anyway, if he announced to the parties that there would be a pause? Stay at home and do what exactly? Funeral arrangements were on hold, thanks to that arrogant Spalding, who acted so suspiciously about Millie's death, like he was trying to solve a murder and inferring that he was suspect. It would only make matters worse, dwelling on all of it.

And it wouldn't bring his Millie back.

His guilt returning, he corrected himself. No longer could he call her "*his* Millie," not after what he brought about, precipitating her death.

A pause in the trial would also provoke a ton of questions. The parties would be extremely curious as to what brought it about, though they would not inquire about the reason for it. And especially those creeps for the Respondent, they would likely set about trying to learn the reason, maybe even bringing that slime Tranter into it. His office would have questions too. The Chief would not remain silent upon learning there had been a pause, not in a case this big.

As awful as he'd been, he couldn't then invent new lies when questioned. Even claiming he had a cold wouldn't fly.

Given the reality of the situation he faced, it only made sense to proceed with the hearing without a break. He would pretend that all was as it had been. Just another day of the hearing. He would make no mention of his wife's passing to anybody. None. Those damn attorneys for the Respondent knew far too much anyway! That meant no disclosure of her death, even within the office. Nobody's business.

When it came time for the wakeless funeral, he would simply take a personal day and perhaps only half of one, he coldly considered. At most it would require one day off, and that would not be a big deal. Possibly, he continued, the whole business could be completed during a weekend.

And if, somehow, it did come to light about Millie's death, he had a ready excuse – that the whole thing was so overwhelming painful, he could not bear to disclose it. Fortunately, at their advanced age, there was nearly no family to notify on his wife's side. She and he shared that situation, both being only children. As it was dark when the police and the rescue truck arrived, there was less hubbub than if it had happened during daylight. For all the few neighbors knew, EMTs showing up could mean little. He wouldn't be home for any callings from them until the weekend. And if someone came knocking, he would simply not come to the door. No one need learn that his wife had died.

There were also some pluses, he considered, to continuing with the trial. Instead of dwelling on Millie's death all day, as he might if he just sat at home, the proceeding itself would demand his attention. And getting the damn AWC thing over, that was worth it by itself. Finish the lying testimony, issue his fraudulent decision on a fast track, and then immediately retire.

The issues settled in his head for the moment, he promptly dressed, though the emptiness in the house remained eerie. He felt spooked, as if something were relentlessly following him as he moved about, with no relief until he was out the door. He knew it was crazy, having such thoughts, but he could not will them out of his head.

THE CASE OF THE ABNORMAL WHITE CENTER

Arriving at his office, as it was early, only a few employees were present and so he was able to make his departure for court without the need to exchange those annoying pleasantries.

He felt strange in the walk to the courthouse, his first time as a widower, a fact only known to the police and the rescue personnel from last night. Guilt pursued him as he proceeded.

What an awful husband he'd become. That 'affair,' if one could call it that, it didn't deserve such an uncritical, almost guiltless, description. Really, it was just sex. Certainly, it was no more than that for her, that floozy, sex for money. He, temporarily delusional, had thought it was more, a fantasy come true. It was foolishness in the extreme, thinking that a woman with her youth and looks, would be interested in one like him, old and not rich.

And even after that, cheating on Millie, there was a last exit ramp for him to retain some ethics. All he had to do was tell that Tranter guy to go fuck himself. A chance to display some spine. Embarrassment, that would be inescapable, but there was no crime for those transgressions.

But no, then he had to dig a hole that was too deep, inescapable.

Bribed. He'd taken the money, even bought a safe to keep it stored at home. Had he just showed some backbone when confronted, Millie would still be alive. But now, with the bribe and the horrendous result of Millie's death, all from his acts, there was no turning back. Even going to the police, admitting to all of it, would surely land him some significant jail time. And if he outlived his sentence, then what? He would be a pariah, plus penniless and deservedly so.

At his age, such a result was unthinkable. He had to go forward.

When he took the bench that morning and looked out at the two phony cherubs for the Respondent, at least the loss of his wife was unknown to those bastards. Now, he thought, the only goal was to finish the damn trial. Just stay focused on that, he told himself. Keep yourself together. Hear all the Respondent's expert witnesses and then deal with any rebuttal testimony that may arise once the Respondent rested. And then issue the blasted decision and be done with it.

"Good morning," he said, offering nothing more, moving right to the business at hand. He was beyond being greatly irritated as he looked at those two, but he remained expressionless about it, not wanting to display his state of mind. And, he thought, there was no need for any of those empty pleasantries he sometimes would offer at the start of the day, not with those unscrupulous attorneys.

"Call your witness," he then instructed the Respondent's lawyers.

Milo and Winston could tell something was up with the judge, his morning words being so terse. With their plans having proceeded so well up to this point, they worried if the judge's minimal words signaled some ominous development. Though uncomfortable, sensing that something had gone awry, there was nothing they could do about it. Krakovich proceeded as required.

"Good morning your Honor. The defense recalls Dr. Peter Kim."

Kim, oblivious to the tension felt by the defense attorneys, resumed his testimony. After completing his illustrious background, the doctor's testimony then moved to his description of the mind-numbing details of the procedures and investigations that he and his team carried out in their "quest," as he put it, to figure out the sources for the white centers.

Conspicuously, his elaborate studies did not include intentional acts as a cause. His inquiries included, he explained, whether such white centers were actually normal occurrences, a bold assertion. By that, he made it clear with high sounding authority that, as a scientist, he simply couldn't begin with any assumption that the condition was abnormal. To do that would be antithetical to any true assessment. Thus, he presented himself as the epitome of objectivity. Thorough scientists, he asserted, with a tone of educating the uneducated, assume nothing.

Knowing that from here on out, it was all pretense – that show the Respondent was performing, as if the outcome of the decision in this proceeding was uncertain – Gray understood that it was a necessary display for the public, for the record the Respondent was making, and certainly for the

THE CASE OF THE ABNORMAL WHITE CENTER

Secretary to continue mistakenly believing that the hearing was all on the up and up.

Even at midweek, Kim's testimony continued with more of the same, all about the particularity and scientific rigor he employed in his search to discover the source of the white centers. It was all tedious stuff, unobjectionable, and necessary if the proceeding was still to be presented as legitimate. It made no sense for the Secretary to object to any of the preliminary testimony because he would be overruled and the end result would only prolong the time to get through it.

The Secretary and Gray listened to it all, though none of it required great attention. That would come when Kim moved to the heart of the matter; his many 'reasons' to explain away the white centers; Kim's 'phony excuses' as the Secretary privately dubbed them.

It was not until after lunch that day that Kim began testifying about the main event – the various innocent reasons to account for the white centers.

Of course, none of the experts had a clue that Gray had been completely compromised. Neither Malthan nor Krakovich was so foolish as to let on about the judge's inextricable predicament. The circle had to be kept extremely small; to have it be otherwise would invite disaster.

Besides, if any of the experts did know or even had a hint about the judge's situation, it would adversely impact their testimony. Even though paid handsomely for their predetermined innocuous reasons to account for the white centers, presumably even they had their limits. It was one thing to make up blameless reasons for the white centers, but to stand by them if they knew the judge had been compromised, that could be a bridge too far. Their paid-for findings would be dampened if they knew the outcome was already assured.

The doctor led off by challenging which samples were white. Reviewing each of the dust samples for the case, he asserted there was no commonality to them; some were mostly white, while others hardly white. This was all to claim that the Secretary really had no consistent basis for determining when a sample showed a violation. This assertion took several hours of testimony. It appeared to be a good start.

The following day and the next were spent with Kim offering several grounds for disputing the conclusions of the Secretary's experts. Right off the bat he contended that the white centers could occur because of the 'filter to foil' distance and the floppiness of the filters. Thus, Kim's assertion was that white centers could occur innocently due to the inner workings of the cassettes themselves, specifically that manufacturing variations in the filter to the foil distance could cause the white centers.

Gray didn't grasp it, but acted as if he were processing all of it. What he did recall was that the Secretary's two experts could not repeat the results Kim claimed to have discovered. In short, they believed that the filter to foil claim came up short itself.

The expert then turned to more common man explanations for the centers, things that anyone, including Gray, could grasp. Well-schooled, with each new reason he presented, Kim first repeated, to the point of being irritating, his earlier remarks that describing the filter centers as white was a questionable premise. He was simply following the directions from Krakovich and Malthan.

The Secretary was annoyed by the tactic. It wasn't needed before a judge, as it might be in front of a jury, to engage in such repetition. But Sanford remained silent; he didn't want to highlight Lee's challenge about whether white meant white. Besides, there was no basis for a winning objection over it.

Privately, Gray, captive that he was, fumed over it too, but he could only curtail repetitive testimony from a witness, not phrases within an answer.

A prominent assertion was that a host of handling issues were also to blame for their occurrence. Kim asserted that dropping the cassettes from heights a small as three inches could create the white centers. Impacts on the hoses to the device also caused the same result. He was not done, maintaining that his 'simulation' of MSHA's handling practices was yet another source. Not enough, the doctorate holder also stated that 'secondary' impacts on the filters, meaning more than one impact, could produce white centers.

As Sanford sat there, listening to all of it, while waiting for his turn at cross-examination, he grew irritable. Turning to one of his co-counsels, he rolled his eyes as he listened to the expert when the secondary impact claims were asserted.

THE CASE OF THE ABNORMAL WHITE CENTER

Of course, none of this was new. Disclosure, through discovery, had informed him all that business would be voiced. It was just that hearing the nonsense at trial was more maddening than simply reading the claims.

He was tempted to ask if having a conversation near a dust collection unit could also cause the white centers, as a way of conveying the ludicrousness of the expert's claim. But he knew better; it would only bring an objection and likely a remark from the judge that sarcasm was inappropriate.

All the alleged mishaps, he thought, if assumed to be true, meant that the miners who had such experiences during the sampling tests were so inept that one wondered how they could even walk or stand up. The claim, he thought, was farcical, especially with so many white center filters involved.

Keeping his poker face all the while, Gray, now wised up, also thought, maybe a few, maybe a few could occur, but on the order of some seventy-five such events? Why, if it were true that repeatedly dropping tool boxes on the sampling assembly hose produced the AWCs, then these miners were so clumsy that it was a wonder that they could work in a coal mine.

Not done, there was no shortage of others to blame for the white centers. Rough handling could include the U.S. Postal service as a culprit too. Mail delivery was always a favorite subject to criticize; everyone from time to time had experienced a damaged or misdelivered package, rare as they were.

Kim was careful not to directly blame the U.S. Mail, as they had no evidence, such as photos of crushed packages at the MSHA technology center, to support the claim. Rather, he couched it as another example to support his theme that rough handling by anyone, miners or postal workers, could produce the white centers.

The last group, the USPS, rested on the premise that they were careless in their package deliveries. It didn't matter that they lacked actual proof of damaged packages. It was always a safe tactic to blame the mail deliverers, the defense thought. Government workers were always an easy target to level criticisms.

Kim also postulated that the clumsy handling likely occurred in the MSHA office too, pointing out that the whole business began when that Miss Nelson 'confessed' as he put it to dropping the things.

Sanford's objection to Kim's inaccurate description of Nelson's testimony was overruled by Gray, who called it a simple exaggeration, noting that the technician did admit to dropping one of them.

Sanford then went over the line in response to that, stating "That's right your honor, once. One time."

That will be enough, Mr. Sanford, Gray scolded, "I have made my ruling."

Sanford knew the protocol. "Yes, understood. Thank you, your honor."

Thus, if believed, Kim had asserted that there were a multitude of sources for the white centers to result, from the difficult mine environment itself and thereafter from each handler of the samples, right up to the MSHA office where the claims originated.

Gray took no joy in reprimanding Sanford, especially as he had privately determined that Kim could not to be taken seriously. Even so, his decision would be required to give praise and credit for the testimony of the Doctor of Philosophy. Poor Sanford, he thought, so in the dark about the hopelessness of a victory for the Secretary.

Malthan and Krakovich knew the rough handling claim could only carry them so far. Had Gray not been captured and in their pocket, the idea was to present a series of excuses for the white centers, not just one. The plan, hatched when there was still a need to have a defense, was to have a bunch of excuses for their occurrence; a few would be explained away due to the filter-to-foil rubbish and others to dropping them, sometimes twice, and so on.

There was no other practical way to deal with so many AWCs. So, they would claim that there were many causes. That was their defense.

Each excuse amounted to a pebble, as it were, but the hope was that together they would, to use that old phrase, make a mountain out of molehills. Then, perhaps Gray, could be persuaded that the government didn't meet its preponderance of the evidence burden.

Now of course, thanks to dear Marla, persuading his honor no longer mattered. It would still be useful however when the Secretary brought his inevitable appeal to the federal court of appeals. Alleged deficiencies in the judge's decision would be met by the substantial evidence rule, coupled with his unassailable credibility determinations. Even if the federal court privately looked askance at the outcome, they would not be able to overcome those determinations by the trial judge.

Kim's malarkey became even more involved, the idea being that the judge would be unable to untie all the knots being presented. The doctor asserted that the hoses themselves, feeding the air into the filters, could explain the condition of the centers. Soft, medium and hard hoses were tested, with Kim solemnly asserting that the soft hoses were more susceptible to producing those whitish centers.

Akin to the dust sampling devices being dropped was MSHA's own handling practices. The thinking was why limit the blame for these innocent developments to the mine operator? Mailing the things, and rough handling by the MSHA testing office itself, those could account for those centers too. The government's own lead-off witness admitted to her clumsy handling of the cassettes!

There were no surprises. But, whereas before Gray would have been open to hearing what the doctor had to say, now with his entrapment, he was properly jaundiced with all of it. People who would set him up, as they had, people like that were not interested in any legitimate contests of the facts. No, ultimately it was all about securing the outcome by compromising the decision-maker, a failsafe arrangement.

Legitimate advocates, he thought, those truly seeking to determine if the white centers could be explained away as innocent occurrences, they would accept the results and, if those results didn't support their clients' claims, then they would settle the case. Not these pettifoggers though. The search for truth and justice was not part of their vocabulary. It was strictly about winning.

Gray willed himself to appear attentive to what he now knew to be pure bullshit, but his mind was elsewhere. His pretense was suddenly interrupted when his cell phone rang. He had forgotten to mute the sound before the day's testimony began and it had been set on the loudest volume. Everyone heard it.

Startled by the ring, Gray quickly hit the mute button, but as he did so he saw it was a message from Tranter, the person he least wanted to hear from.

Of all times, God damn it, not now from that bastard, he thought.

Flustered, he then announced there would be a fifteen-minute recess, advising that he had to attend to another matter. Wanting to regain the appearance that he was the captain of the ship, he repeated, "Fifteen minutes. We resume promptly then," as if there was a need emphasize his edict.

Once in his chambers, he called Tranter, "Did you forget? I am presiding in court."

Tranter well knew it. Didn't care either. If the judge didn't think much of him, well, the feeling was mutual. And who, he thought, was worse? Himself, a private detective, or the guy wearing the black robe? That wasn't a close call in his estimation. Genuflect for him? No way. He responded with abruptness, "5:00 tonight, G Street."

Though powerless, Gray still decided to push back curtly. "Next time I'll have my cell sound turned off," he warned.

Tranter was not cowed. He countered, "Well, *your honor*," adding the title with a clear tone of derision, better keep the vibrate feature on. You wouldn't want to have a text from me in your records, I would think," his message clear.

Gray was stunned. Hadn't thought of that. The son of bitch was right; he couldn't afford to have a text message in his records. Everyone knew that erasing such a message was impossible. There was always a way to retrieve deleted messages; he'd read about that in the news many times, people thinking their tracks were erased and then finding out that texts are forever.

Reminded again that he was powerless, he responded obediently, "I will be there." Afraid to say anything more, without another word he hung up.

No respect, Gray thought. But he recognized that he was impotent. Others were calling the shots now.

During the time left in the session that afternoon, with the hours of the day's trial testimony mounting, and the stress brought about by Tranter's order to show up at the end of the day, he was feeling depleted. It was difficult for him to appear attentive as the doctor's testimony dragged on. The upcoming meeting with Tranter was at the forefront of his mind.

Kim's testimony on direct continued throughout the remainder of the day. Before the expert turned to the next subject of his findings, Gray, seeing that the day was nearly over, interjected, advising that it was an appropriate time to stop. Anxious about the upcoming meeting, by calling the day's session to an end, there would then be some additional time to return to his office before proceeding without delay to meet Tranter at the bar.

As the day came to an end, Gray was satisfied that he appeared to the witnesses and the attorneys, albeit superficially, as both interested and neutral as he listened to the testimony. He knew the act had to be kept up. But in truth, his only thought was that none of what the doctor spewed mattered anymore. He could not imagine how he would have received Kim's testimony if there had been no Nicole and no bribery. Would he have been skeptical or would he have bought into the doctor's explanations? It was no longer possible to put himself back in that state of mind before everything came crashing down.

As their premier witness, the Respondent's direct exam would take up the remainder of the week. Cross-examination would not begin until Monday. The weekend would not give the Secretary any meaningful advantage. Through their preparation the team already knew what could and could not be accomplished. The weekend would not signal a rest for the Respondent's counsel either; their extra-legal strategies were not finished.

Once in his chambers, Gray hastily grabbed his things and made his way out of the courthouse. Though his return walk had just begun, he was sweating profusely, a condition brought about by his anxiety. It wasn't just the sweating; his heart began racing too and he started to worry whether he was having a cardiac event.

He stopped at a crossing to bring himself under control. Looking back from his direction of travel, he was relieved to see there was no one from the hearing. For the few passersby, he tried to look as if he was waiting for someone. This was no time to fold up, he told himself. Slowly, his symptoms eased, as his heart rate and the sweating both diminished. Calmed somewhat, he looked around again, saw no one he recognized, and reassured, he then resumed his trip to the office, the moment of crisis over for now.

Unfortunately, Larkin was present upon his arrival at the office and he noticed Gray's appearance.

"Time for a recap, Charles?" he inquired politely.

But Gray was still too tense to accommodate the request, a condition made worse given his imminent appointment. Besides, with his attention only faintly following the doctor's testimony that day, he would be unable to give much of recounting, and that would be obvious to his colleague. An honest recounting of the testimony, had he been listening, would have taken considerable time to sum up.

"Can't tonight, Richard," he stated, leaving it abruptly at that, with no excuse offered and no apology for his turn down.

With that short rebuff, Larkin had that troublesome feeling come over him again. Something about Gray's demeanor – it just didn't feel at all right. There was also some shrillness in his voice, detectable even with the short response.

Larkin had no choice but to accept the snub.

"Sure, I understand," he replied, though he did not understand it at all. He couldn't spare a few minutes?

Having Larkin out of the way, Gray nervously looked at his watch. It was nearing the time he was to meet Tranter. More like 'commanded' to meet him, he thought. He exited the building briskly, hoping he would not encounter any other colleagues. To his relief, he did not.

Upon entering the Grill, Jerome noticed his long-standing customer, presenting his traditional nod of recognition to the Judge's appearance.

In response to that, Gray, completely preoccupied, was unable to offer more than a minimal acknowledgement to the barkeep, the warmth they used to exchange with his visits gone.

Whatever had brought about the significant change in his patron's behavior, it was still possessing him, Jerome thought. This was a very different person from the one he had known for years.

Gray's attention was then directed solely to finding Tranter. He located him, as before, in a booth located in a darker section of the bar.

He made only a bare nod to his presence, as he slid into the booth, opposite the side Tranter occupied.

With the judge's cool acknowledgement to the person sitting opposite from him, Jerome realized that Gray's aloofness was not a matter solely between them; his atypical behavior applied to others too, including the person in the booth.

As he focused upon the meeting of the two, he took notice that, as before, there was no handshake or other greeting between the two. Extremely odd and troublesome too, he thought. Who meets someone in such a manner, with almost no acknowledgement? Very strange. Any sort of normal encounter would never go that way.

Whoever this person was that Gray was meeting again, it was clear that they were not friends.

Tranter spoke first. "I understand the trial is not far from coming to an end. So, the payments have been increased," he said, as he then handed a larger envelope across to Gray.

Gray took possession of it, immediately secreting it on the walled side of the booth, away from view by the waitress. He doubted this one, overfilled as it was, could fit in his briefcase.

Both the transfer and the judge's acceptance of the envelope were observed by Jerome. It was clear that something foul was going on. This was not hyperactive imagination on his part. What was up with the judge?

With those thoughts, he realized that his previous high regard for Gray had plummeted. Over those many years, serving the judge drinks, admiration had been part of his attitude. He was a judge after all!

But now, that title was not enough to maintain the respect he had held for him. Considering his own good behavior, now having had several years of being on the straight and narrow road, after some history of trouble with the law in his past, he was not shy about evaluating others, even a judge. One holding such an esteemed position, he believed, was obligated to behave in a manner consistent with that title. His observations of Gray, informed by his prior life experiences when he had skirted with bad choices, and now viewing two occasions of the judge meeting with that shady stranger, it was clear that something, and nothing good, was going on.

Effectively a hostage at the table, Gray was careful to say as little as possible. Trust could never be a part of the equation where this Tranter guy was involved.

Responding to Tranter's remark that the trial would soon be concluded, he informed, "There is no certain time frame for the trial to come to a close. The defense has several witnesses yet. And, even when the testimony does conclude, there will post-hearing briefs filed and then a decision will need to written."

It was annoying having to educate this scoundrel who was utterly ignorant about trials.

Tranter nodded, having been duly enlightened, but not chastened by his minimal understanding of the trial process, he responded, "I see, but we want to make sure all the payments have been made before you release your decision. It's to show our good faith, you understand."

Gray only nodded, sticking to his economy of words approach. Good faith, he thought with revulsion, what a misuse of such a term under these circumstances.

A waitress then appeared. "What will it be for you gentlemen this evening," she asked.

Gray, and Tranter too for that matter, would've preferred to immediately go their separate ways, the exchange having been made, but the circumstances required an order.

As they awaited the drinks, each avoided further conversation; Gray opened his briefcase, a diversion, because he had no purpose to the activity other than to use up time. No way, he figured, could that fat package fit within it.

Tranter, with a similar distaste for the man opposite him, engaged in a similar distraction, checking messages on his cell phone.

Jerome, glancing at their booth, took it all in – the obvious coolness between the two remained.

When the drinks arrived, Tranter placed a Grant down in payment, informing the waitress, at the same time, "that will be it for us, thanks. I won't need change."

She smiled, appreciating the large tip, expressing "thank you so much."

Of course, there was no toast. Not under such circumstances and with neither liking one another. Gray nursed his drink for several minutes, but when it was half-empty, he decided to end the meeting. It had barely lasted fifteen minutes, though it seemed much longer to him.

"Good evening," he simply stated, as he arose.

Tranter nodded, acknowledging the words, replied, "I'll be in touch."

As Gray departed, the puffy envelope tucked under one arm, with the other holding his briefcase, his eyes were fixated on the exit. He made no acknowledgement to Jerome, though passing by the bar was unavoidable.

Realizing that he was intentionally being ignored, the barkeep barely looked up as the judge left, but he did take note that the envelope being carried by Gray was fairly bulging. Though he could not be sure of its contents, money, a lot of it, seemed to be the only logical conclusion.

If nothing else, Jerome had street smarts.

Carrying such an overfilled envelope, Jerome could only imagine how much cash his former friend was carrying. If the judge was now revealed to be dishonest, shouldn't he get a piece of the action? he thought.

Outside the bar, Gray briskly moved to his garage, nervous again, as if a stranger could somehow tell that he was carrying a good deal of money. In that fearful state of mind, just having it was a worrisome event, as he held it ever more tightly, anxious to make it to the safety of his car.

Once inside his car, he exhaled, having made it to the safe harbor it provided. Immediately he locked the doors, hitting the lock button twice, as if somehow the car would be locked tighter if he repeated the act. After looking around to reassure himself that he was still alone, he took another deep breath, the bulky envelope still in his lap.

The imagined threat having passed, he then collected himself. Though he had a strong impulse to open the envelope, he exercised self-control, deciding that with such a large amount of money he should get home as soon as possible.

Can't sit here forever, he admonished himself, as he made another neurotic survey of his surroundings. Satisfied that he remained safe, he leaned over, attempting to stuff the envelope under the passenger seat as before. But, being considerably thicker than the last envelope, it was uncooperative and he could only squeeze about half of it under the seat. It was another reason to return without delay to the safety of his residence.

Having had just one drink, and only half of it at that, he was fine, sobriety-wise, easily able to pass any breathalyzer test. With no worry in that regard, he decided to leave the garage without further delay.

Still, though inebriation was not an issue, he reminded himself to be exceedingly careful driving home. Again, his concern was that if he were pulled over for any reason, exceeding the speed limit, or any other driving infraction, a police officer, peering inside his car with a flashlight, might take note of the envelope bulging from under the passenger seat. It might just pique his curiosity.

And thinking about traffic stops, Gray then worried that the 'plain view' exception to police searches could justify the officer making an inquiry about the stuffed package, protruding as it was. He thought about the stories he'd read over the years where a criminal would be pulled over, not for his crime, but for something avoidable, like running red light or speeding and then be nabbed for the major event.

Just be extra fucking careful driving home! he warned himself. By following those precautions, such an issue would never arise.

To his relief, he did arrive home without incident. But he could hardly call it home now, not after last night. He pulled into the garage and triggered the garage door to close even before he exited the car. Just to be safe.

He then sat in the car, the grief over Millie immediately sweeping over him. There was no need to hurry now; no one was home waiting for his entrance, only two timer lights inside misleadingly suggesting otherwise. He was alone and that would be his future at this house.

The house, so empty, presented a situation matched by his own condition – equally empty. Yes, Millie was an ever-present burden, but at least she was there each night when he came home. Until tonight. After a time of staring out his windshield, thinking of his life as it now was, he then came back to the moment, reaching across to the passenger side as he grabbed the package of cash and then opened the car door.

Upon leaving the garage, he entered the house, too tightly holding the payoff, as if it could somehow disappear. Neurotically, once inside, he locked the side entrance door. Now in the hallway, compulsively, he went back to check that the door was locked. Satisfied that it was secured, a ghostly feeling took its place.

A photo on the hallway table of the two of them, both blissfully smiling, stared back at him. He had to lay it face down. Seeing that each morning and evening was too much.

When he then walked into the kitchen, turning on some lights, the unsettling aura followed him. In the past he scoffed at those who talked of ghosts and the supernatural, but not at this moment. Would he have any peace from this later when in bed?

If only he had taken the right road when that floozy made her move. Okay, there would be no Florida home, consigned to the home he had always hated, until he too passed. But was his life now better? Resoundingly, the answer was no.

A matter of survival, he shook himself out of the disturbing thoughts. His attention then turned to the business at hand, that envelope. Opening it, at the kitchen table, so much cash was before him. $30,000 this time, again all hundreds. As before, he could not resist counting it, and doing so twice. The total was confirmed. $60,000 now in his hands. More cash than he'd ever held. And with $240,000 still coming.

With it all spread out over the table, nervously, he looked outside the kitchen windows. A snoop could see it, he thought. He saw no one, those windows just looked out to his backyard. It was crazy to think someone could be out there.

Still, all that money on the table was unsettling, and what if that suspicious Spalding were to show up unannounced, on some pretext, but really arriving simply as an opportunity to snoop.

Imaginings or not, he rapidly gathered his loot back into the envelope and immediately brought it down to the basement safe.

As he descended the stairs with the latest payoff, he noticed how steep they were, and with narrow landings. It was easy to see how his wife could've tumbled. The guilt following him down to the basement; he was afraid that he too could fall.

A significant difference, if his fate were like Millie's, people would not find him for days. One of them, he neurotically considered would be that son of a bitch investigator discovering his body and with that and all the money in the envelope and more in the safe, his suspicions about him would be confirmed. Not that it would matter if he were dead.

Upon reaching the basement floor, he was then able to stop all the morbid thoughts and return to business, storing the latest payment in the safe. Yet, almost fearful that some sort of cosmic justice would be coming for him, he quickly fled the basement, the crime scene as it were for his wife and the continuing site of his wrongdoings.

Once safely upstairs, still plagued by his neurotic fears, he checked to make sure he had closed the garage door. Satisfied, he then went to the front door, peering outside, the post lamp allowing him to see that all was calm.

So reassured, his structured personality roused him back to his routine as he then ventured outside to retrieve the mail. Upon taking the walk to the box at the end of his driveway, he found again a batch of brochures about the joys of living in Florida.

They were now arriving regularly, coming not long after he made his initial inquiry about homes down there.

Thoughts of Millie returned. She asked him about the brochures, but he'd been able to satisfy her curiosity by dismissing it as his pipe dream that they retire to Florida.

Spalding then entered his mind again. If he were to see all those ads about the Sunshine State, would that pique his already suspicious state of mind? Best not to leave those out in the open, he decided.

But Florida, he thought, the prospect of living there in peace, once he got through this self-inflicted mess, there will be that blessing. Survival mode taking over, he commanded himself to remain strong. No faltering now. Just get through the damn trial and issue the blasted decision. Then, perhaps, in time, peacefulness will return to his life.

He rationalized, excusing his complicity that yes, he'd made a terrible mistake, succumbing to that harlot's trap, but he soothed his culpability, noting that he was not the first to be taken in by such temptations.

Though he felt great shame, he tried to concentrate on the idea of retiring to Florida, and the hope that eventually, with time, perhaps healing would occur, and his transgressions would move to the back of his mind. Perhaps, he thought, recalling his Christian lessons, he could perform some penance, maybe some limited public service volunteering to atone for his wrongdoing and with that some easing of his plagued conscience.

He hoped that a glass of wine and a good night's sleep would restore some balance in his head, all to help him get through the remainder of the week. Though the wine helped him fall to sleep, his dreams were not restful.

In one, there was Millie, vividly coming right to his bedside, asking how he could have cheated on her and then entered that corrupt scheme. It seemed so real that he abruptly sat up in bed reaching out to her, asking her forgiveness. His own Christmas Carol nightmare.

In a sweat, and shaken out of his dream, she was gone. The remaining hours before his alarm were fitful. Tomorrow would be a bitch of a day.

CHAPTER 16

The ensuing days of the hearing seemed interminable. Even at best, there would still be two weeks to endure. He reassured himself that, having made it through the day after Millie's death, and keeping his wife's death unknown to anyone at the hearing, he could manage. He could do it, he must do it, he told himself.

Kim's testimony resumed with Gray listening as the doctor solemnly asserted that the white centers could be created through a tympanic or mechanical wave. To support that claim, the doctor informed that in his experiments the filter capsules were stacked and then 'chucked' into a cardboard box. Those actions created white centers, he informed.

Gray, now wise to the phony defenses, was tempted to laugh, but as he was now owned by the defense, he could not express such a reaction. He wondered if he would have displayed such disdain, had he not been captured and bribed.

It seemed that the defense had no end to the number of innocent causes creating the white centers. The government's use of a desiccator for the filters was yet another reason for those white centers, the doctor maintained. Just as with 'mechanical and tympanic waves,' Gray had never heard of desiccators prior to the hearing. The government's experts, aware through discovery that both those claims would be asserted, had earlier presented testimony through their own testing that neither of those alleged sources produced white centers.

It was the best the defense could create; the Respondent advancing all those causes for white centers, while the government was asserting that they could not create white centers applying those methods.

He tried to imagine, if his objectivity had remained, how he would have resolved the quandary created by the competing claims. It wasn't possible.

Then, thinking of his entrapped state, he hit upon one of the reasons he could present to rule against the Secretary. He could simply say that there were too many competing claims to conclude that one side or the other convincingly established their theories. Upon that safe premise, he could then state that the Secretary failed to establish by a preponderance of the evidence that it had refuted the theories.

Knowing what he did about the whole defense charade, he felt some shame about resorting to that, but he reminded himself that now this was a matter of survival. His survival.

To his relief, Kim finished his testimony on direct that afternoon. Between the cross-examination and the inevitable redirect, Gray realized that it would consume the rest of the week. He was buoyed only by the awareness that the end of the trial was now in sight.

Upon the day's conclusion, after a brief stop at the office, he headed directly home. There would be no time spent at the Grill. Ironically, he was now meeting Millie's repeated wishes that he return home directly after work, though too late to benefit her. Soberly, he realized that it was his new circumstances, not any change of heart, that brought about his present behavior.

If only, he thought, if only he had listened to his wife and came directly home with no bar stops, there never would have been any sexual setup and, without that, no bribe either. Alone at home, but feeling her presence there each day, some nights he would skip dinner entirely, consuming only his red wine.

It was now only about making it to the finish line.

When the proceeding resumed that Friday, Gray's dominant thought was, with that day's end, there would be the weekend to gather himself together for the next week. Even if his sleep remained fitful, it would offer some respite, providing two days of relief from the hearing.

Sanford, contemptuous of Kim's testimony on direct, was anxious to get started with his cross-exam. The government's disdain wasn't unfounded. It arose from the information the Secretary learned during discovery. As he saw it, the good doctor's many theories to explain away the white centers tended to show that none of them had merit. It didn't stand to reason, Sanford thought. If the AWCs were not the result of intentional manipulation, then only one or at most two explanations would suffice. Not here though, this team had so many excuses, hoping that something would stick with the judge. If they were all believed, one would think that there could be no such thing as a sample that did not have a white center!

The government began with the doctor's assertion that the Secretary's evaluations of the dust samples were inconsistent, pointing out that the doctor's analysis lacked consistency itself. When presented with his own classifications of more than a hundred filter samples, at trial he named less than a third of them the same.

As Sanford put that to him, he asked the doctor if his inconsistent determinations could be called a good batting average.

Malthan objected to the question but was overruled by Gray.

As the objection failed, that only served to highlight the doctor's poor score on his own evaluations.

Sanford suppressed a smile. It was a good way to start, especially with Malthan's objection making the doctor's deficiency more prominent.

From that good start, Sanford methodically went through each of Kim's asserted explanations for the white centers. He did so with a consistent tone of incredulity.

"So, you're telling us doctor that *all* these white centers came about through various non-intentional actions?"

Malthan objected to the tone of his questioning, but Sanford noted that, however the Respondent's attorney may interpret his speaking voice, a purely speculative claim, it was not a basis to make an objection.

In a different case, Gray might have instructed the attorney to try to refrain from employing a scornful tone, but here he had no sympathy. Yes, the scoundrels had won, but at least he could take some pleasure, whenever possible, of slapping them down when a dubious objection was made. It was a form of payback, however small. He enjoyed knowing that the two smarted whenever overruled.

As he anticipated, the cross and redirect examinations of Kim ate up the remainder of the week. The good news was that there would only be two more expert witnesses for the defense.

When Kim's testimony concluded, Gray again tried to take a step back from it all, asking himself if the competing sides' witnesses essentially had produced a draw, and there was no clear winner, would he find for the mine operator? This time his answer was a guilt-reducing yes. That conclusion would help ensure that his theory would be upheld – the Secretary hadn't met his burden of proof.

The Friday return commute to his home was a slog, as usual, for the end of the work week. At least, he thought, there would be two days of relief. And while the weekend did give him a break from the marathon of a trial, his home environment did not present a peaceful retreat. The emptiness was palpable. While Millie was gone, eerily she was still very much present.

Buck up, he scolded himself.

Heeding his self-criticism, he forced himself to microwave a meal. Can't stop eating, he told himself.

If slowly killing himself was the plan, he might as well drive right into the Potomac, he thought, windows open with all the cash loose in his car, the evidence floating away down the river. Of course, it would be obvious that he took his life, and that would prompt a serious investigation.

But, he considered further, it was unlikely that the trial would start anew. Oh, there would be loud complaints about having a new judge start presiding so late in the trial. However, that would also be a reason to move ahead.

Besides, he thought, the Respondent would probably prevail. Many of his colleagues would take the path of least resistance by finding for the mine operator. Sure, there would be wailing by the Secretary, but the forces for ending the matter, putting the whole mess in the past, that would prevail.

Given the mess he'd created and with no likely revenge even if he opted for suicide, he would just have to see it through, retire without delay and hope that, in time, peace would come to him in Florida.

While trying to hold onto the thought that calm would eventually arrive, the phone rang, startling him.

It was that detective, Spalding.

"Good evening, Mr. Gray," he began.

He was immediately irritated, the arrogant prick once again calling him 'Mr. Gray.'

"Yes," was his curt response.

With no apology for the evening call, the detective simply informed, "You may proceed with the funeral arrangements for your wife."

Gray wanted to ask about the cause of death, a natural question to pose, were it not for that guy's arrogant behavior toward him on Monday. That the detective didn't offer any information about the coroner's findings was clearly an admission that Gray had no culpability, he concluded. No doubt the son of a bitch was sorely disappointed about that outcome, he smiled to himself. The suspicious SOB had lost.

Knowing that he had the upper hand, he decided to respond in kind to the detective's curt remark. "I will be taking care of the arrangements then. Good evening, Mr. Spalding."

Spalding did not miss the slight, ignoring that he had not been courteous himself.

Though he had nothing to go on but his gut, he still felt something was amiss with that guy. It gnawed at him but, absent some unexpected development, there was nothing he could do.

Although Gray convinced himself that he won the exchange with the detective, the call had spoiled his appetite. The microwaved meal would remain untouched.

After a poor night's sleep, he forced himself to eat some breakfast. Promptly at nine, he called a local funeral home, making the arrangements for Millie.

The funeral manager was surprised at the judge's wishes. A person of his station, while not always lavish, rarely spent so little. Cheap, is what it was, he privately thought, while he responded with a professional attitude, hiding his view.

Gray had no hesitations over his choices: cremation, no announcement in any newspaper, and no visiting services. He even declined an urn, though the manager had advised they had several "economical selections" as he put it.

Gray ordered only a plain cardboard case for his wife's remains. One phone call and it was all resolved. The funeral home would retrieve the body from the coroner's office and the cremation would be carried out on Monday.

Gray advised that he would retrieve the box soon after the process had been completed. Her ashes would be spread in their backyard, no physical memories of their home or marriage would be brought to Florida and that included Millie herself.

Despite having that business out of the way, he spent the remainder of the weekend unable to relax, his mind hoping from one matter to another. He would read for a time, but his thoughts would wander, unable to have sustained attention on any book. For some of the time he would review the Florida brochures, with new ones arriving daily. But guilt was with him as he looked them over, spoiling what could have been a pleasant distraction. And he feared, without cause, that Spalding guy might show up unannounced, and then see all those getaway brochures, elevating his suspicious attitude towards him. With that fear in his head, and finding no real pleasure in reviewing them, he scooped them up, placing them in a kitchen drawer.

Even retiring for the night was no haven, not with one side of the bed now so obviously vacant.

When Monday finally arrived, his weekend unrestful, at least it marked the point where the finish line was in sight. Even though there would be significant hours to spend writing the decision, it would be restful by comparison, with the solitude of his office, and his door closed, the seclusion would be welcomed. And as those in the office would know that he was busy writing the important decision, they would not bother him. For the few interrupters, he could effectively shoo them away because of that work.

The morning began with Milo calling its second expert, Dr. Melvin Broccoli. His resume was just as gleaming as Kim's. It took nearly all of the morning session to review his credentials but, before the noon break, he had started, in the same fashion as Kim, to recount the procedures he put in place to determine the sources for the white centers. Like his colleague, Broccoli avoided, wherever possible, use of the word 'abnormal' when describing the filter centers.

All the experts for the Respondent knew of the uniform approach they would be providing – challenging the idea that a white center was anything more than a common and random occurrence.

The quicker pace continued with the afternoon session. By the end of the day the expert had completed most of his testimony on direct. Gray knew this was because his testimony was essentially an affirmation of Kim's.

Now, Gray thought, whether this second expert truly arrived at the same conclusions as the first without any communication or consultation between the two, he could not know. But, based on the tactics employed by those scoundrel lawyers against him, it would be naïve to think that such complete independence occurred. Of course, none of such ruminations mattered now.

In any event, Gray considered it to be anticlimactic as Broccoli's testimony could be summed up as nothing more than a reaffirmation of Kim's assertions. Sure, it was presented as an entirely independent study of the white centers, but to no one's surprise the expert came to the same findings as the first expert.

With each expert trotted out by the Respondent following Kim, Gray knew he had to maintain the appearance that he was closely listening to their findings and opinions. It was all an act, but under the circumstances, it was important that both sides perceived him as the attentive, deeply thoughtful, jurist he held himself out to be.

And, ironically, but for all that had happened, ensnared by that woman and then accepting the bribe, he would have been genuinely listening to their words.

But, now knowing that they were nothing more than expensive hired whores, masquerading as serious scientific evaluators of the causes for the abnormal white centers, he knew that their "conclusions" were purchased, not found through scientific rigor. As he listened to the second expert, the two of them, equally so professorial in their demeanor, this witness also asserted, without blinking, that the AWCs can result from incidental or accidental events and a host of other causes.

Once the day was over, to his relief, Gray was pleased that he was able to return to his office without encountering other employees. Increasing his odds of avoiding such meetings, he took the back entrance. He especially wanted to avoid coming upon Larkin, so it was a relief that both his entrance and exit did not involve seeing him.

Those moments the two had during those post-hearing day reviews, when Larkin occasionally expressed his mild skepticism, were annoying. Oh, he didn't miss the import of his colleague's remarks, not one bit, and so he was in no mood for more of that superior attitude from him this evening.

Safely outside, this time the lure of a drink before returning to his now empty home was too much to ignore. True, the G Street had lost its appeal, what with that whore who entrapped him there and now spoiled further as the place where Tranter transferred the bribe money. But Gray hadn't frequented many other bars in the vicinity, so he returned to his familiar place, tainted now though it was.

When he entered, Jerome, the familiar figure he had known for so many years, was in his dependable location, tending bar. This time Gray acknowledged him, but barely.

That the gesture was minimal did not escape the barkeep. Too important now to be courteous, he thought of the judge's slight. Also, another insult, he did not sit at the bar, his usual location over the years. He was alone this time but still he opted for the privacy of a booth. That was atypical too.

Though his formal education was limited, Jerome's street-wise schooling was solid. And all those years tending bar, if one paid attention, one learned from that experience too. So, he knew, he just knew for sure, that the old judge had gone down the wrong road.

It wasn't hard for him to put it together. That important dust sampling case Gray was handling, it was all in the papers; nearly every day there was a story about the trial. And then, he recalled, there was that woman who appeared at the bar not too long ago. She had no business being a customer at the G Street. Never saw a woman who looked that good in all his years working there. So, she was definitely out of place. She must be a part of it, he thought, trying to connect the dots. Never saw her again, just those two times, but it couldn't have been happenstance that she happened to be there, showing off her allure, just a few bar stools down from his honor.

Added to that was the stranger, that guy who just gave off all kinds of negative vibes to Jerome. He could smell out the types, not your average Joe, just there for a drink. It didn't add up; that out of place guy, who had met twice now with the judge, handing over those large envelopes both times. The contents of those envelopes were not a challenge to figure out.

And so, thought Jerome, the man he believed he had known so well, and a judge no less, turned out to be no better than anyone else. He'd been bought. No doubt about it. Hell, he didn't even need all those years of dealing with characters at the bar to know that.

Jerome saw the situation as his moment. The judge was unaccompanied, at least for the time being, so it was important to act without delay, in case someone else showed up to join him. Best to seize the opportunity and now. He told his assistant at the bar to take care of things, he would be occupied for a short time.

He strode right over to the booth Gray was occupying. This time he arrived as an equal and in that new stature there was none of that previous subservient mien, no asking first for permission to join the judge.

Sliding into the bench on the opposite side, Gray was taken aback by the boldness of the barkeep. Immediately he knew nothing good was coming. Silenced by this abrupt intercession, Gray simply looked back at him, a grim look displayed.

Jerome wasted no time beginning. "Sir," he began, omitting Gray's title, "I want you to know that I am a very observant person. Very observant," he repeated.

"And I keep up with the news too," he informed. "So, I'll get right to the point. I saw you and that seedy guy you've sat with, now twice, in a booth, just like you and me are doing right now." Choosing the word 'observed,' instead of repeating 'saw,' to emphasize its importance, he continued, "I also observed that strange character hand you an envelope on both occasions, the latest one being larger than the first. See, so now you know that I pay attention."

"And as said, I read the papers. I keep up with the news. I can put two and two together. You get what I mean, *sir*?" He emphasized that last word, conveying the opposite of its usual respectful meaning.

Gray knew very well what this nosy barkeep was about. But he remained calm, willing himself to look expressionless across the table, as he waited for the hammer to fall.

"But I am not a greedy person. And I know how to keep my mouth shut too. I can assure you about that. I have no interest in running to the authorities and ruining your career. I just want a fair share, not a lot of money, just a fair share," he repeated.

Gray held his position. Sure, that Tranter guy had him over a barrel. But who was this guy, a mere bartender, that's all he was, nothing more. Minimally educated, he thought, not the type he would ever associate with. Still, he couldn't very well afford any controversy. If this guy started blabbing, even if it was disregarded, it could still create a fuss and who knew where that might lead? Though the chance of his noise causing trouble was slim, he couldn't afford the risk.

Gray looked at him for a time, expressionless. With the silence continuing, he had to fill the void.

"Well, Jerome," he then spoke, careful to keep it all in the hypothetical realm "I have no idea what you're talking about, but for the sake of this silly claim of yours, I'll play along. Hypothetically, what would it take for you to go away?"

This time Jerome was on his heels. Unsure how the judge would react to his implicit threat and the demand that accompanied it, he had not thought through his follow-up. He had not expected such an immediate response from Gray. He was annoyed at his lack of forethought. Should've had an amount in mind, he scolded himself. On the spot, he had to give a figure, or he would seem the fool.

Making matters worse, he knew none of details. What it was exactly that the judge was into, he could not know. His mind raced. He recalled that there was that striking woman and, more recently, that grim guy. Both seemed out of place at the Grill. Were they somehow connected? Neither of them seemed to be people who would be naturally associating with the judge. And then there was the big ongoing trial itself but, none of those things necessarily fit together.

Of course, he thought, it was possible that the judge had multiple, but distinct, problems in his life, an affair going on, and separate and apart from that, money involved with that mining case.

For sure, Gray wasn't about to enlighten him about any of it. Given his own circumstances, not especially well off for his entire life, a paycheck-to-paycheck existence, and that bitch of a girlfriend who nailed him with a paternity suit a decade ago, Jerome thought it was best not to be greedy.

He couldn't delay his answer. "Ten thousand," he informed. For him, that was a lot of money to demand.

Gray, without showing any reaction, was relieved at the relatively small amount. It would only create a small dent in the sum he would be receiving. If he could get away with that and not be subject to new demands, he could easily manage it. His home, all paid off for years now, was worth something, just based on its location. And, the foolish bartender hadn't figured out that, by making the demand, he made himself culpable if things were to hit the fan.

But now, soberly, he realized, there could be no more meetings with Tranter at the Grill. That would only risk more demands from this latest extortionist.

Just a few blocks away, he recalled, there was the Spirit Room. He had been there infrequently, but it did offer secluded seating areas, a must. Not particularly different from the Grill, the only reason he had not gone there more often was the longer walk.

Persisting with the pretense that their whole discussion was fiction, though Jerome was under no such illusion, Gray continued, "So, under this hypothetical, if one were to provide such an amount, what would prevent additional demands later on?"

Again, Jerome had not thought ahead for an answer. He'd never tried to extort anyone before now. He wasn't even sure the 10K would be considered. Lamely, he offered, "I just wouldn't."

Then, considering the question further, he added, "I don't even know what's going on. It may be too risky to my health for all I know, so as I said, I won't be asking for more."

He wanted to add, '*you have my word,*' but realized, given that he was extorting the judge, there was no value to the claim.

Gray seized upon the worry Jerome expressed.

"To continue with this game, because that's all this is between us, that's very wise of you. If I were in your position, I would have the same concern. Getting too involved could have negative health consequences. One could be way out of his depth."

Jerome was unfamiliar with that description, but he understood what Gray meant by it.

Opting for a bluff, Gray then ended the exchange, as if he was the one dictating the terms, informing, "I'll consider this. But I want you to think about taking less. You're asking for a lot."

Having experience and skill in negotiating, he had an upper hand on the bartender. Privately, he knew that even if the demand were twice that amount, he'd probably have no choice but to meet it.

With that, the judge abruptly arose from the booth, closing with "I'll let you know. Good-bye."

Once outside, he moved briskly to his parking location, as if fleeing to that intermediate place of refuge that it had become, until he could reach the safety of his residence. He left the garage without delay, his edginess only lessening as he made the trip home.

With the latest development, he decided to pull over at a shopping center to call Tranter, advising him of the worrisome experience at the Grill, but electing not to disclose the employee making the demand on him. The less said to that guy the better, he thought.

Informed of the problem, it took no persuading to obtain Tranter's agreement for the new meeting location and, to quell his concerns, he assured Gray that the exchanges at the Spirit Room would be more discrete.

Gray was satisfied and it was arranged that they would meet the next evening at the new location at the usual time. He did not seek, nor did Tranter offer, advice about the new issue. He was satisfied that the judge could handle the problem, and if it caused him to part with some of the bribe money, well, too bad for him.

But he did not take the news as if it were nothing. Who knew what could develop from it? It made him rue again that he had gotten involved with this whole thing in the first place. It was too goddamn big was what it was! Sure, it was a disreputable way to make a living, but he had never gone to the extremes used here. He'd gone far over his head and, realizing that, he was anxious about what could develop. Again, he resolved once more to stick to the wayward husband situations. This thing, if it blew up, could spell significant prison time and if it all unraveled, what with that Ruby business, a life sentence could be involved.

Upon arriving home, Gray was totally exhausted. Still, out of compulsion, once inside, he could not resist checking the safe in the basement. Carefully descending the stairs, he was relieved to see that it was intact, an unfounded worry from the start. Even reassured, he decided it was best to add more cover over the thing, make it less obvious to an intruder, should that remote possibility occur. Bad enough that the obnoxious investigator Spalding eyed the thing. Hiding it better, he put some boxes over it, and an old blanket too. It did the trick, creating the appearance of a collection of junk sorely in need of cleaning while still making it accessible for the future deposits without having to relocate it.

Finally, there was time to rest. With a full glass of red in hand, he sat down in the living room. He had nothing planned, but he hoped that the evening would offer some relief from the pressure of the trial and a respite from those meetings with Tranter. It would also give him some time to consider the Jerome problem.

But comfort did not come; with the television off, an eerie feeling once more filled the room. Though more Florida brochures arrived with each day's mail, they were tainted now, with thoughts of Millie remaining prominent in his mind as he glanced through them. Though he told himself it was utterly foolish, it again felt as if Millie was right there in the room. He had no ghostly visions of her presence; things had not gone that far. But even after he finished his first glass of wine, the feeling, so unsettling, remained.

CHAPTER 17

The only good thing about his trip to D.C. that morning was his thought that Dr. Broccoli's testimony was moving at a much faster pace than Kim's. This was understandable, as the second expert's testimony was essentially a reaffirmation of the first expert's findings.

As the afternoon wore on, though he was mindful of the need to appear attentive to the doctor's testimony, he discretely continued to check the time. Shifting in his chair, visibly writing notes, a mild stretch, all those actions afforded the opportunity to glance at his watch.

Winston and Milo noticed his restiveness, but they continued to present the expert's testimony as if the hearing still had legitimacy, not the charade it had become.

The day dragged on, with the second witness' testimony being an echo of the views from the preceding expert. And there was no point to it, given the predetermined outcome. Still, Gray had to make some notes during his testimony, as they would be needed for his decision, giving it authenticity and additional substance for the findings he was now compelled to make. The notes were vital for writing the decision quickly; no way was he going to plod through more than six weeks of transcript testimony!

With it approaching 4:00, he began to look for an appropriate opportunity to call the day to an end. It arrived not long after that, as the defense concluded its direct examination. Though there was time for the Secretary to start its cross, he interceded, advising that, as it was late in the day, testimony would resume the next morning.

The Secretary did not like it. Sanford was ready to challenge the doctor's testimony immediately, but there was no appeal from the judge's determination. It was on Gray's own initiation that the day end, not the Respondent's. Objecting would be fruitless and all it might accomplish would be irritating the judge.

It was obvious to the litigators that it was Gray who wanted to depart, as he immediately arose, rapidly gathering the papers on the bench and exiting to his chambers. Once there, he compulsively checked his watch, to make sure there was sufficient time for him to arrive at the new meeting location.

To avoid the delay that would develop if he were to meet colleagues, especially Larkin, who would undoubtedly ask for a recap of the day's hearing, he decided to walk directly to the Spirit Room. Until his retirement, which would follow shortly after he issued the damned decision, this would now be the routine place for meeting with Tranter. At least there would be anonymity there.

He would still have to settle up, so to speak, with the new troublemaker, that greedy prick Jerome, but once that was done, the extortion money delivered to him, never again would he return to the Grill.

Though he had been there before, entering the new place felt secure, as he was a stranger, no one recognizing him and, God forbid, thankfully, no one from the office was there either. As he scanned the room, he then saw Tranter seated at a booth in a secluded location.

To make sure the judge saw him, he gave him a half-wave. Gray nodded back and moved directly to the booth.

In no sense a friend, far from it, oddly Gray felt some relief seeing the guy. At least their meeting would be without the prying watch of Jerome. Tranter, knowing the judge's preferred liquor choice, had ordered it upon taking the booth, together with his own drink.

Gray took his seat and felt compelled to acknowledge the drink before him, nodding, though annoyed that he had to thank him for anything. When he raised his glass, Tranter thought of clinking it with Gray's but realized it would be too much, considering that the judge was a captive, no companion for sure.

At least there was the envelope to present, as he nonchalantly passed it across the table to him. Gray, gestured again, the minimum acknowledgement, and immediately placed it on the seat next to his thigh. As he did so, he could not resist a quick scan of the nearby patrons. No one took notice of the exchange.

That completed, Tranter began solicitously, "So, you've got a problem with the bartender at the Grill. Do you think you have it under control?"

Gray hadn't identified the employee, but realized Tranter must have made the obvious conclusion about who it was.

"I think so," he answered. "The guy is not sophisticated and his demand is not over the top," oblivious to the fact that Tranter did not care about the amount he would have to pay out. "He made his claim, to which I acknowledged nothing, but he was also tentative, almost fearful, that he was in over his head."

"That's good," Tranter responded. "Fear is a good motivator. Stoke that emotion, if you can, when you meet him. Also tell him that his demand was exorbitant and that you can't meet the full amount. That'll lower his expectation, make him less likely to add new demands."

"I'll do that, minus using words like exorbitant," working in an insult to the bartender's minimal educational background. "The main thing is I want this to be a one and done affair.

I won't ever be returning to that place, so he'd have to search me out if he decides to make a new demand. Of course, as long as I'm in the area, with my office so close, that wouldn't be hard to do. Maybe I should add something along the line that pressing this further could be a health risk. Do you think that would help?"

"That could work. As you said, he seemed nervous. Just don't lay it on too thick," he advised. "You could add that it's a risk to the health of both of you, not just for him. Like it's that big a deal." Tranter paused, adding, "and frankly, it is."

Gray reacted to the sobering words, appreciating the undisguised warning as coming from one that he presumed had some experience in dealing with blackmailers.

Their drinks finished and with neither interested in prolonging the meeting, they agreed to meet again the following week.

Privately, Gray then thought he would address the Jerome problem without delay. Get it over with. By that, he thought, he could avoid having the guy try to extort more out of him.

The walk back to the parking garage, now only a few blocks longer, was uneventful as he avoided coming near the Grill's location. Following his past routine, inside his locked car, and upon checking that no one was around, he could not resist opening the envelope. As with the prior one, this one was fairly bulging too. Showing restraint over compulsion, he counted it just once. Thirty thousand, all hundreds, again. With a last check of his surroundings, he shoved the envelope as far as it could go under the passenger front seat.

Once home, somehow more relaxed this time, upon closing the garage door, he entered the house and promptly put the latest payment in the basement safe. It was almost unbelievable; 90,000 in cash sitting in his basement. They were making good on the arrangement. He was aware that there were still considerable risks involved. How to move that all that money would be an issue, as he knew that the feds tracked cash transactions of $10,000 or more. The IRS requires that such amounts are to be reported and the banks did that. Of course, as all of the money was ill-gotten, he hardly could be reporting it to anyone. It was a problem, but he was confident there would be a way to deal with it.

Following his well-established routine, though now a solo act in his home, he settled down with his red wine. To his relief, no neighbors came by to inquire about the rescue truck at the house. Millie had become a recluse for years, seldom venturing out and never alone. That people didn't notice her absence was not surprising.

On this evening, instead of television, and feeling protected as, given the hour, there was little prospect of any visitors, he started reviewing the pile of ads from Florida displaying new and resale homes. It would not be the same, relocating there alone, but his desire to live in the Sunshine State remained unchanged.

When it was time for sleep, he ascended the stairs with care, remembering his recent near fall event. Despite all of Millie's medical issues and the constant care she required, the bed was a lonely place. There was no refuge from it all; the wrong paths he had gone down, and his wife's premature death, an indirect, but attributable consequence of his acts.

To his surprise he had restful night's sleep, a rare experience of late. When he arose that morning, he hoped it signaled that it was the start of diminishing guilt over Millie's passing. Boldly, he told himself that his wife bore some responsibility for her death. Granting himself absolution, he thought, she had no need to go snooping around. If she had followed her normal routine that fatal tumble would not have happened.

As he drove to the office that morning, the slog being somewhat less congested, a typical mid-week effect, Gray now looked forward to the upcoming end of the week. It should be easy sailing, he thought. There was a good chance that the second expert's testimony would wrap up today and certainly by tomorrow. After that, there would only be one more expert for the defense. Not that he had any plans for the weekend, but it would still be a respite, especially since now, with the trial about to be completed, the end was truly in sight. Considering all that had occurred in those weeks, it was overwhelming.

The biggest case in his life, receiving local attention nearly every day in the Washington newspapers, and even some regular national attention, it truly was that big a deal – effectively the whole coal mining industry indicted for corruption.

And now, they would get off, scot-free, as they say. But he played an essential role in that certain outcome and with his failings, the whole trajectory of his career had now been inalterably changed from the upstanding, respected, judge he had been for decades to one who made a serious moral mistake and then compounded it by being bought.

As if that were not enough, there was his wife's tragic death, an event that would not have occurred but for his late-night actions with the home safe he bought to store his bribe money. The thought of taking his life entered his mind. Because of his shameful acts, he considered that he didn't deserve to live. Certainly, Millie didn't deserve to die that way. It wasn't like she chose to have that MS problem. His problems, though, all of them, those were matters of choice. It was no salve that Millie's passing would not have been far off in any event because of her disease.

An abrupt stop in the traffic flow, causing him to hit his brakes hard, brought him out of his dark thoughts. With his attention minimally on the car ahead, he almost collided with it. Another problem was something he did not need and with that near accident, he willed himself to pay attention to driving, and cease the distracting ruminating.

When the trial resumed that morning, the defense's second expert witness, now under cross-examination, continued his testimony. By the end of the day the government had completed its challenges to the doctor's testimony. Sanford made little progress in that examination. Broccoli stuck to his conclusions, and so the government was left with two experts maintaining, independently they both claimed, that innocent causes could just as well explain those white centers. With several reasons offered to explain the "so-called" white centers, as the expert continually described them, it was clear that both experts blamed the results chiefly on manufacturing differences, the filter-to-foil distances, as the chief culprit. That worked well, as it provided an excuse to explain why the white centers stopped: the manufacturing problems, it was claimed, must have ceased.

It was exasperating to Sanford, but he was left with it, and the hope that the judge would decide that the government's own experts were the more credible witnesses on the issue. Unaware that the fix was in, he consoled himself that any reasonable judge would favor the government's side. After all, there was the large mine that admitted to exactly what the government charged. That had to be in judge's head, even if it never appeared as a basis in any opinion.

On top of that, there was the abrupt stop to the white centers, once word got out that MSHA was on to it. Oh sure, he thought, it was all about manufacturing problems. Pure bullshit. They ceased because the government discovered the scheme.   A clearly guilty reaction if there ever was one. And who could believe that dropping, stepping, mailing and MSHA's own handling could cause so many of those centers? It was all too   far-fetched, he reassured himself.

As the day's testimony came to a close, Gray knew the business requiring his attention was ahead. There was no time for the delay that would be involved with Larkin's continuing requests for updates about the trial, so he would employ his earlier strategy, by going directly to the Grill, avoiding those time-consuming and often annoying conversations with his colleague. Thinking about Larkin, it was especially irritating as he remembered Richard's repeated skeptical comments in reaction to his account of the testimony. And that reaction was even before the mess he got in. He could tell, it was clear, where Larkin was coming from, a reaction which became more transparent as the trial progressed.

The trouble with his colleague's damned superior attitude was that his take was spot-on. For that matter, Millie had it right too. Big judge that he was, with so many years of experience, but his wife saw through it from the start. He didn't wake up to what the two of them clearly saw until after he'd been ensnared.

Making his way to what he hoped it would mark the last visit to his old haunt, the mission was to take care of that Jerome matter and then, hopefully, never see him again. He had packed the cash payoff in an envelope that morning, carrying it in his briefcase all day. Contrary to Tranter's suggestion, he was bringing the full amount, but it would not be handed over until he had sufficient reassurance that there would be no further demands from the guy. When that was done, he would return to the office, confident that by that time the place would be empty, with even Larkin likely gone by then.

On his arrival to the Grill, he immediately saw Jerome at his usual station. They exchanged acknowledgements and Gray then tilted his head signaling his direction toward the booths. Jerome nodded in response to the gesture and joined Gray in his booth without delay. This was no friendly meeting, their past friendship, whatever it had been, was now replaced with a payoff for the bartender to keep his damn mouth closed.

Gray began, "I could've rejected your demand. If you threatened to do something, you would've regretted it, I assure you. But I decided to go along with it," he informed. This is a one-time event. I need your assurance that it's the end of the matter. And, paying you does not mean that I am admitting to any wrongdoing."

Then, vaguely suggesting that he was a victim, he added, "As I told you, this is something bigger than either of us, and because of that I can't say anything more. Let's just say, your health and mine would be in jeopardy and leave it at that." He hoped that his cryptic statement would instill some additional fear in Jerome.

"Do we understand one another?"

The bartender, still soberly nervous about making his demand in the first place, took the warning seriously, assuming, incorrectly, that the danger applied to both of them. In fact, intimidated by the judge's remarks, taking them as genuine, and not a bluff, he did not want to know more about whatever was involved. What he did know was that this case the judge was handling was a very big matter. That was obvious. The daily newspaper and occasional television reports about it confirmed that.

Threats meant something to him. They were to be taken seriously, not dismissed. In the circles he used to travel in, when he was much younger, danger was always in the air. He knew from direct observation that people who crossed the line could find themselves quite dead from such ill-advised behavior. When those events occurred, it was intended as a message for everyone else, not just the victim. He wanted none of that now.

"I get it. I won't be asking for more. That's a promise, though I know that under the circumstances, my word can't be worth much. I don't need more trouble in my life, so again I tell you there will be no more demands."

What more assurance could he receive? thought Gray. It was the best he could do, he realized. And it was good to hear the guy's remark about not wanting more trouble in his life. It revealed that he'd had a taste of trouble in his past, an incentive to avoid more of it.

Still, he felt compelled to add, "Well, I hope so, for the health of both of us," emphasizing the false claim that the risk applied to both of them.

An inopportune interruption, a waitress appeared asking for their orders. Jerome, knowing her, spoke up, "Need a moment to decide," he said congenially.

"Sure, fine, I'll come back in a bit, then," she answered, accepting the delay.

Returning to the business itself, Jerome inquired, "So, the amount, it's as agreed?"

'Agreed,' thought Gray, what a description. There was no agreement earlier; there had only been the demand and he had not said it would be met.

"Yes," he answered, "it's all there," as he passed the envelope across the table to him.

Jerome took it, instinctively placing it next to his thigh, just as he had observed that Gray had done twice before. Awkwardly, given the nature of the exchange, but compelled to say something, he responded, "thank you."

Gray nodded, solemnly, but said nothing in response.

Jerome then arose from the booth, his payoff tightly held.

After a moment, a waitress reappeared, noting that Gray was now alone, with Jerome back at the bar. "So, what will be your pleasure, sir?" she inquired about his order.

Gray was in no mood for a drink, his only goal was to leave. He forced himself to casually respond to her. "You know, I was going to have a drink, but I changed my mind." With those words he handed a fin to her.

She accepted it with a smile. "Thank you. Another time then. Have a good evening, sir."

That 'sir' business, he thought, so commonly added when people spoke to him. His age prominent to others.

"Same to you," he answered.

As he left, he decided to avoid any acknowledgment to Jerome, who was then back at his station, tending bar. He hoped that would underscore the grimness of their meeting, and emphasize the finality of it.

Exiting into the cold, he noted that it marked his last visit to the Grill. Soon, if his plans fell into place, there would be that last visit to the office and the end of his career, now so severely tarnished as it neared the end.

Upon his return to the office, his calculation was confirmed. Not a soul was there. The visit was brief, just checking for any messages before he would be on his way home. He could not help but think that now, his circumstances so dramatically different, there was no longer any need for a timely arrival home, his former spousal duties over.

The evenings in his house continued to provide no refuge. True, Millie was a substantial burden but with his new free-of-responsibilities environment, the emptiness in its place was ever-present, her ghostly presence felt throughout the place, and especially so when in the basement or their bedroom.

Trying to move past that feeling, he willed himself to concentrate on the trial wrapping up, and with that the elements he would include when writing the decision, one that would be solid enough to foreclose a reversal and remand. With his long experience, he was confident that he could write a strong decision. Once that was done, not more than a month, he calculated, after the hearing finished, he would be getting out of Dodge, so to speak. He wished that 'getting out of Dodge' expression had not entered his head, as it was so apt, with he, a judge turned into a criminal, needing to flee Washington.

Attempting to relax from those burdensome issues, perhaps, he hoped, when the time for Florida arrived, Millie's specter would stay behind at their Virginia home, freeing him to make new acquaintances, a fresh start for his life. He resolved that when thoughts of her entered his mind, he would emphasize how much he did for her, over so many years of her illness. He told himself that he deserved some credit for all the efforts he made.

The thoughts of his new destination, and the money he needed to make that happen, brought his mind back to Tranter. He called him and moved right to business. "Good evening," he began, and then, without more, informing "I dealt with that other problem."

Tranter held to his stance that this was Gray's problem, not his. "Okay, fine," was all he offered in response.

From that, Gray understood that Tranter had no interest in the details. He then turned to their business. "When shall we meet next?"

Tranter employing the same economy of words, responded without hesitation. "Tomorrow is fine. Same time."

Gray answered, "Okay, see you then," intentionally ending the call, without adding a 'thank you.' Under these circumstances, he decided, such cordiality was completely unwarranted.

For his part, Jerome, elated, yet fearful over what he had gotten himself into, had immediately placed the payoff from Gray in his locker, secured with a combination lock. He was tempted to open it, but with the risk that another employee might enter the back room, he resisted that urge. The amount was, he trusted, all there. That guy, he wouldn't pull a stunt like that, shorting him.

All that cash, he thought, it would make life easier now. And, it came about without much resistance from the judge. Perhaps, he then contemplated, now feeling outplayed, he should've demanded more. Maybe that threat of harm was just bullshit from him.

Remaining anxious to count his haul, he left work early that evening, telling the manager he was not feeling well.

Once home, in his dreary little apartment, he immediately counted the contents of the envelope. As he expected, it was all there, neat hundreds and not too new either, a good situation. Too many fresh bills, he knew, that would raise eyebrows.

Satisfied for the moment, he then worried about securing it. There had been break-ins in the building, but not in his unit. Still, he realized the money was at risk. There would be a need to put it someplace in safekeeping, though he had no solution in mind at the moment. There were few places in his small apartment to hide anything. Though it felt lame, he decided to spread the cash out under his mattress, and near the center of it too. He imagined that if someone were to break in, any search for valuables would be in his dresser or the closet.

Not long after, he went to bed, his take secured under him. Tomorrow, during the morning, he would figure out a better place for it. No way would he leave it in the apartment, even for a day.

As sleep approached, he mulled over the idea of making a new demand from Gray, his word notwithstanding.

CHAPTER 18

There were reasons for Gray to have a positive attitude with the start of Thursday's proceedings. Soon there would only be Friday to contend with. And the finish line was now very much in site. Considering the approaching end of what had become his ordeal, Gray was fueled with energy from those thoughts. He was pleased that the testimony from the Respondent's second expert was wrapped up as the day came to a close.

Once out of the courthouse, he hurried to his meeting with Tranter, who handed over the latest installment. Less his payoff to Jerome, he now had a net of $110,000. With that much cash, he felt rich. Thinking about his meeting the following week, he would then be over the half-way mark. As the time for post-hearing briefs and the drafting of his decision would involve another four weeks, there was ample time for the balance of the payments due him.

He also informed Tranter that the future meetings would need to be a half-hour later than their usual time. He wrote it off as 'office duties' that could not be deferred.

Undisclosed, was his need to deal with Larkin. Pacifying him had become an obligation. If he avoided the after-trial conferences that had become a regular, but annoying, occurrence, he was concerned that his colleague would become inquisitive if their meetings were suddenly terminated. Once the trial itself was over, those meetings could become infrequent and he would then have no obligation to speak of his decision drafting. Larkin would know and respect that there could be no talk about that. With a nod, Tranter accepted the new time; it was a minimal inconvenience.

His new, solo, routine established, he returned home and promptly deposited the latest payment in the home safe. Before closing it, putting aside thoughts about how he had acquired it, he took a moment to admire the sizeable stash. With the amount growing each week, he made special efforts to cover extra materials over the safe, hiding it more effectively. It wasn't hard to do; the basement was full of junk in need of being trashed anyway.

Feeling comfort from the sizeable amount of cash now in his possession, his anticipation of retirement was growing. But the money could not completely occupy his mind. Millie continued to intrude upon his thoughts, an unsettling thought that made him feel as if she was somehow still residing in the house, but he willed his mind to concentrate on Florida. With brochures continuing daily, his earlier discomfort over their arrival ebbed; it now provided him with the distraction he needed, a form of refuge from his wife's passing, aided by his nightly wine.

He was aware that, ever since her death, his intake of alcohol had spiked. It was a concern, but he was able to put it aside, sympathetically telling himself it was an understandable reaction, given all that had happened to him. Though in need of calming his nerves from the stress he'd been under all these past weeks, he pardoned his role in creating his tense condition by side-stepping that, aside from the complex nature of the trial itself, the rest of the stress, all of it in fact, had been generated by his own poor decisions. He convinced himself that, once he was settled in his new Florida residence, he would be able to curtail his excess wine intake.

On Friday, that day's trial testimony began with the Respondent's third expert, Dr. Calvin Robeson. A math whiz, the preliminaries about his background took nearly two hours, as he droned on presenting his elaborate credentials. Sanford declined to cross-examine about his qualifications. There was no point as his resume was unassailable.

Gray viewed all of it with the jaundice it deserved. It was not news to him that if one has sufficient money, an expert in any field, offering the desired opinion, can be purchased. There were times, in his past cases, when an expert was legitimate, someone to be respected. Not this time. These experts, he now knew to a degree he had never experienced before, were nothing more than whores. Expensive ones to be sure, but still whores. The difference being the amount of money required for testimony from whores with impressive resumes.

Gray did his best to appear attentive, as he knew he was required to present himself that way, while internally noting that it counted for nothing. Occasionally, he would exchange eye contact with those two sharks. Wordless, and with no discernable facial expression, there was still clear communication between them. Gray, unmistakably and understandably, hated the two of them and both knew it.

Tough crap, they thought as they looked back blankly at the judge. Sure, they constructed the trap, but the jurist entered it on his own.

The experts, each of them, though clueless about the crafty setups the Respondents' attorneys had arranged to snare the judge, still knew quite well the purpose behind their employment – dismantle the claims of tampering with the dust sampling in every possible way.

Had any of them not fully understood this and produced findings undercutting the idea that the sampling results were inaccurate, the result of mishandling or whatever, they would've been dismissed, with such adverse findings never seeing the light of day. There is no legal obligation to disclose the identity of witnesses, experts or otherwise, that were not used.

As Robeson then turned to his math and statistical analyses, a mind-dulling topic to all, but a necessary prelude to his conclusions in support of the Respondent's claims, Gray thought that the same biased views might not be said for the Secretary's witnesses. The Secretary, in his estimation, and backed by his long years of trial experience dealing with the government in cases, would be more likely to drop the prosecution if their experts found problems with the tampering claims. In short, if their experts, through tests or statistical analysis, found that tampering was not clearly established, the Secretary would have done the right thing and not proceeded with the matter.

Realizing this, and that his own failings would soon be the cause of denying justice, in order to forgive his culpability, he tried to tamp down the guilt over the impact of his upcoming, predetermined, fraudulent decision.

But it was no use, he knew that his wrongdoing wasn't merely about being unfaithful to his ill wife, nor was it just about the bribe money he was taking weekly.

No, in a greater sense, it was about shortening the lives of all those coal miners who had to inhale the deadly dust, all of them knowing that if they squawked about it to management, unemployment would result.

Those miners, now he knew without doubt, they had all been sucking in that excessive coal dust, the life-shortening price of earning a paycheck. With all his experience of hearing mining cases, Gray was not ignorant of the fact that the miners knew very well what the mine operators were up to and that it was widespread knowledge.

The twelve, who solemnly testified that nothing of the sort occurred, knew this too, the difference being that they were willing to perjure themselves about it. The compensation for their lies being a few nights living it up in Washington, staying at a hotel they could never afford and dining lavishly at expensive restaurants.

The underhanded efforts to fabricate the dust sampling results weren't confined within each mine. Miners, they talk, through family and friends employed at other mines. It was no secret, but no one dared blow the whistle. Those operators, they'd figure out who snitched on them and then it wouldn't take long to invent a reason for firing any traitor.

Yet, Gray considered, those miners who testified could be excused. Yes, they were bought, but they were without bargaining power. Go along, they knew, or in time they would be terminated.

Gray, inattentive to the testimony at hand, returned to the big picture as he thought, I get my damn Florida house, but lose my wife and the integrity I once had, with no one to blame but himself. That was the bargain he made.

And the underground coal miners in those impacted states, all of them, soon would be learning with the issuance of his decision that the requirement to accurately record the amount of coal dust they inhaled was nothing but a joke. Not that they would be surprised; only the new and naïve would not have expected the outcome.

The lesson for all of them would be as it was before, keep your mouth shut and work in the dusty conditions or lose your livelihood.

Only he, as the judge, could've protected all the coal miners from continuing exposure to the debilitating and sometimes fatal lung disease. By his behavior, he had let them all down. No wonder those who made their living through labor were cynical.

It was with all those thoughts in his head that Gray, while displaying his most earnest façade, spent the morning thinking about the mess he had created and the harm his actions had produced. With all of it weighing heavily on him, involuntarily, the thought of taking his life arose again. An unwelcome ideation and to have it enter his head during testimony, the worst possible time of all, left him in disarray.

He knew he had to keep it together. And so, he forced himself to think, not of the testimony, because it was foolish to give it any thought, but of his upcoming Florida location and the fresh start he hoped to establish.

Why, he thought, though retired, he would be quick to reveal to his new neighbors that he had been a judge. Though a veneer, they would not know it was no more than that. And, with that announcement, boasting really was what it would be, ignorant of the real Charles Gray, would come reverence for his former position, and the esteem that would be bestowed upon him, their new, highly regarded, neighbor.

With lunch, keeping to his practice of remaining in chambers, he was able to become became more relaxed, the brief crisis of conscience which had invaded his thoughts during the morning session, having abated for now. He hoped that the momentary suicidal thoughts would not resurface.

From here on out, he privately proclaimed, he would focus on the positive. He must. The past could not be corrected. His guilt was not so overwhelming that he would have no choice but to confess it all publicly. If the present state of his mind created a type of hell, confessing to his wrongs would be much worse.

Holding to the commitment to stay strong, to make it to the finish line, literally and figuratively, he focused on the money. It was coming in regularly. And the indications were that the Jerome extortion had been met. The end was in sight and towards reaching that goal, he resolved to spend some time each evening developing the draft for his decision. It would keep him busy and, perhaps with that, he would be tired enough by nighttime to drop off to sleep quickly, too exhausted to think of his shameful ways. He planned on issuing it not long after the trial concluded, but not too soon, or it would appear to have been issued without due deliberation. Three weeks' time seemed appropriate.

The afternoon session dragged on. Gray had to pretend that he was following the confusing statistical testimony being presented by Robeson. Things like the doctor's chi-square analysis left him baffled. He was left with the easy-to-comprehend point: the expert's conclusion that there was no difference in the numbers of AWCs before the mine operators knew that the government was reviewing them and after the mines learned of it.

But Gray, though flummoxed by the numbers, remembered that the Secretary's statistical expert had stated without contradiction that the AWC rate was 43% before the mines learned that the government was investigating whether tampering was going on and that the rate fell to less than a half a percent after the news got out.

To get around this uncomfortable assertion, Robeson contended that, even if there were differences, they likely were caused by cassette manufacturing changes, a theme that the other experts had asserted, but beyond his expertise. This was echoing one of the several 'null hypotheses' arguments the Respondent had offered; that there was no difference in the before and after rates of AWCs.

It was an audacious claim and Gray hoped he would have recognized it as such even if he had never been compromised. They say, he thought, that numbers don't lie, but here he was learning that, with the right contortions, they could lie, being expertly manipulated to assert whatever result the expert wanted.

Only true mathematical experts could see through the rubbish that was being presented. For him, and really for all judges, even honest ones, they would have to fall back on their credibility determinations for the answer to the conflicting assertions. That, and the stunning numbers of the AWC rates before and then the dramatic drop in those rates once the operators knew the government was onto their industry-wide scheme, would have been the basis for any honest decision.

Mercifully, the numbers expert's direct testimony wrapped up by day's end. Truly, the trial's end was in site. Being Friday, there was also the weekend's reprieve. With no appointment to meet Tranter, he decided there would be no tavern visit. Neither bar was a wise option. His former haunt was now out of the question, what with Jerome, that new extortionist there, and the other, new bar, though safe, was not a place he wished to be seen regularly.

Given those obstacles, he returned directly to the office to drop off his trial materials and then head home. The remaining likelihood of office encounters now dwindling, as he entered the building this time, upon reaching his floor he did so without employing the circuitous route, his prior tactic for reducing the chance of meeting colleagues.

Buoyed by the thought that the whole mess would soon be over, when he came upon Larkin's office, he offered a friendly greeting and initiated the offer for his colleague to come down for a recap of the trial since their last meeting. Best to keep up the pretense, he decided.

Larkin accepted the offer immediately, though by now, based on the cumulative effect of Gray's repeated disparagement of the Secretary's evidence and the comparative exultation he expressed over the witnesses presented by the Respondent's attorneys, the outcome of his colleague's eventual decision was obvious. He knew the Secretary would be losing. Mistakenly, he thought that only Gray and he knew how this litigation would end, clueless that the Respondent's attorneys knew the upcoming result with far more certainty.

"Welcome," Gray began, presenting more friendliness to his colleague than usual, noting that "it's hard to believe but today marked the end of the sixth week for this marathon of a trial. We're approaching the end," he announced. "The Respondent's third, and final, expert began his substantive testimony today," he continued. "He's a well-credentialed statistical expert, and he poked a lot of holes in the conclusions presented by the Secretary's numbers expert."

Again, thought Larkin, nothing has changed. His 'friend,' though now he hesitated in using that term, with his regard for the senior judge having dropped week-by-week during this trial. This 'long-term judge,' he substituted in his head, he hadn't been neutral about this case from the start.

Why? It didn't add up. Not at all. And on top of that, there was that very uncomfortable scene outside the office that he witnessed. It was more than suspicious, as Sandy affirmed when he related the encounter he observed. There was no innocent explanation to be offered for it. But he felt powerless about it. There was nothing he could do. Persuading Gray to reconsider his views was ludicrous. He hadn't made any headway on those few occasions when he delicately suggested a different perspective to him. He was rebuffed each time. With those intermittent diplomatic attempts failing, the idea that he could have him reconsider the whole thing was out of the question.

Despite knowing all that, Larkin could not resist a comment. "But there's been no cross-examination yet?" with feigned ignorance. Though he posed it as a question, he knew full well the answer. In truth, it was another challenge to Gray's one-sided presentation. He knew that the response would be curt.

Gray, already soured over any challenges to his take on the evidence, especially now, given that he'd been compromised, and then bribed, did what Larkin fully anticipated, answering with some unmistakable irritation in his tone.

"Of course not. I didn't suggest otherwise," he said sharply. You asked for a recap and I informed that only his direct testimony had started."

He might as well have told Larkin to leave his office right then, so annoyed with the audacity of Larkin's plain challenge to his objectivity.

This was the tersest response yet from him. To Larkin, the degree of irritation did not seem warranted. Yes, he thought, as he took in Gray's comment, while maintaining a poker face in reaction to it, his remark was critical, an unveiled criticism of Gray's appraisal of the statistical expert, but he was simply trying to point out that only half the story had been heard. His comment just stated that fact.

Beneath the tepid outward civility, there was a full-blown argument going between the two.

So what, he thought, unwilling to offer up some peacemaking remark to the long-term judge's irritated reaction to his views. Nothing Larkin could say would cause the guy to have an epiphany, so he might as well be on the record about the Gray's premature assessment of the latest testimony.

The guy had tilted toward the Respondent from the start and from that early, slanted, view, their friendship had taken a progressive and now deep hit during this trial. He also realized that his present low estimation of the elder judge's attitudes during the trial would not be improving as time passed, not in a case of this significance. If Gray had contempt for Larkin's mild remarks, well, the contempt was mutual.

Larkin could feel the chill permeate the office with Gray's response. Maintaining civility was very difficult. He so wanted to blurt out that he believed something was terribly wrong, that he felt the judge had lost his impartiality from the start of the trial, and then to reveal what he witnessed – that strange exchange, just outside the office building.

Instead, he backed away from uttering those words. Though he didn't mean a word of it, as he arose from the couch, implicitly being asked to leave, he still responded, statesmanlike, but not sincerely, saying "I understand." But he avoided calling him 'judge,' and did not include any personal touch, unable to add 'Charles' to the response.

He then finished with a sterile closing remark, "thank you for the update about the testimony. I know you're anxious to return home to your wife."

That last remark, uniformed and innocent though it was, stung Gray. Though he knew there was no malice behind the reference, the mere mention of Millie opened up his attempts to block thoughts of her death and his role in that event. Apart from the police, the rescue providers and the undertaker, no one knew he was now a widower.

Though shaken by it, Gray recognized that Larkin's tactful remark ending their conversation was sheer diplomacy, a way for him to leave their encounter.

Still, looking directly at Larkin, the innocent mention was received with both shame and anger. Renewed shame over his conduct and how it had impacted his wife with deadly results, and anger, arising from being put in a defensive posture, though Larkin had no clue that he had provoked it.

Being in the wrong was not an obstacle to feeling anger towards Larkin. Excusing the enormity of his failures, as a husband and as a judge, he resented Larkin's superior attitude. His defenses kicked in, equating his failings as no different than others. He thought, had Richard been oh so perfect all his life? He'd never been subject to temptation? He'd always taken the right path? A life free of mistakes?

"Have a good evening yourself," he responded, similarly omitting the respectful title to his colleague, as their sour meeting ended.

With Larkin out of the way, Gray's only thought was to get away from the office, and return to his home, the weekend now temporarily spoiled by Larkin's commentary. Though no longer a place of peace, at least home was better than the office where he had to absorb judgmental remarks from Larkin.

Once home, he got back to business, calling Tranter to arrange the next payment meeting. It was agreed that they would meet at the Spirit Room on Monday, at the newly established time. The next payment, at least that was something positive to focus on, instead of that disagreeable exchange with Larkin.

He then went about his new, single person, routine. Though he could have skipped dinner, relying only upon his wine, he made himself eat, microwaving a meal. With the imminent end to the trial dominating his mind, Gray slept lightly that evening, but now, with the thought that the ordeal would soon be over, a nap to compensate for the insufficient sleep would be available Saturday and Sunday. His retirement not far off, real and daily rest would be available once he relocated to Florida. He could stand strong until then. He had to, he thought.

In his lonely house, he tried to fill up the time by contemplating the outline of the upcoming decision. His earlier formulation held; his finding would rest upon the basis that the Secretary failed to meet his burden of proof.

The weekend time moved slowly, as he tried to rely upon distractions; reviewing more Florida brochures, and deciding what to do with all the home's furnishings. Those belongings, he thought, they would all need to be disposed of, sold for whatever they could bring, or simply donated if necessary. He certainly wasn't about to transport memories of this home down to Florida. No way. Even photos, Millie's clothing and jewelry, none of that could come down there. There could be no 'fresh start,' as he continually described it, if any of those things came with him.

When Monday arrived, marking the start of the seventh week, the weekend devoid of any real respite, at least it marked the last phase of the trial. With cross-examination to start the day, Gray reflected that it was no surprise that the Respondent's statistics expert had taken issue with every claim that the Secretary's numbers expert made.

The expert had an answer for everything, or at least he presented one. That the number of AWCs dropped dramatically once the word got out that the government discovered them, statistically, the expert contended, using indecipherable mathematical models, that the numbers actually had not changed dramatically at all.

That expert's many charts and complicated explanations left Gray totally befuddled. He had no clue about what the expert was claiming and the defense traded on that approach: create a complicated picture and thereby instill doubt in the judge's mind about what the truth was.

In the end, they calculated that the judge would not know up from down, throw his hands up over the confusing and conflicting testimony and, by that, necessarily find for the mine operator.

But who could know for sure that a judge would reach that conclusion? Capturing his honor, as they had successfully accomplished, was the sure way to go, removing all doubt about the outcome.

Nevertheless, that the Respondent had the judge in its pocket did not alter their trial strategy – create a sustainable record, as if the judge had not been bought. So, every witness, expert and lay, was presented as if the outcome was not a certainty.

This was obvious to Gray, and annoying too, but he realized that for his decision to withstand a reversal upon the government's inevitable appeal of it, the record had to be solid in order to support his findings. They were doing exactly that but it still rankled Gray, now a judge in title only.

With no background and little facility for figuring out which claim had more substance, had it been a normal trial, one in which the outcome was not preordained, he would've resolved the conflicting views by making credibility determinations, completely apart from their confusing and conflicting charts and numbers. That approach, it usually served him well, that business of making a personal assessment of a witness' testimony. It was like a sixth sense, developed over his many years of observing witnesses.

But now, none of that mattered. Ironically, if he concluded that the experts differing conclusions were a tossup, he would likely have determined that the Secretary failed to meet the preponderance of the evidence test. Such a result would have meant the Respondent could've won without their scheme to entrap him. It was impossible to imagine how he actually would have ruled had he remained a neutral decisionmaker.

Just look like you're listening closely and comprehending the words being uttered, he told himself.

Brief glances to those unscrupulous rats revealed, he believed, that they knew he was acting, as they were too, the three of them, judge and both those attorneys, playing along, with only the Secretary's team remaining clueless.

Sanford tried his best but statistics were not his forte either. As with the other experts the Respondent presented, he could only display doubt about Robeson's conclusions. His attempts to do more did not succeed and one backfired when he asked the expert how his conclusions could be so different from the Secretary's numbers expert.

Robeson enjoyed the misstep, innocently explaining that he couldn't explain the divergent conclusions; he was testifying only about his own studies.

Milo and Winston relished the response. Feeling triumphant, they declined the opportunity for redirect examination, and by that, closed the door on Sanford having a chance to conduct additional cross the next day.

Wasting no time to exit once the day came to a close, Gray proceeded directly to the Spirit Room. Being early, he was the first to arrive. It was such a relief that no one in the place paid attention to him, still an unknown customer, so unlike his recognizable face at his previous haunt.

He ordered a drink but determined it was just too much to provide one for Tranter, though he knew the man's beverage choice. Absolving himself from his lack of courtesy, by being mindful of who that guy was – the source for his utter undoing and the shameful end to his previously unblemished career, there would be no indirect reward for him. Let him pay for his own damn drink, he thought.

When Tranter arrived, if he recognized the implicit slight, as Gray sat there alone with his drink, he did not express it. Taking his position in the booth, he uttered only a single word, "evening," as he took his seat.

Noticing the new patron in the booth, a waiter came over promptly and took his drink order. Without delay, but checking first for prying eyes and finding no one paying attention to them, Tranter then passed the latest envelope across the table. Gray took possession of it immediately, secreting it as before, next to his thigh on the inner side of the booth.

Though it was difficult to utter the words, he spoke the required acknowledgement, expressing a muted 'thank you.'

Small talk had not become a custom between them. They were, after all, adversaries, though ones who had reached a required mutual accommodation. Tranter was able to fill the void on this occasion, while simultaneously displaying that he remained well-informed about the status of the trial.

"Looks like the hearing will wrap-up this week," he remarked.

Gray knew that, as the guy had not ever been in the courtroom for this case, Malthan and Krakovich had kept him up to speed.

He decided to take on the tone of an educator before this likely un-degreed low life before him.

"Trials are unpredictable. I don't engage in such speculation," as he concluded with the truism, "It's over when it's over."

Tranter was unimpressed with the pseudo-lecture, but chose not to make a rejoinder. He was just as anxious to be done with this guy.

"Well, whenever," he responded, dismissive of the correction and knowing that the trial was a farce now anyway. "We will keep meeting regularly after it does conclude, while you're deciding the outcome of the case."

That last comment, 'deciding the outcome,' was an intentional barb. The highfalutin administrative judge deserved it, he thought.

At that, both were ready to go their separate ways. They finished their drinks without delay and soon Gray was on the road home and once there, following his new routine, he stored the latest payment, secreting it in his basement safe.

With the amount growing each week, neurotically, he checked twice to be sure the safe was locked. Compulsively, he then added even more material from the basement to further hide its presence. The area now looked as he intended, a mess under the stairs in need of cleaning up, not a hiding place.

Satisfied, he retreated to the main floor of the house to prepare some dinner. Following that, he ended the evening with his routine glass of the red grape. Given his recent near fall on the stairs to the second floor, he resisted the urge for a refill drink. Too close to the goal line to screw up now, he thought. Even though his intake had been limited, that frightening event compelled him to ascend slowly, holding the railing firmly as he made his way up to bed. The trial's end so near, on this night he slept well, a rare occurrence over the past weeks.

With last night's thoughts of the trial's imminent end still at the forefront of his mind, he felt exuberant as he began his commute that Tuesday morning. Considering all that had happened and the ever-present danger that the whole thing could be exposed, he still had some spring in his steps as he made his way to court that day.

And, though he was correct that, with the Respondent's numbers expert having finished up his testimony, the defense would rest, it was still up to the Secretary to announce if there would be any more witnesses offered in rebuttal testimony. He so hoped that Sanford would advise that the government too had concluded its case. He would have to patiently wait to see if the nettlesome prick would meet his private wish.

Keep it steady, Gray silently told himself. You're almost there. Keep it steady, he repeated, as he maintained a neutral expression upon hearing the news.

That meant the proceeding would go on at least one more day. He knew he had no choice in the matter. The Secretary's right to call one, or for that matter, several rebuttal witnesses, was absolute. No explanation was required. Worse, it could go on for additional rounds if the Respondent then decided to call rebuttal witnesses of its own. That thought was particularly irritating, knowing Malthan and Krakovich, scoundrels both, would do that, play it to the hilt, no matter that it was obviously completely unnecessary and obnoxious too, since the outcome was foregone.

Please God, he thought, as if he had a right to implore Him of such requests, make the trial end this week.

When the Respondent announced, shortly after the lunch break, that it had concluded its defense, Gray felt immense relief. The trial had gone on for a more than six weeks and he was enervated from the long grind. Without delay, he inquired of the Secretary whether there would be any rebuttal testimony.

Sanford responded, "May we have a brief recess, your honor?"

Gray wanted to push for an immediate answer, but it was important to maintain the appearance of neutrality and, beyond that, he did not want to tip the government that his decision had already been reached, the outcome having been determined long ago, following Tranter's informing that he had been trapped.

"Of course," he responded amiably, an insincere presentation of his attitude, especially knowing that no amount of rebuttable testimony would ever alter the outcome. "We will take a recess," he announced. "The Secretary will advise the Court when it has made its determination."

It was his hope, fervently, that the answer would be to decline rebuttal testimony because, if he did not, that could mean as much as another week of testimony. He had that scenario correctly figured out. Though the Respondent had an understandably high degree of confidence about how Gray would rule, covering all their bases, they would present a robust counter argument to whatever the Secretary might offer in rebuttal.

They knew one could never be one hundred percent sure that one who had been bribed would follow through. Things like a conscience, fear of getting caught, and jail time could erupt within one's superego and result in an adverse decision for the Respondent. If that happened, after adamantly denying that any such leverage had been applied to the jurist, they still needed to be armed with a strong record on appeal if the decision was adverse.

After nearly a half-hour, the Secretary conferred with opposing counsel of its decision and then asked the court reporter to contact the judge in his chambers that they were ready to resume. When Gray took the bench, he did not know what the Secretary's determination would be.

"Thank you, your honor," Sanford announced. "The Secretary has made its determination on the issue of rebuttal testimony and we informed opposing counsel of the decision. We will be offering some rebuttal testimony."

Gray maintained a blank expression in reaction to the announcement. To his relief, the Secretary's rebuttal testimony was limited, calling just one witness back to the stand, one of the two particle experts, Dr. Palmer. He addressed the testimony of the Respondent's experts' claims that there were a number of reasons to explain those white centers that had nothing to do with intentional behavior.

Now that Gray knew the score, he listened closely to the expert's additional dismantling of the claims that these white centers just appeared innocently for a variety of reasons. Maybe a few could be attributed to such causes, he thought, but seventy-five such events in a short period of time? Hardly! He privately scoffed at the suggestion.

And then, he recalled that all the white centers just stopped occurring, like magic. Right! Like that sort of thing could just happen. Why, it was clear evidence of guilt by those SOBs. If the AWCs really did occur because of all the innocent reasons suggested by the experts, the logic was inescapable that they would've continued to appear, just as before. No way they would have just stopped cold, as they did. Did they think he was an idiot, not able to put two and two together!

With those thoughts, while necessarily presenting an outwardly professional, and totally unreadable, demeanor, but now wisened up by the fact that they had to set him up to win the litigation, he derided the fabrications rolled out to explain their disappearance. It was disgusting. The defense was contending that suddenly, and at a time that just happened to occur when the mines became aware that MSHA was onto their chicanery, like a water spigot, those white centers stopped, just like that.

Palmer dismissed the idea that it was all a coincidence, that the mine just started being extra careful when handling the sampling units along with the contention that the filter manufacturing differences had ceased.

It made Gray all the more uncomfortable to hear Palmer's debunking of the defenses. There was no greater proof needed that it was all a massive, industry-wide, fraud that had been perpetuated by nearly all of the coal mines, a fraud that continued until MSHA realized what was going on and the information was leaked to them.

With all that had happened to him, now he just couldn't imagine how he would have received the rebuttal testimony. Maybe it would have persuaded him or least given him pause about the mine's claims that all those white centers were the result of non-intentional acts. They just happened to stop was the essence of their explanation.

The abrupt cessation revealed, unmistakably, the hollowness of their excuses. Further, if one really had a valid defense, he knew, there wouldn't have been any need to trap him in bed with that tramp. Such extreme measures only occur when, as the expression goes, one doesn't have a leg to stand on.

Malthan and Krakovich realized that, if they had not executed their failsafe plan against Gray, Palmer's testimony on direct and later upon rebuttal could have been deadly to their claims. Lawyers recite that if you have the law on your side, pound the law. If you have the facts on your side, pound the facts. But, if you have neither, you pound the table.

Having neither of the first two strategies available and the table pounding being insufficient, they had to go to the unspoken next option, entrap the judge. Unable to restrain the urges from his loins, Gray made it easy. Done! Victory, not how it was brought about, that was the most important thing.

Palmer's testimony, shriveling the excuses claimed by the mine's experts, could not go unanswered. Even though Gray's decision was foregone, the Respondent had no choice but to add their own rebuttal testimony to the record.

It wasn't just for appearances either. With the inevitable appeals, first to the Commissioners and then to the Court of Appeals, there had to be a record to point to where their experts repeated their own innocent explanations for the abnormal white centers.

Then, with their experts creating doubt, if not complete confusion as to the reasons for those white centers, those appellate bodies, facing complicated and ostensibly conflicting scientific evidence, and with them being utterly in the dark about the machinations carried out by mine's attorneys, they would have no choice but to throw their hands up. In such matters, they would fall back upon the substantial evidence rule to uphold the judge's decision. Added to that would be the judge's credibility determinations to end the matter. Courts were remiss to second guess a trial judge's findings of credibility. The political proclivities of some Commissioners would also play an unspoken role in their review of his decision.

Beyond those insurmountable factors, neither the Commission nor the Appeals Court, would be disposed to send the matter back for further proceedings. There was too much pressure, it was too big a case to keep the litigation going. Both appellate bodies were fully aware that there would be a prolonged din from the coal mining industry at large, if they didn't go along with the judge's decision.

The Respondent would cry that the government would only accept a guilty verdict. That they were in fact guilty did not matter.

When Palmer's rebuttal testimony was finished, the Respondent's attorneys perhaps concluding that enough was enough, informed Gray that they would not be cross-examining the expert, an announcement made with a dismissive tone, implying that there was no need to conduct it.

No need indeed! thought Gray, as he looked out impassively at the two lowlifes.

The Secretary then announced that there would be no additional rebuttal testimony.

Thank God, thought Gray.

Of necessity, Malthan immediately announced that the defense would be recalling Dr. Kim, its leadoff and star witness.

Upon hearing that it was not over, and that Kim would be making an encore appearance, Gray made eye contact with those two dishonorable attorneys.

They looked right back at him, unintimidated by his stare. But it was clear they knew that, had the game not been rigged, they could've been fucked. Both lawyers, expressionless, but steely, were unfazed by Gray's grim look; neither had any shame over the tactics they had employed.

Winning a lawsuit can involve more than the facts and the law. Sure, they set the judge up, but no one made him take the bait. They had reason to be doubly confident. Even if Gray had considered to owning up to his adultery, that option disappeared when he took the bribe. He had no exit.

Kim's rebuttal testimony did not take long and the Secretary's cross-examination followed suit. It took the rest of the day, but with both sides having rested, Wednesday would mark the end of the trial phase. The doctor's testimony was all repetitive, but that was largely true of Palmer's rebuttal testimony too. Neither expert offered new grounds, nor new theories, but both were allowed to present regurgitations of their previous views. It was just the way litigation worked.

Sanford took a page from the Respondent's playbook, dismissively announcing when Kim's direct testimony had concluded, that there was no need for cross-examination. But he added a comment to make the record clear. "Your honor," he began, "the Secretary has listened carefully to the Respondent's rebuttal witness." Declining to identify the witness with any reverence, he did not utter either his name, nor his title, leaving it with the unadorned description of "rebuttal witness." Continuing, Sanford stated, "The Secretary believes that the witness added no new information, but instead repeated the contentions he made when he first testified. We see no reason to prolong the proceeding and burden his honor with additional cross-examination, those matters having been covered."

Winston and Milo didn't like the commentary, though it was substantively no different than their own approach to diminish Palmer. It was annoying because that prick Sanford said it directly, using no subtlety, as they had. Though it didn't matter, because the win was assured, they were still peeved over it.

Gray could've remarked that Sanford's disparaging commentary about the lack of value of Kim's rebuttal testimony was unnecessary. Had the outcome not been rigged, a result that only he and those two miscreants posing as attorneys for the Respondent knew would be coming, he probably would've said something about it, making a mild rebuke along the lines that the Secretary could have simply announced that he had no questions for the witness. But given all that had been done to him, Gray decided to say nothing.

Though apparent, for the record, Gray formally asked each side if they had rested. Both confirmed their evidence had been concluded. Internally, Gray sighed, the hard part was finally over. Tomorrow would be a breeze. He would make the formal announcement that the testimony phase for the matter had concluded. There would still be closing arguments, but that would all be anti-climactic. He would then set the dates for submission of the post-hearing briefs.

And, when those steps were completed, he knew that, with all that had been done to him, he could not bring himself to include his customary closing remarks, offered in cases big and small, that he appreciated the professionalism presented by both sides. No way. Not this time.

The end of the day could not come quickly enough. Fearful that he not fuck-up in any way, especially not tonight, Gray went straight home. No stops were made, not even at the grocery store, though he was nearly out of his supply of microwave dinners. He felt no elation during the trip home; remorse was his primary emotion.

THE CASE OF THE ABNORMAL WHITE CENTER

His attempt to focus on the sunny and warm new start to his life in Florida, once he issued the decision, failed. The guilt over his actions took command and thoughts of suicide reemerged. He could not push such drastic thoughts away. He deserved it, he thought, death as payment for all that he had done.

But, at least for now, the idea of actually carrying that out, taking his own life, if he even had the courage for that, was not an option. Now, he had to close the hearing and write the shameful decision. Thinking of the task ahead, his addled mind then shifted away from suicide to a brighter ending. Perhaps, given time, his shame and Millie's death would ebb from his conscience and Florida would be his salvation. He hoped the expression that time heals all wounds, even those self-inflicted, was true.

A restless night offered little sleep for him, but it didn't matter. Anticipating that the day in court would be over by lunch, he could deal with his exhaustion. He had made it through the marathon trial; an event made much worse by his own hand.

On that final day of the trial, after the mandatory, but sterile, 'good morning' greeting, with no delay he moved to the next stage of the proceeding. Repeating yesterday's acknowledgement from the parties that the evidentiary phase was over, Gray immediately addressed the final step.

"Are the parties prepared for their closing arguments?" he inquired, thinking that they should be, with the end of the hearing predictable even a week ago. Both sides announced that they were ready.

With a solemnity continuing his pretense of objectivity, he announced, "Counsel for the Secretary, proceed with your closing."

Sanford began, "Thank you, your honor. And especially thank you for the way you conducted this matter, with great attention and objectivity," his praise expressed with uninformed naïveté.

If only the poor bastard knew, thought Gray.

"Your honor, this case could not be clearer. The Secretary believes that it more than met the preponderance of the evidence standard."

Though he appeared to be attentive to the Secretary's closing, in truth, in his head Gray was creating the closing words he would use for his decision, with those thoughts overshadowing the government's summation.

Only half-listening now, Gray had paid enough attention during all those weeks to appreciate the essence of the Secretary's case. Were it not for the mess he had created, the evidence the government had mustered would've been worthy of serious consideration.

Millie and Larkin observed that early on.

Though he had routinely expressed skepticism in front of Larkin when summarizing the testimony before him as the trial proceeded, he could not be so dismissive of it. And Larkin was not the only one to see what was plain about the case. While it was painful to think of the recent death of Millie, she too, despite not being a lawyer, wasn't fooled by any of it. There was no need to possess a law degree. Her nose and a measure of common sense provided the correct answer.

As Sanford continued, Gray was in a world of his own, reviewing the damning evidence independent of the Secretary's oration. All those white centers, he thought, a number so large just that fact alone almost made the case. And then, when it was clear that, once the word got out that MSHA was onto the scheme, those AWC's virtually vanished.

The defense was utterly ridiculous. Come on! Give me a break! he thought.

Still, it was true that the battle of the experts would've been a challenge for him to figure out which position was more credible. Ironically, the defense's 'spaghetti on the wall' approach, blaming those AWCs on multiple causes, actually served to diminish their defense.

Oh sure, he thought derisively, the mail handling, that devices were dropped, that filter-to-foil distance business, and that the number of AWCs was the same in every mine; those falsehoods were all to blame for the white centers.

If one solid theory had been advanced, that would have made for a more convincing defense than the variety of reasons that were asserted. The reason for presenting those multiple claims was simple: there wasn't a single genuine one among them. None existed.

Besides, the whole set up of him was an admission that they knew the defense was phony. It would have been tough for him to reach the right conclusion, but that process was overridden by fucking that whore and then making matters exponentially worse by taking the bribe money.

Game over by his disastrous choices.

It was only when, prompted by Sanford' words, "In closing, your honor," that Gray's attention returned to the Secretary's oration, "for all these reasons, the Secretary believes that it has more than met its burden of proof in this matter. Thank you."

Dutifully, Gray, now tuned back in to the closing remarks, responded, "Thank you, Counsel. And now, I will hear from the Respondent." As he uttered the words, he felt distaste in his mouth.

Milo stood, presenting his most reverent demeanor, as he looked directly, unflinchingly, at the judge's eyes, their secret known to only a few.

"Thank you, your Honor," he began, "the defense does share, in one respect, the remarks made by the Secretary. We appreciate your attentiveness throughout this very long proceeding, and the probing questions you asked of both sides."

Gray was annoyed, listening to this flimflam man with his phony praise.

Milo knew, Gray realized, that he could do it. It was part of the price he had to pay for his foolish and greedy acts.

He loved to lay it on that way, "But aside from our mutual respect for your judicial demeanor and sagacity, we could not disagree more with the Secretary's story. Far from the *preponderance* of the evidence, the Secretary's case is more accurately described as the *preposterousness* of the evidence," he asserted.

Milo was self-satisfied with his opening expression, employing what he believed to be a very clever phrase.

Just like the guy, thought Gray, careful to keep his poker face intact. His panache was not nearly as impressive as Krakovich believed it to be.

"The facts, the *true* facts," Milo said with an authoritative tone, are that the AWCs as the Secretary incorrectly describes them, are anything but abnormal. They appear with the same frequency in this mine as they do in every coal mine, as our statistical expert amply demonstrated."

And beyond that, beyond that," he repeated for emphasis, "we demonstrated all the ways these centers can occur without any intent to manipulate the results. Why, your honor, the event which began this whole event, I want to remind the Court, occurred when the young lab tech dropped a cassette on the floor. It's quite possible, he proclaimed, that the very first AWC was created by the government itself, an innocent mistake by that Ms. Nelson. But, it was hardly the way to properly handle dust samples."

Gray could not help but think, as his mind drifted away from the attorney's blather, that by the Respondent's actions entrapping him, they understood quite well that the mine had done exactly what was alleged – they tampered with the cassettes. And all to the harm of the miners who were sucking in the poisonous coal dust day after day.

Milo's presentation was nothing more than the frequently employed 'alternative facts' bullshit which had become so de rigueur of late.

"And we showed beyond a shadow of doubt," Milo continued, "the many ways these claimed white centers can develop, apart from any sinister actions. I won't belabor all of those harmless sources, as I know the Court listened carefully to both of our science experts' detailed testimony. The manufacturing differences in the filter-to-foil distances and the floppiness of the filters, those scientific explanations were themselves sufficient to knock down the Secretary's claims, but things as innocuous as dropping a cassette, stepping on the air hoses in the rough and tumble working environment present in all coal mines, and the process of mailing them to MSHA also demonstrated entirely innocent explanations for the few so-called white centers to occur."

It went on far too long, but Gray realized that the record had to be made the same way as if he had not been bought.

When it finally came to an end, Gray spoke with his practiced gravitas, thanking the attorneys for the evidence they presented and their 'useful' closings. He had to say those last remarks, though they applied only to the Secretary's side.

He looked at Sanford and his co-counsel as they listened, appreciative of the compliment. Their expressions displayed a confident attitude that the government would prevail. Poor, naïve fools, he thought, unaware that the outcome had been determined weeks earlier.

The post-hearing submission schedule was then set.

Finally, it was over, as Gray made the formal announcement that the hearing was now closed.

Making an undelayed exit, with relief, he walked back to his office, so glad that he would not have to be in that courtroom again, the one to which he brought dishonor. Upon arriving, there would the required, but thankfully last, review with Larkin about the trial's conclusion, but after that, those annoying updates would end.

As he entered the building, he decided to take the initiative and invite his colleague for the recap. That way he could control the start and end of the exchange.

Larkin welcomed the invitation, but it did not take long before he was given a reaffirmation that Gray would almost certainly be finding for the mine operator. Every one of their prior discussions pointed that way and this was no exception.

"It's finally over," Gray began, "six and half weeks of testimony. Next week I'll be starting to write my decision."

With that remark, Larkin thought, Charles Gray was conveying that his mind was already made up. Had it been otherwise, he would have expected something along the lines of the need to weigh the conflicting evidence, but there was no suggestion of that.

Larkin had largely kept quiet through their several meetings over the course of the trial but, for the few times he did opine, none were received well by Gray. Quite the opposite. His gut told him that something was very much amiss. And, it wasn't completely instinct at work; there was that very peculiar meeting with that stranger and the exchange he made to Gray. He witnessed it. That surreptitious scene, it stuck with him.

Bypassing his former reticence, his respect for Gray now seriously diminished, he spoke up.

"Sounds like you've made up your mind," omitting the more personal touch of calling him judge or Charles.

Gray was already testy; the end of the hearing had not softened his attitude. He was offended by Larkin's brazen comment, unmistakably critical of him. Who did he think he was, this new judge, so green, with minimal experience presiding in cases, having the temerity to predict the outcome of his decision.

Making him angrier over the remark was that the little prick was correct.

Defensively, he replied, with plain irritation in his voice, "I don't recall saying that I have decided the case. I said I'll be writing my decision," correcting him.

Of course, he knew better. It was all a lie, but Larkin had no way, beyond surmise, of knowing what his decision would be. More importantly, he was completely ignorant of the developments which mandated the outcome. Not that he would be sympathetic to the reasons. No one would, but this guy, Gray concluded, he'd scream bloody murder for sure, if he ever learned about what happened.

Larkin was unbowed. The idea of keeping the friendship intact took a back seat to the dismay he felt over Gray's clear loss of neutrality, a display he showed even when the Secretary was presenting its case in chief.

He spoke up, "As you say, technically, you did say you would now be writing the decision but throughout our many conversations during the trial, from the very start you seemed to lean against the Secretary's evidence. Evidence, I should add, by your own recounting, that seemed quite formidable. So, while it's true you only said 'writing the decision,' I'd bet my house that your decision will be to dismiss the case."

The arrogance! thought Gray, no matter that the prick nailed it. He didn't have to listen to this sermon from Mr. Sanctimonious. He decided there was no need to take the insult.

"I think we're done here," he said with finality. All but pointing to his door, he added, "Good evening."

But it wasn't just Gray who was miffed. Trusting his own instincts, Larkin was equally angry. He would not back down, unwilling to end the confrontation with some conciliatory remark.

"Yes, I agree we're done," he responded as he rose from the couch and left the office without another word. That friendship, he thought, it's over, but it was hard to think of it as a loss.

Gray was unsettled that the conversation turned into a conflict. The relief from the trial's conclusion was short-lived, with Larkin's belligerent remark. What did he know? Rather arrogant for him to have such an attitude. His pompous view came about simply from Gray's good grace of updating him about the evidence.

Looking back, he now thought that he never should have been so courteous as to the discuss the trial's progress from the get-go. Larkin was never entitled to updates. That new judge's remarks, they were pure arrogance. He was never in the courtroom for the evidence, not for a single day, not for an hour.

No good deed goes unpunished, he thought, that's the thanks I get for briefing him so regularly, something he never had to do at all. Fuming, he considered that, with their angry exchange, at least one good thing came out of it; the two of them would not be having further discussions about the case, nor about anything else for that matter.

Though he stewed over their clash for a time, his attention then shifted abruptly when he realized that it was time to meet Tranter. He grabbed his briefcase, hurrying to his meeting. No guilt from his clash with Larkin tagged along, as his focus shifted to the next cash installment he would soon be receiving.

Upon exiting his building, a consequence of the conflict with Larkin, he could not help but check to see if anyone, especially that superior, Mr. Oh-so-mighty, judge, was tracking him, first looking behind, then up and down the street. Confident that he was alone, he moved briskly to his destination.

Still perturbed by the encounter with Larkin, he tried to put it aside upon joining Tranter at his booth. Best not to convey any troubles to the guy, he thought.

"Good evening," he said impassively.

"And to you," Tranter replied, employing a similar economy of words, not picking up on Gray's recent irritation. Small talk had never been a part of their meetings, but Tranter did reveal that he had been updated about the hearing.

"So, it's come to a conclusion," he remarked.

Gray, irritated anew, this time by Tranter's remark informing him that he knew the status of the matter, answered only, "Yes, the testimony ended today."

Awkward silence followed, made worse by their mutual distaste for one another. It prompted Tranter to present the latest payment, sliding it across the table. Gray quickly removed it from display, placing it next to his thigh, a nod only acknowledging the exchange.

The purpose of the meeting completed, Gray finished his drink without delay, but he had not lost sight of the most important thing. It wasn't the decision; that he could write in his sleep. It was to solidify the arrangements for the payment installments. Though never mentioned, no decision would be issued until he had received all of the promised money. Tranter must have understood this would be the case, he thought. With today's payment, the half-way mark had been reached; $150,000 in hand, less his loss to that blackmailer Jerome. Five more meetings at $30,000 each time and it would be complete.

Gray used the moment to directly raise the subject. "While I am writing my decision, I presume we'll continue meeting at our usual time," he asserted, the purpose clear.

"Of course," Tranter confirmed. He had done the simple calculation as well. "We'll make it Mondays and Wednesdays. By that schedule, we'll have settled up within the next three weeks."

"Agreed," Gray responded, without adding more. He then arose, parting with, "See you Monday, then," as a way to remind the guy of the next meeting day.

On his homeward bound commute Larkin remained agitated over the meeting with Gray. He was certain that when the decision was issued, the Secretary's case would be dismissed.   Of that there was no doubt.

But why? Why did Gray seem so opposed to the Secretary's case, an opposition that he demonstrated from the start and about which his animosity only grew as the trial progressed.

And then there was that meeting he observed, Gray with that stranger and that exchange; that was no happenstance, no way.

When he arrived home, he told Sandy about the contentious exchange. She was on board with his pessimistic take about the matter from the start. There was no need to convince her that something dark was at work. Equally offended, she suggested that Richard go to the authorities, though she retreated from the idea after he reminded her that there was too little to make such a claim.

Gray's take on the evidence during their discussions as the trial proceeded was certainly not enough. Besides, they were private expressions. And the decision had not even been issued, though he had no doubt about the outcome. Nor did that peculiar meeting he witnessed between Gray and that stranger change the equation. Yes, he saw something pass from the stranger to Gray, but that was all. For that matter, he couldn't even identify the stranger. Never laid eyes on the guy before. Though he had his suspicions he could only speculate about the envelope's contents.

Unhappily, the two agreed there was nothing they could do.

CHAPTER 19

With the trial completed, Gray was now in a whole different existence. Two things were on his agenda. Write the damn decision, a process he had been working on sporadically after the fourth week of the trial and then, once it was issued, get the hell out of Washington for good.

Things had progressed satisfactorily with his Florida plan. His house was now on the market and, as sorry a place as it was, it would sell quickly, based on its location alone. With no mortgage, he would be flush with money between the sale of the home and the 'payments,' those made and those yet to come.

Life in Florida would be comfortable. There would be no need for a mortgage in his new digs and, free of such a debt, his retirement income would be unencumbered. His guilt buried for the moment, he thought how he would be a rich man down there. In addition to the money from selling his house, and the cash from Tranter, there would be his monthly retirement, a sizeable sum at eighty percent of his salary. Soon, he thought, it would become a reality. From the continuous flow of housing brochures over the past several weeks, he had narrowed the areas and communities to visit.

As for that decision, it could be done in as little as two weeks' time, but issuing it so soon would create an appearance issue, suggesting he had not given it sufficient thought. Three or four weeks would look better. He would take some leave during those weeks, and, with a weekend built into it, spend four or five days winnowing down his new home location. Nobody would know he was even out of town while on leave and he was not about to disclose his activities to anyone.

THE CASE OF THE ABNORMAL WHITE CENTER

The first two weeks following the close of the hearing went smoothly. Routinely, he would show up early at the office, the better to avoid interactions with others. Once there, he would shut his door, a clear message that he did not want to be disturbed. Everyone at the office knew he was working on the momentous decision, so interruptions were only when necessary. Even Chief Judge Blandford, aware of the significance of the decision Gray was drafting, avoided visits.

To his relief, Gray's pangs of conscience were diminishing, a product of focusing on writing his decision and his anticipated joy once his new life started in the Sunshine State. He became mindful of his health, taking a good walk during lunchtime and then returning to his office until it was time to end the day. Interactions with fellow employees, unavoidable as they were during the course of the day, were limited to polite nods or hellos, but he would not break his stride when coming upon those at the office, an unmistakable message that he did not want conversation. Everyone picked up on it, respectful of the important decision he was writing.

Larkin continued to stew about the inevitable decision. Upon passing Gray in the hallway on occasion, and then returning to his office, he would dwell upon the horrendous decision he knew would be coming.

In contrast, Gray did not suffer or give thought to their conflict upon seeing Larkin, as he resolutely kept his attention on writing a winning, non-reversible, opinion and the new life he would soon be enjoying.

On those days when it was time to meet Tranter, Gray remained careful to scan the street upon exiting his office, neurotically making sure no one was following him. It would be just like that holier-than-thou Larkin to play detective, he thought.

The meetings with Tranter were brief and the payments were made each time. It was almost too much to believe, with the four latest payments, totaling $120,000, he was virtually paid off; one more installment was all that was due. He announced at the meeting for the fourth payment that he would be 'unavailable' the following week.

Anticipating that the decision was not very far off, Tranter took the news without any questions. He was looking forward to the end of this thing as much as Gray. That Ruby thing, it still haunted him. It would have been one thing to have this whole arrangement unravel if it had just been about money. But with the action necessary to deal with that rambunctious woman; what was planned as a pair of simple female traps, her attempt at extortion required action of an entirely drastic order.

Although everything was running smoothly, there were those occasional awkward, even tense, moments when Gray would pass by Larkin in the office hallway. With their offices in close proximity, those interactions were unavoidable. Those unplanned encounters were tension-filled. There would be the briefest of acknowledgements, usually a nod though, due to awkwardness, a good morning or good afternoon would be added as the time of day called for. At times, they would pass one another with no recognition at all, as if they were invisible to one another.

There was no softening of their attitudes. Larkin remained sure that something had gone foul, though he could not know what it was. Maybe, he speculated, there was something in Gray's background that was being held over him or perhaps something worse, plain and simple bribery. It gnawed at him, but nothing had changed. There was nothing he could do, not with the mere unsubstantiated suspicions he harbored.

Effectively cloistered from the others in his office, Gray continued to convey his 'do not disturb' message by keeping his door closed all day. Apart from Larkin, the staff and other judges, very much aware of the significant case he was handling, presumed that the effort of making the decision was consuming all his time.

In truth, Gray was only spending half of his day on the decision, with his focus on making a reversal, and even a remand, unlikely. His other time was devoted to his upcoming relocation.

A lot had been swirling in the two weeks since the hearing concluded. An offer had been made on his home and he had accepted it without delay. This was no time to quibble or delay, not over the chance that, by waiting, he might realize a sale garnering a few thousand more. That was all he needed, the unpleasant prospect of having to remain in Virginia for God knew how much longer, interfering with his relocation.

As he approached the end of two weeks since the close of the hearing, Gray submitted a leave request, with it covering the entire following week. He would fly to Tampa that Saturday, with a full schedule of potential home sites to visit. Only the Chief Judge and the administrative office knew of the leave, which was immediately approved. Though he did not think it would take a whole week to make his selection, he did not want to be hurried, given the significance of the trip. No one thought anything of his brief absence from the office. A little time off after the long trial seemed natural.

The excitement of the trip, finding and plunking down the money to buy his new digs in Florida, dominated his mind.

The flight was uneventful and he was pleased that he didn't run into anyone he knew at the start of the trip, nor upon his arrival in Tampa. Away from the still-cold Washington weather, he was delighted about the 70-degree temperature that day.

As soon as he got off the plane, he opened his carry-on, stuffing his winter coat in it. With a bounce in his step as he headed to the luggage carousel, those pangs of conscience that had regularly appeared after Millie's death had drifted away, the anticipation of his new home overtaking those moments of guilt. When they did arise, though infrequently on the trip, he rationalized that with his wife's illness, worsening as it did, month-by-month, her passing, despite that awful ending, tumbling down those stairs, was a blessing for her.

Such were the inventions he created to absolve himself.

Energetically, he began each morning early, viewing as many as six properties per day. By mid-week of the trip, he had made his selection, a house well within his means. A bonus, given the upcoming sale of his Virginia home, he would be able to stow away a significant amount of money in banks down there, a comfortable nest egg, more than enough to cover any unexpected expenses. And maybe, he thought, a new car would be in the picture. He could pay cash for it.

The new house and a new car, they would both be part of the fresh start for him. Millie was far from his mind as he returned to D.C. With such a fruitful trip, he had renewed vitality, which he committed towards issuing the damned decision. Even better, as he had the remainder of the week off, he could relax before resuming the task on Monday.

When the new week started, he industriously focused on finishing the decision. No dawdling as the work week began, he got down to the business of resuming its completion without delay. Each day his efforts were uninterrupted except for a brief interlude for lunch and the short nap which followed it. That rest, less than thirty minutes, actually made him more productive for the afternoon.

As five o'clock approached, with him quite satisfied about the progress he made drafting his decision, the day would end with another event. Per their arrangement, he would be meeting Tranter at the Spirit Room. That itself was a significant occasion, as it marked the last payment and therefore his final meeting with that seamy character.

His streak of pleasant events continued as he left the office that evening without meeting any other employees, a result helped by his taking the longer exit route, avoiding the need to pass by Larkin's office.

Arriving at the Spirit, Tranter was there, occupying what had become their usual meeting booth. With a nod, he acknowledged Gray's arrival.

Though unexpressed, the feeling that it would be good to no longer be in the others' presence was shared. Without delay, even before the drinks had been ordered, Tranter, after first reflexively scanning the other patrons in the bar, and then reassured that no one was paying attention to them, passed the envelope across the table.

"Final installment," he said, adding no other words.

Gray almost felt the need to say 'thank you,' but resisted the reflexive response, only nodding in acknowledgement. This time, he was determined to stuff the payoff, envelope and all, into his briefcase. It was difficult, as he was barely able to close the thing.

The two looked at one another, awkwardly aware of the absence of words.

Tranter, feeling the need to fill the vacuum more than Gray, then inquired, "Any idea when the decision will be issued?" Almost apologizing for the question, he added, "Just asking is all. Not pressuring, you understand?"

Gray, picking up on the tone that Tranter was not leaning on him, but only trying to reduce the unpleasantness, decided a civil response was due. "Not too long," he answered.   "It's difficult to say exactly. More important to make it solid than to meet an artificial date."

"Understood," Tranter replied, glad that the void had been filled. With little more to say, both attended to finishing their drinks. That done, Gray arose first, unable to bring himself to express any typical parting remark like 'take care.' "I'll be on my way then," he announced.

Neither gestured for a handshake, as Gray tightly grabbed his briefcase. He presented a final nod to Tranter as he left.

Once outside, he took a deep breath. The fresh air felt good, a nice awakening from the stale atmosphere inside. Though there were no Jerome type problems in the Spirit Room, he didn't want to return to the new location again. In the future, if he had a need for a drink before his return commute, it would have to be at yet another bar. There were plenty of them, almost one on every other block.

Perhaps, he thought, for the short time remaining with his employment at the Commission, he could will himself to go home directly after work. Have his drinks at home. But home was no longer a haven either. Millie's presence was always there. It was almost spooky, the way he could feel her continued spirit throughout the house, no room free from her.

As he prepared to head to the garage, it was then that he spotted her, just outside the bar, not more than twenty feet away. No doubt about it. It was that strumpet, Nicole, or whatever her name really was. She was looking in a different direction, unaware of his presence.

Without thinking, fueled with instant anger, he was compelled to approach her.

Instinctively, she then turned, facing him. She froze; the two were then within arm's length of one another. Shocked to see him, a look of fear came across her face. She was about to turn abruptly and get the hell away, but he grabbed her arm.

"Not so fast, bitch!" he said, surprised that those unplanned words came out. Then he blurted, "How does a cunt like you face yourself each day?"

More afraid now, she tried to wrest free of his hold, but he only held it tighter, with a vise-like grip.

Weighing whether to let out a scream, instead she decided to return his insult.

"And you, oh mighty judge," dripping with contempt as she loudly invoked his title. "A judge who cheats on his wife!" she exclaimed, unaware that was only part of Gray's shame.

The few people on the sidewalk stopped in their routes, transfixed by the loud confrontation they were witnessing.

Gray, realizing the peril he was creating for himself, immediately let go of her arm.

She had identified his occupation twice, fairly shouting 'judge.'

Still, he could not resist a parting shot, the gawkers be damned. "You're still a witch, a horrible person is what you are!"

In his excited state, he dropped his briefcase. It hit the sidewalk with a thud and, overfilled as it was, it immediately sprung open, with several of the C-notes scattering about. Panicky over the development, all his attention was immediately directed to it. He dropped to the ground to gather up the bills.

The crowd, now growing, as others joined, was taking it all in, observing the spectacle. Seeing the Franklins intensified their interest. Some of the patrons in the Spirit Room, hearing of the commotion, went outside to gawk, their number growing.

Tranter, who had become aware that something was going on, was also drawn to see just what it was. Immediately he recognized the two and, without wasting a second, backed away, moving to the other side of the street, while still close enough to see the fracas.

Christ! he thought. This whole thing could unravel! She, she had no business being anywhere near the area. How stupid of her! And as for him, had he lost his mind! He was the bigger ass, with so much more to lose.

Freed, Nicole pivoted, briskly moving away from her assailant, with a final remark.

"We'll see who the horrible person is," she warned, as she started to leave the scene.

Tranter, hearing the threat, noted her direction and immediately began to follow her.

Gray, there by himself, saw that the bystanders remained staring at him. This he did not need. Now he was in a full panic, as he thought, oh my God, someone might recognize me! Instantly, he lowered his head as he scooped up the envelope and shoved the few bills that had emerged back inside it and then into his briefcase. Dramatically aware that he was a virtual fugitive, to reduce the chance of being identified, he kept his head focused on the ground, not turning it in any direction, as he began to escape from his fraught location. Continuing his flight from the observers, he crossed the street immediately, with no thought of where he was heading.

The goal was just to get away.

With no looking back, walking briskly, but avoiding running as that might prompt some to follow him, he continued his escape. Changing direction, as he moved further away from the scene he had created, he had become unaware of his location. Sensing that he was not being pursued, he then slowed his pace, though his heart was still racing.

Finally, some three blocks away, he stopped. No one, thank God, was following him.

Very aware of the mess he'd created, he realized that the cops could have arrived at the scene and then what? They'd want to see his briefcase for sure, a reasonable response to make sure he had no weapon in connection with his skirmish, even though that bitch had disappeared.

How could he explain all that cash? There was no way to do it.

Having escaped a near disaster, he paused in front of the window of a store that had closed. Seeing his reflection, his distraught state was in full view. Great shame at what he had become was reflected before him.

Then, checking anew to make sure he was alone, he brought himself back to survival mode. He resumed walking, employing a forced casualness, this time to the end of the block in order to orient himself to his location. The street signs informed where he was. Now aware of his whereabouts, but still conscious that he not be recognized from the scene he had created, he took a circuitous route, first moving further from his garage location and then, reassured once more that he was safe, he moved briskly to his garage.

Once in that haven, and inside his locked car, he needed some time to calm down before driving home. No more asinine events! he scolded himself.

In the safety of his car, his apprehension still intense, he looked around. Fortunately, there was no one.

It was a moment of relief, but the anxiety remained, his heart still racing from the confrontation and the onlookers to the whole spectacle. He sat there for a time, trying to compose himself and lower his blood pressure.

He knew it was an extremely foolish move on his part, confronting her. It served only to compound the mess he had made. As long as no one recognized him, he told himself that the matter was over. A lesson learned.

But she did make that threat. He remembered her words exactly, that 'we'll see who the horrible person is." That was worrisome. He would just have to hope she would not act on it. There was nothing more he could do to defuse the event. If he ever saw her again, he would have the sense to turn in another direction.

Slowly, he began to decelerate his emotions. Reassured that he was still alone, he made a last look around his parking space. Again, no one had followed him. And, no police. The matter was over, he kept trying to convince himself. It could have gotten much worse, he realized. Christ, an arrest could've been the result, right there on the street.

The papers would have reported it too and with that it would be noted he was the judge in the dust tampering case. It wouldn't take a genius to raise serious questions about the event: the judge hearing this mining-wide fraud case and his arrest with a ton of cash in his brief case. The conclusions would be inescapable. All of this new mess brought on by his own spontaneous and foolish anger.

There would be nothing approaching calm for now, but with some controlled breathing, eventually he became composed enough to drive home.

For his part, Tranter, having seen the mess unfold, continued to follow Marla. Once she was a block away from the scene, and seeing that no one was following her, he called out, "Marla. Wait. It's me, Marty."

Recognizing his name, she stopped and turned towards him.

Tranter spoke immediately. "Marla, I saw that mess. That judge was a real ass," he said, putting the blame squarely on Gray.

"That's the truth. I have a mind to fix his wagon, treating me like that. He hurt my arm too, grabbing me like I was under arrest."

"I agree and I understand your anger, Marla. He acted like a jerk," he added, clearly taking her side.

"I'm not done with him, I tell you," she continued, her anger unabated.

Tranter was sympathetic. "I understand. I do. But you can't do anything Marla. Trying to get even, it's not an option. You and me, we're both way in over our heads. You have to let it go. You must."

At least she listened to his last remark.

"Just let him get away with attacking me? I'm supposed to do nothing?" she said incredulously.

Seeing he was making some progress in persuading her, patiently, Tranter added, "Marla, there is so much power and money behind this litigation, they would think nothing of offing both of us. Believe me. I am not exaggerating. For our continued health we must let it go."

His warning was given so firmly and soberly; she knew it was not a bluff.

"You mean it, don't you Marty," she replied, absorbing the seriousness of his remark.

"I do," he said simply, a grim expression on his face.

Reluctant as she was, unlike Ruby, Marla was not of the hot-head variety. Of course, she knew nothing about her, nor that a second setup had been created, nor that it did not end well for the rambunctious West Virginia girl.

"I hate it, Marty. Some judge, treating me like that. He's the one who disgraced himself!"

"I know, Marla, I know. Listen to me though. Acting on this, would make matters worse. Much worse."

"Okay, okay. I will drop it," she relented.

"Good, I knew you'd have the wisdom to take the smart course. I'll check on you in a couple of days."

They parted. Tranter walked a block in the opposite direction, though it had nothing to do with any destination. He needed a few moments to collect himself. A major incident had been avoided. A fire extinguished before it could spread. Jesus, he said to himself, let this be the last problem for this mess. He would say not a word about the incident to either of those lawyers. He put the lid on Marla, but now he would just have to wait and see if any of those who witnessed the fight between Gray and her recognized the judge. That was out of his control. He would just have to sit tight.

Having pulled himself together, with heightened care, Gray left the parking garage. Once on his way, driving as carefully as he would if he had too many drinks, he focused on the road, avoiding even the distraction of the radio.

Upon making it home without incident, Gray felt continued remorse over his idiocy. But the attention gathering spectacle, which he hoped would have no repercussions, made him realize how close he came to having this whole thing come crashing down.

Still shaken about his rash behavior, he wanted to collapse on the living room couch, but he willed himself to put that last payment safely in the basement safe.

But, as he descended the stairs, he misgauged the second step and started to tumble before grabbing the handrail tightly, averting a complete fall. The envelope flew to the bottom, more of its contents spilling out. There it was, the money he valued more than his wife, on the floor. Panicky over the event, just avoiding a second near-fall event, he then held the railing with both hands.

Hyperventilating, still holding the handrail, and unsure of his steadiness, he tried to bring himself back under control. Lightheaded from the near accident, he didn't even dare to sit on a tread, afraid he could fall again upon arising. A minute passed, as he remained fixed to his location. Slowly the scare, and the panic which accompanied it, began to recede.

Cautiously he arose, checked that he was okay, and once reassured, resumed his trip to the basement, this time awkwardly using a hand-over-hand method along the railing for additional security.

Once safely at the basement bottom, he got on his knees, collected the money that had spilled and stuffed it back into the envelope. Next, he uncovered the paraphernalia covering the home safe. Once the new stash had been deposited, he replaced the items that hid its presence. That done, he sat on the first step, a way to make sure he was steady enough to return upstairs.

Now a near fall had happened twice. He thought of Millie. Perhaps she had brought this about, irrationally thinking it was her attempt to punish him. Well, didn't he deserve it!

Slowly, the crazy ideations lifted. Then, realizing that he couldn't very well remain in the basement all night, with a level of caution he'd never taken before, he climbed the stairs to the first floor, gripping the railing all the while.

Once settled in his living room, bolstered by a glass of wine, and not long after the first, a second serving, he brooded over the disastrous start to the new week. In a rare moment of accounting, he considered his calamitous screw up that evening. Now he was left to worry whether there would be any repercussions from it, as his mind raced to fears over whether anyone in that crowd might have recognized him. Then, he thought, and what about her? Would she pursue this? There would be no immediate answer to that worry. He would just have to wait, with no control over what could develop.

The wine, having its effect on his empty stomach, left him in a state of moderate intoxication. With no desire to eat and exhausted from the clash with that bitch, he decided bed was the only option.

Before carefully ascending the stairs to the bedroom, he first removed his shoes and suit jacket. Impacted by Millie's presence again, her rule was no shoes upstairs, as they dirtied the carpeting. He obeyed, though the rule could no longer be enforced. He didn't like it; socks were slippery, increasing the chance of a fall, but for now he complied.

Having safely arrived on the top floor, as he stood before the bed, what had been their bed, it was no welcoming pad, not with the absence of Millie. But it was worse than that because he again felt her ghostly presence, imagining that she was there, her sorrow over his terrible behavior filling the room. How could you, Charles! he envisioned her saying. It was so stark, he considered sleeping on the living room couch, but rejected the idea, as it would involve using the stairs again. In his uneven state, that was a frightening thought.

It was no surprise that he had a fitful night's sleep. When his alarm sounded, he dragged himself through his morning ritual and then gathered himself during the commute to the office, determined to have a reset to ease his agitated state of mind. He would make himself focus on the decision, that was the first, and for now, the only order of business. Those other worries, he had no control over them, so he had to will them away. Dwelling on them was only destructive to his mental state. Focusing upon continuing with the drafting his decision was the best way to divert his attention from the previous night's debacle. It was absolutely a matter of survival.

Though tired from inadequate sleep, he stuck to his plan and with that he made significant headway. All his years of decision writing enabled him to bring his skills to bear, his talent really, for producing a decision that would withstand the inevitable appeal by the Secretary. Credibility determinations, substantial evidence, those were the keys he knew how to employ effectively.

As he called it a day, progress having been made, his anxiety level continued to diminish during the return commute. No Nicole, no one inquiring about the prior night, and thank God, no police dropping by the office. That would've been a disaster; everyone in the office would be speculating over such a development, especially that arrogant Larkin.

Once safely home, a relatively quiet evening followed, as he prepared a simple dinner, which was followed by two glasses of wine, to imbibe slowly, not gulp down, as he had the night before.

He regained his bearings too. No, Millie wasn't spiritually in their bedroom or anywhere else in the house. Those were all crazy thoughts. Get a grip, man, he scolded himself. Think of the great days ahead, he told himself. They were not far off. He resolved there would be a new start, a fresh start, in which he would only do good things, a model citizen once again, repentant until his life was over. It seemed reasonable, he thought, didn't all religions allow for redemption?

The remaining days of the work week proceeded without any consequences from his public skirmish with that floozie, Nicole, or whatever her real name was, and with that passage of time his confidence grew. Surely, he thought, if something were to occur from that event, it would have happened by now. Equally comforting, there had been no appearance of that bartender, Jerome, diminishing his lingering fear that the son of a bitch would come to his office with a new demand.

Interactions with employees in the office had been minimal, but at times unavoidable during bathroom visits and his trip for lunch. They required only the briefest of exchanges, the formulaic 'how are you' and the predictable replies. Even coming upon Larkin, as he did during the week, those exchanges were as superficial as those with the others. With the weekend about to start, and given the progress of the decision drafting, he would be able to complete it by the end of the following week, if not earlier. The end to this mess and the fresh start were truly in sight.

The weekend also served to distract him from his worries and the work remaining for his decision to be completed. There was much to do at home, so much junk to toss throughout the house. And even the furniture, it was all going to go. He wanted the fresh start to be free of his Virginia memories.

The buyers wanted some of the furnishings, which he practically was giving away. For the rest of the stuff, he learned, that Salvation place was happy to come take it away and their arrival was scheduled just two weeks away.

His biggest concern was the basement safe with all that cash. He had deposited some of it in a few safe deposit boxes, but the rest of it, safe and all, that would be in his car's trunk, plainly the most important item for the trip south.

When work began on Monday, taking a fresh look at his decision, which was nearly completed, he was confident that it was solid. To give the appearance that it had not been rushed, he decided to hold back from issuing it for at least one more week.

That assessment prompted him to make the trip down to that blowhard's office, Chief Edward Blandford. Blandford, the II yet, he thought. One Blandford would've been enough! Still, with both sides minding their manners, Gray delivered the news that his decision was nearing completion and that he would be retiring after that.

Blandford received both announcements with ostensible pleasantness. The Chief could have cared less when the old goat hung it up. Some new blood, he thought, that would be good, though he hoped it wouldn't be another Larkin type. That guy, was a bit too independent, for his liking. He preferred judges who wouldn't be prone to rocking the boat, *his* boat.

As for Gray, he only cared that the coal dust decision was issued, a reassurance Gray gave along with his notice. If the Commission were to pick up the case on appeal, Gray informed that it would not delay his retirement, a decision that Blandford could not countermand. Graciously, Gray did announce that he would be willing to be rehired, on a contract basis, if there was a remand from an appeal.

With that, Gray excused himself, informing that he needed to continue applying his final touches to the decision. He gave no hint to the outcome and though he was curious, Blandford resisted the temptation to ask about it. Gray would've demurred had he done so.

The week continued, his solitude still respected by those in the office, and though he could've issued the decision by the week's end, he sat on it, deciding that the following week would be the best timing for its release.

Now confident that his skirmish with that woman would not produce repercussions, he was able to focus on the many tasks yet to be accomplished at home, as he continued to empty out the place for his departure.

THE CASE OF THE ABNORMAL WHITE CENTER

The following week was largely spent readying his office for his departure, though he did read over the decision closely, a last look to make sure he had covered all the bases. Satisfied that it would withstand the Secretary's appeal, he decided to issue it that Friday, at mid-day. He calculated that timing was best, as it would be early enough for the litigants and anyone who was interested to know of it and have time to read it before the weekend began.

When the day arrived, literally at noon, Gray issued it, presenting a lengthy, ostensibly erudite, opinion. He was pleased with his work product, having created the appearance of a thoughtful analysis, free of bias; an almost clinical step-by-step discussion of the evidence from each side. He was clever enough to grant some points to the Secretary's case, rejecting the several null hypotheses claims of the Respondent's case and other weaker assertions, such as the idea that the postal service mailing of the results to MSHA caused those AWCs. The enormous number of those white centers made that claim laughable.

Not buying into some of the Respondent's more outlandish explanations gave the appearance that he was the epitome of the objective judge. It also set up the legitimacy of what counted – his determination that, while the Secretary's case had some meritorious aspects, it failed to meet the preponderance of the evidence burden. Overcoming that conclusion, he knew, would be too tough a hill to climb. This was especially so because he built the outcome on credibility determinations and what he presented as legitimate expert testimony calling into question the Secretary's claims.

One such hook was the claim that manufacturing variations, that filter-to-foil distance business, accounted for some of those AWCs. With all that had happened to him, he knew it was sheer nonsense, but it was one part of the several reasons he accepted to account for his ultimate conclusion.

The Respondent's spaghetti-on-the-wall approach gave him the freedom to accept some of it, while rejecting other parts, presenting the illusion that he was the model of the cold, strictly analytical, reviewer of the evidence, that neutral evaluator of the evidence, who simply called balls and strikes.

It wasn't perfect, he realized. One aspect could be an Achilles' heel, his claim that the Secretary failed to *disprove* each of the Respondent's several bases for the white centers, a determination that was far outside of the normal proof requirements to establish a violation. However, he remained confident that the opinion, detailed as it was in support of his conclusion, would prevail upon any appeals.

With all the continuous coverage of the case, news of the issuance of Gray's decision spread rapidly. The newspapers reported it online within hours. The local TV stations broke in to their programming, proclaiming it as breaking news. No surprise, everyone in the Commission's offices, both the judges' office and the Commissioners' office, were talking about it. Depending upon the orientation of the individuals in those two offices, people were delighted or greatly disappointed with Gray's decision.

Larkin too was immediately aware of it.

Uncharacteristically, as he normally welcomed visitors, he closed his office door in order to read it without interruption. Irrationally, he had still held out that perhaps Gray would have an epiphany and hold the Respondent accountable.

This was not some abstract academic decision. The outcome left thousands of coal miners unprotected from the ravages of breathing excessive amounts of coal dust. Those mines knew it, but production remained king.

As luck would have it, not long after Larkin read it, Gray and he encountered one another in the hallway, neither pleased to see the other. Certain that something had happened causing the judge he formerly held in high esteem to issue a decision at odds with what he viewed as overwhelming evidence that there had been tampering with those dust collectors, he could barely bring himself to make eye contact. It was unavoidable – he couldn't act as if they weren't passing one another – but the most he could offer was a nod. Gray responded with the same minimal recognition. The animosity was mutual.

Larkin's minimal acknowledgement was clear to Gray. He knew that guy was aware of the decision and was contemptuous of both the outcome and him. Defensively, silently, he thought to himself, well what of it, tough if it didn't pass his judgment of the correct outcome.

Unaware that Larkin had more than a contrary opinion, that he saw him take an envelope from someone, Gray considered that his former colleague just carried a superior attitude, a know-it-all perspective, so common, he thought, with these younger judges. It was pure arrogance, he pacified himself, Larkin had not even once been in the courtroom for all those weeks. So he was able to telepathically make credibility determinations of witnesses he never viewed? Such pomposity! he thought, his estimation unburdened by the underlying truth that he'd been snared by that woman, twice, and then bought off.

Even knowing that Larkin, and his Millie too, saw through his unwarranted takes on the evidence as the case proceeded, he would not allow such thoughts to spoil his relief that it was finally over.

Gray's disgusting opinion dominating his Larkin's thoughts the remainder of the day, so much so that he was unable to focus on any of his own cases. Under those circumstances, he dispensed with his usual practice of staying late to wait for the Friday night traffic slog to ease up. He stewed about it the entire trip home and broke the news to Sandy upon his arrival.

Neither was surprised, but it didn't prevent either from expressing their mutual outrage about it. Both concluded that something had been afoot with Gray. Adding to their revulsion, there was nothing they could do about it.

As Larkin remarked to her "sometimes the bad guys win."

As Gray drove home that evening, his burden relieved, he resolved to stop crowding his head with thoughts of the reactions to his decision. If people didn't like it, well, too bad. It was done and now it was time to direct his energy into finalizing all the arrangements for his relocation. His new home in Bradenton would be a two-day journey. He could handle that; there were plenty of motels at the mid-way point.

Some two-weeks after his decision, wonderful news was delivered. No surprise, the Secretary appealed Gray's decision, but the Commission announced that no two members had decided to review it, though one wrote a blistering dissent.

This was not a surprise to Gray. The Commission then had only four commissioners in place. While one Commissioner made it plain that he had multiple issues with the outcome, the other three, conservative members all, had no interest in picking it up.

Gray had anticipated as much. He had written his decision with those three in mind and it had worked. The case was dead, at least as far as the Commission was concerned.

He realized that, in a case of this magnitude, the Secretary could and probably would march to the U.S. Court of Appeals. There too, he was confident that, while covering themselves with remarks that it did not necessarily agree with his decision, finding substantial evidence and deferring to his credibility determinations, they would very likely uphold the decision.

Even if the Court of Appeals were to remand the matter, and though he had already informed Blandford that it would have to be on a contract basis if he wanted him to handle it, he was bluffing.

As he thought about it, he had no choice but to remain employed until the Court of Appeals made a decision. If he quit and some other judge was assigned the remand, the apple cart could be totally upset. A judge like Larkin was just the type to cause such mayhem.

He couldn't take such a risk. So, he marched down to Blandford's office and informed him that 'out of a sense of duty' he would delay his retirement until the matter was closed.

Blandford, understandably clueless about the true reason for Gray staying on the job – that it was driven entirely by self-interest – accepted the gracious offer from the judge. Sensing that he had the upper hand and could extract promises, Gray added that he expected to be assigned no new cases. He would however issue decisions approving settlement motions, work that, as the Commission currently dictated, involved no work, a figurative rubber stamp being all that was required.

Although Congress had directed that all settlements were to be approved upon review by the Commission, it had issued a decision making that review a joke – all settlements, every one, were to be approved by the judges.

Besides, he had plenty of leave to burn, and in his new cash-rich state, he didn't need to hold the leave and take it as an end of employment cash out.

In what seemed like an endless wait, a month later the Court of Appeals issued a brief decision denying the Secretary's challenges to the decision. As Gray had expected, it took the easy route. Apparently skeptical of his decision, as made clear by its protective remark that its denial did not mean that it would have necessarily reached the same conclusion, but rather that it had to respect the substantial evidence rule and the judge's credibility determinations, and therefore, effectively holding its nose, it ruled that it could not substitute its own views of the evidence.

Gray was pleased; his prediction was accurate. By that Court's determination there was a tidy ending to the matter. No way was the Secretary about to try for the Supreme Court to review it. That would be a fool's errand. The Nine wouldn't pick it up anyway, not on the basis of Gray's unassailable decision.

The Commission too was delighted, its decision being affirmed meant there would be none of the headaches, and work, entailed with a remand. With the entire office emailed about it, Larkin had read it too. It was his last hope that justice could still result.

Elated that the matter was truly over, no resurrection possible, Gray immediately went to Blandford's Office announcing that he was retiring as soon as personnel could gather the paperwork. At the end of the next pay period, which happened to be less than a week after the decision from the Appeals' Court, he was done. A few employees inquired if he wanted a send-off party, and he answered, leaving no doubt about it, that he did not want one. To make it abundantly clear, he informed that if an event were planned, he would not attend. With such a remark, that settled the matter.

In that last week, Larkin, still hemorrhaging from the outcome, inevitably saw Gray in the office hallway, but again he could not manage more than a nod, wordlessly acknowledging his presence as they passed one another. Feeling emboldened, even cocky, by the twin victories, first from the Commission and then by the Court of Appeals, Gray responded in kind, with no more than a nod.

Sometimes Larkin would pass by him, as if he was not there at all. Gray didn't care.

Larkin knew, as did everyone in the office, that his former friend was retiring at the end of the week, but he could not offer even the minimal words of noting the event, nor an expression wishing him good luck. Did not deserve it, he thought, unapologetically.

And so, when Friday arrived and with all the administrative retirement papers completed, Gray packed up his few belongings and left the office as if it were without distinction from the end of any other workday.

Under different circumstances, if his career had ended on the same note as he had performed in every other case, honorably and fairly making his decisions, he might have felt some sadness that it was over. The awful things he had done, the harm his actions brought about, including the death of his wife and to the miners who suffocated by inhaling the deadly coal dust, those prevented any feelings of wistfulness.

As he exited the building that final time, the trail of his behavior followed him. Compulsively, he again looked around, assuring himself, now for the last time that there was no Tranter or Jerome present to assail him. Cleared of that worry, he took a deep breath and headed immediately to the garage. There would be no stop for a drink, not anywhere. It would be straight home, but 'home' had become the rented-back unit following his house sale closing, until the appeals had been completed.

He prepacked his car that evening, the items he was taking to Florida meager. His fresh start in Florida included selling his car, replacing it with a shiny new high-end SUV, easily paid for in cash from his payoffs. It was all about removing every item that could remind him of Millie. The thoughts of his former wife could not be similarly disposed of, though he wished they could.

Early the next morning, he began the two-day drive to his new Florida home. Though it was a solitary journey, he knew that feelings of loneliness were not to be entertained, not when he was the cause of being unaccompanied. Millie, though literally not there, was still very much present, as if she were sitting in the passenger seat. He imagined, as was her practice when the two were in the old car, of her routine criticisms that that he was driving too fast or to watch out for other drivers. It was uncomfortable.

He had disposed of every one of the personal items that marked their years of marriage, but, the intangibles, the thoughts in his head, they remained.

Would she always be in his head, even in a completely new location?

Having planned ahead, when he arrived at his new location, the house was ready for him, intentionally devoid of all the furniture from his Virginia residence. In the weeks that followed, the concerns that his 'transgressions,' as he gently labeled them in his head, would be revealed and that he would be handcuffed, doing a perp walk as he was led away in front of his gawking new neighbors, began to ebb.

With each passing day, his confidence that there would be clear sailing ahead grew. That 'new start' he hoped for seemed increasingly attainable.

The kink was that thoughts of Millie kept entering his head. She needed to be put in the past to attain a genuine new start. But, images of his wife on that cold basement floor, the contorted position in which he found her, persisted. It was a horrific and indelible image that refused to go away.

He tried to will it away. As that did not work, he tried rationalizing, an approach that had worked well for him during his life. Focusing on the undeniable, that nothing could be done to bring her back, he tried to lessen his guilt by noting how well he had cared for her over those many years as her illness progressed.

Thinking, as they say, 'like a lawyer,' he came to his own defense by noting that it was only indirectly that he brought about her fatal fall down those steps. He hadn't asked her to go to the basement to retrieve something while he was busy at the trial. No, he added, to further remove his guilt, the fact was that it was her own curiosity, snooping he called it, that led to her death. The blame was squarely on her.

Despite the efforts, none of his justifications made his culpability go away. The mind tricks he employed, they could not wash away the actions he had taken and for which only he was responsible. She was still there in his head, her death inextricably tied to his conduct, not hers.

While those thoughts still haunted him, at least there were distractions from them. The neighbors were pleasant and the community, being gated, was safe. And, he was living quite well. With the development being side-walked, he had taken to the convenient exercise it provided, a two-mile loop around it. On those trips he would inevitably meet neighbors and brief conversations would ensue.

It did not take long for him to drop that he had been a judge. That information caused instant admiration. "A judge!' people would privately admire the disclosure, as if his title added esteem to the entire neighborhood. Word spread quickly about the newcomer's prominence. People, even those Gray had never met before, came to recognize him when passing in the neighborhood. "Oh, you're the judge," they would say, their veneration unmistakably conveyed with the words.

Gray happily received the praise, his ego welcoming it. He didn't offer to educate them that he was an administrative law judge and one whose portfolio was limited to mine safety cases at that. From his experience, the public blurred the distinction, even on those few occasions when he explained the limited nature of his title. Most, even when schooled about it, only remembered that he was a former judge. Accepting the ignorance about it, it was still pleasurable for the nearly universal smiles he would receive when meeting neighbors during his walks. Even in stores, he would be recognized and uniformly addressed as 'judge' when people would encounter him while shopping.

Ever mindful that he could be spotted by neighbors, he was careful to always display good manners during his outings. The inevitable incidents of life, a dispute with a store clerk, a driver cutting him off and things of that ilk, never provoked ill-tempered reactions from him. He was committed to behaving in the manner the public perceived that, as a judge, he should comport himself. In that role, he did not disappoint.

Back in D.C., the memory of Gray, despite his long tenure, faded quickly among the office employees. His decision too was relegated to 'old news' by them, replaced by fresh distractions.

Malthan and Krakovich played up the win to good effect, proclaiming that the judge's decision showed how unfair the charges had been. They never should have been brought, they told the press, the litigation unfairly disparaging the coal mining industry.

Larkin was an exception. He thought of Gray every time he passed by his now vacant office. None of his thoughts were good. He wished that someone might come forward spilling the beans on whatever it was that guy had done. It was with continuing irritation that he realized there was nothing he could do about it.

He'd heard the man had moved to Florida. At moments of peak anger, he was tempted to find his phone number and lay into him, telling him that he knew there had been some sort of corruption going on, revealing that he saw that envelope passing incident with the stranger. He never acted on it, Sandy counseling him that it would accomplish nothing, ironically making him, not Gray, look bad.

The time in Gray's new location passed quickly, again without incident. Florida was, as he had hoped, so much better than his former Virginia location. Each day thoughts of Millie lessened bit by bit.

And then, abruptly, unexpectedly, it came to an end.

His doorbell rang that day. It was almost noon. Without hesitation he answered to meet the caller.

As he opened the door, he instantly knew the visitor's identity and it was not one to be welcomed.

It was she, no doubt about it. That lowlife, Nicole.

Immediately he knew it meant trouble; this was not a friendly encounter.

How the hell did she find me? he thought, his anxiety growing by the second.

He uttered the first words, and with them and admission that he had no confusion about who was before him.

"What do you want?" he asked, as he nervously looked past her to see if any of the neighbors were witnessing the two. To his relief, at the moment, there were no passersby.

She obliged, answering "If you want me to be quiet and not go to the authorities, it's going to cost you," getting right to the point.

With no time to renew his anger towards her and remembering how badly the last confrontation went, he was painfully aware that he didn't need another scene, especially in his new setting where his status was one of adulation.

"I have no idea what you're talking about," he said, mustering as much as an authoritative tone that he could deliver.

"I have no time for your gambit," she came back. "You think I didn't figure out that your screwing with me put you in that mine's pocket? I'm no fool," she informed.

Perhaps it was his new tranquil environs, giving him some time to regain his bearings, but for whatever reason he was not cowed by her charge. Besides, this was very different from Jerome's demand. That guy saw the envelope being passed to him at the Grill. And, apart from the bartender's low-budget extortion, he was not a player in Gray's corrupt actions.

His mind raced as he evaluated how to deal with the situation. Avoid an explosion at all costs, he thought.

He then considered that while it was natural for her to put together that their sex had compromised him, she had no reason to think that he had been bribed. Just the acts, both occasions, would have been enough for them to set the terms for his favorable decision if he wanted to avoid disclosing his perfidy. It was purely a leap for her to even think that he was paid off under such circumstances.

"I still don't know what you're talking about," he insisted, this time saying it with more conviction.

"They must've paid you something," she insisted, surprised that he did not seem to waiver in his denial.

He picked up on her lack of conviction in her assertion. Clearly, she was fishing.

In case the trollop was recording their conversation he then added, "my decision was based solely on my assessment of the evidence."

His instinct was to add an insult with that remark such as 'if you would take the time to read it, assuming you could comprehend it.' But he refrained.

Don't make her angrier, he privately counseled himself. Stay cool. Instead, he added an insincere compliment. "You know, the Commission and the federal court affirmed my decision. You read those opinions, I'm sure," having no doubt that she had not.

She had seen from the newspapers that his claim was true, though she certainly had not read those opinions. There was no point in doing that, all that legal stuff was gibberish to her.

"Demand all you want," he said evenly. "I did nothing wrong."

Strategically, he then added, "my wife died, you know."

She didn't know about that, nor even when it occurred and the news left her deflated. Now her leverage against him had dropped, with no threat remaining to inform his wife about his infidelity.

With his firm denial that he'd done anything wrong and the added news that he was now a widower, she considered that her hand was weak. Having come all this way and unwilling to simply back down, she struggled to continue her threat.

All she had was the sex and now that was weakened, what with him being a widower.

With no choice, she then added another claim for her demand. "You had no right to abuse me outside that bar! You would not look so good if news got out about that and that you had extramarital sex while hearing that big case."

Gray, noting the shift in her assertion, silently knew that this new extortionist was right about that. Even shouting just about the sex, who could know what might develop? Things could unravel. The consequences were unpredictable. It was time to act diplomatically, he thought. See if a solution can be mediated.

Ignoring the threat part of her remark, he addressed only his intemperate behavior.

"You're right about that," he responded with no delay. "I deeply apologize for that. I have only myself to blame for my unwarranted behavior towards you." Again, he added, presenting phony contrition, "I am deeply sorry for that."

He had her again. Apologizing like that, let the air out of her complaint. Flummoxed, she moved back to her original demand.

"They must have paid you something," she then asserted but her voice displayed that no confidence about that claim. Her talent was in bedding wayward spouses, not debating the vagaries of bribery. In this subject she was out of her league, her visit to Gray based on surmise.

With the risk of her recording the conversation front and center in his head, he answered, "Nothing could be further from the truth. True, we had sex, but nothing follows from that beyond my embarrassment."

He paused, then added, "Think about it. They had me just on the sex. If what you claim was true, which it is *not*," he added with apparent certitude, "do you think you could just claim that I was paid too, not just bedded? And do you think if you went public with your completely unsupported claims, do you really think that people like that, engaged in such a scheme, would just let your bald assertion stand?"

"Anyone who would put herself in such a position, claiming I was paid off, would have to be continually concerned about one's health, I'll tell you that," he said, taking the posture of the wise warning giver.

It put her back. Tranter warned of the same risk.

She was astute enough to pick up on that last remark. A denial, wrapped in a warning, all presented as a hypothetical.

Gray, holding the upper hand, determined it best to call this to an end.

"Look, again I'm sorry for my uncouth behavior. I was unquestionably the lout, both by cheating on my very ill wife and also by my inexcusable confrontation with you."

But, hoping some minimal showing of an apology with a dollop of generosity would be a consolation prize, he then offered, "Will you allow me to cover your airfare and motel plus a small expression of appreciation for not embarrassing my family about my unfaithfulness? Say, five thousand? I can't offer you more, I live on my modest retirement. It's the best I can do to atone for my behavior outside that tavern."

Unaware that he had no family to embarrass, and fearful about his warning not to mess with the powerful who brought about the coal mining case win, she accepted the offer. Considering the circumstances and the weak hand she held, she thought it best to accept it, a small victory, and retreat.

Relieved that a crisis had been averted, he responded, "Just a sec. I'll be right back." There was no offer to have her step inside. In a moment, he returned, handing her an envelope. The transaction was no different really from those many envelopes Tranter had passed to him.

Anticipating her reaction, he presented an excuse for having so much cash on hand. "I just closed on this home and between that and payment for unused leave in my former job, I have cash for you."

She seriously doubted his story; it didn't really explain why he would have so much cash on hand. Unconvinced, but seeing no sense in creating a new bone of contention, she accepted the payment, assuming, incorrectly, that she could not extract more from him. A bird in hand, she thought. Her forte was fucking, not finance.

With no further words available, she left, returning to her rental car.

He stood there silently as she departed, aware that even a wave would be inappropriate.

Once she was out of site, he reentered his house, closing the door, resting against it. It was a bargain to have extricated himself from the new mess.

Please God, no more blackmailers. Let it be the last threat from this mess, he thought.

Though it was totally crazy, the thought of wanting to fuck her again involuntarily entered his mind, as she was still as alluring as before. Fortunately, he retained enough sense to realize that the accord they had just reached would blow up at such a suggestion. Don't be an idiot twice, he told himself, quieting the irrational urge from his loins.

In Washington, Milo and Winston continued to ride high on their success. Both calculated that derivative benefits would flow from their enormous victory, as they considered the potential prestigious government positions that might develop. Working from the inside, influencing regulatory policy, they could strengthen the mining industry broadly, not being limited to individual cases.

THE MINE SAFETY TRILOGY PART II

They received a standing ovation when the attorneys for all the mines which had been charged gathered in the grand meeting room of their firm. They marveled at the talents of the two leaders, glad that they had put their trust in them, in total ignorance of how the results were actually achieved.

Before the press, they boldly, calmly, extolled the American justice system. It was simply a matter of the Secretary failing to prove his case as applied by the judge with his long experience and his applied wisdom. Justice had prevailed! they exclaimed.

Though time had passed since Gray's decision was issued, Larkin continued to brood over it, convinced that corruption had occurred. That his assessment was correct was confirmed in a sense when, months later, the newspapers announced that another coal mine operation admitted to tampering with the dust collection devices. The mine was not one of the mines originally charged.

That made two such confessions of guilt; the one brought out by the government brought out during the trial and then this new one. To Larkin it was proof that, emboldened by Gray's corrupt decision, mines believed they could resume tampering. Though using the crudest of tactics, the papers disclosed that, for the new case, the mine had simply placed the dust collection devices outside, on the surface for some hours, skewing the results.

With nothing to support a different outcome, reducing it to a pipe dream, Larkin still hoped that someday there would be a reckoning.

Sandy had suggested justice could still occur, eventually, invoking that expression 'what goes around comes around.'

Larkin wished that might occur, but at the end, as he had told her before, 'sometimes the bad guys win.'

Whether ultimate justice occurs is the subject of the upcoming Mine Safety Trilogy Part III.

www.ingramcontent.com/pod-product-compliance
Lightning Source LLC
Jackson TN
JSHW022339050625
85686JS00008B/21